Katy Carter Keeps a Secret

Ruth Saberton

Copyright

All characters, organisations and events in this publication, other than those clearly in the public domain, are fictitious and any resemblance to real persons, living or dead, is purely coincidental.

The opinions expressed in this book are solely the opinions of the author and do not represent the opinions or thoughts of the publisher. The author has represented and warranted full ownership and / or legal right to publish all materials in this book.

Copyright © 2016 Ruth Saberton
Editor: Jane Griffiths

The moral right of the author has been asserted.

All rights reserved. No part of this publication may be reproduced, stored in a retrieval system or transmitted, in any form or by any means, without the prior permission of the publisher. If you wish to share this book please do so through the proper channels.

www.ruthsaberton.com

All rights reserved.

Author's Note

Dear Reader,

In 2010 my first novel, KATY CARTER WANTS A HERO, was published and my life changed forever. It had always been a cherished dream of mine to be an author and I'd written ever since I was a child – mostly stories about ponies – and as I grew older the passion for telling stories only grew stronger (as did my love of horses and horse riding, although that's another story!) In between teaching English at a big comprehensive school and moving to Cornwall, I wrote several novels – all of which were rejected by agents and publishers. Many times I felt close to giving up, but when I met a well-known author who advised me to "write about what you know and never give up" I picked myself up and penned KATY CARTER WANTS A HERO, the story of an English teacher who moves to Cornwall to follow her dream of being a writer.

The rest is history. The novel attracted the attention of TV's Richard Madeley and Judy Finnigan as well as being splashed across the national press – feel free to Google that! Katy's adventures and her pet lobster, Pinchy, touched a chord with readers and to my delight many people enjoyed the book and were kind enough to write and tell me. It was even shortlisted for the UK Romantic Novelists' Association's ROMANTIC COMEDY OF THE YEAR award in 2011.

As time went on it was unusual for a week to pass without receiving an email asking me what happens next for Katy and whether there would be a sequel. I thought about this and an idea came to me but I knew that, like me, Katy needed a little time to reach the next stage of her life. Has she changed? Is she still as impulsive and scatty? Now that would be telling!

By the start of this year I felt ready to write the next part of Katy's story and it's been the greatest fun to catch up with her. In KATY

CARTER KEEPS A SECRET we rejoin Katy and her friends about five years on from the end of the first book and ready to set out on a new adventure. I have loved writing this story and I really hope you'll have fun reading it. If you do, I would really appreciate a review on Amazon or GoodReads. These make all the difference to the success of a book and are like gold dust for writers.

I love to hear from my readers. Contact me at ruthsabertonpr@nottinghillpress.co.uk and please visit my website, www.ruthsaberton.co.uk for my blog and news of upcoming books.

Brightest wishes,

x **Ruth** x

Chapter 1

Alexi reached forward to unlace Lucinda's tight bodice. Her heart was racing beneath the swell of her breasts and she moaned with desperate need. She wanted him so much it hurt and this desire was the most exquisite torture she'd ever known. If she didn't protest now he would surely ravish her and then…

And then… and then…

My pen hovers over the page, just as up for whatever happens next as good old quivering Lucinda, but unfortunately for my heroine I haven't a clue what that's going to be. I know in *theory* what's supposed to happen next. You don't get to your thirties and not know, do you? Especially when you've been with the love of your life for almost five years. So of course I know. Every time I look at my boyfriend Ollie my insides turn to soggy Weetabix.

Soggy Weetabix? What kind of image is that? I can do better than soggy Weetabix! At least I hope I can, or I can kiss goodbye to securing this latest ghostwriting contract. If not, it'll be even more supply teaching and there'll be no way to mend our leaking cottage roof or clear the overdraft. No wonder my boyfriend – unlike the always-up-for-it Alexi – is so tired all the time. He's exhausted from the constant plugging of leaks and listening to staccato rain dripping into buckets all night long. I have to get this ghostwriting job. I have to!

My love life and our finances depend on it.

Talking of supply teaching, I'd better make sure today's bunch of Year Nines are getting on with the work I've set them. They've been suspiciously quiet for the past twenty minutes, but then it is an ICT lesson and they probably haven't twigged that playing on the computers is actually work.

I glance up from my page and scan the classroom just to make sure that nobody's throttling a friend with a tie/smoking/playing on their phone, but all is calm.

Go me! I've nailed it! Being a supply teacher is a tricky job and some prankster usually feels duty-bound to try and push it with a new face, but this group of students are behaving beautifully so far. I don't *think* this has anything to do with my telling them that their computers are bugged and that the Headmaster can see everything they're up to, or my playful threat of letting them out for lunch so late they'll have no hope of reaching the canteen pre-stampede. I also *may* have let slip that earlier on I overheard the dinner ladies saying there was a shortage of chips today...

I'm sure I was quite a nice person before I was a secondary school teacher. Now I'm a grand master of psychological chess and such an expert teen whisperer I should have my own show on Sky. These are great skills in the classroom, of course, but not much use if you aspire to be a bestselling novelist – which is still what I want more than anything in the world. Actually that should be what I want *almost* more than anything in the world, because what I really want is for Ollie to stop working so hard in his Head of English job. If I could only write a bestseller and make squillions of pounds he wouldn't have to push himself for all these promotions. Then we could go back to the way things used to be before bills and listed cottages and his career got in the way. And if he doesn't fall asleep on the sofa every night we might even put Alexi and Lucinda to shame. You never know!

I chew my pen and return to my notebook. Think, Katy, think. How hard can it be? You've written a screenplay and you've been a ghostwriter in the past too, so this should be a doddle.

It's thanks to my ghostwritten books that I've got a shot at this new series in the first place. You've probably seen them; in fact, if you've been through an airport or a motorway services area in the last three years or trundled your trolley along the paperback aisle in Tesco, then you'll definitely have seen my books. With their scarlet covers, brash gold font and muscle-bound heroes literally bursting off the front of them, they're pretty hard to miss. Subtle isn't the way to describe a Tansy Topham novel.

Yes! I'm Tansy Topham! Me, Katy Carter! Incredible but true!

OK, so I'm not really Tansy. Obviously not! She's a leggy blonde ex glamour model married to a top Plymouth Pirates striker and I'm a short, ginger teacher living with St Jude's Head of English – but the words inside those scarlet covers are all mine, every single breathless one of them. I'm a bestselling novelist in disguise, which is great, of course, but not *quite* how I thought things would turn out.

When my first book, *Heart of the Highwayman*, became a screenplay I really thought that was it; I was up and running. The ink had barely dried on the contract and already I was mentally lobbing my teaching folders into the skip, packing our suitcases and relocating to Hollywood. I'd even picked us a fantastic house to rent in Beverly Hills, close to all the major studios and handy for bumping into film stars and Kardashians – who, as I keep having to explain to Ollie, aren't *Star Trek* aliens but THE most famous family on this planet. It was all looking perfect. Even though Ol kept telling me not to let my imagination run away, I was convinced that this was it. Boy wizards and vampires were so yesterday, and historical blockbusters were the next big thing for sure.

Except they weren't.

Thanks a lot, Christian Grey.

Cable ties and red rooms of pain aren't quite my forte. Just ask Ollie. The wiring in our cottage makes Spaghetti Junction look organised, and when it comes to pain I'm such a wimp that I'll scream the place down if I have a splinter. Every time my best friend Mads tells childbirth horror stories I clap my hands over my ears and sing *la la la* very loudly until she gives up. Seriously, I'm more than happy to believe that Rafferty and Bluebell were delivered by the daft-names stork.

As for sadomasochism and kinky sex? If a girl's spent a long day being mentally beaten in a secondary school classroom, the last thing she needs is another round when she gets home. A hot bubble bath and a big glass of wine are much more like it. And BDSM? I'd thought that was something to do with beefburgers in the eighties, until Mads handed me her copy of *Fifty Shades* and insisted I read it.

"It might help you and Ollie," she'd said kindly. "Richard and I have been very inspired by it."

Ew. Much as I love my best friend and can just about tolerate her vicar husband, the mere thought of how they might have been inspired was enough to put me right off my school lunch. I'd skimmed the book, blushed a bit, then returned it and thought not much more about it until I realised this was what the whole world wanted to read now.

So, to cut a long story short, Ollie and I never did go to LA and I'm still supply teaching at Tregowan Comprehensive School. But I haven't given up my dreams of being a famous writer. Of course not! I know that sweeping romantic sagas will come back around and my time will come. All I have to do is wait.

In the meantime I've needed to find a way of making enough money to keep our cottage from falling down around our ears. Listed cottages that dip their toes into one of England's most picturesque harbours are all very well in theory, but maintaining one costs more than a class-A drug habit. And this isn't an exaggeration, because our friend Gabriel Winters – yes *the* Gabriel Winters the movie star – told Ollie just how much that might be. And honestly? I actually think a cocaine addiction would be cheaper than running the gauntlet with the planning people and English Heritage.

Maintaining our cottage was certainly getting tricky on just Ollie's teaching salary and my dwindling royalties from *Highwayman*. I'd needed a solution and fast. When Tansy Topham's agent contacted me looking for a ghostwriter for a series of "light-hearted sexy romps" I'd been thrilled. It didn't matter that I was only top of a very short shortlist because I was the writer nearest to Plymouth and Tansy couldn't be bothered travelling far to attend meetings in between her hectic schedule of manicures and shopping. Nor was I worried that these books were hardly works of great literature. I didn't even care that there'd be no ongoing royalties for me after the initial payment. No! In a fit of agentless and leaky-roofed desperation I signed the contract and grabbed the one-off advance with both hands.

Hmm. Possibly *not* my wisest financial decision, seeing as the books have sold squillions and kept Tansy very nicely in designer bags and Caribbean holidays. And I probably should have spotted the clause which stipulated I couldn't write for anyone else while I was under contract, buy hey! These things are all a learning curve, right? And besides, Tansy's great fun and we've had a hoot coming up with plotlines together. What I actually mean by this is that I drive over to Tansy and Tommy's mock-Tudor house, chat to Tansy and give her some ideas, she nods and says, "Sounds great, babes," and then I go home and write them into books. It's hours of work and a few quid for me and about five minutes and loadsamoney for her, but then she's the famous WAG and I'm just an English teacher from a small Cornish fishing village. I don't mind really. After all, it's good experience and I can genuinely say that I am a bestselling novelist, even if this is in disguise and I still have to grovel to the bank manager.

It's a lesson in looking at contracts closely too, and I'll never make the same mistake again. Of course not! And anyway, Tansy's great fun to hang out with and writing for her won't do my CV any harm. She's not signed another contract with me though, because apparently she's far too busy with a new project – something to do with catering I think, although to be honest I wasn't really listening. While she was talking I was trying to do some rapid mental arithmetic, in a panic-stricken attempt to work out whether we'd still be able to pay the bills without the income of a fourth Tansy book.

I'm pretty rubbish at maths, but even I could figure out that the answer to this was a very depressing "no".

Luckily for me and my cottage roof, Tansy's publishers have a new ghostwritten project in mind and they've asked me if I want to try out for it. The good news is that in all there are three books up for grabs and the royalties are much better than the Tansy ones. The bad news is that the genre they want me to write in isn't exactly romance.

OK. I won't beat about the bush – although this is exactly what my characters probably *will* be doing if I'm chosen to write the books – this new series is an erotic one. Not quite my forte, but how hard can it be?

How *hard* can it be? See, I'm practically there already! I'm a natural!

I glance down at the notes Throb Publishing have emailed over and I have a hot flush just looking at the top sheet. It's a miracle the staffroom printer didn't combust when I ran this lot off before assembly. I had to snatch my pages from old Miss Myers, who'd picked them up with her RE worksheets by accident and was squinting down in amazement.

"A-level creative writing project!" I'd said hastily, almost rugby tackling her to the floor in my desperation to grab the printout. "Writing in the style of err... popular modern authors. Exam boards today, eh! What will they think of next?"

I think I've got away with it. I mean, exam boards do come up with the weirdest assignments, don't they? The other day my bottom-set Year Eleven class had to write in role as creatures from *Animal Farm*. After I'd explained that this was *Animal Farm* the political allegory and not the dodgy movie they all thought I meant, I spent twenty minutes arguing with Josh Johns about whether or not animals could actually write and, if not, then why bother with the assignment? He had a good point; after all, how many bestselling novels are written by animals? About as many as are really written by celebrities, I reckon.

So, like I say, I think I got away with it. Using the school printer for personal use is a big no-no anyway, but using it to print out the brief from Throb Publishing most definitely wouldn't put me in the good books, so to speak. Tregowan Comp's not a bad place to work but they're not keen on me being Tansy Topham as it is. In fact, one of the conditions of my working here is keeping this quiet in case the parents get upset and it tarnishes the school's reputation.

I can't see an issue myself. Most of our kids and parents love Plymouth Pirates and are glued to Tansy's reality show. Tansy might be an ex glamour model but she's a business woman too, isn't she? And her handbag collection alone is probably worth more than most people's houses. Still, beggars who need supply work can't be choosers, and so I do my best to keep my alter ego under wraps – a bit like Bruce Wayne, I like to think. Or Wonder Woman, although I'm not sure I could get away with wearing the satin tights these days.

Just thinking about my narrow escape at the printer makes me feel a little hot under the collar. I think I need a moment to cool down before I risk another attempt with Lucinda and Alexi. Time for a stroll around the classroom to check on these students. One's swinging on the back two legs of his chair, so I give him my best stare of death, which does the trick. Everyone else looks like they're on task and utterly fascinated by the pie-chart lesson their usual teacher has set, so all is well. They're probably just superfast at minimising the browser screen, which I do secretly admire; I'm an expert at this myself, given my tendency to scoot around the Internet when I'm supposed to be concentrating on my job. Still, at least they're nice and quiet, which means I can get back to work.

Right, Katy, focus on this sample chapter. You can do this. Of course you can.

I pick up my pen, turn the top sheet of paper over and take a deep breath. It's not as though I haven't done this before. Writing to a plan is how the Tansy books work and this is no different, just a bit more… err… a bit more naked and grunty. All very natural though, I'm sure, and if you like experimenting with B&Q's cable-tie selection probably nothing out of the ordinary. I've even got a very helpful synopsis and chapter breakdown of this novel right in front of me. Basically, Throb just want an author who can churn out the next *Fifty Shades* for them. I can do this!

Except I can't. How on earth am I supposed to give this publisher the sample first chapter of a novel that's meant to be hotter than Brad Pitt's Aga, when my own love life is quieter than Cornwall in January?

Brad Pitt's *Aga*? Seriously? What's happening to me? I used to be able to write steamy stuff with my eyes closed, or at least with thirty teenagers creating havoc around me – and I've got gorgeous, sexy Ollie to inspire me too, my own perfect romantic hero. The words ought to be flowing onto the page.

Let's try again.

Alexi drew her into his arms and she felt the silken heat of his flesh as he pulled her into a burning kiss. The press of his…

Of his… his…

I chew my biro. Meat? Sausage? Baguette?

Oh Lord. Have I spent too much time eating Ollie's lovely cooking and not nearly enough having wild and crazy sex? Will I ever be able to fix the cottage roof so that my boyfriend can finally get a good night's sleep and remember that there's more to do in bed than fall unconscious?

I push the papers back into the folder and heave a sigh of relief when I see it's lunchtime in five minutes. Time to finish the lesson, scoop up the paper aeroplanes and make my students tuck in their shirts. In a moment I'll be hotfooting it to the school canteen to try to grab my lunch before being trampled by the hungry teen stampede, and then I'll be enjoying a welcome coffee in the staffroom.

Alexi and his sausage will just have to wait until later on.

Chapter 2

One of the best things about being a supply teacher at Tregowan Comp, apart from the obvious joy of educating young minds and exploring my subject, is the macaroni cheese served in the school canteen. Sometimes the only thing that gets me through a double period of bottom-set Year Eleven English without hurling myself out of the window and onto the chewing-gum-freckled concrete below is holding out for a dish of piping hot pasta with gooey cheese on the top. Occasionally I really push the boat out and have chips too, and then the day doesn't seem so bad, not even when Luke Harries tells me to eff off or Bryan Kay (aged sixteen) calls his mummy to come and beat me up because I'm cruel enough to suggest he actually takes his head off the desk for two minutes and does some coursework. Sorry to disillusion you, Jamie Oliver, but junk food really does make everything better – and if you had to do my job you'd be guzzling Turkey Twizzlers by morning break, trust me.

Luckily no education secretary has yet twigged that teachers are easily placated by a free bun or a good lunch, and as I weave my way through the corridor crush – my plate held high to avoid being taken out by monster rucksacks and flailing elbows – all is well in my world. I've jumped to the front of the lunch queue and grabbed my food without sustaining a serious injury, coffee will be brewing in the staffroom, and then I've got an easy afternoon covering an art lesson. I love covering art lessons! Kids listen to their iPods and splash paint about with total concentration while I get on with my own work, which today means writing some X-rated action for Alexi and Lucinda. With some stodgy calories inside me and another read-through of the notes, I'm sure I'll get there. I don't actually need to be having mind-blowing sex myself to write about it, do I? That's what imaginations are for. After all, Tolkien wasn't a hobbit and I'm pretty sure J K Rowling isn't a wizard.

Yes, I'm feeling so much more positive about this sample chapter, and that's *before* I've even eaten my lunch.

Throb Publishing, prepare to be amazed!

"That looks good!" Lucy Tyler, one of the English teachers, peers longingly at my lunch as I settle myself into a saggy chair and prepare to tuck in. "I'm starving. I wish I wasn't having salad."

Lucy is perpetually on a diet and, like me, has the willpower of a very weak-willpowered gnat. As she gazes down sadly at her Tupperware tub of limp green leaves, I can't help but notice that the small coffee table between us is littered with sweet wrappers. Seeing me look, she turns pink.

"Rob from IT sent them over. He said they were for all of us because it's a special day."

Rob from IT has had a crush on Lucy for just about forever. Cue lots of blushing (him) and hair twiddling (her, not him, since he's one of those guys who shaves his head and thinks it fools everyone into not noticing he's going bald). It's really quite romantic, in a *just get on with it* kind of way. Their eyes meet across the crowded staffroom, him sitting with the geeky IT crowd and her with the cool and sassy English teachers, just like Romeo and Juliet at the Montagues' party. Sometimes they might bump into each other at the photocopier, or maybe their hands will brush when they reach for the same worksheet on teacher training days, but neither dares cross the acres of scratchy blue school carpet to declare their love. So longing looks and shared pedagogy is as far as it goes…

Hmm. Not quite the loin-grinding and nipple-hardening detail that Throb are asking me to produce, but it's sweet nonetheless. Maybe teacher romance is the next big thing? Snogging in the staffroom? Passion in the PE office? I make a mental note to jot some ideas down once lunch is over. Ollie's a teacher too, so maybe he could help me with some practical research? All in the name of literature, of course, which means he can't plead being too tired.

That's genius! I can hardly wait to get home and—

Well, yes. That.

Lucy's staring at me. "Are you all right, Katy? Your eyes have gone all weird and your mouth's hanging open."

I yank myself out of my steamy-novel planning and back into the present. I feel quite hot and bothered, and I don't think it's from the molten lava temperature of my macaroni cheese either.

"I'm fine. I was just thinking about the chocolates. But what's Rob on about, saying it's a special day?"

She turns even pinker. "It's Valentine's Day."

You know that dream where you suddenly find yourself naked in the middle of the high street? Well, I have a very similar feeling right now.

Oh. My. God.

Call myself a romantic novelist?

I've totally forgotten Valentine's Day!

No, that's not quite right. I haven't *totally* forgotten Valentine's Day. Like Christmas, Halloween and Easter, it's hardwired into my consciousness thanks to an endless barrage of adverts. And at this time of year the supermarket shelves are filled with so many hearts it's tricky to know whether you're in Tesco or a cardio ward. So on some level I'd known that Valentine's Day was almost upon me; it's just that lately I haven't been able to think about anything else except having to produce this flipping sample chapter in record time. It's how I get when I'm writing.

And now I've missed Valentine's Day? Poor, poor Ollie! What must he think? I know it was still dark when he left this morning, and I think I kissed him goodbye (although I *might* have just rolled over and gone back to sleep), but how could I have let him drive to Plymouth without saying a big Valentine's *I love you*?

Hold on. Did he wish me happy Valentine's Day? Was there a card or present left somewhere for me to find? Is he right now waiting for his mobile to beep with a huge *thank you* from me? Or maybe there's a dozen red roses in the sitting room that I didn't notice because I slept through the alarm again and only just escaped getting marked late for school myself?

I fish my phone out of my bag in case I've missed a call from him. I sent a text at break time and usually he replies. Aha! I knew it. There's a text.

Ring later x

A ring! Is that a cryptic comment or what? Does he mean he's going to call me or does he mean more? He loves to play word games and he knows how my mind works. Some people might call it jumping to conclusions but they don't know Ollie like I do.

And I may have been hinting just a little bit…

Let's look at that text again and deconstruct it.

Ring later

Ring. Later.

There's a deeper meaning to this. I should know. I'm an English teacher. I spend all day analysing this kind of thing. What if he's left a ring for me to find when I get home?

He might have done! He really might! I bet that's what he means!

Years ago when we first got together, Ollie said he wanted us to get married and not mess about wasting time. He said we knew each other so well that there was no need to wait. I'd totally agreed because I loved him and knew there and then that there would never be anyone else. As far as I was concerned we were technically engaged and all I needed was a ring. So I waited.

And waited.

And waited a bit more.

And waited even a bit more than that, but still no ring.

You know when you're introduced to somebody and don't take their name in properly and then for ever afterwards you can't ask again for fear of seeming rude? Well, that's the kind of situation I'm in with getting engaged properly. I daren't keep asking because it will sound dead pushy, and everyone knows guys like to do things according to their own timing, don't they? Besides, we've been so busy with sorting the house and paying off student debts and the general day-to-day busyness of living that the wedding thing has gone right to the bottom of the list. I know Ollie hasn't forgotten though, because he would never have said it if he didn't mean it. He'll be waiting for the right time – and what better time than Valentine's

Day?

My imagination is really up and running now. Desert Orchid has nothing on me. I know it's totally unfeminist, and my parents would be bitterly disappointed in me ("Marriage is just so *bourgeois*, Katy!"), but I would really, really like to get married.

There. I've said it. Embarrassing or what? So *not* cool or twenty-first century or feminist. I'm supposed to want to be an astronaut or a nuclear physicist or prime minister or something like that, not harbour secret dreams of white dresses, bridesmaids and glittery diamond rings.

I know my mother would roll her eyes and make some remark about slavery to patriarchy (which is pretty ironic, since I don't think my father has done any of his own ironing since about 1979), but the truth is I don't like heights, I'm rubbish at science, and the House of Commons is far too similar to the school playground for my liking. I'd just like to be Mrs Oliver Burrows.

(And a bestselling novelist, of course.)

Anyway, I think I've kept my thoughts on all this pretty much to myself. In an age when experimenting with gender, sexuality and even cable ties is the norm, it feels as though the last and biggest taboo of all is wanting to get married.

Did I say married?

Shush!

Not so loud, Katy!

Seriously, when I paid for my latest copy of *Brides* magazine yesterday, I couldn't have felt more self-conscious if I'd been buying hard-core porn. As I passed my money over I muttered, "It's for a friend", then shoved the magazine in my bag as fast as possible. As soon as I was home I hid it in the drawer where I keep my Tampax and all the other girl-specific stuff Ol's never likely to root through when hunting for a spanner or something. My credit card statements live there too now, since he busted me by finding them under the sink. Anyway, so far so good. I don't want to look desperate or for him to feel under any pressure. When Ol proposes properly (and I'm sure he will one day soon because, leaky roof and quiet love life aside, we really have had a brilliant five years together) I don't want him to feel railroaded into it. I actually think I've done a good job of not looking too needy or too desperate; any hints I drop are so subtle Ollie probably doesn't even notice them. The couple of times I have *accidentally* left wedding magazines lying about he's used them as coasters and I don't think he even realised what they were.

Subliminal and subtle. That's the best way.

I just wish it wasn't so slow.

But now my hopes are sky high because it's Valentine's Day, Ol's said nothing and I'm one hundred percent certain he's planning something amazing.

"Katy! I said are you all right?"

Lucy's voice, fully trained in the art of silencing thirty teenagers at fifty paces, rips me out of a very pleasant daydream where Ol is slipping a gorgeous diamond ring onto my finger (and not one from a Haribo packet like he once threatened) and saying all the romantic things that he's been waiting five years to say. It's pretty depressing to find myself in the staffroom, surrounded by the detritus of a tub of Miniature Heroes and a plate of congealing macaroni cheese.

"Fine! Fine!" I say quickly.

"You haven't touched your lunch." Lucy's eyeing up my food the way teenage girls eye up Harry Styles. It's weird but I'm so excited at the thought of what's going to happen when I get home this evening that my appetite's totally vanished.

"Do you know what? I don't think I want it after all. You have it," I say, and Lucy's forking up the macaroni cheese even before I've finished speaking.

"You must eat something," she says through a huge mouthful. "Have a chocolate."

My hand hovers over a miniature Flake. I shouldn't really stuff my face with sweets though, if I'm going to be squeezing into a wedding dress any time soon.

"One won't hurt," Lucy adds.

"Bloody hell!" exclaims a voice from the coffee machine. "You're not still scoffing sweets are you, Luce? Thought you said you were on a diet?"

Steph, our Head of English, weaves her way through the heaving staffroom and slops a stained coffee mug onto the table, liberally coating Lucy's marking, before hurling herself into a chair. Pushing her long hair back from her face, she helps herself to a mini Crunchie and munches furiously.

"I'm starving! What moron decided to move lunchtime to one-fifteen? I was almost gnawing my desk."

"The later lunchtime is better for the students," Lucy says piously. "They learn more consistently in the mornings. It's all about accelerated learning."

Steph helps herself to another chocolate. "Bugger the students. What about me? And Katy. She looks bloody awful. What's happened? Just found out you're covering bottom set Year Seven art this afternoon? They painted the last supply teacher blue and chased him out of the room with the lino-cutting knives. Ha! Ha!"

Bollocks. That's the exact class I have this afternoon. Goodbye quiet hour with Alexi and Lucinda, and hello *Lord of the Flies* with paint. Just my luck.

"Katy forgot Valentine's Day," Lucy tells Steph, who raises her eyebrows.

"You're a disgrace, woman. How dare you neglect the lovely Mr Burrows? I've a good mind to steal him away from you."

"Get in the queue," Lucy sighs. "I saw him before you."

"Hello, people? I am here," I say. "Me. Katy Carter? Ollie's girlfriend?"

"Did you hear something?" Steph asks Lucy, who shakes her head. And then they cackle like something out of *Macbeth*.

I raise my eyes to the suspended ceiling. My colleagues are staunch members of the Ollie Burrows Fan Club and, in spite of the fact that *I* am the founder member thank you very much, they never miss a chance to tell me how wonderful my boyfriend is. As if I didn't know! Everyone adores Ollie, from Sasha our dog to my parents to the grumpy woman in the petrol station who can just about grunt when I go in but is all smiles for Ol. He's got that special magic: everything from his twinkly toffee eyes to his cute smile to his personality is gorgeous, and people just love him.

I love him.

Anyway, before he headed off to Plymouth to become a very serious Head of English, Ollie worked at Tregowan Comp and he was popular with everyone – from the dinner ladies who gave him extra-big portions to the hardest kids and even Steph, who for all her talk about *little sods* and *buggers* is one of the most dedicated teachers I've ever come across. When Ollie left the school it was like somebody had died, and even though I'm sometimes drafted in on supply to fill the gaps I know I'm a very poor second.

Even a year on since he left, Steph's still mourning Ollie's departure. She and Lucy are talking now about what a fantastic job he's doing in his new school. I'm sure he is too (he certainly works hard enough), but I can't help thinking life was more fun when he worked here and was home by five most evenings, and when the extent of his ambition was going out to grab a kebab. Nevertheless, I arrange my face into an *I totally agree* expression and nod sagely. A couple of times I check my phone, just in case, but no such luck.

Maybe he's waiting for me to find the engagement ring and call him?

Yes! I bet that's it! Come on, three-thirty! I have to get home!

"Is Carolyn Miles still Deputy Head at St Jude's?" Steph is asking, unwrapping her fifth chocolate and ignoring the look of panic on Lucy's face. "Blonde? Scarily efficient? Drives a red convertible?"

"The one who looks like a model?" Lucy pushes the empty pasta plate aside and grabs a handful of sweets while she still has the chance. "I met her on a course once. She scared the life out of me."

Lucy isn't alone. I've met Carolyn Miles a few times and she scares the life out of me too. Tall, slim and blonde, she's like some data-crunching senior management Bond villainess, and whenever our paths cross I feel like I've been sent to her office for a stern telling off. Ollie works very closely with her, but that doesn't worry me because I know he loves me and Carolyn is my total opposite so, ha! She doesn't stand a chance.

I hope...

"Wouldn't want her working with *my* boyfriend," says Steph.

"You don't have a boyfriend," Lucy points out.

Steph shrugs. "Well if I did have one, especially one as lush as Ollie, then. No way would I want him working with Carolyn. From what I've heard, all her male colleagues end up joining the Miles High Club!"

I'm hoping this is a joke but even if it is, I'm not laughing. I'm trying to come up with a mature and sensible retort (other than *sod off, Steph*) when the end-of-break bell sounds. Not one member of staff stirs – apart from Lucy, who sweeps up her books, shrugs her bag onto her shoulder and scurries out. Outside, I watch the kids moving as slowly as it's possible for teenagers to move. As one they chew and swear their way across the campus. Well, there's no putting it off any longer; death by art class it is.

I really hope I make it home in one piece. I can hardly wait to find my engagement ring, and I've had a brilliant idea about what I can do to prove to Ollie just how much I love him too.

This is going to be the best Valentine's Day ever, I just know it!

Chapter 3

Alexi's eyes glittered dangerously as they raked Lucinda's flesh.

"Delicious," he murmured. "Now, step forward and take off the rest of your clothes."

Lucinda's mouth trembled. She was consumed with such longing that she thought she would swoon. Her gaze dropped to the cable ties held in his strong and pleasure-promising hands and her heart raced. She ought to step away, run back to the office and back to her job as a sous chef at Alexi Gould Hotels International, but Lucinda's inner goddess was telling her…

Telling her…

Oh Lordy. I have no idea what Lucinda's inner goddess is telling her.

Run for the hills? Take the cable ties home and sort out the macramé behind the telly? Never cover a bottom-set Year Seven art lesson again if you like classroom ceilings that aren't splattered with paint and don't think having KIK ME! daubed on your back in vermillion is amusing? Maybe the inner goddess is saying give up trying to write erotica, Katy?

Forget writer's block. I should be so lucky. This is writer's constipation and unless I can find the literary equivalent of syrup of figs very soon I'm in big trouble, and so are my finances. Usually I can write anywhere. On a train. In a classroom. Even in the bath. Voices come into my head and chat away to me and I write it all down as soon as I have a pen and paper to hand. Alexi and Lucinda just don't want to play ball – presumably because it's adult games they ought to be playing and, good as my imagination is, I can't quite stretch it far enough. I need a little real-life inspiration, hence why I'm in the Tregowan general store with a wire basket looped over the crook of my arm.

And, FYI, I am not looking for cable ties.

It's after school now and, having made it out alive, I'm in the village shop cruising the aisles for romantic dinner inspiration. Like writing erotic novels, cooking isn't really my forte. Fortunately Ollie, who's a brilliant chef thanks to a stint in culinary boot camp courtesy of his ex, generally takes care of the meals and does all of our cooking. If I say so myself I do make a mean slice of toast and Marmite and I have been known to stretch to pesto and pasta, but generally (and so that we don't starve or die from food poisoning) we divide the labour up so that he cooks and I do other stuff. Like… like…

Well. Lots of things, I'm sure. Far too many to even start to list, which is why I'm struggling to think of any.

Anyway, Ollie knows I'm no cook, so preparing a really romantic dinner says loads about just how much I love him. And hopefully I won't poison him either. But what's easy to make and won't take very long? I don't want to waste valuable ring-hunting time sautéing and blanching and all those other weird and wonderful things they do on MasterChef. Basically if it doesn't take sixty seconds and go ping then I don't want to know.

During the few blissful moments when the bottom-set art class weren't trying to flick paint at the ceiling or graffiti on me, I managed to Google "easy recipes" and I think I've found one for risotto that fits the bill. It's only rice and a few other bits and bobs, so how hard can it be? I never knew there were quite so many varieties of rice though. Call me stupid but I thought rice was rice; pop it in the microwave for two minutes and ping! Ben's your Uncle!

But no. Apparently it's not that simple because there are endless varieties of rice to choose from. Pudding. Basmati. Arborio. Jasmine. Brown. White. Green with pink spots. OK, I may have made that last one up, but you get the drift. I feel overwhelmed looking at them all. Since when did the Tregowan village shop get so sophisticated? This isn't trendy Rock or foodie heaven Padstow. I'm feeling a bit cross-eyed actually.

I'm still squinting at the packets and wondering which variety to use when Maddy bowls in with Bluebell and Rafferty in tow. At least I think it's my godchildren whose wrists are clamped inside her fingers, but it's hard to tell since one's dressed as Spiderman and the other appears to be some kind of Ninja Turtle.

"Fancy-dress party," Mads explains when I enquire about their attire. "As if I don't have enough to do without having to try and make costumes and bake fairy cakes, now I've got to find a sodding card."

"Don't swear, Mummy," says Spiderman piously. This has to be Rafferty because he sounds just like his father. How terrifying is that? I'm nervous; he'll be asking me where I stand with Jesus if I don't get out of here pronto.

"I said spodding," Mads tells him, rolling her eyes at me. "Never have kids, Katy. It's like living with the bloody Gestapo."

"You said bloody," pipes up Donatello or whichever turtle Bluebell has chosen as her alter ego today. "Daddy will be very cross and Jesus will be very sad."

My best friend sighs. "Fine. You win. Go and choose some forgetful sweets."

Olympic runners off the block don't move as fast as the Lomax twins tear over to the pick 'n' mix. This is obviously a very familiar activity, although that's hardly surprising: before she was married to a vicar, Maddy's vocabulary made Gordon Ramsay sound like Mary Poppins. If Bluebell and Rafferty have any teeth left by the time they're ten it will be a miracle.

"Forgetful sweets?"

"Don't look at me like that." Mads grabs the first card she sees and stuffs it into her basket. I don't really think with deepest sympathy is the most appropriate choice for a five-year-old's birthday party, but the expression on her face is one I know from experience not to mess with, so I keep quiet. "Seriously, Katy. If Richard so much as thinks I've said 'bum' in front of the twins he'll go mental. You know what he's like."

I certainly do. He's only just about forgiven me for the twins chirping bollocks merrily to themselves. Apparently it was my fault because it happened to coincide with the time I fetched them from nursery and wrote my car off driving through a deep puddle. This was over two years ago – and since Richard, being a vicar, is pretty much obliged to forgive people, it gives you an idea of just how seriously he takes these things.

"You'd better start finding different words to use before all their teeth fall out," I suggest, and Mads nods.

"Yep, you're right, or otherwise when they hit their teens and start demanding iPads, I'm screwed." She claps her hand over her mouth. "Oops. I mean, I'm in trouble."

"I heard that. Can I have some sweets too?" I ask, and Mads wallops me with her basket.

"Don't you start. Anyway, what are you doing in here? Are you food shopping?" My best friend's brow crinkles as she peers into my basket and clocks the lone onion and packet of bacon I've chucked in. "I thought Ollie did the food shopping? And the cooking?"

I ignore this comment. I do food shopping too. Of course I do. I often phone the Indian and sometimes the pizza place too.

Joking aside, Ol likes to cruise the aisles of Waitrose. He says after a day at school the supermarket relaxes him. I love my boyfriend very much but even I find this a bit weird and I have a sneaking suspicion he only says this to keep me from going myself and filling the trolley with scented candles and paperbacks.

"I'm cooking risotto," I tell her proudly. "It's Valentine's Day."

"So you thought you'd poison Ol? I thought you liked the guy? Can't you just jump his bones? He'll probably survive that."

I doubt it. He'd probably die of shock.

"Very funny," I say and then, because I can't keep it to myself any longer, I whisper, "I want to do something special that he knows will have taken an effort. I think he's bought me an engagement ring at last!"

Maddy's dark eyebrows shoot into her curly hair. "No way! Seriously? What makes you think that?"

Actually, I'm not sure I can remember now, but I haven't thought about much else for hours and now it seems totally possible.

"Just a feeling. He left early and didn't leave me anything. I think he's hidden a ring in the house."

Maddy looks worried. "Did he mention doing that?"

"Not exactly," I admit. I might have mentioned it a few times though, and Ollie's bound to have got the hint. This tactic worked a treat with getting him to start putting the loo seat down and to stop eating pickled onions before bedtime, so why not for engagement rings too? "He did text ring later though."

"As in ring?" She mimes a phone with her hand. "Or ring as in finger?"

I'm not sure to be honest. Put like this it does seem a rather tenuous link.

"I don't know," I confess.

"So he might not have done it?"

Talk about raining on my parade. Maddy Lomax is more like a monsoon.

"I'm pretty sure he has," I say firmly. "Come on, Mads! Isn't it romantic? Ollie wouldn't have just gone to work without wishing me happy Valentine's Day, would he?"

"He might if he'd forgotten."

As if Ollie would ever forget Valentine's Day! He knows how much it means to me. Every year since we've been together he's always come up with something thoughtful. From midnight picnics on the beach with thermoses of tea to a little treasure hunt in the cottage, he's always made it special.

"There's no way he'd forget," I reassure her. "This year is just going to be the best Valentine's of all and I know exactly why. I really think he's going to propose!"

"In that case all those wedding magazines you keep leaving around the house will have been worth every penny," she says.

"I don't keep leaving them around the house!"

"Of course you do." Maddy grins at me. "It's not the subtlest hint but fingers crossed it's worked."

"It's not hinting. It's… subliminal!"

"Don't get all huffy. I'm not criticising you," my best friend says, selecting a packet of Arborio rice and dropping it into my basket. "I definitely think it's time you and Ollie got married and were as miserable as the rest of us. Joke!" she adds when she catches my expression. "You've been together for ages and you're perfect together, we can all see that. Sometimes guys just need a bit of a prod."

"Did Richard?" I'm curious about this. The way the Rev goes on I half suspect God nipped down from heaven and told him to pop the question.

"Duh! Of course. You know how long it takes him to make his mind up about anything," Mads says. "Remember how I had to persuade him to have the kids?"

Actually I'm trying very hard to forget. Mads was a woman on a mission and got me embroiled in all kinds of mad schemes in her raise money for a second honeymoon plan. In a weird twist of fate Richard's plans turned out to be even more hare-brained, and traumatic enough to send me screaming to the educational psychologist's office.

On cue, Spiderman and Donatello come charging by on a circuit of the village shop, cheeks bulging hamster fashion with sweets, and buzzing with sugar. Those two should come into school for the sex ed lessons. Ten minutes with the Lomax twins would put any horny teenager off the concept of unprotected sex, and I'd never have to teach the dreaded condom-on-the-banana lesson again.

"I have to be the first to officially congratulate you. Don't you dare show Frankie first or even your sister," she orders, making a swipe for Rafferty and missing. "Come here, you little bu— buttercup!"

"You're my oldest friend, so of course I'll tell you first."

"I'll hold you to that. And how's the porn book going?" she says, so loudly that lost tribes in the Amazon look up.

"Shh!" I glance around the shop in terror that the head of Tregowan Comp has popped in to do some shopping and my supply work will vanish faster than sweets into my godchildren's mouths. Once I'm sure nobody's looking my way or listening, I lower my voice. "It's not. In fact, I'm really struggling to write a paragraph, let alone a chapter. I don't think I can do this, Mads. My mind isn't filthy enough."

She looks at me thoughtfully. "Too much of a romantic to write about the nuts and bolts of the whole process?"

Hmm. She's onto something there. I do think that might be the problem.

"Maybe," I agree. "But the trouble is I really need the money, so not being able to write about the nuts and bolts is a luxury I can't afford. Tansy's had enough of books and I've just had a quote for the roof which makes me feel sick. If I get the Throb job the royalties look good and it would pay for the roof and take the pressure off Ollie."

"And pay for a wedding too?"

Crap. I hadn't even thought about the cost of the wedding. From the state of our bank balance I'll be wrapping myself in a net curtain and using Hula Hoops for rings at this rate. Traditionally I know the bride's parents help, but the last time I spoke to mine they were heading off to Spain in their camper van – and besides, they tend to have even less money than me. Maybe Frankie and Gabriel could adopt me? I bet they'd love to plan another wedding. Their own was totally flamboyant (twenty peacocks, anyone?) and even Elton John looked impressed. They'll probably have me dressed up like something out of Big Fat Gypsy Weddings but it'll be worth it. I might even get featured in OK! magazine...

"I can see from your face how dire this is, my pure and innocent friend," says Mads. "Fear not. I have a mind like an open sewer and I'm sure I can help. Let's have a girls' night and a brainstorm. I'm sure we'll come up with something. I'll give Frankie a call too. He's bound to have some ideas. By the time we've finished your new hero will make Christian Grey look like a well-adjusted human being!"

I'm rather alarmed. Much as I love Ollie's cousin, rock star Frankie Burrows, he's far too over the top at times and possibly the most indiscreet person on the planet.

"Don't tell Frankie. You know how hopeless he is at keeping a secret. If I get the contract with Throb it has to be hush-hush, remember? And if Tregowan Comp isn't keen on having a bodice-ripping novel writer on the books, just imagine what Ollie's school will be like if they so much as think he's linked to me. They'll freak."

Maddy's nose crinkles. "St Jude's sounds like a right barrel of laughs. Not."

I nod. St Jude's is dead strict. The kids actually wear their ties around their necks rather than knotted around their heads like Rambo, and they have blazers too. Ol did tell me lots about their place in the league table and the latest Ofsted report but I'd had half an eye on TOWIE at the time and, besides, there's a magic switch in my brain which flicks off from school stuff after three-thirty. Apart from the terrifying Carolyn Miles, she of the long legs and blonde hair, all I know about St Jude's is that as an establishment it takes itself extremely seriously. Ollie was thrilled to get a job there. He did say it was never his kind of place (Tregowan Comp being more his style), but he reckoned St Jude's offered him an excellent opportunity for career development. At this point I nearly fell off our sofa. Career development? Since when had Ol been interested in career development? In fact, I was sure I could remember him telling me he'd only gone into teaching so he could spend the six-week summer holidays surfing.

But no. It appears that something has changed and Ollie now takes his career Very Seriously Indeed. I even caught him reading The Guardian the other day, and a few nights ago he shouted "attainment targets" in his sleep. I'm a bit worried to be honest, but he seems keen and I'll do anything I can to support him.

I. Must. Not. Let. Ollie. Down.

Mads and I make plans for a brainstorming session in the vicarage when the Rev is busy with the parish council and safely out of the way. Then she rounds up the twins, both on major sugar highs, and heads off to their party. Feeling far more optimistic now about the chances of Lucinda and Alexi actually getting down to basics, I practically skip round the shop. Even the astronomical price of what looks like a pretty puny selection of goods can't dent my excitement. What cost an engagement dinner and feeding the man I love? I even throw in a bottle of fizzy wine for good measure. This is going to be a wonderful evening; I just know it!

Now all I have to do is get home and find that ring.

Chapter 4

Whoever knew that a tiny two-bedroomed cottage could have so many possible hiding places? I must have been searching for at least two hours and I can't find any trace of an engagement ring or even a card. I've tried everywhere too, from the bottom of Sasha's basket to the ironing pile (somewhere I never venture – after all, what are tumble driers for?) to the top of the kitchen units, and still no joy. I've searched drawers, cupboards, under the sink, the garden shed – but there's still no ring. Ollie's found an amazingly safe location for it, that's for sure. I've searched so hard I feel like Frodo.

At least *my* Valentine's gift is well under way. The kitchen might look a bit like an explosion's gone off and I *may* have helped myself to a glass or two of the cooking wine, but the lump of goo bubbling away on the hob certainly looks like it has potential and it doesn't smell too bad either.

I really do hate cooking. It's like I have cookery dyslexia or something. I always *think* I'm following the recipe, measuring carefully, blending religiously and, unlike Nigella, resisting the temptation to dip my fingers into anything nice, but this domestic-goddess lark is way harder than it looks. As I survey the war zone that is my kitchen I promise I will never again look down on the Food Technology teachers. So they might have sod all marking to do, but just imagine the washing up! And as for kids near hobs and blenders? I shudder at the thought. If today's art class was anything to judge by, then the Food Tech crew are lucky to make it out alive.

Anyway, my dinner's looking really good, if I do say so myself, and if Ollie makes it home soon then it should be just perfect. The pretendy champagne is cooling, Nora Jones is crooning in the background and I've lit a few candles too. Ol reckons my candle habit is a fire hazard, and he's always paranoid at bedtime just in case I've left one alight to burn us all to a crisp, but I always think they make the atmosphere very romantic. I bet Alexi and Lucinda would find plenty of interesting uses for candles and hot wax—

Quick! Write that down! Maybe they can do something naughty with risotto too? Nibble grains of rice from all kinds of exciting places? Dust themselves with Parmesan cheese? I'll ask Mads what she thinks. It could work; everyone's *MasterChef* and *Bake Off* mad these days, so some food-themed cheekiness might be the very thing to hit the spot.

I'm just hunting for a notebook (which is something of a challenge, seeing as I've turned the desk inside out and everything's now in a bit of a muddle), when I hear the front door open. Moments later Sasha, our Irish setter, hurls herself at me as though she's been away for twenty years rather than just with the dog sitter since eight a.m. Shortly afterwards Ollie walks into the kitchen, staring about the place in disbelief.

"Bloody hell! Have we been burgled?"

Honestly, what's Ollie like? "No, of course not. Whatever makes you say that?"

My boyfriend runs a hand through his curly brown hair. "Err, the fact that it looks like the entire house has been ransacked? The contents of the cupboard under the stairs have been emptied out all over the hall? And what on earth's happened to our kitchen?"

Ah. The kitchen. Earlier I rummaged through every drawer, examined the oven and even scaled the worktops in my search, but somehow I don't think he's referring to my new Olympic sport *find the ring*. A lot else has gone on in the kitchen since then.

"I'm cooking dinner," I say, reaching onto my tiptoes and kissing him, but he's far too busy gazing around wide-eyed to pay me much attention. Is he looking to see if I've found the hiding place? Oh! I can hardly wait! Come on, Ollie! It's all I can do not to just shriek "Give me my engagement ring!" and jump up and down at him a bit like Sasha does when she thinks we're off for a walk.

"Well, that explains the mess in here," he says with a wry smile, then winces as he peers into the bubbling saucepan.

"That looks very… err… unusual."

It does? What's risotto supposed to look like? I thought it was meant to have some texture to it, although maybe those lumps and the black crusty bits shouldn't be there. Oh well, if not we can always pick them out.

"It's mushroom risotto," I announce. "With bacon. And wine and chocolate mousse too."

"In the risotto?" He steps backwards in alarm.

"No, silly! Prosecco to drink and chocolate mousse for pudding."

Ollie takes off his steamed-up glasses, wipes them on his sleeve and looks at me long and hard with those amazing brown eyes flecked with gold, which always make me melt just like the spatula did earlier on the Aga hotplate. (Hopefully dousing the house in Febreze earlier has disguised the stench of this disaster. Poor Ol's only recently finished removing the soldered-on remnants of the last one. I have a very bad track record when it comes to melting things on the hotplate.)

"OK," he says slowly. "What have I done wrong?"

"Nothing!"

Ol replaces his glasses. "All right then. What have *you* done wrong?"

Isn't that nice? Here I am cooking my (nearly) fiancé a romantic

Valentine's dinner and he instantly assumes I've done something terrible.

"Any lobsters hiding? Giant cactus under a pile of coats? Dog shredded a valuable document?" he asks, pulling me into his arms and tickling me just under the ribs, in the one place he knows is guaranteed to have me pleading for mercy in about two seconds flat. I gasp and writhe while Ollie continues to tickle me and describes the disastrous dinner party I once threw for my ex-boyfriend and his dreadfully strait-laced boss.

"No! No! Nothing like that!" Managing to pull myself away and escape to the far end of the kitchen, I just about suck in enough air to gasp, "It's Valentine's Day!"

The grin vanishes from Ollie's face in a nanosecond. He stops laughing instantly and my stomach swoops from excitement to crushing despair. I know my boyfriend inside out and I can tell from the horrified expression on his face that he's totally and utterly forgotten. There's no surprise and there's no ring. Mads was right: Ollie's text meant he was going to call me, not propose. I've been so stupid. Me and my bloody, busy, overactive imagination. Why couldn't it just have been content with writing blue scenes for Throb Publishing? Isn't that enough for it? Did it really need to make me believe I was about to get engaged? Or was I just choosing to believe this was possible because I want it so much? I've been kidding myself, haven't I? Nothing could be further from Ollie's mind. He wasn't gearing up to propose at all. He can't even be bothered to remember bloody Valentine's Day.

Yes, I know I forgot it too, but that's different. Totally different!

"Oh shit!" Ollie looks at me aghast. "I'm so sorry. I completely forgot."

I try to say something but all I do is make a feeble little squeak because there's a lump in my throat so huge it makes the risotto look smooth.

"I knew Valentine's Day was coming up and I meant to do something," Ol continues, looking absolutely mortified, "honestly I did, baby, but I've just been so busy. We had a massive meeting after school about Progress 8 and the new GCSE bandings, and I had to make sure my analysis of the Key Stage 2 data was spot on for Carolyn's presentation, otherwise come three years' time our value added will be a negative residual and we're all screwed."

I stare at him. Firstly, because I have no idea what on earth he's talking about, secondly because who gives a toss about what might happen three years away, and thirdly because he's mentioned Carolyn. Steph's comment earlier today about male staff enjoying the "Miles High Club" has triggered such a big red alert in my brain I can almost hear the claxons sounding.

Ollie's forgotten Valentine's Day because he's been working on a presentation with Carolyn Miles?

Seriously?

"You were at a meeting?" I ask, and Ollie nods wearily.

"Of course I was. I always have a middle leaders' meeting on Tuesdays. This was a long one too; I think the dog sitter thought I'd abandoned Sasha. I'm sorry to be back so late, Katy, and even sorrier I forgot it's Valentine's Day."

He puts his glasses on the kitchen table, pushing aside a pile of plates I plonked there earlier while emptying the dresser in my ring search, and grinds his knuckles into his eyes. He looks absolutely exhausted and I notice just how pale he is and how deep the shadows are under his eyes. He's working far too hard in this new job and I wish with all my heart that he didn't have to. Suddenly Valentine's Day doesn't matter half as much as it did.

"It's OK, Ol," I say, stepping forward and hugging him. "It doesn't matter. I only remembered at lunchtime myself."

Ollie pulls an outraged face. "I see. So you don't love me anymore?"

"How can you say that when I've made you dinner?"

He drops a weary kiss onto the top of my head. "Is that the dinner I can smell burning?"

We both look at the risotto pan. A plume of black smoke is starting to rise and with a shriek I dash forward to snatch the saucepan from the hotplate and plunge it into the sink. There's a sizzle and a hiss and then – voila! I have made risotto soup.

Ollie's laughing so hard that tears are running down his cheeks.

"I do love you, Katy Carter," he gasps. "Don't ever change, will you?"

I look around at our kitchen – with the cupboard doors open, contents strewn all over the place and yet another ruined saucepan languishing in the sink – and feel very lucky that he loves me just the way I am because, to be quite honest, I don't think I *can* change. I'm a disaster zone. A lesser man would have given up years ago.

"I don't think I could handle living with a normal woman," Ollie adds, and I dig him in the ribs before kissing him. His lips taste of the cold air outside and I pull him closer, thinking that maybe burning the dinner was a blessing in disguise and there are far more interesting things to do than eat dinner. And we still have the chocolate mousse too…

But I'm not the only person thinking about food; at this point Sasha bounds back into the kitchen, tongue lolling and gazing beseechingly up at us with big brown eyes, which is Red Setter for *please feed me*. Since we both know from bitter experience that a hungry Sasha is likely to chew her way through coursework folders/important documents/Ollie's most expensive wetsuit, any hopes of passion are hastily put aside for the very important job of filling her bowl.

"Why were you rummaging through the cupboards anyway?" Ollie asks me as he hunts for the dog food. He's looking totally confused, which is fair enough seeing as I relocated all twenty tins underneath the kitchen table while searching for the ring that never was.

"I was spring cleaning."

"In February?" He raises his eyebrows. "There's still frost outside most mornings, Katy."

"It never hurts to start early," I say piously.

"We've lived here nearly five years and this is the first time I've ever heard you mention spring cleaning." Ollie locates a tin, tugs the ring pull and forks the contents into Sasha's bowl while she dances about ecstatically. He grins at me over his shoulder. "I'd hardly call that starting early! Are you sure you weren't looking for something?"

"Of course not!" I cross my fingers behind my back and pray very hard that he never guesses what I was actually up to. I think I'd die of mortification. There was I thinking he was planning to give me a ring, when in reality nothing could have been further from Ollie's mind. Far better he thinks I'm a bit unhinged – which to be fair he always has done anyway – than he suspects I was hoping for an engagement ring. He must have forgotten what he said to me on the quay all that time ago, and I really haven't the heart to remind him.

Luckily my prayers are answered (take that, Reverend Rich!) and Ollie seems to accept my spring-cleaning explanation. Once Sasha's fed and the kitchen's been restored to something like order, we peer into the fridge in the hope that something to eat might have miraculously appeared. Alas, even the chocolate mousse looks unfit for consumption. Unless we want to make an onion-and-jelly baby omelette, starvation is imminent.

"Let's go to the pub for dinner," Ol suggests.

I almost collapse onto the kitchen floor with shock because it's Tuesday and teachers never, ever go out on a school night. Our pupils might be up until the small hours playing *Call of Duty* or sending pictures to total strangers on Chatroulette, but rest assured that most of their teachers are tucked up by ten o'clock with a mug of Horlicks. Any who *are* still up are scaling mountains of marking while necking Red Bull to keep their heavy eyes open.

"Really?"

"Really," Ollie replies. "It's Valentine's Day and I'm bloody well going to have a night off from working and take my gorgeous girlfriend out for dinner."

"Can't wait to meet her," I say. "Will she mind if I'm there too?"

Ollie's answer to this is to kiss me again. "You *are* gorgeous, Katy, even if you make a total mess and cost us a fortune in ruined saucepans!"

And he says this with his glasses on too. How lucky am I?

I do up my coat and pull on my pink spotty wellies before Ollie can change his mind, and moments later we're walking hand in hand through the village towards the Mermaid Inn with Sasha lolloping ahead, ears flapping and her excited barks punctuating the still evening air.

It's a perfect Valentine's night. The twinkly stars and smile of moon are reflected in the still water of Tregowan Harbour, while the tide beyond it laps against the harbour walls and smoke drifts softly from cottage chimneys. It's bitterly cold and the narrow streets are deserted. With our breath rising in front of us and our faces tingling in the chilly air, we walk along the quay, past fish boxes piled like yellow Lego bricks, before turning sharp right and climbing the crooked steps that lead into the pub.

The minute the door opens the peace of the outside world evaporates because the Mermaid's absolutely heaving. No wonder the village is empty: everyone's in here celebrating Valentine's Day. Red paper hearts are strung across the low beams, the menu's offering two-for-one steak dinners with free bubbly, and over the ancient sound system Chris de Burgh is warbling about a lady in red dancing with him.

"Not in here she won't," Ollie says drily as we elbow our way to the bar. "There's hardly any room to stand, never mind dance. Tell you what, why don't you see if you can grab us a table while I order the food?"

I look around but if there's even room to swing a gnat I can't see it. Golly, I had no idea Tregowan was such a loved-up village. Usually on a Tuesday in February the pub's deserted apart from a few diehard drinkers and the occasional piece of tumbleweed blowing by. Today, however, practically everyone we know is out and about. I even spot my sister and her fisherman boyfriend sitting in the window seat tucking into steaks. I'm gobsmacked, because if there was ever a prize for the world's most unromantic couple then they'd be the winners by a mile. Holly's true passion is applied mathematics, and the only fishnets that turn Guy on are the ones dragged behind his trawler. They're the most unlikely couple in the world; they bicker non-stop and only see each other in passing when he's off to the pub and she's coming in from lecturing. Then again, maybe that's why it works? I'm very fond of Guy but he'd drive me mad in twenty seconds flat. Saying that, I feel exactly the same way about my sister, so it's probably a match made in heaven after all.

Mads reckons the sex must be good. ("Because, let's face it, Katy, all he thinks about is fishing and all she talks about is numbers!") And she could be onto something, I guess – not that I really want to think about it for too long. Besides, it's not my sister's relationship I'm worried about; I can't help feeling it doesn't bode well for me and Ollie if *even* Guy Tregarten can remember Valentine's Day…

"Guy and Holly are over there," I tell Ollie, pointing in their direction.

"Blimey," he says, glancing across the bar. "That's a bit out of character for Guy, isn't it? Maybe they ran out of beer at home?"

I laugh. "That's probably it. If they move up, then maybe we can join them? You know those two, they won't mind if we crash their Valentine's dinner."

"Guy certainly won't if we get a round or two in," agrees Ol, "and I think I can brave an hour talking about the Common Fisheries Policy if it means we get a seat."

"You must be hungry," I say.

"You'd better believe it. I'll even talk about fishing if it means I get to eat," he tells me.

Leaving Ollie to wait in the queue, I thread my way through the press of bodies to join my sister. I wave and call out, but either Chris de Burgh is too loud or I'm so short that she can't see my little ginger head above the crush. Being five feet three is such a curse, and in my flat wellies I don't even have the advantage of the platform boots I usually wear to crowded places – so I give up trying to attract their attention and focus instead on not being elbowed in the head or dunked in beer.

Once I'm closer, however, I soon realise that even if I were eight feet tall, painted blue and tap-dancing naked through the Mermaid, Holly and Guy still wouldn't notice me. Squashed up in the window seat with their knees rammed under a tiny table and their heads close together, they're completely engrossed in one another. Guy is actually stroking Holly's face and gazing at her with such blatant adoration that it brings a lump to my throat. And what's this? Is he really holding her hand?

Crikey! Maybe they're not quite as unromantic as Mads and I thought?

I'm just backing away quietly, not wanting to interrupt their Valentine's Day, when Holly spots me.

"Katy! What on earth are you doing skulking away from us?"

"I wasn't skulking!" I protest. "I just didn't want to disturb you."

"You were totally skulking, you harris," grins Guy. "Skulk. Skulk. Skulk. That's you, Katy Carter, although those bloody silly wellies stand out a mile. Nobody could miss those."

"They're not silly! They're Joules."

He shrugs. "I don't care who you borrowed them off. They'd be no use on a wet deck in a force nine. You'd slide everywhere."

I'm more likely to join the Mars mission than I am to go deep-sea fishing in a storm, but that won't stop Guy from telling me what I should wear.

"Put a sock in it, Guy," my sister orders. To me she says, "Just ignore him. You know Guy would like us all to dress in smocks and rigger boots, a bit like him, and wear oilskins in the rain."

"Makes sense to me," Guy says sulkily.

"Well we're not all you, Guy Tregarten," retorts my sister, and then they're up and running – bickering about the right clothing to wear, whether Holly really needs more than three pairs of shoes and why Guy needs to brave a trip across the Tamar and go clothes shopping.

Time for me to escape…

"I'll catch you guys later," I say quickly while Holly pauses for breath and Guy's still searching for counterarguments. "Have a lovely night!"

"Don't go," my sister cries. "Come and join us! It'll be fun."

Fun? I think I'd have a more peaceful evening hanging out with Tom and Jerry.

"Oh no, no. You two are having a romantic meal together," I insist, poised for flight. Out of the corner of my eye I spot Ollie, armed with a tray of drinks and several packets of pork scratchings (allegedly to keep Sasha quiet, but which I know are to tide him over until our food arrives). If Guy clocks the beers, we'll never escape. "We'll catch you later."

"No you bloody won't," says Guy, moving up and patting the space next to him. "We've got some bloody brilliant news and who better to celebrate with than you two?"

They have? Has Guy caught a giant fish? Or maybe Holly 's discovered a new magical prime number or something?

My sister's nodding. "He's right for once! We really do have some good news! Look!"

Slowly, she slips her left hand from Guy's and holds it up proudly – and a big diamond on her third finger sparkles in the candlelight.

My mouth swings open. Is that what I think it is? Seriously?

"Guy's asked me to marry him!" my sister says happily. "On Valentine's Day too! Isn't it romantic! I'm engaged, Katy! Guy and I are going to get married! How exciting is that?"

Chapter 5

"Get this down your neck and tell me all about it."

Mads hands me a glass of wine, tucks her legs underneath her and curls up on the sofa. The twins are both in bed, the Rev's safely out of the way and Ollie has after-school training, so here I am at the vicarage armed with my brief from Throb Publishing, a notebook and about ten million woes. It's just as well my best friend's sitting comfortably, because I'm about to begin and it could take some time.

"There's Pringles too," Maddy adds, "but I think the rug rats may have been at them. One of Richard's really interfering parishioners knocked earlier, so I hid behind the sofa with the twins and the only way I could keep them quiet was to fill their faces with crisps."

"You hid from your flock? That's wasn't very charitable. Where would Christianity be today if Jesus had done the same?" I tease.

"Believe me, even the good Lord would want to hide from this one," my friend sighs. "She picks holes in everything we do, and you know how hard Richard works here. I sometimes think she's just looking for an excuse for the diocese to find a new vicar she and her cronies can control."

Richard isn't one of my favourite people, and I'm sure he would say the same about me, but he's certainly dedicated to his work – and Mads, for all her flippant comments, is one hundred percent behind him.

"She's the one who's dumped all this crap on me to sort out for the next jumble sale," Mads continues, waving her hand at the towering pile of bric-a-brac dominating the back half of the tiny sitting room. "It's going to take hours to sort through and goodness knows what kinds of awful things I'll find. I'll have to bathe in Dettol afterwards and fumigate the place."

"You're really expected to organise all of that?" I gaze up at the jumble mountain, half expecting to see a couple of Sherpas waving from the summit.

"Of course. It's all part of the fun life I lead as a vicar's wife. Don't even get me started on the flower arranging and coffee mornings. Anyway, enough of all that! Time for some comfort eating." Mads pops the Pringles lid, fishes out a couple and crams them into her mouth. "Mmmph mmm mumph ooo!"

After sharing a student house together and spending many evenings drinking wine and eating junk food, Mads and I are fluent in Pringle. This mumbling is her asking what's going on with me.

It's a good question. I only wish I knew myself.

I take a big gulp of wine. "You already know about the lack of ring."

She swallows and nods.

"Yeah, that's a shame – but we did think it was a bit of a long shot that Ollie might have hidden one, didn't we?"

Did we? That's news to me; I'd been pretty convinced myself, and I seem to remember Mads making me swear she'd be the first of our friends to see the ring. But since I'm now starting to doubt my grasp on reality, I stare sadly down at my Chardonnay.

"It's not just that. He'd totally forgotten it was Valentine's Day and he's never done that before. Ollie's always been brilliant at remembering birthdays and special occasions." I begin to gnaw at the skin around my thumbnail. "What do you think it means?"

"That he's busy? You said yourself he's been really stressed at work and is up all hours planning lessons and marking books."

"But Ollie never forgets anything!"

"Great as Ollie is, Katy, he's still a bloke and they're not like us. They do that kind of stuff. It's in their genetic code to be a bit crap at times."

"Does Richard forget special occasions?" I ask, curious.

"He wouldn't bloody dare! His life wouldn't be worth living and he'd certainly never get sex again," Maddy says. "Anyway, I've got a giant calendar on the fridge door with all the important dates highlighted in fluorescent colours, and another identical one in his study. Richard couldn't miss a special occasion even if he wanted to – which he doesn't because he knows what's good for him. Honestly, it's a brilliant system. Why don't you try it?"

To be honest this a) sounds more like the sort of thing I should be doing for myself and b) surely defeats the object? If Ollie only remembers Valentine's Day or an anniversary because I nag him via a huge visual aid rather than because these things are actually important to him, then what's the point?

"The point is, this way Ollie can't forget," Mads explains when I voice my concerns. "Which means you're happy and he's off the hook. Everyone's a winner. Ta-da!"

I'm still unconvinced, but since she's the one who's happily married and has a big bunch of red roses taking pride of place on the mantelpiece I guess Mads must know what she's talking about. I suppose I could give it a try – although Ollie will probably think I've flipped, given that I'm possibly one of the most disorganised people on the planet. He's usually the one who gives *me* a list or makes sure I'm going to the right school on my supply days. Besides, I still can't shake the feeling that all this is missing the point. It isn't so much that Ollie forgot Valentine's but *why*.

"It isn't very me," I say doubtfully. "It sounds more like the sort of thing Holly would do."

"My point exactly. And who just got engaged? Holly! Not you!"

Ouch. This certainly hits me where it hurts. As much as I'm thrilled for my sister and Guy, there's a little part of me that's bright green with envy and can't quite believe it's true. Holly and Guy getting married? I never ever saw that one coming.

"I'm sorry if that was a bit tactless," says Mads, leaning over and sloshing more wine into my glass.

"*If?*" I take a big gulp of my topped-up drink.

"OK, so it was totally tactless, but don't you think it's a fair point? Men need a bit of help sometimes with these things. Holly probably gave Guy a few hints."

My sister's hinting would be as subtle as a wrecking ball swinging around with Miley Cyrus gyrating on it, but I don't actually think she did have to hint. Holly seemed genuinely surprised and Guy couldn't have been any prouder if he'd just caught the world's biggest fish, which in a way I suppose he has. No, it looks to me as though this was very much his idea. Guy wants to marry my sister.

He's not forgotten…

"But I don't want to hint, Mads. Ollie and I aren't like that. We don't play games and there's no way I'd ever want him to feel pressured, so I really don't think a cork board with highlighted dates is the way forward. I want him to still *want* to get married, not feel he has to because I've written it on a to-do list. That's not very romantic."

"Who said anything about romance? I thought it was marriage we were discussing?" Mads says. "Still, up to you. Stick to leaving the wedding magazines around the house and rummaging through cupboards if you want, but take it from me, sometimes a girl has to take matters into her own hands. If you sit in the passenger seat too long you forget how to drive."

"I hope that's just a metaphor," I say gloomily. "Since Ollie takes the car to school and drops me off on the way, I haven't driven anywhere for ages. We keep meaning to buy a second car, but it's just more expense – and until our roof's fixed there's no way we can do it. Not unless I win the lottery."

My best friend looks alarmed. "You're not pinning all your hopes on winning the jackpot are you?"

Truth is I'm Camelot's bitch, but it's probably better to keep my lucky-dip habit to myself. Twice a week I have a little glimmer of hope that maybe, just maybe, my numbers will come in and I'll be able to rescue Ollie from dripping ceilings and marking hell without having to resort to writing for Throb. Besides, what's a few quid in return for several days of optimistic daydreaming? It's a bargain if you think about it, and certainly cheaper than therapy. They should have the lottery on the NHS.

"Of course not," I say.

"Fibber," laughs Mads, topping up her own glass. "I bet you're spending a fortune on tickets. Just don't forget your friends when the millions come in. I want my cut or I'm telling Ollie he's shacked up with a gambler."

"I'm hardly a gambler! Anyway, I thought Richard didn't believe in the lottery? How could you possibly justify getting your hands dirty with my ill-gotten gains from Mammon? Won't you go straight to hell?"

"Lobbing a load into the collection will help me get to heaven. And somebody has to keep Louis Vuitton in business, so buying a few bags is practically charity," she says airily. "But never mind me. Your lottery-ticket addiction and lack of engagement ring aside, how are things with you and Ollie? Seriously, I mean. Is everything all right?"

I stare past her and into the leaping flames of the wood burner. I tell Mads pretty much everything and she knows me inside out, but there's one thing I haven't said to her, because I'm scared that voicing it aloud will make it real. It's a little worry that's been worming its way gradually into my subconscious thanks to comments from Steph or the odd throwaway remark from Ollie, and it's probably paranoia on my part…

What do I mean, *probably*? Of course it is.

"He's fine," I say firmly. "We're fine, I think."

Mads, who's been carefully extracting Pringle crumbs from the bottom of the tube, looks up in alarm.

"You only *think* you're fine?"

I gulp. I did think we were fine until Steph mentioned Carolyn "Miles High Club" and Ollie let slip that he'd been working late on a presentation with her. He collaborates very closely with Carolyn, but she's his line manager so this is hardly surprising. I know he loves me and I trust him, of course I do, but he's been so obsessed with work lately and all he talks about is school…

And she's gorgeous. Tall and blonde and so ambitious she makes Donald Trump look half-hearted. I bet Carolyn Miles can analyse data in her sleep and has never burned a risotto in her life. She looks organised and thorough and is totally career driven.

In other words, she's the complete opposite of me.

Mads sets down the tube, brushes sour-cream-and-chive dust from her fingertips and gives me her best *tell all* look.

"He's working really long hours," I say, reluctant to mention Carolyn. "Honestly, Mads, I'm not exaggerating. He's hardly ever home before seven and we never have any time together because if he's not marking he's planning or at some St Jude's function."

"Sounds like he's just working super hard, babes."

I nod, because there's no denying it. "Tonight he says he's got after-school training until eight."

Mads knows me well enough to pick up the subtext. "He *says*? And you don't think that's true?"

I shrug. "It probably is true. Schools always have twilight training."

"What the fuck is *twilight training*? Something to do with werewolves and vampires?"

If only. I'm sure I'd have listened far more attentively in the past if we'd been gazing at R-Patz in the school hall rather than at the head teacher and a mind-numbing selection of PowerPoint slides telling us things we already knew (and at a time in the day when all any teacher wants to do is collapse in a heap and sob).

"Nothing so exciting. It's evening teacher training," I tell her. "Ollie has to deliver a session on data analysis and exam-grade predictions. It's all really complicated stuff."

"Blimey," says Mads. "And there was me thinking it was all about chalk, leather elbow patches and confiscating fags."

"Where on earth do you get your ideas about school? *Grange Hill*? It's all interactive whiteboards and suits these days, and the kids are way too busy sexting to worry about cigarettes. Just you wait until the twins are teenagers."

She grimaces. "I'm dreading it already; believe me, nursery school's bad enough. But, listen, if Ollie's got all this extra responsibility with data, surely that explains why he's working so hard and staying late at school? If it's as complex as it sounds then he's got to be right on top of it all, hasn't he? Especially if he wants to be promoted in the future or something."

"But that's the thing, Mads! This is Ollie we're talking about here. Ollie! The man who likes surfing and rock climbing and playing on his Xbox. Since when was he worried about being promoted? It's not like him at all. He's totally changed since he moved to St Jude's! He's become so ambitious."

And what if Carolyn Miles is the reason? I add silently. I'm not going to say anything about my fears to Mads yet. I know that if I do she'll be like a dog with a bone and there won't be a minute's peace until we've done something hare-brained like staking out St Jude's so that Maddy can have a good gander at the opposition. But the worry is still there and, like a pair of too-tight leggings, is making me very uncomfortable. I trust Ollie, I do, but Carolyn's so groomed, so driven, so *grown up* – and I'm just none of those things, am I? What if somebody like her is actually what he needs, rather than daydreaming me with my trail of toast crumbs and ink-stained fingers?

I love Ollie with all my heart and soul. He's my special best friend, my other half and the person whose very existence makes me smile every day – but what if I'm no longer what he needs?

This thought makes my stomach swoop with horror.

"More wine," Mads says, catching sight of my face. Jumping up, she heads for the fridge. Returning with another bottle and twisting off the screw cap, she refills our glasses and settles back onto the sofa. "I think you're worrying too much about Ollie, babes. None of us are twenty-five anymore and it's not unusual for a guy to want promotion at our age. Richard was just the same: he wanted his own parish and the chance to prove himself. That's why we came to Tregowan."

I nod but I'm not convinced. Richard and Ollie are nothing alike. The Rev probably won't be happy until he's Archbishop of Canterbury or something, but Ollie's never been the kind of person who wanted to follow the management route. Something's changed but I've no idea what.

"My guess is he wants to prove himself in his new school," Mads concludes. "From what you tell me that's going to be really hard work, so he'll have to put in a lot of time and effort. I wouldn't read too much into any of it if I was you."

She's right. Of course she is. I know how hard heads of departments in secondary schools have to work, and this certainly accounts for Ollie being exhausted and stressed. I'm shattered after just a day of supply teaching, so it's no wonder he's worn out. But what this doesn't explain is why he felt the urge to take the job in the first place. If it's because we need the money, then I'd feel dreadful. I have to find a way of taking the pressure off him and pulling my weight financially, which could start with winning the contract to write for Throb…

Writer's block is not an option. It's time for that brainstorming session.

I'm just reaching into my bag to dig out the brief when a pyjama-clad Rafferty pads into the sitting room demanding a drink. With ruffled dark curls, pink chubby cheeks and a teddy bear clutched to his chest he looks so cute that even my hard teenager-teaching heart melts. I have the cutest godchildren! OK, so as a godmother I'm a bit lacking in the moral and religious parts of my duties, but with Richard at the helm I'm sure they're more than well provided for on that score. I'm very good at other bits such as the buying of McDonald's and accidentally teaching them swear words. I'm also an excellent teller of bedtime stories and, as soon as he clocks me, Rafferty demands one.

"No way," his mother says sternly. "It's way past bedtime. You need to get straight back up those stairs."

Rafferty's bottom lip juts out. Then he sees the two wine bottles on the table and his eyes widen.

"Grown-up drink! Daddy says no grown-up drink! Naughty Mummy!"

Ah yes. Just to complicate life Richard and Maddy have given up alcohol for Lent, or rather Richard has and his wife is humouring him. Personally, I'd have given up being bossed about by the Rev, and for a bit longer than Lent too – but Mads says give and take is all part of a marriage and, anyway, what Richard doesn't know won't hurt him.

"But isn't that lying?" I'd asked, a bit confused by the moral quicksand I'd found myself immersed in. But Mads just grinned and said she'd crossed her fingers when they'd agreed. I'm still not convinced this would stand up in a court of law or with Jesus either if he were to pop in and enquire, but since I'm not a vicar's wife, or anyone's wife actually, what do I know?

"That's Katy's drink," Mads says swiftly, shooting me a look that says part of being a godmother is very definitely letting Mummy off the hook while I look like a complete booze hound. "Mummy's going to have a nice cup of tea."

"One bottle. Two bottles." Rafferty counts. "Is Katy always very thirsty, Mummy? Is that why Daddy says she drinks too much?"

"Daddy doesn't say that!" Mads is bright red. And so she should be. I'm losing count of how many times I've taken the blame for whatever madcap scheme she's dreamt up. Thinking I'm a lush is probably one of the nicer opinions Richard holds of yours truly.

"He does! And he said—"

"Bed! Now!" With a face hotter than the wood burner, Mads leaps up from the sofa and scoops her son into her arms, presumably before he can drop his parents in it any further.

"I'll pop the *kettle* on shall I?" I say sweetly, and Mads flushes an even deeper crimson.

"Back in a minute," she promises and heads upstairs. With every step I hear Rafferty demanding a story and, suspecting that stories operate in a similar fashion to forgetful sweets, I distract myself by having a rummage through the jumble. Several avalanches later I've unearthed a couple of dog-eared Jilly Coopers and a funky lava lamp that wouldn't look out of place in Austin Power's shag pit.

"Have it," Mads insists when she eventually rejoins me. "I'll pop a donation into the funds on your behalf."

"Feeling guilty about letting your son believe his godmother is Tregowan's answer to George Best?" I ask, and Mads sighs.

"You know how seriously Richard takes these things. If he thought I'd cheated he'd feel utterly betrayed. I can't let him down. Not when he's trying so hard and hasn't cracked at all. I really appreciate you covering for me when I slip up."

"Slip up? Mads, you've had the best part of a bottle!"

"So would you if you had to sort out all that jumble! Besides, I can't help it if I'm not as strong-minded as Richard, can I?"

Strong-minded is a nice way of putting it. The Rev's about as flexible as a steel girder and Mads has the self-control of... of... well, of something with zero self-control. Every year she cheats at Lent and every year I end up covering for her. It wasn't so bad when it was chocolate or shopping she'd given up; I could take the blame for those and just look like a greedy spendthrift. But appearing to be a raging alcoholic is hardly conducive to my reputation – or Ollie's, for that matter. The last thing Ollie needs now that he's so career-minded is anyone at St Jude's hearing *that* about me.

"Let me make it up to you by coming up with some amazing ideas for your sample chapter," says Mads, who knows exactly how to get around me. "Let's have another *cup of tea* and get brainstorming. Just you wait! In a couple of hours' time your notebook will be so hot it'll burst into flames!"

So, fortified by more wine, we work our way through the guidelines from Throb and Mads puts her thinking cap on. Before long I'm making notes on things I haven't even imagined and she's right! It's so hot I'm having to fan my cheeks with the A4 sheets. By the time Richard arrives home (the wine glasses having been safely washed up and put away, and two mugs of very non-alcoholic coffee having been placed innocently in front of us), I have so many ideas that my head's spinning. I kiss my best friend goodnight, wave to Richard and head back home, filled with optimism.

I can do this. I know I can. The Throb contract is as good as in the bag. Alexi and Lucinda had better be ready – they're in for a very busy time!

Chapter 6

I love Saturdays! There's nothing better than waking up with the blissful knowledge that the whole weekend is still ahead, brimful of possibilities and acres of free time. It's impossible to lie in when there are seagulls tap-dancing on the rooftop and a boisterous red setter leaping onto the bed demanding walks and attention, so usually Ollie and I get up early and have breakfast together before taking Sasha for a long walk.

OK, maybe I'm using a little bit of artistic licence here. What I should say is that we have breakfast together and then Ollie and Sasha go for a long walk while I potter around the house and think about writing my book, which can take ages. Sometimes they're back before I've even typed a word. This is because thinking about writing a book is a very serious thing indeed, and although Ollie reckons I'm just wasting time checking Facebook and Instagram, what he doesn't realise is that this is all a major part of the creative process. All the famous writers are on the Internet – and very busy they are too, tweeting and Facebooking and pinning things on virtual pinboards. Reading what they put there is like attending a digital masterclass, and there are loads of funny video clips of cats too (although I only look at those as a break from research, of course). But honestly, I can spend hours just getting into the writing zone.

Anyway, Saturday's usually a relaxed day of writing and chilling out and generally just enjoying some spare time together, although recently Ollie hasn't had much of this. He's been spending Saturday afternoons planning lessons or grading coursework while I pop over to see Mads or to visit Holly. I hadn't realised quite how much his job had been eating into our time together until I started to really think about it, but now that I have noticed I'm worried.

Ollie is working far too hard.

Take this Saturday, for example. It's one of those beautiful crisp and sunshiny days, without the usual rain and sea mists that tend to be wrapped around Tregowan like a scarf for most of the winter. Even *I* woke up feeling eager to go for a walk. I didn't bark or jump around on the bed like Sasha but I did share her enthusiasm for going out along the cliffs and letting the cold air blast the cobwebs away. I've been working pretty hard on my sample chapter too, and unless I want to contract a bad case of writer's bum, going for a walk is a great idea – especially if we make it as far as the next town and can buy pasties. A pasty always motivates me to do some exercise.

"I can't," Ollie says. Even though it's not yet nine o'clock he's already settling down at the kitchen table and spreading out folders and books. "I need to get this A-level coursework ready for moderation on Monday."

"But it's Saturday!" I exclaim. "Ol, you need a day off."

He laughs bleakly. "I can't have a day off; there's far too much to do. Anyway, I didn't work last night, did I?"

"Only because you fell asleep in front of the telly!"

"That's because I was exhausted after three hours spent trying to fix the electrics in this place," he reminds me with a wry smile. "Don't blame St Jude's for that one, Katy Carter! Blame your lava lamp."

Ah. Yes. My lava lamp. It seemed like such a good idea at the time…

"There was a very good reason why somebody donated it to a jumble sale," my boyfriend continues, fishing out a red pen and flipping open his mark book. "They probably weren't huge fans of having all their wiring blown up either."

"I didn't know that at the time! I just thought it looked like fun and would cheer up the kitchen," I protest. "And in fairness to me I was right; it looked brilliant."

Ollie nods. "It certainly did until it shorted out the entire house and melted the circuit boards. Then we couldn't see anything. Not even our hands in front of our faces. And I'd hardly describe the bill from the emergency electrician as *fun*, although he's certainly laughing all the way to the bank!"

He's got a point. I never knew an electrician could put so many noughts onto a bill. He said he'd put together a quote for having the whole cottage rewired too, which apparently is what we need to do if we don't want the place to go up in flames. All this makes the advance from Throb look even more attractive. I must give Mads the final draft of my first chapter, for the bonk queen's seal of approval before I email it across to them – because, thanks to me and my jumble-sale find, Ollie and I need some extra cash. And fast.

Ollie's rubbing his eyes and replacing his glasses, which always heralds a bout of serious concentration. So, feeling dreadful for being the cause of yet more financial woe, I fetch Sasha's lead and allow her to drag me out into the stinging cold. We walk down the beach and play stick for an hour and then do a loop around the harbour, and by the time I'm heading back through the village I feel slightly better. I'm just crossing the little bridge at the foot of the quay when my phone rings and Tansy Topham's beaming face flashes across the screen.

"Katy!" she squeals as I answer. "How are you? It's been too long!"

It's been about three weeks but a lot can happen in three weeks if you're Tansy. I've been reading in *Hiya!* all about her romantic Caribbean getaway with Tommy, *Closer*'s just published an interview about her latest fashion fail and yesterday she popped up on *Loose Women*. Not that I was watching telly when I was meant to be writing; I only had it on in the background.

"I've got a window in my diary for today," Tansy carries on, not pausing for me to say "hi" back or tell her how I've been. "Do you fancy meeting up for some shopping and some lunch? Tommy's training and the nanny's got the kids and I am so bored it's untrue! We so need a girly catch-up. There's a really cool new wine bar on the Barbican and you'll love it. What do you think? Have you got time?"

I think I really should be working on my chapter, but the idea of a little bit of time out with Tansy is very appealing – as is being able to enjoy a glass of wine without constantly looking over my shoulder in case the Reverend Richard Lomax appears. For a few seconds I'm torn, before reminding myself that getting out and about and seeing the world is all part of being a writer. Visiting a new wine bar with Tansy's practically research, isn't it? I might find something to inspire me to write the definitive great British novel which would never happen if I just stayed at home. I'm actually doing my creativity a favour by meeting her.

"I'd love to," I say, and we arrange to meet in an hour. Plymouth is only forty minutes away so I should make it with acres of time to spare and, anyway, Tansy's always late everywhere she goes.

Back in the kitchen Ollie's almost through his pile of marking and looking far more cheerful. Three coffee cups are lined up on the table and his hair's all messed up where he's been running his fingers through it, something he always does when he's concentrating very hard. Last night it was practically standing on end as he did his best to figure out how to get our electricity back – and mine was certainly standing on end when I saw the electrician's bill.

His face lights up as he sees me, and my heart melts. I love him so much. There *has* to be a way I can make his life easier.

"Tansy's invited me for lunch," I tell him, winding my arms around his neck and dropping a kiss onto his head.

Ollie pulls me onto his lap and kisses me back. "Since when did Tansy eat?"

It's a good point. Tansy thinks champagne is a food group. I guess that's why she's a size zero and I'm… not.

"She said she wants a girly catch-up," I tell him.

Ollie grimaces. "You mean she wants to moan about Tommy. Poor man. I wonder what he's done now? Not bought her this season's LV bag in the right colour?"

Tansy famously rules her footballer husband with a rod of iron. She might only be a size-zero slip of a thing, but Tommy's absolutely terrified of her. And yes, she has an amazing handbag collection in all kinds of colours and fabrics. The only person with a selection that comes anything close is

Frankie.

"I'll come into town with you," Ol says, tipping me off his lap and starting to gather up his work, "but I'll give the girl talk a miss. You can drop me into school and I'll pop this data onto the system. I may as well get ahead."

"On a Saturday?" I can hardly keep the horror from my voice. "Who are you and what have you done with the real Ollie Burrows?"

He laughs. "I know; I would never have believed it either, but I might as well play catch-up while you're busy with Tansy. That way we can have some time together later."

Well, I'm not going to argue with this. Three days sitting at my laptop dreaming up steamy scenarios for Alexi and Lucinda have left me very hot under the collar and some time together with Ollie is exactly what I need! He can input data all afternoon if it means we get some quality time later on.

Maddy's comment about my being a passenger is in the back of my mind and Ollie is nervously relegated to co-driver while I take the wheel and steer us to Plymouth. Our car is a rather featureless Focus and I do miss the quirky little Beetle he owned for years. Still, there's a lot to be said for not breaking down every five miles or being gassed by carbon-monoxide fumes. We sail along the A38 and over the Tamar Bridge, except for Ollie yelling "Stop!" when I'm so busy looking at the view I almost forget to brake at the toll barrier. Then we head into town. The car has more acceleration than I remember, and I have a lot of fun seeing how fast I can pull away at the traffic lights. Nowhere near as fast as Tansy in her Lotus but pretty good for me, I think – and everyone knows that speed cameras don't really have film in them, do they?

I hope not, anyway…

"I feel like kissing the ground," Ollie remarks when I pull up outside St Jude's and he opens the door. "You've missed your vocation in Formula One, that's for sure."

"Stop exaggerating and go and do some work," I say, leaning across and kissing him goodbye.

Leaving Ollie and his giant wheelie bag of work outside the side entrance, I pull away from St Jude's. Unlike Tregowan Comp, which is situated slap bang in the middle of the local council estate, my boyfriend's school is in a very smart residential area and at the end of a neat tree-lined drive. Not a scrap of litter or a scavenging seagull is to be seen and nobody's graffitied the St Jude's sign either. What kind of school is this? It's so posh it's making me nervous.

I'm trying to recall how Ollie said to reach the Barbican from here (although it doesn't help that I struggle with remembering my left and right), when a red car turns off the main road and into the school drive. It's a very sexy convertible with the hood down on such a gorgeous day, and as it bowls past I can't help but look – which I guess is the point of cars like this. Nobody does a double take at me in the Ford Focus. Well, not unless I cut them up at the roundabout. (That wasn't strictly my fault, by the way; the road markings were very faint.) No, this is a sleek little number with a curvy bonnet and cheeky pop-up headlights, which is practically yelling *look at me!* So of course I look and, surprise surprise, it's being driven by a glamorous blonde in giant sunglasses and wearing a black leather jacket.

Wait a minute. I recognise that driver. I know I do! I last saw her at the St Jude's staff Christmas dinner when she was poured into black velvet and wearing lipstick the exact colour of that car.

It's Carolyn Miles. What on earth is she doing here on a Saturday?

Unless… unless…

Unless she's meeting Ollie?

My brain has taken a few seconds to click into gear but now it's made the connection it's whizzing away. Has Ollie arranged to meet Carolyn at St Jude's while I'm out of the way with Tansy?

I go cold all over and a horrible churning sensation grips my stomach. I crane my neck to see over my shoulder and, sure enough, the car is pulling up outside the school and a pair of long, denim-clad legs are stretching out as Carolyn uncoils herself from the low-slung seat.

Bugger. I haven't imagined it. She really *is* here, on a Saturday, in an empty school where my boyfriend is supposed to be working.

Supposed to be working? Is that what I really think? I'm horrified with myself. I trust Ollie one hundred percent! Of course I do. Over the past few days I've managed to convince myself I'm being ridiculous and paranoid about Carolyn, but seeing her now and in the well-toned flesh makes me wobble.

Come on, Katy, you're being ridiculous!

Ollie loves me and we're happy together, I'm sure we are, and there's no way he'd cheat. No way at all. Yet how come Carolyn's here too and Ollie didn't think to mention it to me? Is she the real reason he's so keen to come in to work on a Saturday?

It's a coincidence. Of course it is! I'm sure I'm jumping to all kinds of conclusions here, but as I head off to meet Tansy there's one thing I do know for certain: if I don't find out soon what's going on I'll drive myself round the bend.

And given today's success with roundabouts, that won't be a pretty sight.

Chapter 7

Pop! The champagne cork explodes out of the bottle and flies across the wine bar, narrowly missing a couple of lunchtime diners.

"Oops!" giggles Tansy, waving at them apologetically. "I must stop doing that. I almost took Tommy out the other day, and that could have cost us a place in the Premier League."

We're balancing precariously on the most uncomfortable bar stools imaginable at a tiny weeny table slap bang in the window of Plymouth's newest and most achingly trendy wine bar. I'm suffering from a severe case of bum overhang while Tansy, who as usual is wearing a very short skirt, flashes her gusset to all the passers-by and the somewhat jaded photographer from the local rag. Everyone who passes the window cranes their neck to have a good look in and does a double a take when they realise who I'm sitting with.

It's a bit like being a goldfish in a very posh bowl.

"To us!" Tansy declares, raising her glass and tossing her glossy blonde extensions. "The bestselling authors! And to my new business, BBs!"

We chink glasses, although I'm not really sure I have quite as much to celebrate. Writing for Tansy might have been a small income stream but it was better than nothing, and without it my literary career is looking very precarious indeed.

Almost as precarious as my relationship's beginning to feel…

I still can't believe Ollie's arranged to meet Carolyn Miles at school and hasn't told me. Every time I think about this my insides turn into tangled knitting. It must mean something, but what?

"What's wrong?" Tansy's brow is fighting Botox in an attempt to furrow. "You look really down. I know what will cheer you up – let's go to Waterstones after lunch and face out all my books. That's always fun!"

I laugh. "Maybe not. You caused havoc last time when all those people wanting autographs blocked the shop."

"Can't help being popular, hon," Tansy says, passing me a menu and casting a critical eye over it. "Bollocks. There's hardly anything low fat on this."

She's right – and usually I'd say that was a good thing, especially since what *is* on the menu is the most delicious selection, all moules-frites this and baked-brie that – but my appetite's totally vanished. I don't even think I could manage one of the sea-salt-crusted artisan breadsticks.

What a waste.

"I'll have the chicken and radicchio salad, no dressing and no chicken," Tansy tells the waiter. "Katy? Choose whatever you like. It's on me."

"I'll have the same," I say, snapping my menu shut and passing it over. Yes, I know I've just ordered a bowl of leaves but at least I'll be skinny and miserable.

Tansy stares at me. "Is that it? Don't you want the fries with truffle shavings? Or the blue cheese and wild boar burger?"

I shake my head. "Salad's fine."

"Salad's fine?" Tansy echoes. She couldn't look more shocked. "What's going on? Are you leaving Ollie and becoming a footballer's wife? Should I sign you up for my gym and take you on a trolley dash round Louis Vuitton?"

Louis Vuitton? After we've paid for the damage caused by my lava-lamp disaster I'll be lucky to afford a trolley dash around Lidl.

Tansy crosses her arms – quite a feat with E-cup fake boobs – and narrows her blue eyes. "I don't think I've ever seen you looking so down. What's wrong?"

Where do I start?

"And don't say nothing, either," she adds, mind reading clearly being another of her skills, alongside her talents as author/chef/fashion designer. "You should tell me because *Hiya!* magazine have just given me an agony aunt column and I need to practise."

"So I'm your problem-page guinea pig?"

"What an unkind way to put it. No, you can be my dry run and I might be able to help, you never know. I'm good at solving problems. Everyone always says so."

Since Tansy's usual idea of solving problems is getting someone else to do things for her (I need to write a book! Hire Katy! I need to look after my children! Hire a nanny!), I don't hold out much hope, not unless she can reroof and rewire cottages and make Carolyn Miles vanish. But she means well, and as our salads arrive I find myself telling her all my woes.

"Shit," Tansy says once I draw to a close. "No wonder you're off your food with all that lot going on."

I gaze down at my bowl of glossy leaves. Yum.

"Yes," she continues, steepling her fingers beneath her pointed chin, tilting her head and adopting a caring agony aunt expression, "I can see it's upsetting when your long-term partner doesn't love you enough to want to commit, forgets Valentine's Day and sneaks around with another woman. You're bound to feel awful. It's a rejection in every possible way. I'd be devastated. Broken-hearted. Suicidal even."

I blink. "Err, Tansy, do you really think a career as an agony aunt is for you?"

"Of course! *Tell it like it is Tansy* is what they're going to call me. It's tough love. None of your pussyfooting around nonsense with me!"

"Pussyfooting? That was more like stomping all over my feelings in Tommy's football boots! Ollie isn't sneaking around with another woman anyway! It could be a perfectly innocent meeting with a work colleague for all I know. And anyone could forget Valentine's Day if they're as busy as he is! It doesn't mean he doesn't love me! You're talking utter rubbish. Everything is absolutely fine."

"Ta-da! Problem solved!" Tansy cries triumphantly. "God, I'm bloody good, even if I do say so myself! Bet you're feeling better already, aren't you?"

She's right! I am! I was so stung by what she said that I leapt to Ollie's defence and, do you know what? I was totally able to justify his actions. She's a genius!

"I'm so going to get my agent to make *Hiya!* pay me an extra twenty percent," Tansy decides, attacking her salad with gusto. "Oh, sod it! Thirty percent, why not? I'm saving lives here."

I hardly hear her. What on earth have I been stressing about? This is Ollie! My lovely dog-loving, nacho-eating, comfort blanket, gorgeous Ollie! Not the Casanova of Cornwall.

Everything's OK!

And I'm starving!

"Can I have a side of truffle-shaved fries?" I ask a passing waiter. "And a portion of baked brie too?"

"Phew," says Tansy. "That's more like it. You had me worried for a minute there."

I had myself worried too. Thank goodness I've seen the light! Maybe I should have some garlic bread too in celebration?

"Still," she continues, spearing a leaf thoughtfully, "if this Carolyn is as good-looking as you say she is then I can see why there might be a problem."

There is? She can?

"What do you mean?" I ask.

Tansy puts her fork down and, reaching across the table, places her well-manicured hand on my ink-stained and gnawed paw.

"Now, Katy, you know I love you and think the world of you, don't you?"

I'm a bit alarmed. This sounds dangerously like one of those *it's not you, it's me* speeches.

"But," she continues, turning my hand over and tutting at the state of my nails, "you really could do with a bit of a makeover. You've let yourself go a little, haven't you? It's understandable. People do that when they're happy and comfortable in a relationship. And why bother making an effort with clothes and make-up when you've already got your man?"

"Err, I hate to break it to you, Tans, but I have made an effort. I've dressed up today."

Her eyes widen. "In that case, girlfriend, it's even worse than I thought. We really do have a problem."

We do? I didn't think I looked too bad. My hair's probably a bit wild and curly at the moment, but it's held back with a glittery clip – and I've even put some make-up on today in honour of having lunch out. I'd thought my outfit of flared jeans, floaty green top and New Rock boots was cool and funky too, especially teamed with a battered biker jacket that I salvaged a while back from Maddy's jumble-sale stash. Put it this way, no small children have run away screaming yet. Granted, I'm not dolled up to the nines like Tansy, but if I dressed like that in Tregowan I'd a) freeze to death and b) break my ankle just trying to walk to the car.

"What's wrong with what I'm wearing?" I ask, stung.

"Nothing! Nothing! Forget I said anything!"

There's nothing worse than people starting to tell you something and then stopping halfway through, is there? Now I'm totally paranoid and even the arrival of golden fries and gooey brie can't distract me. Any minute now I'll be trying to catch sight of my reflection in the window or the back of a teaspoon or something just like Frankie's husband, Gabriel.

"What? What is it?" I really am behaving like Gabriel now; I grab a spoon and peer into it, as if it might yield some answers. "Come on! You've obviously got a problem with my outfit!"

"Sweetie, I adore your outfit. It's very… very…" She pauses to search for the right word and, even though as Tansy's ghostwriter I know her vocabulary is limited, I'm still alarmed.

"Very?"

"Very studenty! Yes, babes, you really rock that nineties student vibe."

"That's probably because I *was* a nineties student – years and years ago! I'm not still dressing like a student!"

"I'm afraid you are though, hon, but I'm not criticising. Clompy boots, baggy tops and shaggy perms suit some people."

"That's not a perm! It's my real hair!"

She claps her hand over her mouth. "Oops!"

"So my hair's wrong, my clothes are wrong and I'm several decades out of date? Anything else you'd like to add?"

Tansy can't quite look me in the eye. Even she knows this sounds bad, and she's not the most *subtle* girl in the world. Of course she isn't. Some of the outfits she's worn out and about make Katie Price's look demure. And at least Liz Hurley bothered to safety-pin her dress.

"It's all great, hon, but from what you're telling me about this Carolyn she sounds like a woman who works on her image. A more mature look. Sophisticated."

"Mature and sophisticated? Sounds like a smelly cheese."

And talking of cheese, I dip some crusty bread into my baked brie and munch contentedly while Tansy winces. There are probably more calories in that mouthful than she sees in a week.

"Is she groomed? Is she gorgeous? Is she successful? Is she alone with your man right now?" she presses.

The bread's suddenly claggy in my mouth and my stomach lurches because the answer to all these questions is a resounding *yes*.

"So you need to give her a run for her money, babes. You need to make a little more effort." Sensing weakness, Tansy goes in for the kill. "You need to remind your man just what he's got at home! Dress up! Make an effort for him! Don't just sit around in your onesie eating Wotsits and watching Jeremy Kyle."

"I don't own a onesie!" I protest.

I do love a good packet of Wotsits though. Who doesn't? And I've always found Jeremy Kyle very entertaining.

"It's a simile. Or a metaphor. Or something like that anyway," Tansy says airily, the finer points of figurative language being something for lesser mortals like me to worry about. "You know what I mean. Anyway, like I said, sweetie, we need to give you a makeover."

"We do?"

She claps her hands. "It'll be fun. Who better to give you a hand with your image and fashion than me? I'm an expert after all."

"Because you do a lot of shopping?" I ask, feeling doubtful about taking fashion advice from someone who once went to a Bond premier dressed in nothing more than black shoelaces. She did. Seriously. Google it.

"Duh!" laughs Tansy. "No, because I had my show, *SOS Makeover*, silly! It was on the Style Channel, remember?"

Ollie and I don't have satellite TV (we can only just scrape together enough to afford the BBC) but I don't have the heart to tell Tansy this, because she's looking so proud.

"So why don't I give you a makeover this afternoon?" she continues, pushing her salad aside in excitement. "No protests, sweetie! It's my treat as a thank you for the books! It'll be so much fun."

I'm not convinced. I might not have seen Tansy's show but I can only imagine what the end result will be. I'll look like the love child of an Oompa-Loompa and a drag queen.

"We can go into town and find everything we need," Tansy declares, a fanatical gleam in her eyes now. "My salon will squeeze you in if I ask them to, and so will the beauticians. How do you feel about Botox?"

I can't say I've ever had any feelings either way. Botox is for the likes of Simon Cowell and *TOWIE* stars, not mere mortals like me. But now that I think about it, I'm not overly thrilled by the idea of needles and a shiny forehead.

"You really could do with sorting out those wrinkles before they get any worse," Tansy adds. "And maybe a bit of filler?"

I don't have any wrinkles! I don't!

Do I?

I can't help it; I pick up the spoon and peer into it again. My face, bulbous and distorted, looms back at me. With my ginger person's pale skin, I might well look like the undead – but I can't see any wrinkles.

"Where are these wrinkles?" As if I don't have enough to worry about already with our leaky roof, the rewiring, the Throb sample and Carolyn Miles, now I have to fret about wrinkles too?

Someone dunk me in a vat of Oil of Olay.

Fast.

"Did I say wrinkles? Duh! I meant laughter lines," Tansy amends swiftly, but I'm not laughing. "All the girls have a touch of Botox on their laughter lines, hon. It's just another treatment to us."

By "girls" she means her fellow WAGs. They also all have rather startled expressions and gleaming foreheads. I want to improve my appearance, but I'm not sure looking like a surprised boiled egg is the way to go.

"I'll pass on the needles, thanks," I say.

"How about a facial then?" Tansy suggests. "A blow-dry, a treatment and some shopping. That's just what you need. Trust me, hon. By the time I've finished Ollie won't be able to take his eyes off you. This Carolyn ho will be toast."

"She's hardly a ho, Tansy! She's the Deputy Head of one of Britain's highest-performing secondary schools."

"If she messing with your man, then she a ho, girlfriend."

Going all "from the hood" suddenly and with her voice far too loud for the small wine bar, Tansy's attracting a lot of attention – and I know from experience that she's only going to get worse. Once she has an idea lodged in her head nothing stops her. I won't have a minute's peace until I cave in.

Besides, what if she's right? What if I have let myself go and a groomed Carolyn type is what Ollie really needs these days? If he's as career ambitious as he now seems to be, then Carolyn in her smart suits and tailored chic fits the bill far more neatly than me.

I feel a bit sick at this idea. Perhaps I do need Tansy's help. Anyway, how bad can it be? She's had a TV show, after all. They wouldn't give her one of those if she wasn't any good, would they? Perhaps a shopping trip with Tansy is *exactly* what I need?

"Well?" Tansy says. "Ready to give this Carolyn a run for her money?"

I nod slowly. After all, what have I got to lose?

Project makeover it is.

Four hours later and en route to pick up Ollie, I'm starting to think that maybe I had a little more to lose than I'd realised. Like my dignity, for instance? Believe me, what small tatters I did have remaining after over a decade of teaching are well and truly shredded now. Until you've stood in the middle of a changing room with the stark lighting making your backside look like a bowl of porridge (at least, I hope that was just a nasty trick of the light) and with a size-zero WAG helping to shoehorn your squidgy bits into a pair of control pants, you haven't known what total humiliation is. The pants were so tight and required such contortions for me to even haul them over my knees that after just a few moments I was gasping and sweating like Alexi and Lucinda in my first chapter. Not that Lucinda would be seen dead in these putty-coloured monstrosities.

And neither, just for the record, would Alexi.

"Are you sure about this?" I'd puffed once the pants were in position and I'd surveyed my bulging backside from several very unflattering angles. "I think Ollie's more of a black lace and red ribbon kind of man."

"Aren't they all?" Tansy had laughed. "No, hon, Ollie isn't going to see these. As if! They exist just to give you a sleek silhouette under your clothes. They hide all those flabby bits you don't want anyone to see. Trust me. All the celebs wear them, and sometimes on special occasions we even double up. Or triple. Maybe you could too?"

As I try to change gear and almost rupture my intestines in the process, I really regret agreeing to give the double-shapewear thing a go. I can hardly breathe and it feels a bit like I'm being cut in half by cheese wire, but Tansy's the expert here and she insists that good underwear is the key.

Ironic really, since she's famous for not wearing any herself...

Still, the very tight green wrap dress she'd picked up for me would have shown every lump and bump, so I guess not being able to breathe is a small price to pay for not looking like Jabba the Hutt. I'm not one hundred percent convinced about the plunging neckline, but since this frock is from Tansy's own range I didn't dare protest in case it sounded ungrateful. Just as I didn't like to point out that false nails would play havoc with trying to type novels and that I quite like my hair curly rather than straightened and backcombed into a huge high ponytail. And as for make-up? A slick of mascara and some lip gloss is usually enough for me, so to be wearing a full face feels weird, like I'm about to step onto the stage or juggle custard pies.

I pull down the sun visor to sneak a look at myself in the vanity mirror, and almost swerve into the central reservation when I catch sight of my reflection.

Yikes!

What the heck did they do to my eyebrows? Apart from having a black humpbacked bridge above each eye, I've got bright pink stripes too. I *knew* that wax was too hot. It was all very well for Tansy to tell me to stop making such a fuss. She wasn't the one being boiled alive, was she? And why on earth am I orange? I look like a baked bean!

What was Tansy thinking? And what was *I* thinking to listen to her in the first place? Looking like this isn't elegant or sophisticated. Far from it. Oh Lord! I have to do something before Ollie sees me, because Tansy's spot on: he'll be gobsmacked, all right. I look utterly ridiculous and nothing like myself at all. And unless he's suddenly started fancying drag queens, this scary new me isn't going to win him away from Carolyn Miles.

As soon as I pull into the school car park I yank the sun visor down again, spit on my forefinger and start to scrub my face frantically. Unfortunately, the neon-orange foundation Tansy's chosen would survive a nuclear bomb and my saliva's no match for it. No matter how hard I grind my finger against my cheek, nothing shifts.

I'm trying to figure out how on earth I can tear back into town to give myself an anti-makeover, when the school door swings open and Ollie steps out into the sunshine with none other than Carolyn Miles. They're deep in conversation and something he says makes her laugh so much that she tips back her head, tosses her golden mane and pokes him in the arm. They look so chummy and in tune with each other that I freeze.

This turns out to be a big mistake. What I should have done is throw the tartan car blanket over my head, put the Focus in reverse and screech out of there like Vin Diesel. Instead, I sit as motionless as my sprayed hair, before recovering myself sufficiently to dive into the passenger footwell. I don't even care that the gearstick's stabbing me in the tummy or that my control pants are cutting off my circulation. All I care about is that Ollie doesn't see me looking like this, especially not while he has the gorgeous Carolyn Miles in tow. Better he thinks I've been beamed up by aliens rather than beaten by the WAG stick.

"Katy? What are you doing down there? Are you ill?"

Darn! Too late! Ollie opens the car door and peers at me in alarm.

"I dropped an earring," I mumble. Luckily the passenger footwell is full of old magazines and sweet wrappers, so finding anything in there could take a while – certainly long enough for him to get shot of Carolyn and for me to try making myself look a little more normal.

But unfortunately Ollie isn't prepared to let me rummage in peace.

"Don't worry, we'll find it in a minute," he says. "Come and say hi to Carolyn. She's been helping me with the Key Stage 3 data analysis. Come on, Katy! Forget the earring for a minute."

There's nothing for it. I'm trapped. Reluctantly, I sit up in all my WAG-tastic glory.

Ollie's eyes widen behind his glasses and then he starts to laugh. "Blimey, Katy! I thought you were off to have lunch with Tansy? Not swinging around a pole! How is Peter Stringfellow these days?"

"Very funny!" My face is bright red. "Look, Tansy thought it would be nice to give me a makeover as a thank you for the books."

"Bloody hell! What does she do to people she doesn't feel grateful to?" Still laughing, he turns to Carolyn who, joy of joy, has now joined us. "Caro, you remember my girlfriend Katy, don't you? Although I won't be offended if you don't recognise her!"

"Nice to see you again, Katy," says Carolyn Miles politely. Her grey eyes flicker over me with total disinterest before she turns back to Ollie. "Great work today. Remember what I said about applying for the Assistant Head Teacher post. I really think you're ready."

Ollie lights up like Oxford Street on Christmas Eve. "Seriously? You really think so?"

"I know so," Carolyn says warmly, giving his arm a little squeeze. "There's no one else I would want to work with that closely. You're the person for the job. We'll talk on Monday and discuss an application. My office at seven-thirty. See you then."

And, with this order issued, she's sashaying across to her little red car, spike-heeled boots scrunching on the gravel and blonde ponytail bouncing with every step.

I stare after her. My orange face and daft outfit are totally forgotten.

What's going on? Ollie is seriously considering applying to be school senior management? He's never mentioned this to me.

Just like he never mentioned he was meeting Carolyn today. My skin starts to prickle, and not just from where I've been scalded either. I have a terrible sense of unease. Ollie's keeping secrets from me and he's never, ever done that before. We've always told each other everything.

I need to find out what's going on here, and I will do too – just as soon as I've got home, scrubbed away the make-up and managed to get these control pants off.

Chapter 8

"Don't keep me in suspense, Mads. What do you think? Is it good enough to send?"

It's Monday evening and Maddy and I are having a long-overdue girls' night at the pub. Ollie's at a parents' evening, Richard's looking after the twins and Holly won't be here until after seven, so we've had a window of time to look over my sample chapter for Throb.

I'm gripping the stem of my wine glass so tightly I'm half expecting it to shatter. I don't think I've ever felt so nervous about showing my best friend something I've written. Mads has been my critique partner and beta reader for as long as I've been writing, but showing her this sample chapter is absolutely terrifying. I couldn't feel more exposed if I were sitting in the Mermaid stark naked. I mean, what if she thinks all that *stuff* I've described is based on my own sex life? What if she thinks Ollie and I actually do these things ourselves? Like the bit when Alexi rips Lucinda's tights off with his teeth, lashes her to the kitchen table, fetches the clothes pegs and—

Well *that*. Good Lord. I'm embarrassed just thinking about the scene I've handed her. I'm surprised my poor little laptop didn't burst into flames while I was typing it, too. I know I'm pretty new to this erotic fiction lark, and it isn't really my bag at all, but it's amazing just how motivating a big electrician's bill and the possibility of complete financial annihilation can be. Over the past few days the words have poured from my imagination and onto the screen in an X-rated torrent. I'm actually rather shocked at myself. Who knew what darkness was lurking in the depths of my mind?

If I get this gig, I'll have to have a pen name. What if people think I'm writing from experience? And even worse, what if Ollie does? He'll know we've never got down and dirty on the kitchen floor – well, nothing more exciting than sweeping and scrubbing the grubby quarry tiles, anyway! Even worse, will he think I've been up to no good with somebody else?

I gnaw at my thumb. This alter ego stuff is certainly complicated. How Bruce Wayne and Peter Parker cope I'll never know.

Mads looks up and fans herself with the printed pages.

"Bloody hell, Katy Carter! You're a dark horse. That thing Alexi did with the courgettes! I'm blushing!"

I'm blushing too. This little detail came to me when I was peering in the fridge looking for something to eat and contemplating a courgette and margarine sandwich…

"Don't look so worried; I don't think you and Ollie have a vegetable fetish," she continues, returning to the manuscript and thumbing through it. "Ditto golden syrup, clothes pegs and cocktail sticks. No, girlfriend, unless the mild-mannered Mr Burrows is a serious deviant, you have got one twisted imagination. Congratulations. You've written a perfect porny sample chapter."

"It's erotica!" I protest.

"You just keep on telling yourself that," Mads says kindly. "Is there any more? I can't wait to find out what Alexi finds next. How about the Hoover? Or a feather duster?"

I place my head in my hands. "This is all wrong. I want to write romance!"

"I thought Alexi was very romantic with the clothes pegs and washing line," grins Maddy. "Next time I'm hanging out the laundry I'll make sure I call Richard over!"

This image is enough to make me reach for my drink.

"Anyway," my best friend continues, "romance isn't paying the bills, but I'm sure this will. Email it to Throb, babes. Our work here is done."

My thumb hovers over my phone. The sample chapter is attached to an email to my (potential) editor, and it's ready to fire into the ether.

"Send it," says Mads sternly. "Stop being such a jelly."

My thumb's still poised over *send*. I know we need the money, I know this chapter ticks all the boxes in the brief and I know I can deliver the goods, but something deep down inside me is saying this might not be my brightest idea. I'm aware that Ollie's been keeping secrets from me too – meeting Carolyn for one, and his head-teacherly ambitions for another – but it just doesn't feel right. Besides, it was bad enough when I was writing for Tansy. How would St Jude's feel if their prospective Assistant Head Teacher was living with Tregowan's answer to E L James?

"I'm not sure," I say cautiously. "Maybe I should run it by Ollie first?"

"What will that achieve? It'll only stress him out," Mads points out. "What our other halves don't know won't hurt them."

"Err, that wasn't what you said a moment ago when I told you Ollie hadn't mentioned the Assistant Head thing."

"Different rules for us, babes. Never forget that. Anyway, didn't you say that Throb would give you a pen name? Ollie won't even know it's you and neither will anyone else. Now stop making such a fuss, think of the money and send the bloody email!"

For a vicar's wife Mads is pretty happy to tempt me with Mammon – which, let's be honest, isn't very hard. The local sparky pushed his estimate for the rewiring through the door this morning and, ever since I scraped myself off the floor after the shock, I've been trying to figure out how to pay him. Is Maddy right? Is this the only way? I just don't know.

"Mads! Katy! I knew I'd find you in here, darlings! Let me buy us some drinks to celebrate my return to the motherland!"

Frankie Burrows – Ollie's cousin, who also happens to be a rock icon – bursts into the pub and flings his arms around us both. I'm caught in a wiry embrace and tangled in his flowing Hermès scarf; my thumb slips on the iPhone screen and oops! The email is sent. Call it fate, call it coincidence or just call it *my sodding bad luck as usual*, but the issue has been decided for me. I have just submitted a sample chapter to Throb.

"Shall we have champagne, darlings! On me?" Frankie trills. "Bolly? Cristal? Dom P?"

"Stop being such a show-off," Mads scolds. "You're in Cornwall now, not L bloody A. Seriously, Frankie, you're spending far too much time with celebs and not nearly enough with the peasants! Get over yourself and drink house white like the rest us."

"Righty-ho," says Frankie, who by now is used to Maddy's razor-blade put-downs. "Three glasses of paupers' white it is. Oh! Here's Holly! Hello, angel! Wine for you as well? Celebrate that sparkly ring and marrying the delicious Guy?"

My sister joins us, pulling off her bobble hat and running her hands through her red curls.

"Believe me, he's far from delicious when he rolls in at midnight reeking of fish and booze."

"Ooo! How manly!" Frankie shivers theatrically. "I'm just picturing him now, naked except for his oilskins and his skin glistening from the storm."

Holly gives him a pitying look. "Guy doesn't wear his oilskins at home, and if there's bad weather the last place you'll find him is at sea because he'll be in here, propping up the bar. This is real life, not *The Perfect Storm*."

"No prizes for guessing who got all the imagination in the Carter family," Frankie says.

"Frankie was just offering to get a round in," Mads tells Holly, stuffing my printed chapter into her bag. "White wine for you?"

My sister shakes her head. "No, not for me thanks. I'll just have a mineral water."

"Mineral water?" Frankie looks shocked. "Are you ill?"

"I'm fine," Holly says, pulling herself onto a bar stool. "I just don't need a drink. It's been a long day. I wouldn't mind some food though. Maybe a portion of cheesy chips."

I look at my sister a little more closely. Never an outdoors person, she looks even paler than usual and there are dark smudges beneath her eyes. She works far too hard at the uni. This doesn't usually stop her having a drink though. Holly and Guy are such regular fixtures in the pub they ought to have shares in the local brewery.

"Don't look at me like I've grown two heads, Katy!" Holly snaps. "I don't have to have a drink to have a good time, you know."

"I know that," I say, feeling hurt.

"Well, I *do* need a drink. Good times, bad times or indifferent," Maddy declares. "And since I'm on a rare night out, I'm going to have another."

I open my mouth to remind her about the Lenten ban, then shut it quickly. Mads didn't listen to me when I protested earlier, so nothing much will have changed. If Frankie drops her in it with the Rev, then it's her bad luck.

We all perch at the bar and Frankie has a lovely time ordering drinks and being over-the-top camp just to wind up Derrick the landlord and some of the more conservative locals. Much as they dine out on having a rock musician and his film-star husband as part-time residents, this is Tregowan and attitudes can still be quite traditional – something I know only too well.

"So what are you going to do about rewiring the cottage, not to mention getting the roof fixed?" Holly asks me when we've all settled down to the serious business of eating and drinking, once our plates of chips are in front of us too.

"Are you trying to drive me to alcohol?" I groan.

"I didn't know electricians could charge that much. I might retrain," says Maddy thoughtfully. "Then I could run an all-female team of electricians. We could have pink dungarees and vans and tools! It would be brilliant."

"You could call your firm Pussy Power," suggests Frankie, and Maddy laughs so hard at this that she snorts her drink all over the bar.

"I don't know what you're laughing about. It was your lava lamp that caused all my problems," I point out after she's recovered sufficiently to breathe. "Or the electrician's bill, at least. I ought to be making you pay for it!"

"I never talked you into taking it or said it was working. I seem to remember you were the one who wanted the bloody thing," Maddy reminds me, mopping up her drink with a bar towel. "Did I tell you to plug it in without testing it? Did I?"

"No," I mutter sulkily.

"I'd offer to get it all fixed, sweetie, but Ollie will only say no," says Frankie. "That boy is too proud for his own good."

He's right. Ollie will say no. He's scarily independent and never wants handouts or help of any kind. When my godmother died and left us enough money to put a big deposit on our cottage I had a hard time persuading him to accept it, and that was when we were first together and *persuading* him was fairly easy! I don't stand a chance these days.

Especially since he's still laughing about my WAG-over. He'll probably never take me seriously again after that.

"You could always look for the loot," chips in Derrick the landlord, who's polishing glasses behind the bar and listening in to our conversation. "That would pay for you to get the place rewired. Probably take care of the leaky roof and the mortgage too."

My ears prick up. At the moment *rewiring*, *roof* and *mortgage* are words that wake me up in the night. Along with *overdraft* and *Carolyn* and *secret writing job*, obviously. It's amazing I get any sleep at all.

"What loot?"

"The loot that's buried in your cottage," Derrick says patiently. "Old Cecily Greville's life savings."

He's got my attention now. When Ollie and I bought our cottage it was in a really bad way – even worse than it is now, which I know you'll find hard to believe. It had belonged to an old lady who'd lived there for donkey's years; in fact, nobody in Tregowan could agree on just how long she had lived there. Bob the postie reckoned at least forty years because he remembered her in the cottage when he was a boy, but Penny Pengelley from the sweet shop was convinced Cecily had bought the cottage before the First World War. Whatever the truth, Cecily Greville had been quite a recluse and when she died, without family or friends, she'd left her cottage to an animal shelter.

"She never left any money to anyone but she was supposed to be one of the wealthiest women in the village," Derrick continues, enjoying having a captive audience. "Where did all her valuables go? The jewellery? The money she'd stashed away for a rainy day?"

"This is Cornwall, where it rains all the time, so she'd have spent all that." Holly pulls a face, but the landlord isn't put off by my sister's cynicism.

"Mock all you like, Holly Carter, but Cecily Greville came from one of the richest families in the area. Her father was a wine merchant, and believe me she'd have been worth something in any age. Before she died she told the old vicar she'd buried her life savings under the floor of the sitting room. He didn't take her seriously, as she was quite muddled towards the end, but maybe she wasn't as confused as we all thought?"

I'm staring at him. "She told the vicar her life savings were buried under her sitting room floor? *My* sitting room floor? And you never thought to mention that before? Not in nearly five years?"

Derrick shrugs his plump shoulders. "Sorry, maid. Never occurred to me before. Truth be told I'd all but forgotten it."

Derrick might have been able to forget that there's a fortune buried under my sitting room but I know I won't be able to. It's going to drive me mad! How on earth can I sit on my sofa now watching *EastEnders* when underneath me are squillions of pounds? I'll never sit still again.

It's going to be *unbearable!*

If I find the missing money all our problems will be solved! I can get the roof fixed, rewire the cottage, pay off the mortgage and not write for Throb, and Ollie won't have to work so hard. That's what I call a result!

I *have* to find out what's under my floor! I have to!"

"Don't you dare," Holly says.

"Dare what?"

"Dare even think about pulling up the floorboards and looking underneath. It's all nonsense, Katy."

It's scary sometimes just how well my sister knows me. Then again, she's seen me tear my parents' place upside down hunting for our Christmas presents.

"It might not be nonsense though. It could be true!" Frankie's eyes are enormous. "Oh my God! Katy! There's a fortune underneath your house, angel! I just know it!"

Frankie has a fortune in his wallet and an even bigger one in his bank account, but he couldn't look more excited as he clutches my arm and makes plans.

"Even if there is, the money isn't Katy's," says Maddy, pouring a gallon of water on my lovely sunshiny parade. "We know who it belonged to, don't we? So it's part of Miss Greville's estate."

"Which Katy purchased," says Derrick. "The house and all that's in it are hers."

"And you said she had no family," adds Frankie excitedly. "So it's legally Katy's! Finders keepers!"

Although Frankie is a rock star and not a lawyer, he's speaking with such conviction that I'm convinced. "Let's go and look now! Before Ollie comes home and tells us we're being daft!" I say.

"You *are* being daft!" Holly's practically shouting now. "It's just a story!"

But my poor sister might as well talk to the beer pumps because Mads, Frankie and I are now so worked up we can hardly sit still, and no matter how many times Holly tries to calm us down we're quite unable to hear reason. By the time we leave the pub I'm one hundred percent certain I'm only metres and minutes away from financial salvation. As soon as I've found a way to lift the floorboards and pull out the treasure, my lottery habit, leaky roof and rewiring bill will all be history!

"If you find anything, call me straight away," Mads insists when we part company by the fish market.

"And if Ollie kicks you out for being a total lunatic you can sleep on our sofa," Holly tells me. "But you'll have to watch *Ice Road Truckers* and *Trawlermen* with Guy when he comes in from the pub, so don't say you haven't been warned."

With this parting shot my sister gives me a hug and then she and Mads set off for their houses on the left-hand side of the valley. Frankie lives this way too, in a beautiful big house called Smuggler's Rest, but he's far too excited to think about going home. Besides, it's only nine o'clock, the night is still young and Ollie will only just be finishing parents' evening. I reckon this gives me at least half an hour to peek under the floor without causing him any stress.

Once back at home I fob Sasha off with a doggy chew so that she'll leave us in peace, then I pour Frankie and myself a couple of glasses of wine and survey the sitting room thoughtfully.

It's a tiny cottage. How hard can this be? All I have to do is find the right spot, pull out the loot and ta-da! No more almost electrocuting myself every time I plug the telly in. Simples.

"Right," says Frankie, rubbing his hands together gleefully, "where shall we start?"

"Derrick said the living room," I recall. It seems an obvious choice. From what I can remember about moving in, Miss Greville had been using the living room as a bedroom during her last few months. Of course she'd have kept her life savings here where she could keep her eye on them.

"So let's get stuck in!" Peeling off his beautiful leather jacket and the Hermès scarf, Frankie is rolling up the rug before I even draw breath to reply. He stares at the nailed-down floorboards and then asks, "Where do you keep your crowbar, sweetie?"

"My crowbar?"

"Yes, your crowbar," Frankie repeats, hopping from foot to foot now in agitation. "We need it to prise these mofos up!"

Do you know, it's the strangest thing but in over thirty years on this planet it's never before occurred to me that I'm lacking one of these. But apparently, it is a truth universally acknowledged that a young woman in possession of a potential fortune must be in want of a crowbar.

"I don't have one," I confess.

At least, I don't think we do — unless it's in the shed with all the boy stuff Ollie keeps in there like... like... well, anyway, like his tools and things.

Frankie looks pained. "I love you, angel girl, but fancy not knowing where your crowbar is. It's an utter disgrace!"

"And I suppose you know exactly where to find one at your house?"

"Of course. Gabe keeps ours under the bed."

"Too much information!" I tell him.

Frankie laughs. "Not for anything naughty. We're mega-famous remember? We might get a stalker or a deranged fan breaking in. Mufty can't defend us from everyone."

Mufty is Gabriel's toy poodle and he has teeth like needles. If I were a stalker, I'd take the crowbar any day.

"We'll just have to see if we can use brute strength," Frankie decides.

Since he's stick thin and I've got all the muscle tone of a rice pudding, this idea lasts for about five seconds. Several snapped fingernails (Frankie) and one giant splinter (me) later, we've totally lost heart with pulling up the floorboards by hand. Instead, we're lying on our stomachs peering down through the cracks between the boards when Ollie walks in.

"Unless snorting dust is the latest A-list vice of choice, what on earth are you two doing?"

Frankie and I leap up as though scalded. We'd been so engrossed in shining the iPhone torch through the floorboard gaps that we hadn't even heard the door open, although that could have been down to all Frankie's screeching when a spider crawled across his hand. Frankie catches my eye and I know straight away that he's not going to say anything.

Ollie slumps onto the sofa, leaning right back and closing his eyes. "Don't tell me. Katy's lost another earring, but without the fancy dress this time?"

"Eh?" says Frankie.

"You promised not to bring that up again," I remind Ollie.

One eye opens and his lovely mouth curls into a smile. "I can't resist. You made such a lovely WAG and it was such good fun helping you out of that sexy underwear."

Frankie claps his hands over his ears. "Enough already."

Ollie laughs. "Chillax, Frankie. Katy thought it might be a good idea to wear two pairs of control pants – until she needed the loo. Then we had an underwear trauma."

"Double-Spanx bladder?" Frankie nods sympathetically. "Total red carpet nightmare. I feel your pain, girlfriend."

I feel it too. Even if I live to be as old as Cecily Greville I don't think I'll get over the humiliation of my boyfriend having to tug putty-hued spandex over my knees. Ollie almost passed out with the effort.

"I'm not even going to ask what you two are up to now," Ollie continues, taking off his glasses and grinding his knuckles into his eyes. "I'm so tired I can hardly think. Just don't switch on any lava lamps."

"Ha. Ha," I say, getting to my feet and rolling the carpet back into place. "Actually, Ol, we were looking for hidden treasure."

"Of course you were," Ollie agrees wearily. "And when you've had enough of looking for it, could you maybe find the kettle and pop that on? I'm going to have a bath and go to bed."

I've told the truth and he doesn't believe me. How ironic is that? I have every sympathy for the little boy who cried wolf.

"He looks awful," Frankie says once Ollie's dragged himself off the sofa and up the stairs to run a bath. "I've never seen him look so tired."

"I told you he was working too hard. He's even going for an Assistant Head Teacher job."

Frankie looks alarmed. "That doesn't sound like Ol. Doesn't he think all managers are tossers?"

He used to, until Carolyn Miles came along, but I don't tell Frankie about her. So far I haven't told anyone except Tansy. I don't dare.

"I need to do something to take the pressure off him," is all I say. "And soon."

"And you will." Frankie gives me a hug. "We'll find that loot. It's down there, I just know it – and I am never wrong. It's all going to be fine, Katy, trust me."

All I can do is nod because I really hope he's right.

And if not? Well then, I just don't know.

Chapter 9

There's nothing harder than trying to write a book with a potential fortune underneath your feet. Never mind the temptation of Jeremy Kyle or Facebook; those I can handle. The possibility of treasure under my living room floor I simply can't ignore.

It's going to drive me crazy. I have to know!

It's been four days since Derrick mentioned Cecily Greville's life savings – four days during which I've been slowly and steadily going mad with not knowing. Frankie's gone back to London to see his agent so I've not had access to his crowbar and, as hard as I've tried, my kitchen knives are no match for heavy-duty nails. So far I've bent three and practically severed one of my fingers in the attempt so, unless I want to type with my nose for the rest of my life, I'll have to abandon my feeble attempts to lift the floorboards until Frankie returns. He's made me promise I won't peep without him being present but it's proving very difficult to resist.

Focus on the job in hand, Katy! Focus! It's not as though I have time to waste either, because the pressure is well and truly on since Lisa Armstrong, Throb's Senior Commissioning Editor, called earlier with the news that they love my chapter and are hiring me as Isara Lovett, their hottest new erotic novelist.

I Lovett? Seriously? I have to admit that, cash-strapped as I am, I almost baulked at this one. I mean, it's hardly subtle, is it? Then again, *Kitchen of Correction* is hardly a subtle book. Alexi, the sexy Russian billionaire chef, isn't really a subtle kind of guy either, not when he gets going with the marrows...

Still, beggars with big rewiring bills, leaky roofs and stressed boyfriends can't be choosers, so I've said yes and the contracts are in the post. The Booker Prize is still a distant dream and I don't think Radio 4 will be wanting to interview me on *Woman's Hour* any time soon, but at least there's a couple of grand on its way. The deadline's very tight, though. I only have six weeks to write the thing, so I can't waste a second.

"Is that going to be all right for you, Katy?" the editor had asked. "We appreciate it's a very short time frame. Will you be able to make the deadline?"

"Of course!" I'd crossed my fingers, toes and eyes at this point. Anything to get my mitts on that money.

One hundred thousand words in six weeks seems perfectly doable. Even my hopeless maths is able to calculate it's only sixteen thousand words or so a week and only just over two thousand a day. I can do that. OK, so this isn't exactly my usual genre and I'll have to do a little more research than I normally would (i.e. collude with Mads), but it's perfectly possible. Kinky kitchen here I come! Or rather, kinky kitchen here Alexi and Lucinda come!

So for now I have to forget the fortune under my sofa and concentrate on justifying my advance. I have to be professional and produce the novel I've been paid to write. I can do this. Of course I can. It's just like the Tansy books, only a bit more thrusty…

I take a deep breath and begin to type.

CHAPTER 2

Great! That's a start. Maybe I should make a coffee now and have a biscuit while the muse wakes up? Or perhaps have another go at swinging Maddy's lucky crystal over the carpet? It was a bit confused earlier and swung just about everywhere, which wasn't quite what *Fate and Destiny* said it would do. Left for yes and right for no, I think it was. Or maybe the other way around? I'm always getting left and right muddled up, so perhaps the crystal does too – or else there's so much treasure under there that the crystal doesn't know what to do first? Oh my God! Of course! That's exactly what it is! And didn't my *Fate and Destiny* horoscope also say something about fortune's finger pointing my way in a very unexpected manner? What could be more unexpected than finding lost loot under my own sitting room? Fortune's finger is pointing at me! It really is!

Hold on. Didn't the National Lottery once use a pointing finger in its advertising campaign? What if the horoscope's saying I ought to buy some lottery tickets? And tonight the EuroMillions jackpot is meant for me?

Lord. It's tricky trying to decipher all this cosmic stuff, but I'm feeling lucky and if I don't act on my intuition it could cost us a fortune. Thirty quid out of the emergency bills account won't hurt, not when this week's jackpot is so high. Buying tickets is practically an investment!

A few mouse clicks later I'm feeling very optimistic. The winning tickets have been purchased and my success is in the bag, I just know it. Now the pressure's off I'm sure I can settle down and write today's chapter. Let Holly scoff all she likes about the mathematical odds of lottery success.

Tonight I'm sure it's going to be me.

Before settling down to work I'll just have a quick scoot round the Rightmove site to pick my dream properties, and maybe I'll have a little peek at Facebook too. Then I'll be in a better position to start my chapter. All this is planning and preparation and vitally important. You have to be in the right space to create. You can't force these things. It's all about being in a creative state of mind.

Once I've chosen our would-be mansion and Range Rover as well as clicking *like* on a cute Facebook video of dancing kittens, I'm more than ready to return to my book. It's time to create.

Brace yourself, Chapter 2. Here I come.

Lucinda awoke on the kitchen floor. The vegetable rack was toppled over and her buttocks stung.

Yuk. Not sure I like the juxtaposition of buttocks and vegetables. It's putting me off my lunch. Let's delete that bit.

Alexi's disdainful glance swept over Lucinda. The cabbages were ruined and the courgettes squashed. There was no way he could use them now. He smiled cruelly. Lucinda was only the starter and it was time the other billionaire diners enjoyed a special main course.

Ooo. Main courses. Like steak or maybe pizza? My stomach rumbles. It's already apparent that writing about food isn't going to help my waistline, if even cabbages and courgettes are making me peckish.

And never mind billionaire diners. What about the billions under my floor?

Drat. It's no use. I can't think about writing when there are squillions of pounds just inches away from me. I don't think even Frankie's most devoted fan could want to see him as much as I do at this moment: I need him and his crowbar right now. I have to get under the floor! I have to!

I won't be able to write a word until those sodding floorboards are up.

I'll distract myself with a quick visit to the fridge. Maybe some of last night's leftover lasagne will take my mind off it all? It's lunchtime anyway and I'm sure there's some law somewhere which dictates that workers need regular breaks. I'll heat up the lasagne, watch *Loose Women* and then go back to work. I can write two thousand words in an afternoon. How hard can it be? I've got the detailed synopsis and the chapter breakdowns spread out in front of me. All I have to do is follow them and concentrate.

I've just heaped a generous dollop of Ollie's lasagne into a bowl and am about to pop it into the microwave when a furious hammering of fists on our front door makes me jump out of my skin. The cottage is tiny and the kitchen opens straight out onto the narrow lane outside. Usually the top half of the stable door is ajar so that I can wave at anyone going by and watch the fishing boats bobbing on the tide while I'm writing, but today it's closed because I haven't wanted to stray far from the living room. It would be just my luck if burglars got wind of the loot now and decided to search for it *Home Alone* style.

"Hello?" calls a voice as the door swings open. "Anyone in?"

Sasha leaps up from her basket, barking furiously and bouncing up and down at the door. As I dive to grab her collar my bowl goes flying. Lasagne drips onto the floor and shards of crockery are everywhere. Experience tells me that I'll be getting splinters of ceramic in my bare feet for months.

"This is all I bloody need!" I wail.

"Pleased to see you too," says the visitor (and cause of my lunch fail) as he shuffles into the kitchen. Familiar toffee-coloured eyes stare at me mournfully from beneath a shaggy fringe, and as an enormous rucksack is deposited at my feet I find myself crushed in a bony bear hug.

It's Ollie's little brother, Nicky, only not so little anymore; in the six months since I last saw him he's shot up like a weed and has even grown some stubble. How ancient does this make me feel? When I first met Ollie, Nicky was five years old. It's hard to reconcile the cute kid with a passion for Lego and Thomas the Tank Engine with this six-foot skater dude sporting long hair, a beanie hat and a suspicious-looking roll-up tucked behind his ear.

"God, that smells good. Has Ol been cooking? Can I have some? And are there any biscuits?" Letting go of me, Nicky's already rifling through the cupboards in search of food. My own starvation is imminent, since his appetite makes a horde of locusts look restrained. When Nicky came to stay last summer our grocery bill trebled and even Sasha feared for her dog biscuits.

"Sweet! There's some left." Without waiting for a reply or permission, my boyfriend's teenage brother dives into the fridge, fishes out the remainder of the lasagne and shovels it into his mouth with a teaspoon. "God, I'm bloody starving," he says through mouthfuls.

I'm lost for words, partly because most of the air has been squeezed from my lungs and partly because I'm so surprised to see him. Shouldn't Nicky be safely locked away in his very posh boarding school? A *surprise* child and eighteen years Ollie's junior, he's very much the baby of the family. He's also hell in converse boots and broke more hearts last summer than I did diets. Just looking at him makes me feel about one hundred and eighty.

"Shouldn't you be at school?" I ask, wincing to hear myself. Lord. I sound like such a teacher. Just when did I get so old?

Nicky hauls himself up onto the worktop and continues to inhale lasagne while Sasha, who in all the excitement has gobbled up the food I spilled, gazes adoringly up at him in the hope of more.

"Nope. Got kicked out," he says cheerfully. "Mmm! This is bloody good. Is there any more?"

"Kicked out?" I stare at him. "As in expelled?"

"Yep, although permanent exclusion was what they were calling it," Nicky says. "It's more PC apparently. Doesn't freak the crumblies out as much."

"And they asked you to leave? Just like that?" I'm into teacher mode now and my brain is whirling. What about his A-levels? What about his place at Oxford reading politics? And I can't imagine Nicky has his parents' consent to travel alone from Sussex to Cornwall.

"How did you get here?" I ask. Tregowan's impossible to get to by public transport.

"I hitched," Nicky says airily. "Don't look like that. I didn't get snatched by a danger stranger. It's all groovy gravy."

Groovy gravy? I don't think so! There's a serious safeguarding issue here, since he's supposed to be in the care of the school! It's shocking!

"And the school just let you leave?"

His bowl now empty, Nicky hops down from the worktop and begins to rummage through the biscuit tin.

"Cool! Chocolate ones! Can I finish them?"

Unfortunately for Nicky, I'm an expert on teenagers avoiding telling me the truth. You can't play *Where's Your Coursework?* for as long as I have and not know when big porkie pies are being told, deliberately or by omission.

"Nicky? What happened? Did they tell you to go? Or," I pause and give him my best stern look, "did you just walk out?"

"Don't give me that teacher face," says Nicky, selecting two chocolate digestives, which he crams into his mouth. "Mmmph mmm a urgh!"

I translate this easily enough, since it's a lament I hear most days when I'm in the classroom.

"I'm not having a go," I say. "But, Nicky, you've just turned up in my house, in the middle of term and telling me you've been kicked out of school. So what happened? I need to know."

He shrugs one shoulder. "They were all having a right go at me and said I was going to be excluded, so I saved them the trouble and went."

"You walked out? They don't know where you are?"

"Chill out, Katy. I'm eighteen. I can do what I want because I'm actually an adult," he huffs, with a jutting bottom lip. "Hey! Have you still got that stuff that makes chocolate milk?"

"Cupboard by the Aga," I reply automatically.

"Cool," says Nicky and, helping himself to a jug, he proceeds to make enough for the whole village. Once he's sitting at the table, his long skinny-jeaned legs stretched out while he dunks biscuits in his chocolate milk, he adds, "I thought you or Ollie might call school for me and tell them I'm all right? Let them know I'm living with you now? Then tell the olds too?"

It's just as well I'm leaning against the kitchen units at this point.

"Err, I hate to break it to you, Nicky, but you're *not* living with us. Absolutely no way. Of course I'll phone the school and I'm sure Ollie will drive you back tomorrow, but you can't stay here. You've got your A-levels coming up."

"Haven't you listened to me? I can't go back to school. They've kicked me out."

"I'm sure we can sort that," I say. At least I bloody well hope we can, because if Ollie's mum gets wind of this she'll go mental. It'll be the Home Counties' very own version of Hiroshima. Even worse, she might turn up here, and *that* I could really do without. Ann Burrows is a nice lady but she's very churchgoing and has a horror of dust and dirt. If she sees the state of our cottage, she'll freak. For that matter, I must have a really good clean of the place before she next comes to visit.

I smile sympathetically at Nicky. Whatever he's done it can't be that terrible, surely? I know he was in trouble last year for flogging cigarettes to other sixth-formers – but his head teacher had privately confided to Ollie's father that Nicky Burrows was bound to be the first ex-pupil to make a billion. It was enterprising if not strictly moral.

"Whatever it is, it can't be that bad," I say in my best form-tutor voice. "We can make it better and put it right."

"I don't think we can," sighs Nicky. "You see, Katy, the headmaster caught me and his daughter."

I wait for the rest of the sentence but it doesn't come.

"Caught you and his daughter what?" I ask.

Then a horrible and very heavy penny drops. Surely not *that*? Not sweet little Nicky who wanted to be Harry Potter when he grew up? I *knew* mixed schools were a bad idea. No wonder nobody can concentrate or meet their target grades. They're all too busy thinking about sex!

I gulp.

"You weren't… you weren't… doing bad stuff?"

Nicky gives me a pitying look. "*Bad stuff*? Jesus, Katy, your generation is so obsessed with sex. It's totally boring. My English teachers talk about nothing else. Is that really all you can think about?"

Actually at the moment it is, which reminds me – I must move the Throb notes before he sees them.

And anyway, what does he mean *my generation*? We're in the same one. Aren't we?

"FYI I wasn't shagging Cassie, although she's well fit and I so would if she asked," Nicky continues, locating the Nutella now and scooping it out with his forefinger. "No, her dad caught us sneaking out to a meeting of the Socialist Workers Party and we've all been told that's banned. Christ, I think he'd far rather we were shagging than I might have turned his daughter into a—" Nicky makes speech marks with his chocolatey fingers, "commie-loving tree-hugger."

I'm outraged. "He can't kick you out for having a political conscience and an independent mind. That's the whole point of education!"

"You know it isn't. The point of the current education system is to pass exams," he reminds me as he lets Sasha lick his fingers clean. "Anyway, he *can* kick me out for hijacking the PA system and calling him a fascist in front of all the parents on speech day."

I stare at him, half impressed and half horrified. "You didn't?"

"I did," says Nicky. "So you and Ollie *have* to take me in. I'm being politically persecuted at Adolf Hitler High and I'm officially an oppressed mass. In fact, we should probably contact Amnesty and get them on the case."

I can honestly say I've never met an oppressed mass before. I must admit I would have thought there'd be more of them than just one gangly sixth-former eating his way through my kitchen cupboards.

Nicky, sensing his advantage, presses it home. "So I thought I could live with you guys and transfer to Tregowan Comp and do my A-levels here. The olds will go for it once you and Ol have explained everything. There's room in the cottage and I'll even have two teachers at home to force me to study. So I'm sorted. I'll be an A-grade student again before you know it."

I open my mouth to protest but I can't think what to say. After all, he's Ollie's brother and Ollie loves Nicky and I love Ollie. How can I say no?

While my head spins, Nicky makes a giant triple-decker sandwich and then collapses onto the sofa in front of *Loose Women*. I shut the laptop and hurriedly gather up my notes. Writing about the antics of Alexi and Lucinda and the contents of their vegetable rack seems wildly inappropriate now that I'm suddenly *in loco parentis*.

For better or worse, it appears that I am now the owner of a teenager.

Chapter 10

There's only one thing worse than a job interview and that's knowing that the man you love is having one. I keep looking at the kitchen clock, thinking how right now Ollie is in the head teacher's office looking smart and slightly uncomfortable in his best suit and having to think of all kinds of clever answers as a panel of governors fire questions at him. Which he can easily do, of course, because he's super intelligent, has prepared very hard for today and really does know his stuff. I've never known him be so focused on something or pursue it so wholeheartedly. It's actually been quite scary.

Where is the real Ollie and what has this career-minded impostor done with him?

I tap a few more words into my laptop, but my mind isn't really on it. Alexi the chef and Lucinda his assistant are supposed to be serving up one of their special banquets for a rich sheikh and I ought to be getting on with things, but all I can think about is Ollie and how much he wants this Assistant Headship. He's prepared non-stop, and last night in bed I tested him on the data he'd analysed – which to be honest wasn't really what I'd had in mind for him after a steamy day of writing for Throb. Still, I did my very best to help. If not, I feared Carolyn Miles might be more than happy to oblige…

I don't think I'm being paranoid on this score. In the last week Carolyn's called Ollie constantly and he's been closeted away in the kitchen, surrounded by files and printed spreadsheets and having low-voiced and intense conversations with her while I work in the sitting room, guard Cecily Greville's loot and develop RSI from minimising the screen every time Nicky saunters in.

Lord, but teenagers have a lot of energy. He might sleep until noon most days but once he's up Nicky's constantly bouncing around the house like Sasha – except that he spends ages media stacking, which for the uninitiated and from what I've seen means watching telly, listening to his music, surfing the Internet and playing on his Xbox all at once. It's awesome multitasking and I feel very inadequate, since I can hardly string a sentence together at the moment. My target of two thousand words a day might as well be two billion. Right now I'd be happy to write two hundred.

To all those parents I've met during my teaching career – I totally take it back. Having a teenager is way, way harder than it looks. I seriously feel like my brain's turning to cream cheese, and if Nicky plays much more Xbox then I'm sure his will too.

To cut a long and very involved story short, it's been agreed that Nicky can stay with us until he sits his exams in the summer. Once his parents were over the shock (more that their youngest son was left wing than that he'd been excluded), Ollie managed to convince them that the state system was more than capable of delivering A-levels and that we'd make sure Nicky attended school and studied hard.

"I must be mad," Ollie said to me once the decision had been made and we were now the proud owners of an A-level student. "I know this is the last thing we need right now, but I couldn't make him go back to that bloody awful prison of a school, Katy. I was so miserable there."

It had been on the tip of my tongue to point out that Nicky hadn't seemed miserable in the slightest to me; in fact he'd been having a lovely old time flogging black-market goods to his peers and being a rebellious left-wing anarchist too when it suited him. But knowing how much Ollie adores his little brother I kept quiet. Besides, this was only going to be for a few months. Just how hard could it be?

The answer is: blooming hard.

Seriously.

Until this past week I had no idea just how difficult parenting is. I might have spent years teaching, but having kids at home? I'm soon discovering that this is a whole new ball game. All of a sudden I totally get why Bluebell and Rafferty can tie Maddy up in knots – and even local artist Jason Howard's exhausted resignation regarding his evil offspring, Luke and Leia, makes sense now. (I hadn't thought they could get any worse than they were as young children, but they're truly demonic now that they've hit puberty. Poor Jason.) Being on somebody's case 24/7 is exhausting.

If I've ever felt the teeniest bit broody watching cute babies in TV adverts, then the last few days have put paid to that. The reality of life with a teenager is a world away from sweet tiny tots and designer buggies. So far as I can tell, it's all about empty milk cartons put back in the fridge and trails of dirty socks. And I've fallen down the loo more times than I can count because Nicky has an inability to put the seat down. Then there's his sleeping in till noon and the constant grazing on anything remotely edible. (I had to forcibly take Sasha's biscuits away from him.) That's not to mention the mysterious disappearance of Ollie's beer and the miracle of the emptying wine box…

Ollie's trying to work, I'm trying to write and in the middle of all this we've also been frantically doing our best to persuade Tregowan Comp that a late-entry sixth-former who's been kicked out of public school is exactly what they want.

"Sleep with the Head if you have to," Ollie had said to me last night after the oversubscribed St Jude's turned his brother down flat. "Do whatever you can to get Nicky a place."

"Don't even joke about it," I'd shuddered, and Ollie had raised his eyebrows.

"Who says I'm joking? If we don't do something soon he'll lose the use of his legs and never get out of bed again!"

It was a fair point.

"Maybe's he's nocturnal?" I'd suggested.

"I wish I was," Ollie had yawned. "I've been up all hours trying to prepare for tomorrow."

I'd been about to propose an early night – Nicky having vanished out for the evening with some new-found village friends – when Carolyn had phoned and embroiled Ollie in a fascinating discussion about Ofsted reports. Knowing that this conversation could well go on for several hours, I gave up and went to pace the living room, swing my crystal and attempt to pour all my frustrations into Alexi and Lucinda. But even they weren't in the mood, so I ended up slamming my laptop lid closed in annoyance.

Anyway, today's been far more successful because Nicky now has a school place and I didn't have to use my womanly wiles either. The Head wasn't keen at first, but I swung it by pointing out that Nicky was already an Oxbridge success, which would look good on our league tables in such data-driven times and also be a great bragging point at sixth-form recruitment evenings.

See. I have learned something from listening in to Ollie and Carolyn's conversations, although I'm far from thrilled with myself. It feels as though these days both my literary and my educational morals are going down the swanny.

Anyway, Nicky's sorted and so I'm writing in the kitchen this morning and guarding the fridge. It was a tough call between the treasure and the milk, but the milk's won because I'm getting very tired of black coffee and empty Nutella pots. Worse, when Ollie went to make his packed lunch he discovered tooth marks in the cheese, so enough is enough. Until Nicky's safely in school I'm a human shield between him and our groceries.

I've opened the kitchen half-door and glorious golden sunshine is streaming in and dancing across the tiles. Seagulls are squabbling outside, the air's sharp and I can hear the chugging of small fishing boats as they put out to sea for a couple of hours' netting. Surely on a day like this everything's going to go well? Ollie will get his job, I'll write a brilliant chapter and life will start to look up! I might not have won the lottery last week but I've bought a few more tickets and I feel certain that tonight's my night. Fate's lucky finger is pointing at me!

"More likely it's giving you the bird," Mads grins, when I voice my optimism. She's sitting next to me at the table, nursing a cup of coffee and turning the air blue with all her ideas for today's chapter. At this rate poor

Alexi will be too exhausted to open his naughty restaurant. "The lottery's a loser's game, babes. Don't be fooled."

I know she's right but those big-money numbers are to me what gin was to desperate Victorians.

"Besides, don't forget the loot under the floor," she continues. "As soon as we've got a clear evening and a crowbar we'll pull the boards up and have a good hunt, and hopefully all your problems will be solved."

I open my mouth to ask whether she thinks finding the treasure will solve my Carolyn problem. But then I shut it again quickly, because I still haven't told Mads any of this. I'm teetering on the brink of confessing my deepest fears when Frankie arrives with Gabriel in tow. They're both brimming over with excitement because they're off to New York while Gabe stars on Broadway, and they'll be renting an apartment on Central Park.

"I'm going to do some recording too," Frankie announces, in between a flurry of air kisses (me and Mads) and enthusiastic patting (Sasha). Meanwhile Gabriel, who's so ridiculously good-looking it almost hurts to look at him, checks out his hair in the microwave window.

"Brilliant news," says Maddy, giving Frankie a hug. "Your solo album will be amazing."

"It probably won't be, but hopefully everyone will buy it anyway," Frankie grins. "And then I'll get billions of downloads, be number one all over the world and One Direction can kiss my arse!"

"In your dreams, darling," says Gabriel, and then they squabble happily for a bit over who gets Harry Styles and who can have Bieber as a consolation prize, while Mads and I roll our eyes indulgently.

"Frankie's been quite low since the Queens have been on a break. This is going to be wonderful for him," Gabriel says eventually, squeezing his husband's hand. "A change of scene and some quality shopping are just what he needs. New York's got it all."

I'm pea-green with envy. Ever since watching my first episode of *Sex and the City* I've hankered after a trip to the Big Apple, where I just know I'd channel my inner Carrie Bradshaw and become a celebrated writer. I'd also have the designer wardrobe and shoe collection too, of course, although I might draw the line at the tutu. Much as I'd love to wear it, I'd look like a ginger loo-roll dolly.

"What Gabe actually means is that I've been feeling broody," Frankie sighs. "It must be my age or something, but the last time we were over at Victoria and David's I couldn't help thinking how adorable their kids are."

"I've got a cure for that," Mads tells him. "Feel free to borrow my two whenever you want. You'll soon be glad you've only got a poodle."

But Frankie isn't having this. "Bluebell and Raffy are simply gorge!"

"Tell me that when they wake you up at five a.m. every day," Mads says.

"No wonder I'm haggard."

Gabriel looks horrified. "I can't afford to look tired, Frankie. I'll lose some of my modelling work and the film roles will go to younger guys."

"That's what Botox's for," Frankie reassures him.

"If you're feeling broody, help yourself to Nicky," I offer as, right on cue, in he shuffles clad in baggy tracksuit pants and with his hair on end. Yawning widely and heading for the fridge as though pulled there by a tractor beam, Nicky selects the milk and proceeds to knock it back from the carton, his eyes still shut and totally oblivious to his audience. Drink finished, he belches happily and wipes his mouth on his hoody sleeve before placing the empty carton back in the fridge.

"Err, maybe not?" says Gabriel nervously to Frankie. "How about another dog?"

Maddy's eyes are wide. "Dear God. Is that what I have to look forward to?"

I nod. "Times two. Good luck."

As though on autopilot, Nicky's now heading for the kitchen cupboard where, by some amazing feat of psychic prowess, he selects a packet of Frosties without looking – then tips it straight into his mouth. Munching contentedly and trailing cereal all over the floor, he shuffles past and vanishes into the living room.

"It's like watching a cereal-eating Lady Macbeth," says Gabriel in awe. "Is he still asleep?"

I nod. "Nicky's eyes don't open until noon. This is early for him." I'm actually starting to wonder how I'll manage to get him up, dressed and into school on time. Maybe an electric cattle prod? The farmer down the road probably has one. If not, then cold water should do the trick.

"How much does he cost to feed?" asks Mads.

"Put it this way, Nicky's been with us less than a week and already I'm thinking of calling Geldof and arranging a *Feed the Teen* concert," I say.

"Since when did little Nicky get so big?" wonders Frankie. "I feel old!"

I sigh. "How do you think *I* feel? He won't even friend me on Facebook."

In fact, it's even worse than this; I'm still smarting because, according to Nicky, only "olds" go on Facebook anyway, and all the cool young people are on Snapchat and Instagram or vlogging. Vlogging? What on earth is that? It sounds like a disease. Nicky also tried to give me a lecture on YouTubers, who apparently make a fortune. I'm starting to feel a bit like my dad must have done when Holly and I gave him an iPad ("Where's the on button, Katy? What do you mean I swipe it?") and my brain is clearly turning to mush.

I've been in a state of growing alarm ever since. Until Nicky arrived I'd thought I was young and cool and up to date. Now I feel about as relevant as a VHS video recorder.

"I'll friend you on Facebook if you like," offers Bob the postie, reaching in through the open stable door with today's mail. "I've got eight hundred and thirty friends but I can probably fit you in."

Mads winks at me. "I bet you feel really special to be number eight hundred and thirty-one!"

"Right now I'll take anyone," I say.

"No change there, darling!" Frankie teases, and I wallop him with the big brown envelope Bob's just handed me, while he yelps and hides behind his husband.

"Careful with that," Bob warns me. "Looks like a publishing contract to me."

He's right. Closer inspection reveals this to be my contract with Throb, raced through for me to sign as promised. All I need to do is squiggle my signature on the dotted line, pop it in an envelope to send back and bingo! The advance is in my bank account and all will be well. There isn't a second to waste. I need to get this bad boy signed and back in the post.

I rip open the envelope and pull out the contract. There's pages and pages of it and, as if this wasn't enough, the whole thing's in triplicate too. While Mads makes some tea and Gabriel delightedly signs autographs for Bob's five sisters (nobody has the heart to tell him Bob's an only child and these will be up on eBay before the postie's finished his round), I skim-read the first few pages before going cross-eyed. How many clauses? And what exactly does it all mean?

I squint at the small print but it's no good. Even if I turned the thing upside down it wouldn't make any more sense; there's way too much legalese. I'm sure it's all fine though. I mean, how complicated can it be? They want to pay a writer to ghostwrite *Kitchen of Correction* and I'll write the thing and get paid. There really isn't any more to it than that.

Of course there isn't.

I bet they just make these contracts super complicated so that lawyers can feel clever and agents can justify their twenty percent. It's like the emperor's new clothes!

Picking up one of Ollie's stray pens from the table, I sign my name with a flourish. Once, twice and then three times in bright red ink.

There! The contacts are completed and it's only a matter of days before the money is on its way. That was actually very easy. I can't imagine what agents make such a fuss about.

"Err, is that a good idea?" Frankie asks as I stuff the signed paperwork into the return envelope and seal it.

"Of course! This book's going to get our house rewired."

"Not writing the book," he says. "I meant signing a contract without getting your agent to check it through. Is that wise? Loads of bands get totally ripped off that way."

I'm touched that Frankie thinks I might have a literary agent. In my dreams.

"I don't have an agent," I confess. In the past Tansy's agent did all that stuff and I just got paid. Admittedly it was a pittance, so maybe I *should* have looked a little more closely at the paperwork?

"OK, at least read it carefully then? What if there's something in there that you don't like?"

"Such as?"

"I don't know, sweetie! That's what I pay my manager for! Do you want Seb to have a look at this? He's done such wonders for Gabe that I've hired him for myself as well. Honestly, angel, he's one of the best there is."

I laugh at the very thought of being able to hire Seb Sharp. One of the media industry's top managers, anything he charges for looking at a contract will make my rewiring bill look small.

"It's fine, Frankie. Don't look so worried. This is just a standard industry thing for a spot of ghostwriting. It's just a formality."

He looks doubtful. "Really?"

"Really!" I promise. "I've signed loads of these. It's fine. Stop stressing."

Frankie holds his hands up. "OK! I'm sure you know what you're doing. I just hope they haven't got some hidden clause in there that you have to paint yourself pink and dance naked or something."

It's scary what goes on in some people's minds, isn't it? And even scarier that I can't help thinking that this is *exactly* the kind of thing Throb might want their authors to do…

Come on, Katy! You're being ridiculous. Of course they won't! Still, this has given me a very good idea of what Alexi can do with strawberry custard…

I just need to get on with writing the book, banking the money and fixing this lava-lamp disaster. It's too late now to start worrying: the contracts are signed and the money will soon be in the account. This is all good. I bet Ollie even gets his job too.

Today is going really well. Nothing can possibly go wrong. Signing that contract was definitely the right thing to do.

Chapter 11

"Katy," calls Nicky. "What's this?"

I almost jump out of my skin, nearly dropping my toast and Marmite on the kitchen floor. It's only half past ten on a Saturday morning and, thinking myself safe because Ollie's yet again in school and Nicky never rises before noon, I've been working on *Kitchen of Correction* in the sitting room. Needing inspiration for my latest chapter, I've headed to my own far less exciting kitchen to refuel, foolishly leaving my laptop and notes unguarded.

Toast abandoned mid-butter, I dash back to my laptop. But it's too late: Nicky's sprawled on the sofa reading through my notes with eyes like saucers and his mouth hanging open.

"Sick!" he breathes. I know this is teen for *wow*, but it makes my heart sink all the same. Today's chapter is set in Alexi's special bakery and although "sick" isn't quite the right adjective, once I'd read the synopsis through I was certainly put off glacé cherries for life…

"Are you writing porn?"

"Of course not! And that's my private work! You shouldn't be looking at it!" I fly at the laptop, slam the lid shut and gather all my papers into a pile – as if hiding the evidence will make any difference now. Never mind shutting the stable door after the horse has bolted; this one has just done several laps of Aintree and is now enjoying a press call with its owner.

I'm so busted.

"If it's private you shouldn't be leaving it lying around for everyone to look at," Nicky points out.

Is nothing sacred? Can't a girl even write a book in peace?

"It wasn't lying around for everyone to read," I say huffily. "It was on the table where I was working. In my own home and in private! And anyway, what are you doing up? It's daylight. Shouldn't you still be in your pit?"

"I thought you'd be pleased to see me up early." Nicky looks offended. "I thought this was what you wanted? Why else pour cold water on me yesterday and hide an alarm clock under my bed the day before that?"

"To wake you up for school! You have to be up for school but it's Saturday today. You can sleep in all day if you feel like it!"

No wonder parents feel like tearing their hair out. At this rate I'll be bald by half-term. Nicky's managed fifteen schooldays at Tregowan Comp so far and every one of these has seen him arrive late. I've already had a stern phone call from the attendance secretary, and when I did a day's supply on Friday I was too ashamed to look the Head of Sixth Form in the eye. Then Steph took me to task about several missed deadlines. I am now officially the guardian of a problem pupil, and although I share this joy with Ollie I haven't managed to talk to him about Nicky yet. Since he became the Assistant Head at St Jude's, Ollie's been busier than ever. Forget ships that pass in the night; we're sailing different oceans altogether, and these days the good ship Ollie Burrows has Carolyn Miles firmly at the helm…

"I felt like getting up early. I thought you'd be pleased," Nicky complains, interrupting my musings on Carolyn and her endless calls.

"I am pleased, but not when you go nosing through my work!"

"I wasn't nosing. I was being your beta reader. And talking of beating, I like that bit with the egg whisk. Kinky!"

My face is hotter than the earth's core. Oh God! I can't believe he's read *that* bit! I knew I should never have let Mads persuade me to include it. I'll have social services knocking on my door any minute to take Nicky away from my dubious care.

Now there's a thought… Do they take eighteen-year-olds away, I wonder?

"You look well guilty! I take it Ollie doesn't know?" Nicky fans my red face. "Don't worry, your secret's safe with me. I won't tell." He pauses and then adds slyly, "Or rather, I won't tell Ollie as long as you stop throwing cold water on me."

Bollocks. There goes any vain hope of ever having any authority over him. I know when I'm beaten. Nicky's so sharp Alexi could chop carrots with him in the fictional kitchen.

"Do you know, it's actually not bad," Nicky continues, his toffee-brown eyes narrowed critically. "The syntax needs a little work and you've got a few typos there, but the shagging's red hot. And that bit where they get the wet tea towels and—"

I clap my hands over my ears. Apart from being critiqued by an A-level English student, even one that's a potential Oxbridge high-flyer, I can hardly bear to hear any of this. I want to write romance! How did it all go so wrong?

"I'm only writing this to get the house rewired!"

"I didn't think you were writing it because you wanted to or liked it. Let's face it, you and Ollie are a bit past all that stuff anyway at your age," Nicky says pityingly.

We are not! Of course we're not!

Are we?

Maybe he has a point, because come to think of it when was the last time Ollie and I did much more in bed than pass out or drink tea? Even the seagulls on the rooftop get more action than us lately. No matter how many wedding magazines I leave about – because I'm through with subtle, Goddammit – or how much of my best underwear I dig out, all Ollie can think about is his new job.

His new job or, says a nasty little voice deep down inside, *Carolyn Miles?*

"To be honest," Nicky continues thoughtfully while I panic about my (lack of) love life, "I can see straight away this isn't one consistent style. I take it Maddy's helping you with the book?"

There's no point hiding anything now, so I nod.

"She comes up with the err… material and I write it up," I confess. "I know it's not great literature but it'll pay some bills."

"Sod great literature. Write what pays," says Nicky, who for a socialist seems to have some very capitalist leanings. "So why doesn't my big brother know about this?"

"I haven't said anything because his school wouldn't approve and I don't want to compromise him," I explain, and Nicky nods sagely. Having been rejected by St Jude's, he totally gets it.

"Look, don't take this personally, and you can tell me to get lost if you want, but your book's a bit clichéd in parts," Nicky tells me kindly. "I'm pretty good at creative writing myself and I could give you some help. If you like?"

I'm even more horrified at this thought than I am at being patronised by an A-level student. "Absolutely not! You can't write this kind of thing at your age!"

"I'm eighteen," he says patiently. "I've had Internet access all my life, not like you lot. There's not much my generation haven't seen. Besides, what do you think is in all those A-level English literature texts? Chaucer? Byron? *Fanny Hill*? Sex, Katy. S. E. X. Pure filth, that's what. We can be a writers' collective. You, me and Maddy. What do you say? It'll be fun."

It would? Personally I can't think of anything worse. It'll be like writing a book with Beavis and Butt-Head. My head's already aching just imagining all the sniggering.

"It won't count towards your English language coursework," I warn, and Nicky laughs.

"No, but you donating a few pennies for my consultancy input will be brilliant for my gap-year fund! Just think of me as your editor at home. That way I'll *have* to make sure I don't *accidentally* mention anything to Ol because I'll be in on it too! Don't think of my contribution to all this as a literary experience. Think of it as insurance!"

And with this Nicky jumps up, kisses me on the cheek and bounds out of the room whistling while I stare after him incredulously. I can't believe it! I've just been well and truly stitched up – and I can't help admiring his nerve.

One thing's for sure: Nicky Burrows has got a great career ahead of him as a politician.

"That's brilliant!" Mads wipes her eyes when I recount this episode over a pub lunch. "Fantastic! I love it! Or should that be, *I Lovett*?"

"Very funny," I say gloomily. "Do you see me laughing? This is terrible! Apart from the fact I'm keeping a huge secret from Ollie, which feels really wrong, I can't possibly let Nicky look at the synopsis. He's far too young!"

"He's eighteen!"

"Exactly!"

"And what were you up to at eighteen? Knitting? Baking fairy cakes? Or red-hot shagging?"

The answer to this is none of the above, not that I'm going to let on to Mads just how dull my teenage years were. The nearest I got to sex was sneaking a copy of *Riders* into my school bag.

"Anyway, you can bet your life Nicky knows way more than we did at his age," Maddy continues. "You're a teacher, you must know that."

I nod miserably. Even though I know she's right I'm horrified at the thought of sweet little Nicky reading up on Alexi and Lucinda's shenanigans. The fact that sweet little Nicky is blackmailing me, albeit in an amusing and helpful way, is totally beside the point.

"But I'm in a position of authority! I can't let him read this stuff."

"Katy, it's just a book and Nicky's right: it's not even a very naughty book really compared to some of his A-level texts. It's just worse for you because you're—"

"What?"

Mads shakes her head. "No, I can't say it."

"What? What am I?"

"You're a prude!"

I stare at her. "I am not."

"Are too," says Mads. "You read *Fifty Shades* with a Jane Austen dust cover over it."

"I was protecting my intellectual reputation!"

"No you weren't," she says fondly. "But it doesn't matter anyway because we all love you. Nicky and I will help you deliver this bloody book – but then step away from the erotic literature, please? For your own sanity? And mine?"

"I will, I will." I nod fervently. From now on in, I swear to God the most action anyone in my novels will get is a spot of chaste handholding.

Mads dunks a cheesy chip in ketchup and munches thoughtfully.

"So now I've set your mind at rest about sweet innocent Nicky, we've just planned chapter five of the book and the advance has landed in your savings account. I would have thought all was well, so why do you look so miserable?"

"I don't look miserable."

"I'm afraid you do. Never take up acting, Katy, because you're crap."

This is a blow indeed, because I'd thought I was doing a sterling job of putting on a brave face. The thing is, all this business with Carolyn is starting to really get to me. As much as I appreciate that Ollie needed to be at work today, I have a horrible feeling she'll be there too, all bright-eyed and flippy-ponytailed, and they'll be able to talk data and learning strategies to their hearts' content. Then they'll probably go for lunch and laugh at school in-jokes, just like we used to do.

There's a lump the size of a trawl float in my throat and my eyes fill.

"Tell me," Mads orders, and so I do. By the time I've talked myself into a standstill our lunch is cold.

"Fuck a duck," she breathes. "You did well to keep this to yourself. I'd have been climbing the walls."

"I've been digging the floors. Does that count?"

"I guess so. Now listen, I don't believe for one minute that Ollie would even look at another woman when he's bonkers about you."

"You haven't seen her," I point out gloomily.

"We can soon sort that. I take it there's a St Jude's website? She'll be on there, I should think," says Mads, plucking her phone from her bag and selecting the Internet browser.

I nod. "They have a staff page. Ollie's has just been updated. He had a new picture too. He even had a haircut."

"Blimey," says Maddy. "He is taking this new job seriously."

She isn't wrong. I'd shed a secret tear when Ollie had come home with his gorgeous shaggy curls lopped off and his earring gone. He'd looked so serious all of a sudden. I know an Assistant Head Teacher can't look like a gangly surfer dude, but it feels as though another part of him has stepped out of my reach.

"Found it. St Jude's, blah blah, senior leaders, Carolyn Miles… oh. Oh dear."

My stomach lurches. "What's that supposed to mean?"

"It means that…" Mads squints at the screen. "It means that it's worse than I thought. But look, I'm a woman, so what do I know? Give me a minute."

She hops up from her seat and wanders across to the far end of the bar where Guy and a bunch of his fishermen pals are playing cards and squabbling. Moments later cries of "Phwoar!" and "I would!" ring through the pub.

Oh.

"Houston, we may have a problem," Maddy announces, sitting back down. "The general consensus among the fishermen is that she's well fit, so I totally see why you'd be worried. *But*," she presses on before I can interrupt, "this doesn't mean a thing. Ollie loves you and I don't think anything's changed there, although I appreciate that you need to prove that for yourself. You need to see them together so that you know once and for all that there's nothing going on."

I do? I mean, I do!

"And luckily for you," Mads says, "I have a plan that's going to help you do exactly that. So drink up, sit up and listen to me!"

Chapter 12

Why oh why do I listen to Maddy Lomax? By now I should surely know better. Her good ideas always end in total disaster, so whatever made me think this time it would be any different?

Desperation. That's what.

"Well, go on then," Mads says, giving me a little shove. "Get out the car and go kick ass. Give that slapper a run for her money."

I can honestly say I have never wanted to get out of a car less in my life or felt less inclined to kick ass.

"I'm not sure—" I begin, but Mads leans across and pokes me so hard in the ribs that I'm out of the seat before I have a chance to finish my sentence.

"We've been through this, Katy! No more chickening out!" Mads scolds, tossing my bag after me. "You said you wanted to see for yourself once and for all what's really going on with this Carolyn floozy, so now's your chance. I don't know what you're waiting for!"

"I don't know, Mads," I say nervously. "I'm not sure this is a good idea."

"It's not a 'good idea'. It's a bloody *genius* idea, that's what it is. How else will you ever know for certain there's nothing going on? Now, go and get 'em!"

The car door slams and tyres spin on gravel as Mads tears away, waving merrily and leaving me staring after her in shock. I can't believe she's just abandoned me! She wouldn't really, surely?

She'll be back in a minute.

Or maybe two?

But five? Five minutes is seriously pushing her luck and this is when I realise Maddy isn't returning. *Thank you very much,* I think as I shoulder my bag and try to decide what to do next. She really has driven off and dumped me and Tansy's cast-off bag in the St Jude's car park and, as agreed, I know she won't be back until three-thirty. So until then it looks as though I'm on my own.

It's ten to nine on Tuesday morning, smartly attired students are scurrying through the school gates before the bell has even sounded, and several teachers are circling the playground just in case there's a whiff of bad behaviour or, heaven forbid, somebody isn't wearing their blazer. If the lack of swearing/footballing/shirts hanging out isn't already unnerving enough, knowing I could bump into Ollie at any minute is even more terrifying. He's no idea that I've booked a supply day here with the express purpose of seeing first-hand what goes on between him and Carolyn at work, and that's the way I'm intending to keep it – hence the blonde wig I've borrowed from Gabriel and the trendy clear-glass specs that Frankie's loaned me. (They're both away at the moment, but they said I was welcome to let myself into Smuggler's Rest and rummage for stuff in their wardrobe.) Having teamed these with a suit from Maddy's jumble mountain and a pair of heels I could barely walk in, I hardly recognised myself when I peered in the mirror.

"That's the whole point," Mads said, while I tottered up and down the vicarage kitchen in an attempt to walk. "You look totally professional and nothing like your usual self."

I chose to ignore this comment. Still, if I looked nothing like myself I supposed it was job done. If I accidentally bumped into Ollie in a corridor, he wouldn't know it was me.

It's strange how what seemed like such a great plan after a few glasses of wine doesn't feel quite as clever in the cold light of day. What am I doing here in a second-hand and rather musty disguise, spying on the man I love and wearing a vain film star's hairpiece?

I must have been drunk. This is a crazy idea!

I'm contemplating turning tail and heading out of the gates in search of a bus when an efficient-looking teacher comes over. Glancing down at her clipboard she says in a bright voice, "On supply? Mrs Carter?"

"Err, yes," I agree, caught on the hop and not able to think fast enough to deny it.

"Well, no point standing in the playground. You need to book in at reception, pick up a lanyard and then Ms Miles will show you where to find your first class. It's Mass first though, so you'll have time to grab a coffee and a biscuit."

Mass? Coffee and a biscuit? Feeling as though I've been dropped into a strange parallel universe where teachers actually have time for snacks, I follow her into St Jude's and, just like that, the decision is out of my hands. Heart beating hard, I head towards the reception where I'm signed in, given a lanyard and badge to wear and then asked to wait outside Carolyn's office. Children flow past with shirts tucked in and their ties done up rather around their heads Rambo style, and then the corridors empty as if by magic when they go into the chapel. Chapel? Can you believe it? At Tregowan Comp I'm delighted if the kids sit down at their desks, never mind go to church. What kind of a place is this?

I'd completely forgotten that St Jude's is a Catholic school; Ollie, a very lapsed Catholic indeed, had to brush up on the Hail Marys and other bits when he'd applied for the job. He kept quiet about living in sin with me too, which seemed a bit bonkers in the twenty-first century. While I sit outside the school office like a naughty girl, I contemplate the agonised Jesus hanging from a crucifix on the far side of the corridor and start to feel very uneasy indeed. What if there are nuns lurking about who can tell just by looking at me that I'm LYING about who I am? Will I get dragged to confession? Have to say some chants? Go to hell, do not pass go and do not collect two hundred pounds? Beneath my borrowed polyester suit I begin to sweat. Is it my imagination or is Jesus looking at me in a particularly disappointed manner? Has he been chatting with the Reverend Richard?

I shift nervously on the hard plastic seat and try looking at the floor, but I'm sure I can still sense Jesus's scrutiny and His sadness that I've let Him down. Any minute a lightning bolt will fry me. Or maybe I'll be eaten by a swarm of locusts or something? To be honest, I'm not altogether sure. My knowledge of Catholicism is a bit sparse. For a start, my parents are totally against organised religion, and apart from watching *Sister Act* and reading *The Da Vinci Code*, my education on all things religious is rather vague.

I *knew* I shouldn't have bunked those lectures on Dante when I was at uni…

Anyway, my own personal circle of hell is heating up fast, because now the office door is opening and none other than Carolyn and Ollie are emerging. They're deep in discussion and Ol is clutching a huge pile of paperwork, so I'm sure they've just been planning the day ahead and nothing more. I duck my head down but luckily Ollie's too busy looking through one of his folders to notice a lowly supply teacher, and Carolyn's preoccupied by touching his arm and flicking her hair at him. Floozy.

"Catch you afterwards, OK?" she says, and Ollie nods.

"Sure. Better get to chapel. See you later, C."

C? He even has a pet name for her? Never mind the hair flicking. This is way worse than I thought.

As Ollie walks away I stare after him, wanting nothing more than to follow, throw my arms around him and tell him just how worried I am. Normally I can tell Ollie anything and he always makes it better. Of course he does. He's my best friend. Lately though it's starting to feel as though there are so many misunderstandings and secrets between us that I simply don't know where to start when it comes to unravelling them all.

"Mrs Carter? Welcome to St Jude's." Carolyn is holding out her hand. As though in a dream I find myself taking it and having my own hand pumped up and down. "Here's your map and your timetable for the day. Chapel finishes at nine-twenty and then you'll have lower fourth English in the Loyola Suite."

I have absolutely no idea what she's on about but I nod manically. At this point my wig starts to slip over my eyes, so I have to shove it back hastily. Coils of ginger hair make a bid for freedom and I push them out of sight.

"Have we met before?" Carolyn asks, looking confused.

"I've not done supply here before," I hedge, which isn't fibbing, is it? There's no way I can tell a bare-faced lie with Jesus watching.

"You look very familiar," she says thoughtfully. "And, I don't mean to be rude or ask personal questions, but why are you wearing a wig?"

"I've got very brightly coloured hair," I improvise. "Pink and green and, err, ginger. It doesn't look professional does it? And the prospectus rules say quite clearly that natural hair colours only are allowed, so I didn't want to start the day with a black mark. Ha ha!"

"Those rules are generally applied to the students rather than the teachers," Carolyn tells me slowly. "We don't expect our staff to wear the uniform either, you know."

"I like to set a good example," I say piously, folding my hands in front of me and raising my eyes to the crucifix in a saintly manner. "It's what our Lord would want, after all."

She looks rather alarmed by all this and I make a mental note not to over-egg my religious pudding too much in future.

"Right," Carolyn says with a frown. "Anyway, here's your map of the school and the number of our emergency mobile in case you have an issue. One of the senior teachers always carries it. My advice is to pop the number into your own mobile when you're in the staffroom."

I nod. "Thanks. I will."

Feeling like I've landed in an Enid Blyton novel I set off along a clean and gum-free corridor, clutching my map and doing my best not to break my ankles in the heels Mads lent me. After I've gone a little way I slow down because I have no intention of wasting time in the staffroom. No. I need to find Ollie's classroom and have a look for any evidence. If he's in the chapel then it's the perfect time to snoop around. There are no children about, most of the teachers are occupied and I've got my lanyard ID on, so I'm good to go.

The trouble is I have absolutely no idea where I am. The bloody map's so small I can hardly make out anything and all these white corridors look exactly the same. I daren't retrace my steps in case I bump into Carolyn again and she rumbles me, and I don't dare ask anyone where Ollie's office is because I have no right or need to be there. I guess I'll just keep doing circuits of the school until I see his name on a door or catch sight of him again.

I round another corner and pass down a flight of steps before crossing a courtyard. Aha! Ollie's mentioned that courtyard. All the teachers hate it because it isn't covered; when the rain comes down, which it tends to do on a very regular basis in the West Country, they get soaked going to and from their classrooms. Ollie's office can't be far away.

And then suddenly I'm right on top of it, and because this is St Jude's and not Tregowan Comp, the door's unlocked and I'm in. For a second I dither in the doorway, all too aware that this is wrong and I shouldn't be here. But then a picture on top of a filing cabinet catches my eye.

Oh! It's of me!

I step forward for a closer look and there's a big lump in my throat because it's a picture I know very well. It's one Ollie took when we went travelling around Europe in his old camper van, back when we were first together and before we'd bought the cottage. I'm sitting in the camper's doorway with my arms around Sasha and beaming at the camera. The sun's setting behind us but it's not the golden rays making me glow: it's love and happiness. Just recalling what happened shortly after the photo was taken is enough to bring a similar flush to my cheeks now, and I know that every time Ol looks at it he'll remember too. Of course he will. That's why it's there.

I'm such an idiot. Ollie isn't having a fling with Carolyn. It's obvious that he isn't. Ollie loves me, just like I love him. That picture says it all.

I'm just picking it up for a closer look when the door flies open and Carolyn strides in.

"What do you think you're doing?" she demands, and I jump out of my skin. Bollocks!

My heart's racing as I put the photo back. I can't be discovered now, I can't! If Ollie finds out I've been spying on him he'll be absolutely devastated.

"Oh! Hello again!" I do my best to sound normal, as though I haven't been caught snooping around the Assistant Head's office. "I'm afraid I got a bit lost. I was looking for—" I glance down at the crumpled map clutched in my hand, "the Loyola Suite?"

She frowns. "Your map's upside down. You're in totally the wrong part of the school. This is the Assistant Head's office."

"It is?" I hope I'm doing a good job of looking surprised. "Oh dear! Just as well I'm not here to teach geography. Ha ha!"

Carolyn stares at me as though I'm deranged. She's probably wondering how anyone remotely sane could confuse an office with a classroom. She'll be looking up the results of my criminal record check as soon as she can, and I don't blame her either. Heaven only knows what she'll say to the supply agency. I'll probably never work again.

"If you follow me, I'll show you where you should be," she says briskly.

Where I should be? My heart sinks. The last thing I want to do is stay here now. All I want is to get out of here as fast as I can and before I bump into Ollie. And once I'm home I am never listening to Maddy Lomax and her bright ideas again.

"I'll find it," I begin, but Carolyn isn't having this.

"I really don't have the time to hunt you down if you get lost a second time. I'll take you to the Loyola Suite." She checks her watch and clicks her tongue in irritation. "We're running late as it is and I expect Mr Burrows is already there settling them down for you. It's his classes you're looking after today."

I'm covering Ollie's lessons? But why? He's here! I've just seen him.

I gawp at her. "But isn't Ol – I mean Mr Burrows here today? Why am I covering his classes?"

Carolyn Miles looks taken aback to have a lowly supply teacher demanding to know the ins and outs of the Assistant Head's whereabouts.

"He and I are off timetable at Burrington Hall today."

Every cell in my body freezes. Burrington Hall? As in the plush country house hotel just outside the city? Ollie's going there for the day with Carolyn? He never mentioned it to me.

Trust, Katy, trust. Remember the photo? There's bound to be an innocent explanation.

"Right," I say, and it sounds as though I've been strangled.

"So if you don't mind, maybe we could get going? Senior management inset days cost time and money and we can't afford to wait around," she barks. "It's why you're here, after all."

"Oh! A training day! That's OK then!" I follow her out of the room and into the corridor, full now of children fresh out of Mass and keen to let off steam. I need to get out of here and fast, but before I even have the chance to make an excuse, she clamps her hand onto my shoulder and steers me towards a classroom.

Shit! It's Ollie's classroom! And there he is on the other side of it (with his back to me, thank heavens), writing on the whiteboard. It's only a matter of seconds before he turns around and sees me. Seconds I cannot waste.

I have to get out of here!

"Right, this is where you need to be. Lower fourth form war poetry. They should get on quietly," Carolyn tells me. "I'll let Mr Burrows explain what he needs you to do, but all the work is set and taped to the desk."

"Actually, I've just realised that there's somewhere else I need to be. Sorry!" I attempt to spin on my heel but that iron hand holds me so tightly I can hardly move, while another tortured Jesus gazes at me with sympathy from His position above the whiteboard. I know this is a Catholic school and everything, but I have absolutely no desire to confess everything at this moment in time.

If I don't escape now I'll have some serious explaining to do – and the worst of it is that even to *me* this all sounds insane, so goodness only knows what Ollie will think.

"Good God!" Carolyn roars, and I jump so hard that my feet leave the ground. "I've just spent the best part of twenty minutes looking for you. You're not going anywhere! You're here on supply and you're going to teach this class. Now get on with it!"

Never mind the kids being scared of her.

I'm bloody terrified.

"I think I need a change of vocation!" I yank myself away and make a bolt for freedom. "I've just realised I don't want to teach anymore! It's not for me! Blame the Education Secretary. Blame the government, but I just can't handle it. Too much stress! Sorry!"

Carolyn's mouth is open and she's frozen with disbelief, which is just the chance I need. Before she can come to her senses and grab me or, even worse, Ollie comes out of his classroom, I'm off as fast as my legs and high heels can carry me. Even when she shouts after me I don't stop, and as soon as I'm across the courtyard and in the car park I kick off my shoes and start to run.

There's no way I dare stick around. I'm out of here.

Chapter 13

This morning has been a total nightmare. I may be closer to proving my fears about Carolyn to be unfounded – at least on my boyfriend's part – but in the process I could have caused Ollie a lot of embarrassment. And I should imagine that, thanks to me, St Jude's senior leaders never got to have their relaxing day out of school. If Ollie ever finds out that the mad runaway supply teacher was me I don't know what I'll do. Die of humiliation probably.

As I sit in the kitchen trying to write another episode in the quite frankly knackering sex lives of Alexi and Lucinda, I'm feeling utterly despondent. Even Nicky's tongue-in-cheek input doesn't cheer me up, and neither does the big packet of chocolate biscuits Maddy's brought round as a peace offering.

I can't eat a chocolate biscuit? Things must be really serious. And anyway, it's going to take her more than a packet of digestives to make up for this latest near miss.

"How many more times can I apologise?" Mads asks. "It seemed like a great idea at the time. How was I to know you'd be asked to cover Ollie's lessons? I'm not a sodding psychic."

It's a fair point but I'm not willing to concede it yet. She needs to grovel a bit more first.

"Besides," she continues, "I still think it was a good idea. At least you saw for yourself that there was nothing going on. I'd say that's a bloody good result actually. You ought to be thanking me, not sulking."

"Don't push it," I say.

"This might seem a really obvious point," Nicky butts in, looking up from the chapter notes, "but speaking in my limited capacity as a guy, why on earth did you go to all this trouble rather than just talking to my brother?"

When Mads and I have recovered sufficiently from laughing at such a crazy notion Nicky adds, with all the wisdom of someone who's been an adult for about fifteen minutes, "What you two need to know about blokes is that we're not actually very complicated. There's no subtext. Just ask us and we'll tell you what you need to know."

"That," says Maddy sternly while I gnaw my thumbnail, "has to be the worst advice I've ever heard. If Katy had asked Ollie whether he's boffing Carolyn, then he'd think she doesn't trust him."

"Well she doesn't, does she?" remarks Nicky. "Not if she thinks he'd cheat. Next?"

Mads is stumped and I search for an answer. I mean, I do trust Ollie. Of course I do. It's just that he's been a bit weird lately. And I certainly don't trust Carolyn. Why all the phone calls and late meetings and now even Saturday mornings in school?

"On the other hand," Nicky adds, considering me through narrowed eyes, "I'd say that what you did this morning, Katy, is classic of a passive-aggressive female pattern of behaviour and even maybe borders on the psychotic. Have you ever seen a shrink?"

I lay my head on the table and groan. "Are you trying to make me feel even worse? And anyway, it wasn't my idea: it was Maddy's!"

He laughs. "Then you definitely need to see a shrink for listening to anything she says!"

"Oi, watch it, squirt," Mads warns. "Anyway, shouldn't you be in school?"

"Free lesson," says Nicky quickly. I strongly suspect this is a fib but I feel way too exhausted to push it. Besides, he's doing a sterling job of knocking my latest chapter into shape.

"I'm only kidding," Nicky says. "You don't need a shrink, Katy. You're just a typical complicated woman. Why ask my brother if he's shagging somebody else – which he isn't by the way – when you can go to all the effort of spying on him while he's at work? For fuck's sake! Just talk to him. Work it out. Communicate. Relationships are all about communication."

"Are you the next Jeremy Kyle?" Mads asks. "What's next? A lie-detector test? Or a DNA revelation? DNA! Now that's a thought! That could prove everything."

"Don't even go there," I warn. "Step away from my mess."

"Spoilsport," sighs Maddy, rising from the kitchen table and putting the kettle on. "I'm a vicar's wife, remember? I have to get my fun somewhere."

"What will I tell Ollie if he asks about today?" I wonder.

"Crazy notion, but how about the truth?" suggests Nicky. "Why don't you 'fess up about this bloody book for a start? It's not good to keep secrets."

You're telling me it isn't, but own up about this book? Now I've seen first-hand just how weird they are at St Jude's there's no way I can burden Ollie with the knowledge that I'm writing for Throb. Apart from the fact that I've already given most of my advance to the local sparky and couldn't pay it back even if I wanted to, I had a little peek at the contract earlier on and it didn't make good reading. Although I'm no lawyer, it looks to me as though there's a nasty little clause in it that suggests they can sue my ass should I back out. We struggle to pay the council tax, so we'd never afford a lawsuit. It's official. I'm stuffed.

So, I can't tell Ollie the truth – not when I know how much his career means to him. I'll just have to carry on writing the book in secret. Or as much in secret as I can now that just about everyone else I know is in on it.

Besides, Ollie's not been one hundred percent truthful with me either, has he? I had no idea he was off to Burrington Hall today and I still have a nagging feeling that there's more he's hiding. His mobile phone even has a PIN on it these days, and I guess I didn't really need to call the psychic hotline to be told that this is a very bad sign indeed. To be honest I shouldn't be calling the telephone psychics anyway, but they're cheaper than counselling and, unlike my best friend, they don't persuade me into pursuing ridiculous so-called master plans. So all in all, premium-rate phone charges aside, I'd say they're excellent value for money.

While Maddy makes tea, I sink back into my chair and continue to chew my fingernails. Nicky taps away at the laptop, occasionally asking me for my opinion. To be honest I'm not really paying much attention, and before long he and Mads are having an in-depth discussion about washing lines versus duct tape, while I occupy myself with trying to find a way to ask Ollie exactly what's going on. I'm so lost in thought that even when the top half of the kitchen door swings open and Britain's favourite WAG pops her head through, I barely notice.

"Is this the house of sin and ill repute?" grins Tansy Topham, letting herself in and sashaying across the kitchen. Today her long extensions are piled high on her head like a blonde pineapple. She's wearing sprayed-on skinny jeans and spike-heeled boots, and her famous chest is spilling out of a very tight vest top. When she bends over to kiss me, Nicky almost falls off his chair.

"More like the house of darkness and despair. But enough of me. What are you doing in Tregowan? You do know this isn't the city?"

Tansy's surgery-perfect nose crinkles. "Like, duh. I've just had to walk miles from the car park to get here, and in my Louboutins. Will the Lotus be safe parked there?"

I nod. "It'll be covered in seagull crap but, yes, it'll still have four wheels."

"That's the main thing. Tommy can always wash it or have it resprayed." Tansy sits at the table, her heavily laden charm bracelet chinking on her twiggy arms. "Anyway, I had to come. You weren't answering your phone."

Ah yes. That'll be the phone I switched off in order to avoid the irate calls from the supply agency. Looks like my change of career is coming faster than I'd anticipated.

"Katy's had a rough morning," Maddy explains, setting a mug of hot water and lemon in front of Tansy. Everyone knows Tansy doesn't do caffeine.

"Yeah, she looks like shit," Tansy agrees with her usual tact. Turning to me she says, "Babes, I'm afraid things might be about to get a whole lot worse. I'm a bit worried I *may* have put my foot in it."

When Tansy says she *may* have done something there's usually no *may* about it. I'm instantly alarmed.

"Tansy," I say, "what have you done?"

She fiddles nervously with her bracelet. "I *might* have accidentally mentioned to a journalist that I don't write my own books."

Is that all? I mean, this is hardly going to come as a surprise to the general public. Still, I don't want to hurt her feelings so I say gently, "I think people have already guessed that."

"Really?"

"Really," I promise.

"Phew," says Tansy. "So if I'd said an English teacher from Tregowan wrote my books instead of me it wouldn't be a problem?"

"I can't imagine so. I'm not that exciting."

"What about school?" Maddy asks.

"Tregowan Comp already know about the books," I say slowly. "They're not thrilled but it'll be no surprise to them. Ollie's school might not be too impressed, but since it's my writing not his I really don't think it's going to be an issue."

Tansy claps her hands. "That's such a relief. I'd hate to drop you in it."

"No, I think I'm more than capable of doing that myself," I say bleakly.

While we drink tea and Nicky continues to stare at my visitor in disbelief, the conversation turns to BBs, Tansy's new catering business – which she's very excited about for a girl who seldom eats. Still deep in thought about what may or may not be going on with Ollie, I tune in and out of the conversation, letting it wash over me just like the waves washing up the beach beyond the harbour wall. Mads is nodding absently and Nicky's asking whether there would be any part-time work for him. I can't say that I've ever imagined him as a waiter, but anything that gets him out of bed and away from extorting funds from me can only be a good thing. Tansy certainly seems to think this is a possibility and takes his number.

"If either of you ever want to book with us I'll give you a huge discount too," Tansy is saying now. "I think you'll love what we do."

"Maybe Katy could book you for her next book launch?" says Maddy, grinning at me.

Very funny. I'm actually planning to be very far away indeed when *Kitchen of Correction* hits the shops. I hear the Mars mission might have spaces?

"I mean it," insists Tansy. "Big discounts all around. Tell your friends!"

Tansy is nothing if not generous. Take the old beach bag she gave me last year, for instance. It only turned out to be a Louis Vuitton and worth more than our car. I wouldn't dream of taking advantage of her kindness, but it could be handy having a catering contact. My brain's whirring already.

Ollie's mum is celebrating her sixtieth birthday later on this year and has been threatening – err, I mean talking about – spending it in Tregowan. Ann Burrows is very proper and I can't help suspecting she thinks Ollie could have done better for himself. His wine-buff father, Geoff, is much easier to get along with, although I do wish he'd just drink the stuff rather than pontificating about it. He even described my father's nettle wine as having a bouquet of "wild thyme and ambrosia", which delighted Dad because most people think it smells like wee. It certainly looks like it.

Hey! If I throw Ann a wonderful surprise birthday party it will really impress her and it'll be one less thing for Ollie to worry about. I know he's been racking his brains for what to do for her. Maybe I can pay for it with the remainder of my advance from Throb? That way at least some good might come from my having written this secret book. I know we need to get our roof fixed as well at some point, but there'll be another two novels in the series to help cover that.

Hugely cheered by the notion of doing something nice with my guilty money, I don't take a lot of persuading to go to the pub for lunch. By the time I return to the cottage, a few glasses of wine down, I'm feeling far more mellow. Tansy and her seagull-crap speckled Lotus have roared back to Plymouth, Mads has gone to collect the twins from school and Nicky's sloped off somewhere. All is quiet in the cottage. All is still. I can get on with my work in peace, make a bit of money, retire from writing mummy porn and all will be well. Ollie and I will be the way we always have been and life will go back to normal.

Of course it will.

I scoop my laptop from the kitchen table and relocate to the living room, followed closely by Sasha. Then I position myself on the sofa and flex my fingers over the keyboard. Right Alexi and Lucinda. Where were you?

Oh.

Oh my goodness!

They can't do that!

Can they?

I slam the lid shut and fan my flaming cheeks. That is the last time I am letting Maddy and Nicky loose on this novel. Even Throb has limits. There has to be another way I can earn money. Do I really need both kidneys?

And then I have my eureka moment, only without a bath and in the sitting room instead. The answer to everything is right beneath my feet!

Maybe it's inspiration? Maybe I'm tuning into the spirit of Cecily Greville? Or maybe it's the wine talking, but I really feel that I'm onto something! And I might not have a crowbar but the fireside poker looks sturdy enough to do the job. I'm not going to wait for Frankie to get his butt in gear. I know I've promised to put the treasure hunt on hold until he comes back, but it's been over a month and I'm fast running out of patience.

Patience and cash.

I'm going to do this myself.

Girl power!

I feel energised! I feel like lightning is zinging through me! I feel alive!

Leaping to my feet I shove the coffee table out the way, roll back the carpet and then grab the poker, wielding it in the style of Luke Skywalker with a lightsabre. The treasure is only inches away from me, I can feel it!

"Let's do this," I say to Sasha, who raises her head from her paws and regards me with sad brown eyes. "Don't look so worried. This is going to be great."

Now. Where to start? How about that floorboard over there? It's always been a bit loose and squeaky; it's right by the door too, so it's easy to access. Yes, it's the perfect hiding place. I can't believe I haven't thought about it before. That's bound to be where an old lady would hide her life savings.

I ram the poker into the gap between the floorboards and heave with all my weight but the bloody thing doesn't give an inch. Think, Katy, think! You need to wedge the board up a bit to ease the poker along. Something small and flat should be just the job. I know! Those glittery flip-flops Tansy gave me last summer will be just the thing. OK, so this probably wasn't *quite* what Jimmy Choo had in mind, but I think it only proves just how versatile these sandals are and that they were worth every penny. I don't suppose my Primarni ones would be nearly as good at wedging open gaps in floorboards.

I slide the poker in, lean on it with all my might and *pop*! Up comes the floorboard. Elated, I shine my iPhone torch into the void and see... nothing.

Oh.

I sit back on my heels feeling totally deflated. I'd been so sure that this was the spot. Maddy's crystal went bonkers here the other day.

OK. This is not defeat. This is just a minor setback. There's a whole floor here. I'm in the wrong place, that's all. Just keep digging!

You know when you have a spot on your face and you think to yourself that you'll just have a little squeeze? And then that little squeeze turns into a medium squeeze and looks a bit red, so you squeeze just a bit more? And then another pimple catches your attention and before you know it your entire face is under attack? Well, after about twenty minutes our sitting room floor has succumbed to a similar fate. I haven't lifted all the boards, but I'm going that way – until my torch beam picks up a cobwebby corner of sacking and my heart thuds.

Is this it?

I sit bolt upright, my despair evaporating. I've found it! I've really found it! Who needs the lottery! I have found Cecily Greville's treasure!

My fear of spiders has been miraculously overcome as I reach my hand down into the gap. My skin's tingling and my heart's racing as my fingers close around the rough fabric. Golly! It's really heavy. There must be a fortune in here. Gold coins maybe, or jewels or even ingots? To be honest I'm not certain what an ingot is exactly, but I think finding a couple could be very good news for us. Beyond excited, I grit my teeth and heave with all my might. There's a jolt, then a clanking a bit like Maddy makes when she sneaks a couple of bottles into the vicarage. And finally I fall backwards onto the floor as the loot pops out of the hole in the floorboards.

Success!

Closer inspection reveals my find to be a hessian sack tied up with scraps of lace and ribbon, beautiful fabric remnants that surely must have once belonged to old Miss Greville. This bag has to be where she put her life savings.

"I've found it, Sasha," I breathe. The dog barks excitedly and bounds around the room, leaping the holes in the floor with canine ease and waving her plumy tail in delight. I feel like doing exactly the same and if I had a tail it'd be wagging for sure because this is it! I've found the treasure!

Feeling as though I'm about to pass out with anticipation, I unknot the ribbon with trembling fingers and then peer into the bag.

What?

This doesn't look much like somebody's life savings to me. More like the recycling.

Six dusty old bottles with 1805 on them? Seriously? This can't be right! I thought I'd dug up treasure, not Cecily Greville's trash.

I place the bottles on the floor, very carefully because surprisingly they seem to still be full. Then I shake the bag hopefully, but there's nothing except for a cloud of dust and a rather disgruntled spider.

I slump back against the sofa, deflated. This isn't what I was expecting. Not at all.

I'm contemplating heading to the fridge and pouring myself an enormous glass of wine before beginning Operation Fix the Floor when I hear the kitchen door slam.

"Katy! I'm home."

Shit! Ollie doesn't usually get home before at least seven and it's only five now. If he sees the state of this room he'll flip! I'd hoped the treasure would have smoothed things over but unless he wants a glass of ancient home-made plonk I'm in big trouble.

"I'm in the sitting room," I call back, jumping to my feet and doing my best to push the floorboards back into place. But will the bloody things fit? Of course not. They might have been perfectly happy to slot together for the past four hundred years but they don't want to play now. I shove as hard as I can but still no joy.

Bollocks!

"Katy?"

"Be right with you!" I trill. "Just finishing this sentence!"

I hear the fridge door open and the hiss of a ring pull as Ollie opens a can.

"How about we grab a takeaway?" he continues. "I've had the most bloody awful day. I was meant to be on a leadership training course but the bloody supply teacher did a runner at the eleventh hour and we had to cancel. I nearly called the agency and got you in."

I feel faint at the very idea. Thank God he didn't.

"Anyway, all I want to do now is collapse in front of some mindless telly with a Chinese and my gorgeous girlfriend," he says, and he sounds so tired that my heart goes out to him. Without intending to I've totally ruined both ends of the day for the man I love. The fridge door shuts and there's a long pause, followed by the sound of an empty can being tossed into the recycling. Then I hear him chatting to Sasha and finally his footsteps as he heads to the sitting room.

Three, two, one—

Ollie's standing in the doorway; his eyes are enormous behind his glasses. "What the fuck?"

"Don't panic!" I say, jumping to my feet while he gazes around in shock. "It looks worse than it is!"

The trouble is that as I say this I don't quite believe it myself. Our floor has more craters than the surface of the moon and the air's thick with the dust of centuries. Oh dear. I think this looks just as bad as it really is.

"I can explain!" I cry when he shakes his head in disbelief. "You see, I—"

But Ollie holds his hands up. "Do you know what, Katy? I'm too tired to even hear it. All I wanted to do was come home and relax. Is that too much to ask?"

"I was looking for treasure!"

"Katy, I don't care if you were looking for sodding Godot," he replies wearily. "All I want is a rest but I can't even have that."

"You can! Of course you can. This won't take me a minute to fix. Why don't you have a bath while I do it?" I say desperately. I can't bear to see him look so defeated. All I wanted to do was help but I've gone and made things ten times worse.

In fact, forget ten. I've made things *twenty* times worse.

"I'm going to the pub," Ollie says, "and I might be some time because I bloody well need another drink. Possibly two. Maybe when I come home we might have a floor again? Just a thought. Up to you. Floors are probably overrated."

I don't think I've ever seen Ollie this fed up. Not even when I accidentally flooded the bathroom or dyed all his clothes pink by leaving a rogue sock in the wash. No, usually he finds my disasters amusing and we have a laugh about them. Then he helps to put things right, and we end up having a lot of fun before sloping off upstairs for even more fun. That's what we normally do.

But not today. No, today he looks scarily like a man who is at the very end of his tether.

I lapse into silence as Ollie picks up Sasha's lead and calls her. Moments later I hear the front door slam shut and his footsteps passing the cottage. He's gone, and if I want him to come back and stay I'll need to fix a bit more than just this floor.

I pick up the dusty bottles and stow them under the stairs. Then, and with a very heavy heart, I make a start on replacing the floorboards. I don't care about how awkward they are, or about splinters and spiders. I only care about Ollie. I hope I can as easily sort out all the other gaps that have suddenly appeared in my life.

Chapter 14

DAILY DAGGER

CORNISH TEACHER'S SEXY SECRET

BY: Staff Show Business Reporter

TANSY TOPHAM REVEALS: "I didn't write a word of my bestselling novels!"

SHE'S HAD an amazing career, from lads' mag pin-up to WAG to fashion designer to bestselling novelist. Incredibly, Tansy Topham's literary efforts have even outsold the Booker list.

But far from writing the books herself, Tansy – wife of England striker Tommy Topham – leaves the hard work to a ghostwriter.

"I'm far too busy with my fashion lines and being on telly!" Tansy boasts. "Anyway, have you ever tried typing with acrylics? I just say I want a story written and there it is! It's easy!"

So far Ms Topham has 'written' three novels. Her first book, *Thrilled by His Touch*, sold 200,000 copies in six weeks and her second, *Tamed by His Touch*, stormed straight to the top of the bestsellers list. The books might be simplistic and downmarket but they are undeniably racy.

"My books are about WAGs and sexy footballers. I haven't read them yet but everyone tells me they're dead good," Tansy explains.

"I'm lucky to have a really talented writer in Cornwall who does the books for me. I can't say who it is because it might get them into trouble at work, as they're an English teacher and my books are full of sex! Oh! You won't put that bit in, will you?"

Do you know the identity of Tansy's saucy ghostwriter? Contact the newsroom on the number below, or drop us an email.

"The press think it's me!" Ollie exclaims. "They've been camped outside school all day trying to get comments from parents and kids. We've had complaints, the school governors have called an emergency meeting, the Head's going crazy and the priest has had a fit. It's a disaster."

He's sitting at the kitchen table with his head in his hands and an expression of utter despair on his face. He's had the day from hell and it's all my fault.

Again.

He's only just about forgiven me for the pulling-up-the-floor episode. Putting it all back proved a lot trickier than I'd thought and I'd had to pay a local builder to give me a hand. Ollie winced when he saw the bill but didn't say anything. He hadn't needed to. I already felt bad enough and there wasn't even any treasure to show for all the grief either, just six dusty bottles of plonk. And now this.

I smooth the tabloid out onto the table and scan it again. *Simplistic and downmarket*? How very dare they! I slaved over those books. I polished that prose. It was art!

"What the hell was Tansy thinking?" Ollie groans. "She's created havoc."

"She *wasn't* thinking," I sigh. "This is Tansy, after all. Thinking isn't really her forte. In fairness she did mention she might have said something, but I didn't worry too much since they all know at the comp that I write books. It never occurred to me for a minute that the press might think it was you."

He sighs wearily. "I guess it makes more of a story if the writer of sexy books is the Assistant Head of a Catholic school. That way they can dig up all kinds of salacious stories. What does it matter whether or not they've outed the wrong person? Papers are selling."

Books are too, but I keep this observation to myself because I think it would be the last straw for Ollie. I only received a one-off fee but Tansy will be doing very nicely as the royalties flood in. The last time I checked Amazon, *Thrilled* was riding high at the top of the charts, with the rest of the series catching up fast. At this rate Tansy will be choosing a new Lotus by bedtime.

This story, or rather non-story, of a celeb hiring a ghostwriter really has been blown out of all proportion. Within literally minutes of the *Dagger*'s online newspaper running the piece Mads was banging on my door and the village shop was doing a roaring trade in selling papers and spreading gossip. Somebody somewhere had called the newsroom with the information that a teacher from Tregowan was the culprit – and because Ollie's the only one of us officially teaching he's been mistakenly outed as Tansy Topham's ghostwriter. The "sexy bonkbusters penned by a teacher at a strict Catholic school" angle is the hook the press have run with and, unsurprisingly, the management at St Jude's are most unimpressed.

Poor Ollie has had a lot of explaining to do.

It's seven p.m. now and we've been sitting in the kitchen for the past couple of hours, trawling through the stories and shaking our heads at the ridiculous amount of interest. We've given up any hope of trying to put the record straight. After all, we've spent enough time with Gabriel and Frankie to know that unless we have huge amounts of money and a Rottweiler of an agent there's no point protesting. We just have to ride it out.

Or rather poor Ollie does.

Oh God! What if they find out about *Kitchen of Correction?* It'd destroy him and probably lose him his job. What have I done?

I *have* to stop getting into these scrapes. And I will too. Just as soon as this latest book is delivered I'll tell the editor that I simply can't write another one. Maybe Maddy could take over? Richard would flip but he'd get over it eventually, and Maddy could always give the royalties to the church. In a way I'd actually be doing good!

Feeling cheered by this idea, I wind my arms around Ollie's neck and kiss the top of his shorn head.

"But your Head Teacher was all right in the end, wasn't he?" I ask hopefully. "Now he knows it's me and not you?"

Ollie nods. "Once I scraped him down from the ceiling and apologised profusely to Father O' Neill, he calmed down a bit. I think I still have a job."

"Think?"

He pulls me onto his lap. "Don't look so worried. I'm teasing you. Of course I still have a job. But," he pauses and rests his nose against mine, "I have been told in no uncertain terms that the reputation of St Jude's is not to be dragged into the mud for a second time. You have no idea just how old-fashioned that place is."

Actually I do, but of course I can't tell him this.

"Apparently my partner's behaviour reflects on me and therefore the good name of the school," Ollie continues. "So maybe no more trashy books, Katy?"

I'm offended on the behalf of my Tansy books. "My books aren't trashy! The last Tansy one outsold Dan Brown!"

Ollie kisses my nose. "You know what I mean. Look, I don't want to sound like some nineteen-fifties throwback here, but with my new salary and your supply wages I think we'll be OK financially without any more ghostwriting income. Why don't you step back from all that now and concentrate on your own stuff? You could write a novel or even another screenplay."

I can't think of anything I'd like better, but I have a very big Throb-shaped cloud looming over me. I have no choice but to finish that book now. If I don't then their lawyers will tear me to shreds and feed me to the sharks. Or something like that. Whatever lawyers do to people who break contracts. For a moment I teeter on the brink of confessing all. I hold back though, because I feel there's a "but" hovering.

"But?" I prompt.

Ollie grins. "But nothing too sexy? It's more than my job's worth. OK?"

"OK," I say reluctantly. There goes any hope of confessing. Maybe I should pop over to St Jude's and just collar the priest instead? I certainly can't burden Ollie any further. I've caused him quite enough stress.

He gives me a hug. "Don't look so worried, Katy. It's not your fault St Jude's is so uptight."

No, I think, but it is my fault I signed a contract with Throb which I never bothered to read carefully. Why didn't I listen to Frankie? How typical that the one time he spoke sense I ignored him.

"And all this fuss will soon go away and everything will go back to normal," Ollie adds. "You'll see. Now, why don't we open a bottle of wine and forget about today?"

I know that even a year in therapy won't come close to helping me forget about today. In fact, it's not today I'm worried about so much as the unseen days that lurk ahead. Days when my literary secret could be revealed at any time.

I'm going to be a nervous wreck!

OK. Don't panic. It's all going to be fine. All I have to do is finish the book. It's almost completed anyway and I know I'll make the deadline. Then I can forget all about it.

I hope.

I slither off Ollie's lap and fetch us both a big glass of wine – which, let's face it, we both need. I know it won't make much difference though. This is the first time I've deliberately withheld something from him and it doesn't feel right at all. I'm so tired of all the secrets.

It's no good. I'm going to have to tell the truth.

Deep breath, Katy. You can do it.

"Ollie, I—"

The sudden hammering at the door makes us both jump and interrupts the confession that's poised on my lips like a diver about to leap from the highest board.

Thud! Thud! Thud! goes the door, while the cottage shakes with each blow. *Thud! Thud! Thud!*

"There's only one person I know who knocks like that," says Ollie, hauling himself out of his chair. "Shall I let your future brother-in-law in?"

"If you don't the whole place will fall down," I say.

"Wait a minute, Guy," calls Ollie, unfastening the kitchen door. "The door's locked."

"What have you locked it for?" grumbles Guy, ducking his head as he steps inside. "Hope you two weren't at it?"

"Don't be ridiculous; of course they weren't. It's locked to keep out all the nosy reporters," snaps my sister, who's hard on his heels. "Everyone's talking about Tansy Topham's ghostwriter. Don't you ever listen to a word I say?"

"Try not to, babe," replies Guy. "Easier that way and it's probably why we're still together."

"We're together because nobody else would put up with you," Holly says darkly. "And, if you read anything more than the *Beano* you'd know that the press is full of the story."

Knowing from experience that this pair can squabble all day once they start, I do my best to get a word in while I still have the chance.

"Is there something you two need? Only we're pretty busy right now."

"Looks like it," Guy remarks, nodding towards the wine glasses and plonking himself down at the table. "Busy on the piss more like. Typical teachers. No wonder the country's going to a bag of maggots. Go on then, don't mind if I do. Pour us a glass."

As he makes himself at home I give in and fetch a couple of glasses from the dresser.

"Not for me, thanks," Holly says quickly. "I'm off alcohol at the moment."

"I'll have hers," Guy says. "Top yours up, you two, and then sit down. We've got some big news."

I glance at my sister, then at Guy holding two wine glasses, and suddenly the penny drops. I can't believe I didn't twig sooner!

"Oh my God! You're having a baby!"

Holly nods and Guy beams, and then I'm hugging them and kissing them and the men are shaking hands and clapping each other on the back. Wow! I'm going to be an aunty! Me! An aunty! I don't think I've been this excited since *Take That* got back together!

When we've all finished crying/hugging/knocking back the wine, Guy says casually, "So now we all know Holly's up the duff can I tell you the big news?"

I'm confused. "You mean that wasn't it?"

Holly laughs. "Oh yes, there's far more exciting news than a baby, at least as far as Guy's concerned!"

Her fiancé looks hurt. "That's not true, babe. Nothing's more important than Turpin Tregarten."

"We are *not* calling our baby Turpin!" Holly says, and they're off again, bickering about what to call their child while Ollie and I wait for them to draw breath.

"Your other news?" Ollie prompts.

"Oh yes," says Holly. "Go on, Guy! Tell them!"

My future brother-in-law beams at me. "You're going to love this, Katy, since it was your pet in the first place."

"What pet?" I'm totally blank. Sometimes I really think too much beer and rough seas have done Guy some sort of damage, because he talks utter nonsense half the time.

"Your lobster," he says impatiently. "Jeez! Don't tell me you've forgotten it already? Not when you made me take the bloody thing miles out to sea and release it. Twenty quid I could have got for that on the fish stall, but no. You had to release it into the wild. And now it's back."

I stare at Guy in disbelief. Five years ago I was throwing a dinner party for my then tosser of a boyfriend and his odious boss, something that was bound to be an absolute disaster for a girl with my culinary talents. In desperation I'd bribed Ollie to do the cooking by promising to mark his GCSE coursework in return. All was going well until his speciality dish turned out to be a lobster.

A lobster that was very much alive.

It's a long story but Pinchy, as my starter course became known, ended up travelling with me to Tregowan – where he spent a few happy days splashing around in Maddy's bath before Reverend Rich lost what small sense of humour he did possess. Cue one voyage out to sea with Guy and one released lobster, and the rest was history.

Or so I'd thought...

"No way! Not Pinchy?" I gasp, and Guy snorts.

"Pinchy! Ha! Who names a twatting lobster?"

Ollie puts his arm around me. "Katy does. Come on, Guy! Don't keep us all in suspense. What's the news?"

Guy knocks his entire glass of wine back and wipes his mouth on the back of his hand. "When I released *Pinchy*, I made a note and tagged the lobster – a mate of mine was involved in a research project and suggested I could take part – and I let the hatchery in Padstow know too for their records."

"Conservation and sustainable fishing are important to Guy," Holly explains, catching my blank expression. "He's not a philistine, you know."

This is reassuring, because he certainly does a bloody good impression of one.

"Course I'm not. I'm bloody well Cornish," Guy agrees. "Anyway, let's forget talking about foreigners for a minute, because what I'm about to tell you is far more interesting. I've just had a call from the hatchery – they've only had bloody New York on the phone." He pauses for dramatic effect. "Katy, your lobster is in New fucking York!"

"What? That's impossible!"

Impossible and totally unfair! Even I haven't been to New York yet! How on earth has Pinchy the lobster managed to get there first?

"Apparently not impossible at all. A fishing boat caught your lobster off Cape Cod and because it was tagged they've traced it back to here," Guy explains.

"Blimey," says Ollie. "Pinchy swam all the way to America?"

"Well he didn't take a jumbo jet!" says Guy. "Of course it bloody swam, you harris!"

"Technically, we don't know that for sure," Holly corrects him. "Pinchy could have been in currents, hopped into another pot and been turfed out, or even caught in flotsam and sailed across. The marine biologists are speculating like crazy because this is unprecedented. So unprecedented, in fact, that there's a film crew making a documentary about it all now, which is why Guy's been contacted."

"Wow," I say, impressed. "Pinchy gets to star in a documentary? Like with David Attenborough?"

"It's more of a dramality show set in the city's aquarium," Holly explains and, when Ollie looks at her blankly, adds, "like *TOWIE* or *Keeping Up with the Kardashians*? Apparently the Pinchy story is going to be featured as a thread."

"*The Only Way is Lobster*," grins Ollie. "Especially for dinner! Or how about *I'm a Lobster Get Me Out of Here*?"

I thump him. "I did not drag Pinchy all the way from London to Cornwall just so somebody could cook him, thank you very much!"

My sister ignores our comments. She's wearing her Very Serious expression, so I do my best to look serious too.

"The film crew and the aquarium team want Guy to be in the episodes about Pinchy because he released the lobster and knows so much about sustainable fisheries," my sister says, slipping her small hand into Guy's giant paw and smiling proudly up at him. "They've invited him out to New York."

"That's brilliant! How exciting!" Ollie says warmly.

"I seem to remember that you wanted to cook Pinchy," I remind Guy. Is he really the right choice? Pinchy should be very afraid if Guy Tregarten gets too close.

"I was only joking about all that!" Guy says, but he can't quite look me in the eye. "The thing is, I do want to go to New York and be in the documentary and say my bit about the state of the fishing industry here, but… but…"

"But he's too scared to go on his own," Holly finishes. "Guy's never flown before or even been abroad."

This doesn't surprise me. Guy thinks Devon is a foreign land and gets vertigo crossing the Tamar Bridge.

"So go with him, Holly," I say. "It'll be amazing. I'm dead jealous."

"I can't go. I've got way too much on at the uni with the run-up to finals, and besides, I don't want to risk flying in my condition." She places a hand on her pancake-flat tummy. Honestly, I look more pregnant after eating a biscuit. "So Guy and I wondered whether you would go with him, Katy?"

"Me?"

"It's your bloody lobster," Guy says.

"Technically I think you'll find it was mine first," Ollie points out, squeezing my hand. "But since I love Katy I'll let her go in my place. She's a lobster mummy and, anyway, I'd look stupid in a tutu."

Poor Ollie has sat through more episodes of *Sex and the City* than any man should ever have to. He knows all the plots inside out and how I'd love to be Carrie Bradshaw just for five minutes.

Guy looks at me pleadingly.

"Go on, Katy," he says. "You know you want to."

Of course I know I want to. My heart is doing this weird boingy thing in my chest and I can't quite believe it. New York. Seriously? Me?

"You want *me* to go to New York with you?" I ask, hardly able to take this in.

"Guy can't go on his own. You're terrified, aren't you, sweetie?" says Holly.

Her six-foot strapping fisherman fiancé nods miserably. "I'm crapping myself about being in a city, never mind getting on a bloody plane."

"So why put yourself through it, mate?" Ollie asks.

"Because if I can get some publicity through a documentary I'll be able to raise a lot more awareness of how the politicians have stitched up the British fishing fleet," Guy replies, as though this should be totally obvious. "Bloody good idea, eh?"

I'm sure it would be if I had a clue what he's on about. Seeing my confused expression, my sister adds, "Think about Jamie Oliver and the school dinners thing. If Guy gets a bit of media exposure he might be able to do something similar for the fishing industry. Unfair fishing quotas will be the new junk food and everyone will be talking about them. You wait and see. He'll be TV gold. Look how much the Americans love Gordon Ramsay. They'll go bonkers for Guy."

Sometimes I think my sister's spent far too much time with her fiancé. She's as nuts as he is.

"Don't look at me like that. It really could work," Holly says firmly. "There's a whole new political and media career waiting for Guy if he can just pull this off. He can't go to sea forever; it's too dangerous, especially now he's going to be a dad."

Guy kisses her cheek and then nods. "I can't be a coward and chicken out on this, no matter how much I hate bloody cities or the thought of flying. So I guess what I'm saying is: Katy Carter, how do you feel about coming with me on an all-expenses-paid trip to visit Pinchy in New York?"

And of course there's only one answer to a question like that, isn't there?

It looks as though I'm going to New York!

Chapter 15

Throb

Fiction that's red hot and ready!

Eros Towers * Sherrington Boulevard * W14 6BY

Dear Katy,

Many thanks on the behalf of Throb for delivering *Kitchen of Correction* ahead of schedule. We are delighted to tell you that we are able to push publication forward as a result of this and look forward to the book being a big success.

Everyone on the team was surprised by the imaginative energy and vivid detail of the work. None of us will ever be able to see clothes pegs or cabbages in the same way again. Your author copies will be delivered shortly by courier.

We do hope you like them!

Thanks also for the parcel of Cornish pasties. Yes, you were correct in fearing that they might arrive a little bit squashed.

We donated your kind gift to the builders working next door. They were thrilled and send their regards.

Unfortunately, we cannot forget about the 'small clause' which says the author must be available and willing to promote the novel. If you look carefully at the third paragraph in your contract you will see that it is clearly stated that once the document is signed it is legally binding.

We look forward to seeing I Lovett out and about very soon!

Best wishes,

Lisa Armstrong (Senior Commissioning Editor)

"Don't look so worried!" Mads says as she wheels my suitcase towards the check-in desk. "The flight will be a piece of cake. All you need to do is sit back, watch a few movies and enjoy all the booze. I can't tell you how jealous I am."

"I'm not worried about the flight," I say, which is one hundred percent true. Any nerves I may have harboured about flying have been well and truly overshadowed by the letter from Throb that arrived this morning and the threat of Bob the postie handing Ollie the parcel full of my author copies. In terms of the carnage it could cause, it might as well be a bomb with a lit fuse. Mads has promised to do her best to pre-empt the delivery, but short of staking out the Post Office or camping on our doorstep I can't see how. My only hope is that the books arrive on a school day and have to be collected later on. If not, I'm going to have an awful lot of explaining to do. So is Mads, since she helped me to finish the book in record time. And Nicky too, who I have to say was the real genius behind it all.

The problem is that even if Ollie *doesn't* see the books I have a nasty feeling that I'll still have a lot of explaining to do, since Throb are insisting on promotion and publicity. After everything I've promised him too about not bringing St Jude's into disrepute! I can't believe that in spite of all my best efforts Throb are refusing to release me from that annoying clause in the contract – almost as much as I can't believe I never spotted it. OK, maybe I *can* believe I never spotted it, since I didn't read the contract in the first place. I'm going to be kicking myself all the way to the United States.

There has to be a way of getting out of this. I just haven't thought of it yet, that's all. I've got all those hours of transatlantic flight to come up with something, and then ten days in America. I'll go and find Frankie and Gabriel. Maybe they can help? Otherwise I'm doomed. Ollie will never forgive me and he'll run away with Carolyn and I'll die of a broken heart. The thought of living for even a millisecond without Ol makes my heart lurch and my eyes prickle. What am I thinking, going the USA when there's all this mess to deal with and the man I love is miles away? I can't go to New York! I need to get back to Cornwall immediately!

I know I've thought of nothing else but this trip for the past few weeks, but I've changed my mind.

I want to go home!

I stop dead in my tracks. All around me the airport throngs with travellers lugging cases, queuing at the check-in desks or craning their necks to peer up at the information boards. I'm sure it's very noisy but I can't hear a sound and everything's slowing down. I think I'm having a panic attack. To be honest I don't know how it's taken me this long. Should I ask for a paper bag? And what would I do with one anyway?

Maddy stops wheeling, places her hands on my shoulders and peers at me intently. "Babes, are you all right? You're ever such a funny colour. Are you worried about the flight?"

I shake my head but my best friend isn't convinced. "You looked like this when we went to Shagaluf on that girls' holiday. You had a meltdown at the boarding gate and we had to score some Valium off an old lady, remember?"

I don't stand a chance of *not* remembering with Maddy constantly reminding me of it. It wasn't one of my finest moments – but in fairness to me we had been binge-watching the *Lost* boxset the night before and my imagination was working overtime. Mads has never forgotten, which is why she's insisted on accompanying me to Bristol Airport today. Ollie's working and I was quite happy to travel up with Guy and Holly, but my best friend wasn't having it.

"The truth of the matter is I need some respite from the twins," she'd confessed. "And I'll be able to go to shopping on the way home without Richard having a hissy fit or checking the bank balance afterwards. You'd be doing me a favour if you said you needed a bit of handholding."

So an elaborate charade had followed, with Mads playing the role of supportive friend while I took the part of nervous traveller, or at least when Richard was around anyway. Ollie thought I was mad, but then again this was nothing new. He's looking totally frazzled and I have a horrible feeling he's secretly looking forward to a break from lava-lamp disasters and living-room excavations.

"It's not the flight," I say, and I sound as though I've been inhaling helium. "It's all this business with the book."

Mads nods. "I can see why that could be stressful, but the way I see it is that nobody knows who the mysterious I Lovett is yet, do they? And nobody from the publishing house has met you yet either, have they?"

It's a good point.

"And if they do want to see you," Maddy continues, "then they'll just have to wait because you're out of the country. That'll give us enough time to figure out what to do."

I ought to feel reassured by the way she's including herself in this mess but somehow I don't, probably because whenever Maddy gets involved everything in my life becomes far more complicated.

"I'll get Nicky to keep an eye out for those books," she continues, grabbing the case in one hand and my arm in the other as she propels us to the check-in. "Fear not, between us we'll sort it."

"Nicky should be focusing on his A-levels, not sitting around waiting for the postman! I'm worried enough as it is that he'll get distracted doing all that work for Tansy."

Maddy grins. "The amount he's earning I'm not surprised. Are you sure Tansy isn't a secret drug dealer?"

"Ssh!" I glance around nervously. Call me paranoid but I'm always terrified there's a stray reporter lurking in wait for a Tansy story and I'll have a writ slapped on me before you can say "lawsuit". I'm not kidding: the paperwork I signed when I became Tansy's ghostwriter made the Throb contract look like a comic.

Still, it's certainly true that Nicky's been working very hard for Tansy's new venture. He's already earned enough to buy a scooter, and all his spare time's spent driving to various venues. I never thought Nicky would enjoy waiting tables quite so much but he actually seems to be thriving on it. Last week he even had a haircut and got Maddy to tweeze his eyebrows, so it's nice he's interested in looking smart for work. He's stopped asking me if he can borrow money too, which is a bonus. In fact, I had to beg a twenty from *him* yesterday.

If I'd known how lucrative waiting tables could be I'd never have become an English teacher.

Maddy hugs me. "That was a joke! Relax, everything's going to be fine this end, I promise. All you have to do is explore the Big Apple and babysit Guy. And if you don't eat pastrami on rye, wear a tutu and drink a cosmo on my behalf then I'm never talking to you again!"

As we take our place in the check-in queue for JFK I'm feeling slightly more reassured but I'm also really wishing Ollie was coming with me. Just think of the fun we could have had together! Shopping in Macy's, walking hand in hand through Central Park, cruising up the Hudson, visiting the Statue of Liberty… I feel quite sad that I'll be having all of these amazing experiences without him. But of course Ollie is working and since it's the run-up to the exam season there's no way he can come too. In his usual generous way he's told me to go and have the time of my life, and I know he means it too, but this doesn't stop me wishing things were different. I know if we could only have some time away together we'd be able to talk properly.

I might even pluck up the courage to tell him about my secret alter ego…

But this is all hypothetical, and since Ollie's busy taking extra revision classes and crammer sessions even at the weekends I'll be exploring New York with my prospective brother-in-law instead. Never mind *Crocodile Dundee*; Guy is Fish Cornwall. And, talk of the devil, here he comes now, dressed as though he's about to hop aboard his trawler rather than fly across the pond.

"He's wearing a smock and rigger boots," giggles Mads, watching Guy trail behind my sister – who's striding across the concourse with an expression of grim determination all over her face.

"Sorry we're late," Holly puffs. "We've parked miles away and then Guy insisted on checking out the shops. I lost him for ages before I eventually found him in Dixons."

Guy, clutching a giant Toblerone to his chest, looks mutinous.

"Of course I was in Dixons. Where did you think I'd be? Claire's sodding Accessories?"

Holly ignores him and pushes her glasses up her nose with her forefinger, always a sign of intense concentration. "Now, Katy, you'll have to look after his wallet, tickets and passport because he'll only lose them. I've also packed him a pasty to eat in Departures and he's got a couple of diazepam too for if he gets nervous on the flight. Make sure he doesn't drink with them, OK? He mustn't mix those with alcohol. "

That'll be easier said than done, since it's lager rather than blood that flows through Guy's arteries.

"You're giving Katy the passports and tickets?" Mads looks worried. "Is that wise?"

"I think I can cope," I say.

"You left your rucksack on the airport shuttle earlier," she reminds me.

Yes. OK. I did. And I also had a big telling-off from the security man, who was apparently only minutes away from cordoning the area off and blowing my poor bag up. I still feel a bit hot under the collar just thinking about some of the things he said to me. But I won't do it again. No way. From now until we reach our hotel I'm not letting my bag out of my sight.

"Guy can't have them. His smock pockets are full and he won't carry a manbag," Holly says.

"Manbag? Who do you think I am? Bloody Frankie?" grumbles Guy. He glances across the concourse to the café. "Christ. I need a beer."

"I don't think I can keep Guy away from booze," I say to my sister. "Maybe he shouldn't have any tablets?"

"He needs them. He's absolutely terrified," Holly whispers as we edge closer to the desk and her fiancé shuffles miserably forward. "He's never flown – he's hardly even left Cornwall. Look after him for me, Katy? Please? I know Guy makes a big noise but he's a jelly underneath. It's all bluster and I'm not sure how he'll cope in a city. Oh God, I wish I was coming too, to look after him."

I give her a hug. "He'll be fine. Don't worry."

But my sister isn't convinced. "The thing is, Katy, that I actually *did* find him in Claire's Accessories at one point – and unless my fiancé has developed a sudden liking for glittery hair slides, it's obvious he was hiding. If you hang onto his wallet, he can't go to ground in the bar. Make sure you don't let him out of your sight!"

As we check in I bear her comments in mind. It's true to say that Guy has gone a very funny colour, and several times he's looked as though he's about to make a break for freedom. How I'll keep hold of him is anyone's guess. Parking him in the bar had been my preferred plan of action, but now I'll have to drag him through duty-free with me. Perhaps that's a good thing? As always he smells of diesel and fish, so if by the time we board he's a pungent mix of every aftershave Chanel makes, that can only be an improvement.

Once we're through security, where Guy's steel toecaps set off every alarm going, I heave a sigh of relief. Apart from one hairy moment when Guy had his fisherman's knife confiscated and another when his pasty was flattened, we seem to have made it through in one piece. Guy might be as gutted as the fish his knife had dealt with in the past, but at least we haven't been arrested.

Yet.

"That was a bloody good knife," Guy grumbles as we head into Departures. "How am I going to fillet a cod now?"

"We're going to New York to see Pinchy," I remind him. "You'll be far too busy sightseeing and being filmed for the documentary to fillet a fish. Besides, why would you need to?"

He shrugs. "I don't know. It's just what I do. Not going to sea for ten days is going to be bloody weird."

"No it isn't! It's going to be so exciting!" I say, going into full Mary Poppins mode and clapping my hands. "This is the chance of a lifetime! We're travelling the world."

"But I'm happy at home with Holly. Like you are with Ollie." His eyes narrow. "You are happy with Ollie, right?"

"Of course I am!" I say firmly. "It's just that things are a bit complicated at the moment."

Guy shakes his head. "Sounds like an excuse to me. Things are only as complicated as people make them. What's so bloody difficult about that? You love him and he loves you. It'll be fine."

Oh. My. God. He's right! He really is. I should just tell Ollie everything.

And I will. I really will.

Once I'm back from New York.

"So there you go then, you daft cow," says Guy, settling into his new and unlikely role as an agony aunt and regarding me kindly. "All solved. Just stop overthinking it, like I'm about to stop overthinking this flying crap."

He reaches into his pocket and pulls out a blister packet of tablets. Popping several out, he knocks them back and then proceeds to lay himself along a row of seats in the departure lounge, with his head pillowed on his smock.

"Hang on! Where did you get those?" I ask.

Guy winks. "Why do you think I was so keen to carry your tray?"

Even at the time I'd thought this sudden chivalry totally out of character, and now it makes perfect sense. He was stealing the tranquillisers.

"Should you take that many?"

He shrugs. "I've got to get through this somehow. If I've got to fly, then I'd rather do it high as a kite."

Guy faces rough seas that make those in disaster movies look feeble, but I can see how terrified he is. Right now I think he's being the bravest I've ever seen him.

"You'll love New York," I promise. "This is an adventure."

But Guy just looks sad. "Every day that I'm on my trawler is an adventure, and I love it in Tregowan with Holly. Your sister and Turpin are the biggest adventure I could ever have. I knew I should have sold that lobster. If it hadn't been for you, Katy Carter, it would have been someone's dinner five years ago and we could all have stayed at home. Thanks a bloody lot."

He closes his eyes and that's the end of the conversation. Personally I'm planning to give Pinchy the biggest hug a lobster ever had (if a lobster has ever had a hug, of course). Claws and water aside, I don't care because I owe him! Thanks to my old crustacean friend, I've had a reprieve from the demands of Throb and am safely out of the country while I try to think how to disentangle myself from the whole mess. And I get to visit the coolest city in the world too!

No, as far as I'm concerned the day I refused to let Ollie cook lobster thermidor was a very good one, and not just for Pinchy. Even Guy's miserable face and lack of excitement can't dampen my spirits. Leaving him to snooze, I set off to check out the perfume and designer handbags.

New York and Pinchy – here I come!

Chapter 16

Oh my God! I love New York! I mean *seriously* love it! This has to been the most exciting city on the face of the earth and I can't believe I'm really here, in the back of a real live yellow taxi, crawling through the Manhattan traffic while a proper New York cabbie swears at the other drivers and snaps his gum. And everything looks exactly like it does on the telly too! The buildings really are so tall you can't see the sky, and there's the subway and horses pulling carriages round Central Park and everything!

This is amazing!

The sun's even out too and the pavements, or do I mean the *sidewalks*, throng with cool New Yorkers dressed in sharp suits and trainers. As we cross over the Brooklyn Bridge the water below glistens and sparkles just as brightly as the Tiffany's window display. River cruisers are gliding up and down, full of tourists taking in the city, while helicopters buzz above us – and I'm sure I've just seen the Statue of Liberty out of the corner of my eye as well.

I have! I have! Oh my God! I really have! And it's pea-green in the bright sunshine! How amazing is that? The real live Statue of Liberty! It's over there!

"Look, Guy!" I squeal, grabbing his arm. "It's the Statue of Liberty!"

Guy grunts but doesn't look up. In fact, he doesn't even open his eyes. He's been like this ever since we arrived yesterday evening. The monster dose of diazepam he'd taken before the flight, coupled with several sneaky lagers on the plane, meant he snored his way across the pond and throughout the journey to our hotel, oblivious to my shrieks of excitement when the iconic Manhattan skyline loomed on the horizon and we drove past streets with names as familiar to me as my own. Madison Avenue, Fifth Avenue and Times Square passed him by; all the excitement of seeing the city was lost on Guy. Somehow he managed to stumble to his room though, where he remained until I knocked for him this morning.

"Leave me alone," he'd growled when, after much hammering, the door finally swung open. "I'm jet-lagged."

Unshaven, with his hair on end and still wearing yesterday's clothes, Guy had looked more like the undead than the jet-lagged. I was worried because according to our itinerary we were due at the aquarium for ten-thirty. Somehow I needed to persuade him to leave his hotel room.

"It's breakfast time," I'd said brightly. "It smells amazing and there's pancakes and maple syrup and bacon!"

Guy had glowered at me. "Maple and bacon? What the fuck's wrong with cornflakes?"

"Nothing," I'd replied, gritting my teeth and doing my best to bear in mind what my sister had said about Guy's noise being an indication that he was freaked out rather than genuinely irritated. "But you can eat cornflakes any old time. Come on, Guy! We're in America so we need to eat what the Americans eat. Come on! It'll be fun!"

"I don't think I'm well. Maybe I should just stay in my room and sleep it off?"

"Not today, Guy," I'd said in my best bossy teacher voice. "The documentary crew have left a message and they're sending a car at ten to take us to the aquarium. This is your big chance to make an impression, remember? Be the Jamie Oliver of the fishing world?"

At that point there'd been a wailing of sirens and a blast of horns from outside, and Guy had winced. "Am I allowed to change my mind on that?"

"Nope." I'd given him a little shove. "Come on! We need to get going. After that, you can sleep as much as you want. Go and get ready."

"Yes, Miss," Guy had muttered before retreating into the gloom of his hotel room. I'd waited outside, hardly able to contain myself because I was in New York – home of the Empire State Building, *Sex and the City* and some of the best shopping in the world. I couldn't wait to see it all. By the time he'd emerged I was ready to combust with impatience. He'd chosen to wear his usual fishing smock and rigger boots rather than the smart suit Holly had packed, and he still hadn't bothered to shave, but I wasn't about to start complaining. The main thing was that he was up and ready to go. All I had to do was get him fed, into a taxi and across New York to the aquarium.

How hard could that be?

Now, as our cab crawls across this most amazing of cities, I notice that Guy's big hands are bunched tightly into fists and reflect that maybe I've bitten off more than I can chew. Guy's shut his eyes not because he's jet-lagged or in a bad mood but because he's too scared to look. The sheer volume of traffic, pulsing energy and surging tide of humanity are beyond anything he's used to in sleepy Cornwall.

Oh, who am I kidding? They're beyond anything *I'm* used to! But I love it!

I look out of the window and blink because now we're heading through Brooklyn and down towards Coney Island, with its famous boardwalk and rollercoaster and pier. I feel like I'm on a movie set and I shake my head in disbelief.

When our bright yellow cab eventually draws up near the aquarium, my stomach pancake-flips. I know it probably sounds ridiculous to be so excited about seeing a lobster, but this particular lobster and I go way back and we went through a lot together! Pinchy knew me when I was still with my ex, tosser James, and was one of the reasons that Ollie and I got together. Pinchy accompanied me to Cornwall and, like me, survived living with the Reverend Richard. Just. We have a past! We have history!

Do lobsters recognise people and, if they do, will Pinchy recognise me?

"I can't believe Pinchy made it all this way!" I say proudly to Guy as we walk to the reception area. "What a swim! I'm so proud of him for being a transatlantic lobster!"

Guy looks as though he can't quite believe it either, but before he has the chance to reply a woman with bright scarlet hair is bearing down on us. She's waving like crazy and she's followed by a film crew. Hang on. Are the cameras rolling?

"Guy!" she calls. "Guy Tregarten! Hi there! I'm Helen Wales from ACC Productions. Welcome! We're so pleased to see you!"

Guy can't even draw breath because she's kissing him on both cheeks while beaming at the camera. Wow. I didn't know necks could bend quite that far. She's like Mrs Incredible!

"What do you think of New York?" Helen Wales is asking him. "Isn't is awesome?"

Guy considers this for a moment.

"Driving on the wrong side of the road is bloody weird, and what the hell are grits?" he asks. "Something for the road when it snows?"

Helen and her team squeal with laughter as though he's just said something hilarious, and Guy looks perplexed.

"What did I say?" he asks.

"Oh my gawd! I just love your accent," pipes up the blonde who's wielding the boom microphone. "It's adorable!"

"Say something else!" urges a skinny boy in very tight trousers. At least I think it's a boy. "I love the way you speak!"

"So cute!" agrees another.

"Do you know Hugh Grant?"

"Have you met the Queen?"

"Or Princess Kate? Oh my God, I just adore Princess Kate!"

Guy looks at me wild-eyed and for an awful moment I really think he's about to bolt. I'll never find him again if he does; he'll have to swim the Atlantic to get back to Cornwall, like Pinchy in reverse.

"Apart from our driving and our breakfasts, I hope you're enjoying the city so far?" Helen says to us both. I nod and am just about to reply, but she turns her attention back to Guy.

Oh. OK then.

"I just love your outfit, sweetie! It's so authentic. You look just like a fisherman."

"I am a bloody fisherman, that's why," Guy says and his brow wrinkles.

"What am I supposed to look like? A bloody ballet dancer?"

Helen claps her hands and laughs delightedly as though he's just said something amazingly intelligent. "Just wonderful!"

"Do you have those yellow trousers too? And a yellow hat? I'd just adore to see you in those and I know our audience would too," trills a man wearing so much make-up he makes Boy George in his eighties heyday look understated.

Guy looks confused. "Oilskins?"

"If you say so!" giggles Boy George. "You cheeky money!"

"No one wears oilskins on land," Guy tells him scathingly. "Or only if they're a total harris anyway. Fuck me, what a stupid question. Can I go home now please?"

"Oh my God! He's better than Chef Ramsay," Helen breathes. Her eyes are wide and she looks alarmingly like the Reverend Richard giving a sermon – I recognise that fanatical expression. "And those muscles too and that designer stubble. Absolutely wonderful. Just wonderful. TV gold!"

He is? I can't see it myself but then again I've known Guy for a long time. Still, she's the docudrama maker and must know what she's on about. It's certainly true that Guy and Gordon share a love of colourful language, but there I'm afraid the similarities end; according to Holly, Guy's idea of cooking is pouring boiling water into a Pot Noodle.

An hour later and my head is spinning. So far we've both been interviewed, filmed alighting from another taxi (for cutaways, apparently), met the crew and glugged so much mineral water that my poor bladder is about to go on strike. Then we've talked to the sustainable fisheries team and Guy's droned on about fishing at quite some length. But now, at long last and finally, we're on our way to see Pinchy.

Pinchy!

I can't believe how nervous I am – which is ridiculous, because Pinchy was supposed to be dinner, not my pet. But he's swum all the way to the United States, which is pretty darned impressive. I'm actually rather proud of him. This must be how parents feel when their kids pass exams.

I'm also feeling proud of my prospective brother-in-law. If I hadn't seen first-hand just how terrified he was of flying to the States and finding himself in a huge city, I'd never know now. He's risen to the occasion like an utter star. He's answered questions, cracked jokes, given sound bites and been hugely entertaining – however unintentionally – and with every minute that passes Helen Wales looks more and more as though she's going to pop. There was one rather awkward moment when Guy said he could murder a fag, but once the Americans realised he only wanted a cigarette everything was fine. I even heard Helen ask the cameraman whether he'd caught that line because it would be a great teaser.

I wonder if Guy's next career is closer than he thinks?

Anyway, never mind Guy's new-found talents in front of the camera; I'm looking forward to seeing the real star of the show now. We follow Adam, a marine biologist, along a hot and airless corridor, then down a flight of steps and into a vast room lined with glass tanks and which is heavy with a cloying fishy smell. Various species swim leisurely laps while crabs chill on rocks and seahorses jig about, but there's only one tank that catches my eye – and when it does I stop dead in my tracks.

Oh my goodness! Pinchy's looking straight at me!

It's him! It really is! I'd know that black beady gaze anywhere!

I'm truly choked. The last time I thought I saw Pinchy was when Ollie took me in his arms and kissed me on the quayside (the same time he sort of proposed, but the less said about that the better). I'd even thought I'd glimpsed a claw waving at me above the sea. This was purely my imagination, of course, but it had made me happy all the same. As had Ollie's kisses…

"Bloody hell! That bugger must weigh nearly nine pounds!" Guy says, stepping forward. I can practically hear him working out the market value.

"Eight pounds one ounce," Adam tells us. "Not quite the biggest recorded lobster but a beauty nonetheless."

I press my hand to the glass. "Hello, Pinchy. How are you?"

"*How are you?*" Guy mimics. "What's this? *Downton* fucking *Abbey*? It's a bloody lobster, Katy. It's not going to reply, *I'm marvellous, thanks, old sport!*"

"Shut up, Guy," I say mildly. "Or I'll dump you at the subway and leave you to find your own way home."

Guy holds up his hands. "Jesus! I was only teasing. You carry on, Dr Dolittle! Have a little chat with your old lobster pal. Don't mind the rest of us."

Pinchy regards me with his familiar disapproving stare. *Take this numpty away*, he's saying, and I couldn't agree more. But unfortunately for Pinchy and for me, the numpty is the star of the show and also something of an expert, so we're both stuck with him. While I stroke the glass next to my lobster and wonder how on earth my old friend managed to end up here, Guy talks to Adam about sustainable fisheries and the work of the National Lobster Hatchery in Padstow. The cameras whir, especially when he starts telling a tall story about one drunken night in Rock with Prince Harry and a load of his friends…

"Why's Pinchy all on his own? Shouldn't he have a friend?" I interrupt hastily. The last thing we need now is Guy getting us all sent to the Tower of London.

"Not a great idea, since lobsters are cannibalistic," the marine biologist smiles.

"That's why we rubber-band their claws up," Guy adds, neatly distracted from committing treason. "Stops them attacking each other and us. Those claws bloody well hurt."

Lobsters are cannibals. All of a sudden I'm seeing Pinchy in a whole new light. Any minute now he'll be requesting fava beans and a nice Chianti! And where's the mask?

"So what will happen to him now?" I ask Adam. "He won't go to the market will he? Not when he's done so well to get here."

"He'd be worth a mint," says Guy thoughtfully. "Imagine all the canapés you could make from that bugger!"

Adam laughs. "We've had several enquiries already. I'm told one even came from Donald Trump's people, although that could have just been a joke, of course."

Pinchy holds my gaze. He certainly doesn't find it funny.

I run my finger down the glass. It seems very unfair to eat Pinchy now and after all his hard work to get this far. Ungrateful even. Instantly my mind is figuring out how I can rescue him if he's set to become a billionaire's brunch. Breaking him out of here could be tricky, and even if I did manage it could I afford to upgrade my hotel room to one with a bath? And where on earth do you buy sea salt and fish food in Manhattan?

"Don't look so worried. That won't happen, I promise," Adam reassures me. "This lobster is of special scientific interest now. We've still no idea how it managed to travel this far, but the fact that it has and its last known location was logged by Mr Tregarten means we have a wealth of important data to explore. Your friend Pinchy could tell us all sorts about the breeding and migratory patterns of this species."

"That's good to know," I say, relieved. To think that my starter course is now providing scientists with data! It makes my writing career with Tansy and Throb look a bit tame. I've been intellectually bested by a lobster, which says it all.

"We'll liaise with the hatchery in England too," Adam adds. "Your lobster is safe because he's far more interesting and useful to us alive. There are lots of marine biologists very excited about what this could mean for sustainable fisheries projects and breeding patterns. He'll have a lot of visitors here and feature in scientific journals too. This is his tank for life. Your chap's about to become famous in the lobster world."

Pinchy's going to be a celebrity lobster. How cool is that? And all because I rescued him from Ollie's pot!

"Did you hear that? You're about to gain stardom, Pinchy," I tell him.

"And so are you," Helen Wales says to Guy. She's clutching her mobile phone in her hand and beaming from ear to ear. "The *New York at Night Show* has just called. They love this story because it's—" she pauses and makes inverted commas with her free hand, "'quirky and British' and they want Guy to go on! Tonight!"

"Fucking hell," says Guy, and I couldn't put it better myself.

"Guy, honey," says Helen, "if you play your cards right you and your little lobster buddy could be real famous! What do you say to that?"

Guy looks shell-shocked and for once he's totally silent. And as for Pinchy, well, being a lobster he doesn't care for shallow things like fame and fortune. Instead he cleans his antennae and regards me thoughtfully, as though asking quite what I've got him into now. To be honest, I haven't a clue – but whatever it is, it looks as though it's going to be fun. And best of all? I haven't stressed about Throb or Carolyn Miles or my finances for hours.

Coming to New York was a very good idea.

Chapter 17

I can't believe I'm in Saks Fifth Avenue! I'm really, really here wandering through the perfume and make-up departments, and tiptoeing past the Louis Vuitton concession (I'm rocking my hand-me-down bag from Tansy, but nonetheless I imagine I'm probably attracting scorn from some of the customers there because it's *so* last season). And now I'm riding the elegant elevator to the champagne bar where I'm meeting Frankie. This is nothing like my usual life of telling off teenagers and dodging spit balls or paper aeroplanes, that's for sure. I feel as though I've landed on a TV set. In fact, I wouldn't be surprised if Sarah Jessica Parker and Kim Cattrall breezed in at any minute and ordered cosmopolitans.

Maybe I should have one too? After all, I'm a writer in New York City so it's practically the law! And I'm Isara Lovett too, aren't I? So I'll channel my inner Carrie Bradshaw. Perhaps I'll even get my own column and a walk-in shoe wardrobe. Then Ollie and I can get a fashionable loft apartment and spend our days drinking coffee like in *Friends* or walking hand in hand around Central Park. How amazing would that be? I'll be so successful that he'll never have to go to St Jude's again, and I'll wear a tutu dress even if I look ridiculous.

As I perch on a tiny stool to order my drink I feel my mobile buzz in my (so last-season) bag. Maybe it's Ollie wanting to Skype? I do hope so because then I could add the Saks champagne bar to the list of places we've chatted in the days since I arrived in the USA. So far he's joined me at the top of the Rockefeller Center, chatted to me during a boat trip to Liberty Island, watched as I've scoffed pizza under the Brooklyn Bridge, and shared several jaunts through Times Square. I'm missing him hugely and seeing New York on my own isn't nearly as much fun. It's a big city when you're by yourself, and sharing it with Ollie would have been wonderful. I'm determined that one day we'll be here together.

Rooting around in Tansy's bag for my phone I can't help reflecting that this trip's totally wasted on Guy. He's not done any sightseeing at all. In fact, I've hardly seen him because he's been flat out with marine biologists and film crews. And since he went out on prime-time television everything's gone a bit crazy: it seems the Americans can't get enough of him.

I know. It's mad. Five minutes of Guy Tregarten is usually quite enough for most of us.

"He could have a whole new career out here if he wanted it," Frankie had told me on the phone as I sat in my hotel room and watched Guy on

The Late Late Show, stunned that Guy had flown to LA without a fuss. "They absolutely love him! They think he could be the next Chef Ramsay."

"But he doesn't do anything except swear and voice outrageous opinions!" I'd said.

"That never did Gordon any harm, angel," Frankie had pointed out. "And you must admit, Guy's easy on the eye and very entertaining."

I'd shrugged. I guess my prospective brother-in-law is good-looking in a testosterony loud way. All that hauling of nets and lifting of fish boxes has certainly given him a good body, and his skin is tanned and healthy from the outdoors life. So yes, he is attractive – until he opens his mouth. Holly obviously loves him to bits and I know he adores her, but TV stardom? I can't say I saw that coming. Guy wouldn't want that surely? He lives for fishing and his life with Holly. And there's the baby too now.

Anyway, whether he's entertaining by accident or by design, Guy is certainly grabbing attention. No doubt all this is helping to publicise the state of the UK fishing industry, and it's probably even better news for lobster conservation, but it means I've been left at a bit of a loose end. I've visited Pinchy several times for a chat but he's not the greatest conversationalist, and Frankie's been busy. So I've spent the past few days exploring New York on my own. Like I said, it's an amazing city but I miss Ollie desperately. As soon as I get home I'll have to tell him the truth about Throb. We can't have secrets between us anymore and I will never, ever keep anything from Ollie again. Buying new clothes and finishing the chocolate biscuits in one sitting don't count as secrets anyway. Those things are more like just forgetting a few details. But everything else I'll definitely tell him.

I finally locate my phone, and then frown because I don't recognise this caller's number. 020 is a London number, isn't it? Who do I know in London? And why would they be calling me first thing in the morning, UK time?

I have a sudden feeling of foreboding.

"Katy! Angel! Loving the bag! Is it a fake? From off the Fifth Avenue stalls? They have the best fakes ever there! I swear it's where the B-listers really find their Birkins!"

"Frankie!" I spin around, and there he is, those Burrows family toffee-brown eyes twinkling at me from behind his trendy clear glasses. "Oh! You look very… different!"

Usually Frankie rocks heavy eyeliner, long flowing dark hair, swirling coats and dandy highwayman-style boots. A kind of New-Romantic-meets-Ross-Poldark look that would be familiar to any Screaming Queens fan worth their salt. But today I hardly recognise him! His hair is gelled back into a neat ponytail and mostly hidden beneath a jaunty pork-pie hat, the trademark eyeliner has been replaced by sophisticated specs, and he's wearing a pinstriped suit and scarlet snakeskin boots so bright they make me want to head for the sunglasses department.

"I'm trialling my new look, darling," Frankie says, giving me a twirl. "I'm a Serious Artist now, you know. I'm recording."

"Wow! I'm impressed. One of my oldest friends is recording music in New York. How cool is that?"

He nods complacently. "It is, isn't it? I just need to come up with some new tunes and I'll be sorted."

"I thought you said you're recording?"

"I am. I just haven't written any songs yet," Frankie declares airily, hopping up onto the stool next to me. "Ooo! Champagne. Yes, please! I'll have a glass of bubbly too."

"So if you haven't written any new music what were you recording?" Call me stupid but I would have thought recording actual music was key to the entire process.

"I don't need music to start recording!" Frankie laughs, reaching across and patting my hand. "How little you know of the musical world, young Katy! No, before I even think about laying down some tracks I have to make sure my image is right and that I have some wonderful publicity shots. I've been very busy with my stylist. The music is immaterial. Seb says all I have to do is find my niche and then the music will come. It's all about the image here."

I glance around and realise that he's not wrong. Everyone in New York is just so glamorous and so groomed. The women are reed slim and have beautiful waterfalls of blonde hair, while the guys are achingly hip with their funky beards and patent winkle-picker boots. In my ancient jeans, trainers and hoody I stand out a mile, and not in a good way.

"Do you like?" Frankie asks, pouting at me Zoolander style. "Dimitri – my stylist – thought I should go for a fresher, younger look. A bit Harry Styles crossed with Bieber, is how he put it." He leans forward and squints into the mirror at the far side of the counter. "He even suggested Botox. What do you think? Am I wrinkly? Should I indulge?"

Frankie hasn't aged a day since I first met him. Ironic really, as he's certainly been the cause of a fair few of my grey hairs.

"You look great, but won't your fans be disappointed if they expect to get heavy metal but end up with One Direction?"

"You could be right," Frankie agrees, winking at his reflection and batting his lashes. "But in the meantime I shall enjoy! Those cloaks and cravats aren't easy to wear, you know, and the thigh boots really chafed. But never mind me! What about you? Are you ready to shop?"

I nod. "*I* am, but I'm not sure my bank account is."

Frankie sighs. "I'd offer to pay but I know you won't let me. I know! Why don't you just check your balance and see if you can treat yourself to just a teeny tiny little something? I know this store where they make the most divine little pendants that have special spiritual powers. I'm told Katie Holmes has one, and Madonna."

I laugh because one of these pendants will probably cost about the same as my entire cottage, but it makes sense to check my pennies anyway. I've bought quite a few souvenirs since I've been here, including the ubiquitous Statue of Liberty T-shirt and a couple of Empire State Building mugs, but I haven't gone crazy. Hey! Maybe I can find something really lovely for Ollie? Of all the people in the world, he most deserves a treat.

While Frankie orders some drinks I log into an online savings account Ollie and I have. It's not one we use often – in fact I'm under strict instructions not to touch it unless there's a dire emergency – but surely Ol won't mind if I use some for a little weeny splurge?

I type in my password and wait, and when I'm into the account it's lucky I've already had a drink because a huge chunk of money's gone. My heart goes into free fall.

Over a thousand pounds is missing.

One thousand pounds! That's almost everything that was in there!

Have we been robbed?

With a racing pulse I scroll through the statement. Maybe it's a mistake? Or perhaps online fraudsters have struck? Any minute now I'll discover that I supposedly have a porn addiction or a new-found liking for Internet bingo… You read about this kind of thing all the time, don't you?

My shaking finger clicks on the transaction. Oh! It's a transfer to Ollie's credit card company. He must be paying something off. But for over a thousand pounds? What on earth could he have spent a thousand pounds on?

Oh God. Has the roof finally caved in? But if it had then I'd know about it. Maddy would have called me instantly.

Frankie glances at me. "Are you all right?"

"I… I…" I falter because my speech has suddenly dried up. Am I all right? To be honest I'm not sure, because the answer's obvious, isn't it? This is no mistake.

Ollie must have spent the money on somebody else.

And he waited until I was out of the country to do it.

Have I been wrong about Carolyn? Has something been going on all this time? Has he been taking her out to all the best places? Showering her with gifts?

"Katy?" Frankie says again.

"I'm fine," I answer, but my voice sounds all wobbly and weird. "Just not in the mood for shopping."

Frankie looks at me as though I've grown two heads – which is fair enough, because here I am in one of the world's retail-therapy hotspots, with designer stores everywhere I turn, and I'm saying that I don't feel like shopping. But I know that even if I bought twenty handbags and a hundred trinkets from Tiffany's, none of this would make me feel any better. What does shopping matter if I've lost Ollie?

My heart's slamming against my ribcage. There could be a perfectly innocent explanation for why my boyfriend's been secretly splashing the cash while I'm away, but even my active imagination's struggling to offer one. Ann Burrows' sixtieth birthday is coming up soon. Has he bought her a present? But one thousand pounds? I know Ollie loves his mum, but that amount of money on a gift for her is verging on Oedipal.

"There's not as much money in there as I'd hoped," is all I manage to say. "Maybe we could just window-shop?"

Frankie looks horrified. "Darling girl, you can't *window-shop* in New York. It's practically against the law. What I think we should do is—"

But at this point my phone rings again and I snatch it up just in case it's Ollie.

"Hello?" says a clipped voice. "Is that Katy?"

Oh. Not Ollie then. The surge of disappointment I feel is almost unbearable.

"It is," I say.

"Thank God! We've been trying to get hold of you for days," says the voice, sounding exasperated.

"I'm in New York right now," I reply, although I still don't know who's calling.

"We had no idea. You really should tell us if you're out of the country – paragraph four, second clause, just in case you were wondering. Still, as it turns out, the fact that you're in New York at the moment couldn't be better!"

"Who?" mouths Frankie.

"No idea!" I mouth back.

"Sorry, who is this?" I ask when the unknown speaker pauses.

"Lisa Armstrong," she says and, when I don't reply, adds, "Senior Commissioning Editor at Throb Publishing?"

Great. Just great. Can this day get any worse?

"Hi, Lisa," I say, trying to sound thrilled. "What can I do for you?"

So Lisa tells me and by the time the call ends I need the second glass of champagne that Frankie lined up for me, and the third too. There's a huge cloud of doom hovering above my head and I'm finding it hard to find the silver lining.

Probably because there isn't one.

"Spill," says Frankie.

I gulp. "Remember that contract I signed without reading?"

"I certainly do. Don't tell me – it's come back to bite you on the bum?"

"That's one way of putting it," I say. "Throb want me to publicise the book for them. There's a launch planned and I need to be there in role as Isara Lovett."

"Isn't that a good thing? I thought writers loved publicity for their books."

"Usually. The trouble is that this book's a bit on the saucy side."

Frankie's plucked brows shoot under his pork-pie hat.

"I take it by 'saucy' what you actually mean is mind-blowingly blue?"

I blush. "I swear to God I only wrote it to pay some bills. I never thought things would get this out of control."

"Darling, you're very sweet but there's nothing to be ashamed of," says Frankie kindly. "Bondage. BDSM. Whips. It's all mainstream now. In fact, I'd be far more ashamed if I was partaking in what folks used to call 'normal', if I were you. How dull would that be? Kinky is cool now, you know."

I shake my head. "Not if your boyfriend's the Assistant Head of a strict Catholic school, it isn't."

"Ah yes," says Frankie, who gets it at once. "Oh dear. And you haven't told him."

It isn't a question. He knows me far too well by now to need to ask.

"How could I?" I say despairingly. "It would have put Ollie in an impossible position. Besides, we needed the money."

Frankie nods. "I get it. And now they want you to plug the book and your secret could be about to unravel."

It feels a bit like my whole life is unravelling, although that could be down to three alcoholic drinks in quick succession.

"I can't refuse, because it's written into my contract," I say, starting to gnaw on my thumbnail. "They could sue me, couldn't they?"

"I'm afraid so," he agrees. "Darling, I hate to say 'I told you so' but—"

I give him a grim smile. "I told you so?"

We both stare thoughtfully into our drinks. How on earth can I put things right with Ollie, tell the truth and get things sorted, if I'm about to do something that I know will compromise his career? There might be a very good explanation for his recent spending binge (although I'm yet to come up with one), but I won't be able to explain things to *him* very easily if I come out as the appallingly named I Lovett. Ollie will be mortified and I'll never forgive myself if I ruin his career. He loves that job.

Come on, Katy, there has to be a way out of this mess. A way that you can keep Throb happy and not embarrass Ollie. It's all going to be fine. There must be a solution, short of heading for the International Space Station or hiding down in the sewers with the Ninja Turtles. Maybe I could even rock a disguise like Spiderman? Mild-mannered Katy Carter is Throb Woman!

Actually, that sounds a bit dodgy and I'd hate to see the costume.

Costumes. Disguise. Alter egos. Secret identities…

Hang on. I'm onto something…

And then, just like the perfect plot of one of I Lovett's books, it all falls into place in my head. Of course! Secret identities are the key. It's so obvious I can't believe I haven't thought of it already. After all, it wouldn't be for the first time, would it?

"Frankie," I say slowly. "I think I've changed my mind about going shopping…"

Chapter 18

BOOKS AND THE CITY

Exclusive event!

Kitchen of Correction

by

I. Lovett

If you can't stand the heat...

Meet and greet book signing with

Isara Lovett

Saturday 12 noon

Free book for the first thirty!

Well, so far so good. This book-signing lark is actually far less stressful than I thought. I've no idea what all those celebrities make such a song and dance about. All I've had to do is drink several coffees, sit behind a table, scribble my pretend signature onto some books and chat to a few folks about their own writing. It's a bit awkward because some people want to just scuttle past like I'm collecting for charity or something, but others have been very kind. The nun who said she'd pray for me was lovely, and she did seem to really appreciate her free copy. I think it was quite sweet of her to take a few more for her sisters at the convent. The Hell's Angel who insisted on having his photo taken with me was friendly too, and I think it only goes to show that just because someone's got a tattoo of the grim reaper on their face doesn't necessarily mean they're a bad person. And like he said, the murder wasn't really his fault and he's served his time for helping hide the body.

Yes, book signing is fascinating. I'm not sure what I was making such a fuss about. Books and the City is a small independent bookstore in Manhattan and it's fairly quiet. I'm safe enough here. It's not as though CNN are about to burst in and interview me.

So, here I am. It's just gone two p.m. and things seem to be going well. Isara Lovett has made an appearance, the contractual obligations have been met and honour is satisfied. Now I only have to survive for another hour and I can escape back on the subway and into obscurity. Nobody will ever be any the wiser. The book's only been out a couple of days and hopefully it's going to sink without a trace. There are piles of it on the table in front of me and posters in the window and even a massive cardboard cut-out of it by the door, but no one seems very interested. Although I'm sitting here at the table, my pen clutched in my hand and poised for action, my powers of invisibility are strong. Besides, why should people be remotely bothered about an author they've never heard of? On a sunny Saturday New Yorkers have got far more exciting things to do than come and see a nobody called Isara Lovett. They'll all be jogging around Central Park or sipping wheatgrass juice in trendy juice bars.

Luckily for me.

Still, when Lisa called and demanded that I did this signing I had no idea that Books and the City would be so quiet. The customers are certainly giving me quite a wide berth, which I suppose could be something to do with the way I'm dressed, or maybe the cardboard cut-out of Alexi wielding a whisk? It's hard to say. In any case, my shopping trip with Frankie has worked a treat. It was definitely worth maxing out what little credit was left on my Barclaycard: I hardly recognise myself now, thank goodness.

I look like I should be heading for the Playboy Mansion, not flogging books. Frankie's gone totally over the top styling Isara Lovett but the end result looks nothing like me. Even Tansy Topham would be impressed. I think we've got the outfit exactly right in the end, even if it wasn't quite what I'd had in mind initially.

"Are you sure it's not too much?" I'd asked Frankie as I'd stepped out of the Saks fitting room and done a little twirl. "Wouldn't a trouser suit be better? This is a bit revealing."

"You're a purveyor of passion, not a librarian," he'd said, stepping forward and adjusting the lapel of the tight jacket to reveal my new scarlet bra. "Darling, it's perfect. You look very sexy and totally like the writer of erotic romance. Even I think you're hot! Nobody will ever know it's you."

I think that was a double-edged compliment but he's right, thank God: when I catch a glimpse of my reflection in the shop window there's Isara Lovett – writer of steamy books and absolutely nothing to do with Katy Carter.

A bit like Clark Kent to Superman, Isara favours dark colours and glasses, but there the resemblance ends. We might be able to glimpse her pants, but that's because she's wearing a ridiculously short skirt rather than because she's put them on over her tights. As if! Isara Lovett doesn't wear tights. No, she's a stockings girl through and through.

Unfortunately for me.

I shift a bit in my seat because actually stockings are flipping uncomfortable and the suspender belt's cutting into my middle. That could be down to my newly discovered passion for pastrami on rye, or merely because these garments are more torturous than anything good old Alexi could dream up in his kitchen. But if it's good enough for Lucinda then I guess it's good enough for me, even if I feel as though I'm being sliced in half. Add a blonde wig and a full face of make-up into the mix as well as Frankie's cool fashion specs, and ta-da! Isara Lovett has arrived.

It's a good disguise. Even Guy walked straight past me earlier in the hotel lobby. I had to run after him and the expression on his face was priceless.

"It's me!" I'd said, when he'd failed to recognise me. "Katy! I'm off to a book signing."

"Bloody hell! I thought you were a hooker!" Guy had exclaimed. "What kind of a book signing is it?"

"One I'd rather not go to," I'd said darkly, and then the film crew had arrived to collect him and I'd been left to make my own way to Books and the City by subway.

I got some very strange looks.

Anyhow, I think I've got away with it.

As the customers browse the bookshelves and pretend not to see me, I lean back in my seat and watch some tumbleweed blow by. Then I flick through a copy of the book, wincing a little at the scene with the cabbages and the washing line. I'm just about to send Ollie a text when the phone rings. It's Mads.

"Hi!" I say, pleased to hear from her. "You'll never guess what."

"Guy's famous?" says Maddy.

I sit up. "No way! At home too?"

"Absolutely. Holly's just popped in. Apparently *Question Time* want him as a panellist as soon as he's back, and UKIP have called too."

"Crikey," I say. "That's just insane. All he's done is stomp about, make crazy comments and shoot his mouth off."

"Sounds like he has a great career in politics ahead of him," Mads muses. "Get him home fast or he'll probably be running for president by tonight."

"Poor old Pinchy's hardly getting a look-in – and the docudrama was supposed to be about his epic journey, not Guy goes to the city," I sigh.

My best friend laughs. "I bet he's amusing to watch but I'm sure the novelty will wear off."

"Maybe," I say doubtfully. It hasn't on Holly though, so why should the media be any different?

"There's lots of talk about the lobster here, so don't worry," Mads reassures me. "Maybe you could write a book about it? *Pinchy's Journey*? That could be fun, although it does sound a bit like a scene from Alexi's kinky kitchen!"

"Don't even joke about it," I say grimly. "I'm never writing a novel again. The stress of this book has well and truly strangled the muse. In fact, if she ever dares come near me again, shoot me."

"Ah yes, the book signing. That was why I called. How's it going? I loved the picture Frankie sent me, by the way. You look like Tansy in her lads'-mags heyday. You should take that outfit home and give Ollie a treat."

"Ha ha," I say. Until I find out where that thousand pounds went, *treats* of any kind are off the table. Not that they've been on it for a while, but you get my point. It's the principle of the thing that counts.

Sensing my mood, Mads changes the subject swiftly. "Have you signed lots of books?"

"Only six," I admit, "and I think they were out of pity. With any luck *Kitchen of Correction* will be a huge flop and never be seen or heard of again, and I'll be left in peace. There are lots of people shopping but I don't think Alexi and Lucinda are their cup of tea."

"Since when did Alexi and Lucinda bother with tea?" Maddy giggles. "Although, saying that, there was the bit where they got the tin of Earl Grey and—"

"Stop right there," I say, wincing. "You need help, coming up with ideas like that."

"That was Nicky's input. I can't take credit. Honestly, that boy is a writing dynamo. And talking of needing help and the Burrows family, do you still want me to ring Tansy's company incognito and book them to do the food for Ollie's mum's birthday bash?" Maddy asks.

"Yes please," I reply. "She'll try and do it for free if she knows it's me."

"OK. Consider it done. Now, I know you booked the hotel but is there anything else you want me to sort out?"

I'm throwing a surprise birthday party for Ann Burrows. Nothing huge, just a some of her closest friends and family at the Tregowan Country Hotel. I posted the invitations just before I left for the airport and already several friends and relatives have emailed to say they'll be there, including Ann's pastor. I just hope Ann never finds out that I'm paying for this with the rest of my advance for *Kitchen*. She's very nice but terribly strait-laced and I think she'd pop. Geoff would love it though – especially after a few glasses of red.

"It's a really nice thing for you to do," Maddy says warmly. "And Ollie has no idea?"

"No, I just told him that I'd take care of his mum's birthday. I've booked a restaurant the day before and he thinks that's it. He's got no idea about the rest of it. I wanted to take as much pressure off him as possible," I tell her.

This seemed like a good plan at the time, but since discovering that Ollie goes on thousand-pound spending sprees as soon as I'm out of sight, I'm wondering if the gesture is quite as deserved as I'd thought. What on earth has he been buying?

"Katy?" Maddy says. "Are you still there?"

"Yes. Still here." In body if not in mind. "Keep everything quiet, Maddy, OK? It's going to be a surprise. Take care when you book that nobody knows it's to do with me. Or you."

"No probs. I'll pretend to be somebody else. Maybe I'll even do an Irish accent? Top of the morning to you!"

"No! Don't do that! They'll think you're a prank caller!"

Maddy rings off laughing and I turn my attention back to the task in hand, namely being Isara and promoting the books. A couple of spotty teenagers sidle up and try to sneak a read of the juicy bits, so I give them my best teacher glare and they soon skulk away. Then all is very still. It's as though my signing table has a force field around it that repels all the customers. I'm contemplating buying an adult colouring book to pass the time, when the shop door bursts open and Guy strides in.

Oh God. Please strike me dead now.

He's brought the film crew with him – and please tell me that isn't Pinchy in that tank?

"Katy! There you are!" Guy booms, waving at me delightedly, while I wonder where to hide. "I've been in nearly every bloody bookshop in this twatting city trying to find you, and nobody's even heard of you! I kept saying, 'Katy Carter, you harries! She's my girlfriend's sister and she's promoting her book.' We're practically family and I'm here on Holly's behalf! We won't let you down. You need our support and you'll bloody well have it!"

"Err, actually I don't," I begin, but Guy isn't listening; he's far too busy berating the bookshop manager while his entourage clap and cheer.

Oh holy crap. They're filming.

"See!" he hollers, jabbing a giant finger in my direction. "I *told you* that was her! Katy Carter, my girlfriend's sister. She's written a book. No idea what it's about though, because I don't read books. You said she wasn't here, you fibbers!"

"That's not Katy Carter. That's Isara Lovett," says the bookstore's manager faintly, looking on in shock while cameras whir and a huge microphone hovers over her head.

"Isaac who?" Guy bellows. "Never heard of him! That's Katy Carter! She's wearing a daft wig but it's definitely our Katy! Give her credit for her own bloody book! Right, Katy?"

Err no, wrong actually – although it's sweet of Guy to be incensed on my behalf. Sweet if misplaced and pretty flipping annoying.

"Who's this Isaac anyway?" he adds, scanning the shop like the Terminator looking for Sarah Connor. "If he's stealing your work he needs sorting."

"*I'm* Isara," I hiss. "It's me!"

Guy stares at me. "Eh?"

"I'm Isara!"

"Don't be stupid! You're Katy!"

"Isara's my pen name."

"A what name?"

"A made-up name to keep my identity secret," I tell him in a whisper. "So nobody at home knows it was me who wrote it. Look at the book! Then you'll see!"

Guy picks up a copy, clocks the cover and does a double take. His jaw drops. "Fucking hell. You wrote that?"

"No, Pinchy did!" I say, before lowering my voice again. "Of course I wrote it, Guy. But look, you can't tell a soul this is me. I mean it! This has to be a secret."

But Guy's too preoccupied with flicking through a copy of *Kitchen* to listen to me. Moments later most of the documentary team have also picked up copies and are engrossed. Cries of "ooo!" and "Read this bit!" ripple through the group, and a crowd of shoppers gather around my table to see what all the fuss is about. Before long all the piles of books have been grabbed by curious hands and the tills are ringing. The crowd's getting bigger and bigger and the film crew are interviewing a couple of excited customers. It even looks as though CNN are here, although I might be mistaken.

I certainly hope so.

Guy's sitting cross-legged on the floor with a paperback in his hand and his mouth hanging open.

"I'll never see that filthy bugger Ollie Burrows the same way again," he says, shaking his head incredulously. "I can't believe what he does with wet tea towels!"

"It's a work of fiction!" I cry. "It's totally made up!"

But of course nobody's listening to me. No, they're all far too busy either reading or speculating about the true identity of Alexi. They don't care if it's all fiction. The story has taken on a monstrous life of its own.

Oh God. All those years spent teaching media studies at A-level and it's only now that I really understand what Roland Barthes was on about. What does it matter what the truth is when there's a good story to spin? And who cares what the author really meant?

This is a disaster! Things couldn't be worse. Now everyone will think that I've based this book on my own love life. Ollie will be mortified and St Jude's will freak. What have I done?

"Katy Carter? *NYC News*! Would you like to tell us about the book? And what input your own life had in the writing of it?"

"*City Tonight*! Do you research all the episodes yourself?"

"*New York Enquirer*! What was the inspiration for the book? And how long have you known Guy?"

"Congratulations," the store manager says, turning to me. Her smile couldn't be wider. "We've sold every single copy and had orders for over a hundred more. You're going to have a bestseller on your hands, no doubt about it. This book is going to be huge!"

I put my head in my hands.

This was *not* what I had in mind. Not at all.

Ollie is going to kill me.

And I don't blame him one bit.

Chapter 19

Throb

Fiction that's red hot and ready!

Eros Towers * Sherrington Boulevard * W14 6BY

Dear Katy,

Many thanks on the behalf of Throb for such a successful international launch for *Kitchen of Correction*. Everyone on the team is delighted and the book is already on its fifth print run. It is now one of our most downloaded products – in both eBook and audio format.

Thanks also for the delivery of the New York pizzas. Yes, you were correct in fearing that they 'might not travel that well'. Again we donated your kind gift to the builders working next door. The foreman sends his thanks and says his wife is a huge fan of your work. He is currently signed off following a mishap involving a cabbage and a washing line, but hopes to make a full recovery.

Unfortunately, we cannot forget about the 'small clause' which says the author must be available to write the next two novels. If you look carefully at the sixth paragraph in your contract you will see it is clearly stated that once signed the document is legally binding.

We look forward to reading the first draft of *Sitting Room of Sin*!

Best wishes,

Lisa Armstrong (Senior Commissioning Editor)

PS. Would it be possible to have some signed pictures of Guy Tregarten? We are all huge fans here!

It's two weeks later. Two very long weeks later. Two weeks in which I've alternated between apologising to Ollie over and over again and feeling so crippled by guilt that even if the St Jude's priest gave me a million Hail Marys to recite it wouldn't make any difference. Not that St Jude's will let me anywhere near the place after the fiasco of the last fourteen days; they're more likely to ward me off with flaming torches and crucifixes *Hammer House of Horror* style – if lightning doesn't sizzle me first, of course.

Since Guy outed me as the author of *Kitchen of Correction* everything's gone quite crazy. This isn't because of me or even because the book's anything special (believe me, it really isn't). No, it's all down to the American public's weird obsession with Guy. Suddenly everything he's associated with is of huge interest, which is good news for lobster conservation and Throb but very bad news for me.

And even worse news for Ollie.

My cover's well and truly blown and I feel terrible. Not only have I caused Ollie huge embarrassment at school but he's incredibly hurt that I kept the book a secret for so long. I've only been home for a short while and the atmosphere between us is so glacial that Sasha's paws are in danger of getting frostbite. And as for Nicky, when he isn't out working he's taken to hiding in his room, muttering that this is just like being back with his parents. I don't know what I can do to make things right again.

Talking of Mr and Mrs Burrows, as if things weren't strained enough already, Ollie and Nicky's parents arrive this afternoon for Ann's birthday celebrations. That means Ollie and I will need to be on our very best behaviour – any indication that something's up and Ann will be straight in there like Sasha after a rabbit. Tonight we're all going to a local seafood restaurant for a smart family meal, which will probably be about as much fun as sleeping naked on a bed of nails. Thank goodness Mads booked Tansy's caterers for tomorrow's surprise party. With the Tregowan Country Hotel as the venue it should be really classy and can't fail to impress Ann. Maybe when Ollie sees all the trouble I've gone to on his mother's behalf he'll forgive me for the whole Throb fiasco.

I can only hope…

"I wouldn't count on it," is my sister's cheerful response when, over tea and cake at her house, I voice this optimistic opinion.

"Thanks," I say. "Remind me again why I'm here with a prophet of doom like you?"

"Because I'm pregnant and sick and my fiancé is still in the States?" Holly says. "You did far too much of a good job looking after him. I'm starting to wonder if he'll come back now he's enjoying his fifteen minutes of fame so much!"

They persuaded Guy to extend his stay for a little bit, so I had to return on my own. For a man terrified of travelling he's certainly making up for it now; when I left he was flying off to San Diego to speak at a conservation expo. While he's abroad I'm keeping Holly company. She's suffering with morning sickness and high blood pressure but has sworn me to secrecy because she wants Guy to make the most of his time away. He's supposed to be catching a flight home tomorrow, but there's no knowing whether they'll talk him into something else instead.

"He's done exactly what he set out to do," I say. "He's raised awareness of fishing, all right."

"By posing bare-chested for *Cosmo* in bib and braces?" She rolls her eyes. "Just wait until he gets home! Tell me again how that's raised awareness of UK fishing quotas?"

I'm not sure either, but it raised a few pulses and there was certainly a lot of talk about his tackle! Guy's a character and a novelty in the States. Apparently the ratings of the dramality show soared when his episodes aired.

"People are talking about sustainable fishing though, and when he gets back he'll be able to use his brush with fame to speak about it all and make a difference," Holly continues. "Guy's no fool. He's using a celebrity lobster and a lucky break to do what he set out to. I can't wait for him to come home."

"You're really missing him," I say sympathetically. I can't imagine ever missing Guy myself, but then I guess you must miss toothache if you've had it long enough.

But Holly snorts. "Don't be so soft! I just need somebody to make me cups of tea and to warm my feet on when they're cold in bed."

"Who says romance is dead?"

"Well not you, with your kinky book and washing lines!" Holly whips out a copy of *Kitchen* with a flourish. "I'm on chapter ten already and it's a lot more exciting than maths! And I've noticed that all my students are reading it rather than revising for their finals. If they fail, then I'll know exactly who to blame."

"I think Ollie has the same problem," I sigh. "He's really upset."

My sister looks at me as though I'm stupid, which is fair enough given recent events. "You've nearly lost Ollie his job and totally humiliated him in front of all his colleagues, and now most of his kids and their mothers are reading the book. Worse still, he didn't even have a clue you'd written it, which has made him look like a right plank. I bet all the kids are really ripping it out of him."

"Thanks, Hol, I feel so much better now." I place my head in my hands. When they were giving out tact my sister must have been right at the back of the queue. No wonder she and Guy get on so well. "What if Ollie dumps me?"

"Of course he won't," says my sister. "Don't be so dramatic."

"That's easy for you to say." Holly hasn't seen how strained Ollie looks. When he came back from his meeting with the senior leaders last week he was grey with stress and certainly didn't want to talk to me – which was hardly surprising since, as usual, I was the cause of his troubles.

"Not now, Katy, all right?" he'd said when I'd asked how he was. "It's been a shit day and it's not going to get better any time soon. Have you any idea how many cabbages and washing lines have been left on my desk since all this got out?"

"Cabbage soup and bondage tonight, honey?" I'd tried to joke, but Ollie understandably hadn't been amused.

"The school governors have called an emergency board meeting," he'd said, throwing his briefcase onto the floor and heading straight for the fridge to grab a beer. "They're going to discuss my future at the school. They've asked me to attend."

He looked so upset and I was devastated for him.

"This isn't anything to do with you!" I'd cried, stepping forward and putting my arms round him. "I wrote that book! I don't even work for St bloody Jude's."

"And you're *my* girlfriend," Ollie had shot back, shaking me off and starting to pace our tiny kitchen. "As far as they're concerned that means this is my cock-up and my responsibility. You've seen the headlines. They love the fact that you live in sin with your partner, who just so happens to be the Assistant Head of a Catholic school."

I'd seen the headlines and they didn't make pretty reading.

"That'll all be fish and chip paper soon, as the saying goes," I'd remarked as cheerfully as I could, but Ollie just gave me a withering look.

"Unfortunately since the advent of the Internet all those platitudes about fish and chip paper no longer count. That story will be there forever. Any parent who Googles St Jude's will be able to read all about it."

"Maybe they'll all buy the book and we'll have so many royalties you'll never have to teach again?" I'd offered hopefully.

"This isn't about you and your royalties!" Ollie had exploded. "This is about my career and our future! Why do you think I'm working so hard in the first place? Do you think it's because I like being up all night marking or coming home late? I'm doing it for us, Katy! So that maybe we can pay the bills and have a family or even manage to retire before we're eighty. I'm doing this so that you can have the chance to write your novel and enjoy it!"

I'd stared at him. Had he really just mentioned starting a family, or had I just dreamed that bit? And was this a good time to point out that if *Kitchen* kept selling at this rate my share of the royalties could be enough to make our lives a lot easier? Maybe neither of us would need to teach…

I'd opened my mouth to say something but then shut it again fast when I'd recalled the part of the contract that stipulated I had to write the next two books in the series. He'd go spare. If only I'd read that contract before signing it! Note to self: literary agents are worth every penny of their commission. I'd tell him about the sequels in a few days, when things were a little less fraught and the royalties were rolling in. This wasn't keeping secrets as much as a case of damage limitation.

"I'm so sorry," I'd said, for what had to be the billionth time. "I never meant any of this to happen. I was trying to help."

"I love you, Katy," Ollie had said wearily, "but maybe be a little less helpful in the future? I'm so tired of all the stress. I'm not twenty-five anymore. I can't drink all night long and not be hung-over to shit the next day. I can't ski as well as I did either, and I certainly can't cope with any more dramas. I just need a quiet life. I think I can weather this at work – just – but it can't go on. Those books have got to stop."

He wasn't wrong there. All I had to do was figure out how. Since pizza wasn't going to do it and even pasties had failed, I was going to have to think more creatively. *Sitting Room of Sin* and *Dining Room of Desire* were starting to keep me up at night – and not in the way that Throb intended, either.

But one week on from this conversation I still haven't come up with a solution. Now I've got the added strain of Ann and Geoff Burrows rocking up. By some miracle they don't seem to know anything about *Kitchen of Correction* and I'm crossing everything that it stays that way. There are some benefits to Geoff thinking about nothing but wine and Ann being busy with the WI and church. Thank God they have no idea that their eldest son's girlfriend, their youngest son and a vicar's wife are jointly responsible for a smutty book that's being talked about everywhere. I think the shock would kill them.

Anyway, as I say, it's one week on – and although he's not nearly as pissed off as he was, Ollie's still far from being over the trauma. Nothing I can say or do can make it up to him. I can't shake the feeling that he's keeping something from me too, but after the hassle I've caused I don't dare raise the matter of that odd transaction. I'm hoping it's a mistake or that he's bought something special for Ann. It's strange he's not mentioned it at all though. What if my worst fears were spot on all along?

What if he's been buying things for another woman?

It's like my heart is a ball of string in my chest and every time I think about losing Ollie somebody tugs it a little tighter. I love him so much. If only I could put things right and life could go back to normal, or our version of it anyway.

"Look," Holly's saying now, joining me at the table with another mug of ginger tea, "the way I see it is that, yes, you made a mistake not telling Ollie about the book, but you had the best intentions. You never set out to hurt or embarrass him."

"Of course not!" I cry. "I was only trying to get some money together and take the pressure off him because he's working so hard."

"And he's working so hard to take the pressure off you." My sister rolls her eyes. "What a pair you are! I don't know why you worry so much. You're made for each other."

I stare down at the grain of her table and the patterns in the wood start to blur. "I used to think so but I'm not sure he feels the same way. I think there's someone else."

Holly splutters ginger tea all over the table. "What! No way! Ollie would never cheat on you."

"So why would he spend nearly a thousand pounds and not tell me?"

It's not often that my super-brain sister is lost for words, but she is now.

"He must have been buying things for Carolyn," I conclude.

"Who the fuck is Carolyn?" Holly asks.

Ah yes, I forgot I'd only told Maddy and Tansy about her.

"She's a teacher at Ollie's school," I explain. "Blonde, skinny and they work together."

"And?" says Holly, looking puzzled.

For a girl with a PhD from Cambridge my sister can be ridiculously slow on the uptake sometimes.

"So maybe he's having an affair with her? She rings all the time and they work together too."

"Guy calls Crab Pot Mike all the time and they work together on the trawler. I don't think they're shagging though, even if Mike has long blond hair," she says. "And before you tell me I'm being absurd, no more so than you. Seriously, Katy? Do you really think Ollie's so shallow he'd fancy somebody just because she's blonde and skinny?"

"He's a bloke," I say.

"Fair point. But I still say you're totally wrong. How about this for a crazy notion. What if he's bought something for you and he's keeping it as a surprise? Hmm?"

For a millisecond hope blossoms in my heart before I slam on the old mental brakes as fast as I possibly can. I've been here before, remember? The Great St Valentine's Ring Hunt? Ollie doesn't do surprises.

"Not Ollie's style," I tell her. "Besides, he couldn't have kept it a secret this long."

Holly shakes her head. "Having a fling isn't his style either but I think—"

At this point there's a knocking on the front door.

"I'll get it," I say to Holly, who has her hand over her heart. Having a pregnant sister is terrifying and I can't wait until Guy's here to take over the responsibility. "Your blood pressure is high enough."

"Hardly any wonder with you around," she says wryly.

Leaving her to sip her tea, I wiggle through the narrow passages of Holly's tiny cottage (which is easier said than done, since the place was built for half-starved Tudor fisher folk rather than size-twelve me) and open the door.

And once I have, I feel like shutting it again.

Fast.

Can life really hate me this much? Any more spanners to throw in my works, Fate?

"Surprise!" booms my father.

Chapter 20

"Dad! What are you doing here?"

To say I'm taken back is an understatement. I haven't seen hide nor hair of my parents for months, so to find one of them literally on the doorstep is indeed something of a surprise.

And not a good one either.

Don't get me wrong, I think the world of my parents. Of course I do! It's just that sometimes they can be a little difficult to love and even more difficult to live with. Pop them on the scene just when my sort-of in-laws are about to arrive and you could have fireworks that would make the New Year's Eve celebrations in Trafalgar Square look half-hearted.

My parents, although well meaning and very easy-going, are also sometimes a little bit embarrassing. I know what you're thinking! You're thinking that all parents are embarrassing. It's practically their duty to remind you of your most awkward teenage moments or whip out the family photo album and show your new boyfriend pictures of you aged one and with more spare tyres than Kwik Fit. Yes, I bet that's cringe-making, but I spent my formative years *longing* for that kind of embarrassment, because naff dad jokes and teasing about the time you played the back end of the donkey in the school nativity are normal, aren't they? Whereas a father with a talent for "organic herbal gardening" and a mother who insists on chatting to her spirit guides halfway through your parents' evening really aren't.

My folks are ageing hippies who still live in a seventies time warp in their ramshackle barn near Totnes, when they're not travelling. They spend a lot of time driving about the continent to various New Age festivals and goddess workshops, in a rusting VW van held together with their own unique blend of patchouli oil, rainbow paint and optimism. No wonder Holly and I rebelled by becoming total squares. The only time I ever saw my mother cry was when I told her I wasn't interested in travelling to an ashram with her and was off to do teacher training. She went to bed for a week and still claims her aura's never recovered from the disappointment.

Anyway, as I said, I love my parents but they're not always the easiest of company, especially in the presence of Ollie's slightly less relaxed folks. I haven't forgotten the last time, when Geoff innocently took a few puffs of one of my father's *herbal* cigarettes – and several hours later ate his way through the entire sherry trifle Ann had prepared for Sunday lunch. Poor Ann had looked as though she'd needed that sherry herself when Mum announced that Ollie's dead grandmother had joined us in the sitting room.

Still, as two sets of in-laws meeting for the first time goes, I guess it could have been a lot worse.

Somehow…

Anyway, since then I've done my best to keep the Burrows and the Carters apart and, unless we ever hold a family gathering in the Large Hadron Collider, that's the way I intend to keep it. I've enough on my plate already with the fallout from Throb and organising Ann's surprise party, without having to manage Quentin and Drusilla Carter. I kid you not, sieving jelly would be easier.

"Do I need a reason to be here? I've come to see my best girls!" my father booms, so loudly that several seagulls just quietly minding their business on the chimney pot opposite take fright. "It's been far too long!"

"You've been travelling around Spain. It wasn't like we could just pop round," I comment, and Dad grins.

"Fair point. I do wish they'd run those goddess workshops a bit closer to home, but what can you do? The sun's out in Spain and we'd freeze our bits off doing naked circle work in Devon."

Ew! I don't want to think about my parents doing naked circle work *ever*. What if they decide to do this in Tregowan? A horrific image of my naked olds doing a sun salutation flashes before my eyes and I feel quite faint. Ann will flip but I guess Geoff might enjoy it. He was very taken with Mum, although I suspect that had more to do with Dad's special cigarettes than a hitherto undiscovered love of tarot cards.

"Come here!" My father engulfs me in a massive bear hug. The wool of his ethnic knit is scratchy and his beard tickles my cheek, but he's solid and cuddly and smells so comfortingly Dad-like that I feel about six again. As I hug him back I decide that it doesn't matter what Ann and Geoff think. My parents are good-hearted people. We can get through a couple of evenings together. Of course we can!

How hard can it be?

"Where's Mum?" I ask, as we step inside. Is it wrong of me to cross my fingers that she's still halfway up a hill in Andalucía, standing on her head and chanting? Like naughty kids in my classroom, Quentin and Drusilla are easier to deal with when split up.

"Mum's on her way," Dad says, cheerfully destroying all hopes of managing them separately. "She was just parking the van on the harbourside and got it a bit stuck. She shouldn't be long."

The road down to the quay is so narrow I can almost touch either side if I walk along and stretch out my arms. Designed for horses not hippy wagons, it's regularly blocked by holidaymakers tricked by the strident tones of their satnavs into ignoring the evidence of their own eyes.

"She'll get it wedged," I warn. "Can't you go and tell her to put it in the car park?"

"O ye of little faith! Silla can back that camper like a pro. None of the old jokes about women being told one inch is actually five for her," he grins, and I wince. "Oh smile, Katy! It's a joke. J. O. K. E. Anyway, have you seen how much they charge for parking here?"

"I have and, believe me, four pounds is a lot cheaper that respraying a wing," I point out.

"Respraying? Any scratches on that van are marks of honour! Badges of distinction! Wounds of the well-travelled," he says while I roll my eyes. "Anyway, why pay to park when Mother Earth belongs to us all? I'm not a slave to the capitalist system!"

"The ground here belongs to me, so take your shoes off! They're filthy!" Holly has left the kitchen and joined us, hands on hips and glowering at my father's muddy wellies.

"Hello fruit of my loins number two!" Dad beams, but he knows my sister well enough to take his boots off before he kisses her. Placing a hand on her belly he adds, "And how's little Mountain Tiger doing?"

"Mountain Tiger?" I echo and Holly shakes her head.

"As if. If it's a boy I'm calling him George," she tells him. "A nice middle-class, sensible name."

"Seriously?" Dad looks devastated. "With a name like that the poor little bugger will end up a bank manager."

"Oh, I do hope so," Holly says with feeling. "Anything but a fisherman or a hippy will be just fine by me."

"What did I do to end up with two such bourgeois daughters?" grumbles my father, sitting down on his younger daughter's bourgeois sofa and making himself very much at home.

"Drag us from pillar to post while you got stoned, but you won't remember that," my sister reminds him tartly. "Now stop complaining and tell us all about Spain. It's been bloody cold here and I'm very jealous of your tan."

While Holly makes tea Dad regales us with tales of their travels. He's a brilliant storyteller, which always made him a firm favourite with all my friends, and I find myself laughing as he describes how he accidentally asked a barman in Castile for two toilets rather than two beers.

"His face! He said 'Qué? Qué?'" Dad guffaws. "I think he thought I had some lavatory fetish because I asked him over and over again and mimed drinking! Then your mother arrived from her rebirthing class and was able to explain what I meant. How we laughed! We had a great night in the bar after that, drinking Spanish beer and smoking until the sun came up, and then José joined us for the next hundred miles."

Mum and Dad always end up collecting waifs and strays. When I was a kid the house was full of them. The one who was convinced he was

Tutankhamun was quite hard work, especially as he had an annoying habit of stealing my eyeliner.

I glance at my watch. Crikey. It's almost six. Where's the time gone? I should be at home getting ready for tonight's meal. Ollie's getting back early and I'm going to do my best to make sure it's a lovely evening. He's had an awful week and I really want him to relax. This is going to be a great weekend.

Even if it kills me.

"I've got to go," I say, putting down my mug.

Dad looks disappointed. "You haven't seen Mum yet."

"She's probably still trying to park," says Holly. "Or else she's met somebody interesting and wandered off. It wouldn't be the first time."

We all fall silent. When I was thirteen Mum went out to do some shopping and didn't come back for two months. Turned out she'd met a toy boy called Rain and her guides had told her she needed to travel with him. Dad was fine about it – my parents have a very peculiar relationship – but Holly and I were horrified. I think it was at this point Holly buried herself in textbooks and I discovered Mills and Boon novels, hoarding them and reading them from cover to cover until they all but disintegrated in my hands. One day I just knew I would find a romantic hero of my very own who would sweep me off my feet and rescue me from these utter lunatics who just so happened to share my DNA. We'd live happily ever after in his castle/Bedouin tent/New York town house (delete as appropriate) and the past would be forgotten.

Or at least as forgotten as it can be when it insists on driving a psychedelic camper van back into the pile-up of my life.

Anyway, I never did hook up with a duke/sheikh/billionaire, but I am lucky enough to have found Ollie Burrows – the only romantic hero I'll ever want in my life. I really want to make everything up to him, which is why I *cannot* let my parents ruin Ann's special dinner.

But quite how I'm going to prevent them doing that is anyone's guess.

"Don't let them out of your sight," I hiss at my sister as I head to the door. "Keep them with you!"

"Err, they're adults," Holly says.

We both glance across at Dad, who's beeping away happily on Guy's Xbox.

"Or maybe not," she grins. "Look, I'll do my best but be prepared for the worst. If he says they've come here especially for Ann's birthday, then there's not much I can do to stop them. Besides, it would be cruel. They don't mean any harm."

"You've changed your tune!" I'm a bit taken aback because usually Holly's the first to moan about our parents while I have to defend them. When Mum took up with Rain, Holly didn't speak to her for months. It didn't matter that Dad was fine with it all (he's generally happy if left to garden and experiment with home-made wine). My sister was incensed.

But no longer, it seems. Instead, she rests a hand on her stomach and a beatific expression settles across her face.

"Now I'm a parent myself I see it all quite differently."

Holly's baby is probably the size of a kidney bean but as usual I'm trumped by the *you're not a mother* card.

"They were only doing their best," she adds sagely.

They were? This is news to me. To be honest, if my parents were students in my class I'd be scrawling *could try harder* and *see me* all over their books, and sod PC green biro; I'd be using blood-red ink.

"Err, Holl, don't you always say that Philip Larkin must have based his famous poem on them?"

But Holly refuses to rise to my bait and I make my way back home feeling disgruntled and hard done by, in other words exactly like I did when I was a teenager. What is it about parents that just minutes in their company whizzes you back in time like something from *Dr Who*?

"What's up with you?" asks Ollie when, ten minutes later, I stomp into our sitting room.

"Mum and Dad have just rocked up."

"Ah," says Ollie. "Now I know why there's a VW wedged between two cottages. Nobody knew where the driver had gone until Betty from the shop traced them to the pub. It's caused chaos."

This sounds about right. I hurl myself onto the sofa and start to gnaw the skin around my thumbnail. If I end up at my elbows it will be all Quentin and Drusilla's fault.

"They've come down to celebrate your mum's birthday," I tell him. "They're threatening to join us for dinner."

Ollie takes his glasses off and grinds his knuckles into his eyes. "Oh Lord, are they? Well, I guess I'd better call the restaurant and see if they can squeeze in another couple of places."

I have a sense of doom, like the one I tend to get when I open my bank statements.

"I can put them off." I cross my fingers behind my back. At least I flipping hope I can. The trouble is, once my mother gets an idea into her head there's usually no stopping her. She also has a habit of saying her spirit guides have told her to do something, which is pretty hard to argue with and jolly convenient too. Maybe I should get a couple of my own?

But Ollie just sighs and shakes his head. "They're your parents and they'd be so hurt if we excluded them. Besides, you haven't seen your folks for ages."

And this is why I love Ollie so much. He knows my parents, has seen first-hand the chaos they can create, but he's still thinking of them and of me. If I didn't already feel bad enough for the havoc I've caused him lately I feel ten times worse now. He's so generous and so kind. If I could only get to the bottom of the savings account thing. Maybe I should ask him?

Never mind what Maddy says; everyone knows relationships should be all about honesty.

"Ol," I say slowly. "Did you go shopping while I was in New York?"

"What kind of a question is that? Of course. I'd have starved otherwise!" He's scrolling through the phonebook of his mobile now, looking for the restaurant number.

"Not food shopping!" Oh sod it, I may as well just ask him outright. "Buying presents for someone? Expensive presents?"

Ollie's finger hovers over the keypad. Time seems to stand still and all I can hear is the ticking of the sitting-room clock and Sasha's gentle snoring from her basket. Even the dust motes seem to pause in mid-air. It feels as though my whole world is holding its breath and that everything depends on what he says next.

Ollie's looking intently at the phone. "No, definitely not. Why on earth would you think that?"

My heart tightens in my chest. He's lying to me. Ollie never lies to me – or at least, I never thought he did. He's honest and true and straightforward, while I'm a bit scatty and forgetful and get into scrapes. That's how it is. How *we* are. I've always trusted him totally. Why would he lie now, unless there really is something he needs to hide?

"I saw the bank statement on our savings account. You transferred more than a thousand pounds to your credit card," I say quietly.

There's a pause, just a millisecond too long, before he nods.

"Oh yeah. I'd totally forgotten that with everything else that's been going on. I bought Mum a necklace for her birthday. It was about a hundred quid, not a thousand, but some numpty must have charged my credit card wrong. I love my mum but not that much! I paid it off while it was being looked into, just in case I got clobbered for interest or it messed up my credit score, but hopefully it's all sorted now. The account should be back to normal and the money back."

"It was a necklace? For Ann?"

"Yep. Why, what did you think it was? Me buying gifts for another woman?"

Err yes, that's exactly what I thought, not that I dare say so.

"I'm not the one who's been leading a double life," he adds. "Am I Katy? Or should I say Isara?"

And what can I say to this? He's right.

"I only took that ghostwriting job to pay the bills and to try and make things easier!" I protest. "I wish I hadn't!"

"Believe me, you're not the only one," says my boyfriend darkly. "But my point is, Katy, I thought we trusted each other. We're best friends, aren't we?"

I nod. Ollie was my best friend in the world way before he was my boyfriend.

"So what's gone wrong?" he asks me, looking so sad that my heart breaks. "Is life here in Tregowan not enough for you anymore? Do you want to be in New York? Live the celeb lifestyle like Frankie and Gabriel?"

I shudder. I tried that before when Gabriel paid me to be his girlfriend. It's a long story but it didn't end well and, believe me, he's far better off with Frankie —who has a greater appreciation of hair and make-up than I ever will.

"I know I'm just a teacher and I'll never be a wealthy guy," Ollie continues, "but I'm working as hard as I can for us, Katy, and I love you. Yes, you're crazy and annoying and even after all these years I still have absolutely no idea quite what goes on in your head, but I do love you. I always have."

There's a lump in my throat like a beach ball and I leap up from the sofa to hug him, but Ollie holds up his hands, warding me off.

"I love you," he repeats, "but, Katy, I can't cope with all these dramas anymore. Maybe I'm getting old, maybe I'm a boring old git, but I just want life to be straightforward. Please can we have no more secrets and no more scrapes? And no more Throb novels? I can still hardly get to my desk for cabbages, and students keep leaving clothes pegs on my chair. I thought maybe they'd get bored of it all after a week or so, but there's been no let-up. My backside's black and blue, and not from washing lines either!"

My eyes are so full of tears I can hardly see.

"No more dramas," I agree. I mean it too. From henceforth I will avoid dramas like the plague!

Ollie opens his arms and I step into them. His embrace is familiar and safe and warm, and I know I love him as much now as I ever have. There's nothing, nothing I wouldn't do for him. Somehow I'll get out of that Throb contract. There has to be a way.

Ollie kisses me and wipes my tears away with his thumbs.

"Now, I know I said no more dramas," he smiles ruefully, "but I'd still better get hold of the restaurant and sort out some extra places for your parents!"

To be honest, my parents are the least of my problems. Love Ollie as I do, at the back of my mind there's still a lurking shadow and no matter how hard I try, it won't go away but insists on creeping forward. I don't dare mention it.

The problem is I've not seen a refund for that necklace land in the account – and I've been checking it non-stop.

Ollie isn't telling me the whole truth.

And I've no idea why.

Chapter 21

Normally I love eating at Joe's. It's a small seafood restaurant tucked down one of Tregowan's narrow backstreets – all low ceilings strung with fishing nets, and crammed with an eclectic mixture of tables and chairs that look as though they've been borrowed from the neighbours (and probably have, since the chef originally opened his restaurant in his front room). The place still has a homely feeling about it and eating there is cosy for sure, as you're usually squashed right up against your neighbour or else balancing on a stool. Nobody ever complains though, because the food's so good.

Getting a seat in Joe's always means a wonderful meal, so Ollie and I go there whenever we have enough spare change in our pot. There's no choice on the menu; Joe serves whatever he's bought from the boats that day and the fish is so fresh it's practically swimming across the plate. Mussels, crabs and, I hate to say it, lobsters backstroke in garlic butter, which you can mop up with wads of freshly baked bread.

There's always a good atmosphere there, too. In the evenings it's dimly lit with candles rammed into wine bottles, the necks of which are stalactited with congealed wax. Conversation flows as readily as the Chianti and the air's so thick with the scent of garlic and fresh bread that you can more or less taste it.

So, as I say, usually I love eating in this place – but tonight is definitely not one of those times. Quite the opposite in fact. I'm so on edge I don't think I'll manage a mouthful.

Ollie's somehow wangled an extra two places, which makes the seating arrangements interesting to say the least. Ann and Geoff Burrows are on one side of the makeshift table, opposite Ollie and Nicky, with me perched at one end and my father at the other. As always the restaurant's packed and we're crammed together like proverbial sardines. Of my mother there's been absolutely no sign whatsoever, so I'm assuming that she's still in the pub – and I'm crossing everything that she stays there. So far all has gone smoothly enough, give or take a couple of dodgy moments (like when Dad and Nicky sneaked outside for a smoke), and now we're tucking into our moules starters while wine expert Geoff takes care of the booze.

"Ah, Châteauneuf-du-Pape 1996," he says, his eyes lighting up when the waiter proffers a dusty bottle. "That's a fine vintage, wouldn't you agree, Quentin?"

My father, utterly clueless, beams at him. "As long as it gets us all pissed it's good by me!"

Nicky snorts with laughter. He's been giggling a lot since he came back inside and his eyes keep crossing. I don't think Ann has noticed but Ollie and I, both well trained in Personal and Social Education, are on full alert. Honestly, I could throttle my father. Will he ever grow up?

Geoff pours the wine now and swirls it thoughtfully. Then, in practised style, he lowers his nose just above the rim of the glass and inhales deeply.

"Drink it, mate, don't snort it," Dad advises. "It's not cocaine! That's for later!"

Ann winces and Geoff splutters. I guess this isn't how their wine-tasting evenings usually go.

"Joke!" Dad says swiftly when he sees my expression. "That was a joke! I can't afford coke! That's a joke too by the way! Ha ha!"

But Nicky's the only person laughing. Ollie raises his eyes to the ceiling, Ann is grimacing and Geoff is back to the serious business of wine tasting.

"Hmm, a bouquet of marzipan and blackcurrant, topped with overtones of citrus and woodsmoke," he pronounces with a serious expression. "And maybe a note of seafood?"

Now, after five years with Ollie, I'm pretty used to Geoff and his wine snobbery; wine for Geoff is Very Serious Indeed. He can be a bit pompous but he means well and, as Ollie always says, at least whenever we spend Christmas in Surrey we're always guaranteed some good wine. My father, however, is more used to his lethal home-made nettle wine and finds this whole performance absolutely hilarious.

"Marzipan and woodsmoke!" he guffaws. "What on earth are you going on about, Geoff? It's just booze! Now let's get stuck in!"

And before Geoff can even draw breath, Dad reaches across and busies himself sloshing sixty-quid claret into everyone's glasses before raising his own.

"To the beautiful Ann!" he says, winking at her. "Sixty and still sexy! Woof woof!"

Oh God. He's hammered. I glance nervously across the table at Ann but luckily she seems thrilled with this toast; she's even blushing a little. I guess the people at her church don't generally call her sexy. It's also true to say that when Dad turns up the smooth talk and goes all twinkly-eyed he still has that magic which makes women of all ages go daft and giggly.

"Quentin, you're such a charmer," Ann says coyly, peeping up at him from under her lashes, Princess Diana style.

Charmer is not the word I'd use to describe my father. *Liability* would come closer. On the other hand, Dad's a great raconteur and people always enjoy his company – easy to do if you're not related to him – and as we eat he regales us with stories of his travels around Europe. I can hardly swallow a mouthful though. I'm way too terrified he's going to launch into tales of the naked goddess workshops. Pillar of the church Ann will have a pink fit, although Geoff will probably be off to Spain to join up before the main courses have even arrived! When Dad goes to show Ann his newest tattoo I nearly faint with fright. Thank goodness this one is on his arm...

Whatever I did in a past life to deserve this must have been really bad. I was probably Mussolini or something.

Ollie, who knows me so well and can interpret the *I'm having a great time* rigor mortis smile on my face, squeezes my hand under the table. "Relax, Katy. Mum and Dad are having fun, the food's great and even Nicky's taken the night off work for once. Your Dad's on form and they're having a really nice evening. Mum can have a sedate time tomorrow when we take her out for afternoon tea."

I nod, although I know full well that tomorrow afternoon will be far from sedate. Tomorrow's Ann's birthday and I've got my surprise gathering planned at the Tregowan Country Hotel, where Ollie thinks we're taking her for a cream tea. I'll make some excuse to join them later on, when really I'll be hiding with the guests, ready to wow Ann with the bespoke catering Tansy's so proud of. I can't say I ever imagined that cooking was Tansy's thing, but Nicky's been inundated with work so BBs must be pretty good. I can't help smiling to myself a little because Nicky's actually working tomorrow night and hasn't a clue he's booked for his own mother's do. I really do think this is utter genius on my part, even if I say so myself! I can't wait to see Ann's face when she sees him. She's going to be so proud.

"And as for that money," Ollie whispers, smoothing my hair away from my face and brushing a kiss across my cheek, "there's no issue with it, I promise. OK?"

"OK," I whisper back. And I totally believe him, of course I do. Everything is about to go back to normal. Better than normal, even. I just know it!

"And I know things have been weird but it's all going to be fine," Ollie adds. "It really is. You'll see."

And at this exact moment, as if just waiting for her cue to prove him totally wrong, my mother arrives. Or maybe I should more accurately say, my mother chooses to make her dramatic entrance. Long purple dress billowing and wild silver curls tumbling down her back, she wiggles her way through the restaurant, cannoning into tables and bumping into diners.

"Silla!" My father leaps up from his seat. "Where were you, babe? I was getting worried!"

"No you weren't," my mother replies, kissing him soundly on the lips and waggling her finger. "If you were, you'd have come and helped rescue me. I had to get some lovely fishermen to drag the van out of the lane with their forklift. It was wedged and they couldn't even get out until they helped!"

"And once you were out you went to the pub," I say. Oh dear. I sound a bit bitter.

Oh! Maybe it's because I am? Why does my mother always get herself into these scrapes? Why can't she just be normal and do embroidery and bake cakes and… and… well, all the stuff that I'm sure normal mothers do?

"Katy!" In a swirl of tasselled skirts, Mum turns to me. "Darling! There you are! Oh, baby girl, I am so, so proud of you! I always was of course, but I was always a little worried too. It's not natural for a young woman to be so uptight and so repressed, so afraid of her own divine femininity and sexuality. I couldn't work out where your father and I had gone wrong. The hours I've spent talking to my guides about you! Even they were at a loss."

I stare at her, lost for words.

"Then I read this and I knew all my worries had been in vain!" My mother reaches into her pocket and out of its depths comes a copy of a horribly familiar scarlet book, which she flourishes proudly. "Darling! I'm so happy! You're totally liberated and so, so at ease with your sexuality. You've written about things even your father and I haven't tried – but we will now!"

"I bought the clothes pegs," my father interrupts. "You just forgot the washing line and cabbages."

Geoff pales. "Never mind that. How about we have a look at the champagne?" He whips out the wine list and shoves it at his wife. "There was a particularly fine 1998 Taittinger on the list and I think we should splash out seeing as it's your special birthday!"

But Ann doesn't hear a word. She looks aghast.

"Isn't that the book everyone's talking about? The one our pastor said not to read?"

"Bet he checked it out first though, the old perv," grins Nicky. "Read all the rude bits just to see how bad they really were. At least, that's his story!"

"Don't be so disrespectful," snaps his mother. "The book is pure filth! It's the pathway to hell."

Oh Lord. She's not wrong there.

"Oh bollocks to all that nonsense!" scoffs my mother, flicking through the book. "It's earthy and sexy and shows a woman in firm control of her sexuality – and *my* little girl wrote it! I'm the proudest mother on earth. I'm telling everyone that Isara Lovett is my daughter!"

It's one of the most bitter ironies of my life that A-levels, an honours degree and even a respectable teaching career have never made my mother as proud as the antics of Alexi and Lucinda. I should have forgotten academia and written erotica years ago if I wanted her to sing my praises.

Ann's mouth is hanging open. A fork laden with mussels hovers between her chin and the plate, while sauce drips onto the table.

"Katy wrote that book?" she says at last.

Mum nods proudly. "She certainly did. I wish they hadn't bothered with the silly pen name though. Quentin and I have to convince everyone it really is our Katy."

Ann turns to Geoff. "Did you know about this?"

Her husband's Adam's apple bobs nervously. "Err... I might have heard about it."

"So how come I had no idea?"

"Because I did my best to keep it quiet," says Geoff miserably.

Ann is whiter than the table linen. "You lied to me?"

"I wouldn't say I lied exactly," replies poor Geoff. "I just hid anything that might link our son's girlfriend to the book and turned the telly off if there was a mention. I didn't want to upset you, love."

"Well, I'm certainly upset now," says Ann, folding her arms and fixing her husband with a steely look. "Who else knew? Quentin and Drusilla, clearly, and Katy of course, but did you, Oliver? Or you Nicolas?"

Her sons don't reply – which, of course, says it all.

This is probably *not* the time to tell Ann that her youngest son actually helped me write huge chunks of the book in question and edited my apparently clunky syntax. (Lisa Armstrong's raving about my *maturation* in narrative style, which is pretty galling.) When it comes to writing women's erotic fiction Nicky Burrows is a natural.

"I see. So you all knew and you chose to keep me in the dark," Ann says quietly. She turns to me. "Katy, whatever possessed you to write that dreadful book?"

I have the horrible sensation that all the blood's freezing in my body, and now the room's starting to whirl.

"I can explain! There was a really good reason and—" I begin, but my boyfriend's mother isn't in the mood to listen.

"I don't want to hear excuses, Katy! There's never an excuse for that kind of filth!"

I open my mouth to plead the lava-lamp explosion and our rewiring trauma, plus our leaky roof that needed fixing – but I shut it again very fast because I can see from her appalled expression that these reasons won't wash with Ann. Besides, I can appreciate that it's all come as a shock for her. *I'm* still shocked and I've been living with Isara Lovett for months.

"What will people think?" Ann is asking now, shaking her head. "And what about Ollie? Did you stop to consider what effect this could have on his career? I can only imagine how it will reflect on him."

I've thought of nothing else and I really can't feel much worse than I already do. Even the settled bills and the beautifully rewired and reroofed cottage don't help. If I could turn back time and never sign with Throb I would happily live with a huge overdraft, buckets of water everywhere and electrics that hiss and crackle whenever we throw a switch.

"I'm really sorry—" I try again to apologise but I'm interrupted by Ollie, who puts his arm around my shoulder and pulls me against him.

"Mum, I know you're upset but this is absolutely none of your business. My girlfriend's literary career," Ann winces at this but Ollie ignores her, "is nothing to do with anyone else but her. Katy's working very hard to succeed as an author and how she goes about that is her decision. She took a pen name and she did her very best to keep the book low-key. It's not her fault things have worked out this way. But do you know what?" He's looking at me now and his eyes are full of such kindness and love that I feel quite choked. "She did it all for us and our future. She carried a huge burden and never once complained or tried to dump it on me. I'm incredibly proud of her."

He is? I could fall off my seat with surprise. Ann looks stunned, Geoff's knocking back the wine in resignation and my parents are clapping.

"Is that true?" I whisper to Ollie. "Do you really mean that?"

He nods. "Of course I do. I've always been proud of you, Katy Carter. I'm so sorry if St Jude's has got in the way at times, and I'm even more sorry you didn't feel able to tell me about the book. I hate that you thought you couldn't share a part of your life with me. I'm sorry too if I've overreacted lately; I've just been a bit stressed, that's all."

"I didn't want to burden you with it. I'd messed up so badly and I really hoped I could sort things without having to worry you," I explain while Ollie shakes his head.

"But that's what I'm here for, you muppet! I never want you to feel you have to protect me from things. We're a team, aren't we?"

"Yes. Of course we are," I agree – because we always were, even back in the long-ago days when we were just colleagues bonding over our experiences with horrible bottom-set classes and disputes over who'd stolen the milk from the staffroom fridge. I'd always told Ollie everything back then and I suddenly realise how daft it is that now we're even closer I've been keeping things back.

"So if we're a team then we share things, good and bad. Right?" he asks.

"Right," I nod, and then I wait for him to tell me the real reason he raided the savings account and why he never told me he was meeting Carolyn that Saturday. But Ollie says nothing; he just kisses the top of my head and ruffles my curls, leaving me none the wiser about whatever's really going on.

Oh.

OK then. Just no more secrets on my side but he can keep his?

I bite back the questions queuing up on my lips. I can't ask them now, because Ann is saying sorry to me, Geoff's ordering more wine and Mum's swinging a crystal over Nicky and predicting his A-level grades (which, believe me, is something I can do without the help of the spirit world). Besides, I'm just making a fuss about nothing, aren't I?

The trouble is, I can't ignore the nagging unease deep in the pit of my stomach, and until I know for sure what Ollie's up to I don't think I'll have much peace. I know I should trust him, and I do. Most of the time. It's just that I have the strongest feeling he's still keeping something from me.

As Geoff pours me a big glass of wine and Ann apologises yet again for interfering in our business, I do my best to reassure her I'm not upset at all, that everything's fine and that my days of writing erotic novels are well and truly over. That isn't strictly true, of course, but I'm looking to find a way around all this – and I'm sure a solution will come to me at some point. At least I flipping well hope it will.

Otherwise I really will be in trouble.

Chapter 22

I have to talk to you right now! It's urgent! DO NOT IGNORE THIS TEXT!

When it comes to having a crisis, Maddy Lomax doesn't half pick her moments! This really isn't the best time, as I'm currently waiting in a darkened room with an assortment of Ann's relatives and oldest friends – all carefully selected by me and Maddy during the party-planning stages – and poised to cry "Surprise!" as soon as the birthday girl arrives. The balloons are all blown up, the banners are strung across the private dining room and even the weather has decided to play ball by allowing the sun to come out. Any minute now Ollie and his parents will arrive for what they think will be a quiet afternoon tea.

They couldn't be more wrong!

I'm so excited I can hardly wait! This is going to be a brilliant party! I've done my research into Ann's nearest and dearest and I've even managed to get hold of her pastor (fingers crossed he doesn't twig who I am) and a couple of very old relatives. I hope they manage to stay alive until Ann gets here. All the guests are staying at the hotel, courtesy of the dregs of my Throb advance, and judging by the bar bill they've been having a high old time. Isara Lovett will need another few outings just to settle that gin-and-tonic fuelled monster, never mind pay for Great Uncle Clifford's accidental watching of Playboy TV and absent-minded ordering of smoked salmon platters from room service at gone midnight. He might claim not to remember any of this and blame old age, but I'm not fooled. There was a knowing glint in his eye, and when I went to fetch him earlier he was scrolling happily through the pay-per-view screen like a pro. He's only just had a pacemaker fitted and I hope it's up to the job. At this rate I'm going to need one myself.

Lord. The sooner this weekend's over the better.

Still, picking up the tab for Ann's birthday is what I promised myself I'd do, and after the trauma of yesterday's revelation it feels even more important to show the Burrows family that I'm a nice person and not a total deviant. Although Ann has apologised for her shocked outburst yesterday, she's been eyeing me rather nervously ever since – and when I went to hang the washing out this morning she blanched at the mere sight of the peg bag. After this afternoon I'm hoping she'll see me in a whole new light, and by that I mean a flattering light rather than a red one. Maybe she'll begin to look on me as a suitable daughter-in-law.

It'll also show Ollie that I'm always thinking of him, even when it might not seem like it. At the moment he's a bit put out that I've made excuses for not being at afternoon tea. I know we promised each other that we'd have no more secrets between us – but surely a surprise party for his mum doesn't count? A surprise party has to be a secret, doesn't it? Otherwise it would just be a party. Anyway, when Ollie sees the look on Ann's face, he's going to be absolutely made up and he won't mind at all that I never told him what I was planning. Then he'll give his mum the necklace, I'll know that it really was for her all along, and everything will be fine.

Yes. That's exactly what's going to happen.

Everyone here is briefed and waiting excitedly for Ann to arrive. Even Great Uncle Clifford's managed to tear himself away from the satellite telly to join in with the surprise. The pastor has agreed to say grace once the food arrives and the hotel manager reassured me earlier that the caterers had arrived and would be getting ready in the cloakroom. I must admit that sounds a little bit odd, but I suppose they're putting on their pinnies and bow ties before they serve the food. And washing their hands or something? Of course, that must be it. Anyway, the food certainly smells good and my mouth's watering already from the delicious aromas wafting from the room next door where the buffet's been set up. For a woman who never eats, Tansy certainly knows what she's on about. No wonder she's booked solid.

Ding! Ding!

My phone again. Honestly! Mads should know better than to try to contact me now. She knows I'm lying low and can't talk. I'll have to put my phone onto silent or else she'll give the entire game away and ruin everything!

Ding! Ding!

Right. OK.

Ding! Ding!

OK, Maddy! I give in!

I'll check it.

DON'T IGNORE ME! STOP EVERYTHING! NOW!

Has nobody ever told Maddy that texting in capitals is considered aggressive? And anyway, what on earth does she mean, telling me to stop everything right now? Our plan's going perfectly and it's almost at completion. I'm not going to back out now. Why would I even want to?

Ding! Ding!

CALL ME! RED ALERT! ABORT MISSION! ABORT!

Mads really needs to kick her closet sci-fi addiction. She'll be asking me to beam up in a second. And what's all this "abort mission" gubbins? I'm in South East Cornwall, not outer space!

She does sound pretty frantic though. Maybe I ought to give her a call.

Perhaps Rafferty's stuffed another marble up his nose? Or Bluebell's high as a kite on forgetful sweets? Or, and this really would be a cause for alarm, Richard's found the hidden stash of wine bottles from Maddy's very unsuccessful Lent? My stomach lurches at this idea, because I'm bound to get the blame for leading her astray.

"Ooo! They're here!" cries Ollie's godmother, who insists on peeking around the edge of the drapes every five seconds. She thinks nobody can see her, but she's as wrong as anyone in a bright scarlet dress and orange feathered hat could ever be. She may as well be wearing a sign saying Ann Burrows' surprise party is in here! I've tugged her away so many times already that I think I've got RSI.

"Get back from the window, you silly old fool!" says Great Uncle Clifford, bundling her behind the curtains. "They're here! They're here! Shh!"

At this point everyone starts shushing one another, except that they're mostly octogenarians and their idea of shushing sounds like a 747 taking off. I'm so busy trying to keep them quiet that I don't have any time to reply to Maddy's texts or to even look at my phone again.

We hear the murmur of voices as Ollie and his parents pass by the window and head towards the reception. I'm so excited I think I'm going to pop. Any minute now Ann is going to have the surprise of her life! The hotel manager's primed to lead them from the lobby through to this room, under the guise of escorting them to afternoon tea. As soon as they open the door we're all going to shout "Surprise!" and fire party poppers and wave balloons. Then the caterers will come in from the far end of the room with a big cake and champagne while Happy Birthday to You plays – after which the party will really get started.

It's going to be brilliant!

Whatever it is that Mads is stressing about will have to wait.

Footsteps are drawing closer to our hiding place and everyone holds their breath. It's so quiet now that I can practically hear Great Uncle Clifford's pacemaker tick.

"And the view from the blue drawing room has to be one of the finest," we hear the hotel manager telling the unsuspecting Burrows family. "You can see almost to Lizard Point."

"It sounds perfect," Ann is replying. "Afternoon tea with a sea view. I can't think of anything better."

No, but luckily for her, I could. Come on! Open the door! I'm going to burst!

Then the handle turns, the door opens and up we all jump, shouting "Surprise!" and "Happy birthday!" while the lights turn on, party poppers explode like gunfire and everyone starts singing. My phone's ringing now, Mads again probably, but I'm far too busy joining in the general excitement to answer it.

Ann's hand flies to her mouth as she gazes around in astonishment at all her nearest and dearest. "What on earth's this? How come all of you are here?"

Before I have a chance to answer, Great Uncle Clifford toots loudly on a party blower and then coughs so violently that the next few seconds are spent slapping him on the back and panicking that he's about to expire.

"It's your birthday party!" he gasps eventually. "It's a surprise!"

"Surprise!" echo the others, dutifully blowing their party trumpets and waving their balloons before stampeding towards Ann, who promptly vanishes into a tangle of hugs, walking frames and streamers.

Ah. Isn't this brilliant? All her favourite people are gathered here and she must feel so loved. Job done, I'd say. Maybe I ought to give up writing and take up party planning instead? I bet I'd be really good at it! I could do all sorts of themes and learn to make amazing cakes and everyone would book me and maybe I could even get to go on Bake Off and meet Mary Berry and everything…

"Katy?" Ollie's voice breaks into a wonderful daydream where Paul Hollywood is gazing into my eyes and telling me that my vanilla sponge is the most delicious thing he's ever tasted. Taking my hand, Ollie draws me away from the others. "Did you organise all this for Mum?"

"I had a bit of help from Mads," I say modestly and I glance down at my phone. Goodness, four missed calls now. She must really want to talk to me. I'll ring her back as soon as the cake's arrived.

Ollie shakes his head in disbelief. "You've managed to find Mum's relatives and some of her oldest friends and a few church people, get them to Cornwall, arrange a party and keep it a secret?"

Put like that it does sound like some feat and I'm quite impressed myself.

"I couldn't have done it without Maddy. She made the arrangements while I was away."

"But it must have cost a fortune," Ollie says, looking around the room. "There are at least fifteen people here and you've paid for them all? You did all this for my mum?"

I shake my head. "No. I did it for you, Ol. I felt awful about just how much money I cost us with the rewiring and the floor, and I knew how much you'd wanted to do something special for Ann's birthday. Then I had the advance from Throb and I realised that there was something good I could do with it. It seemed like a way of making up for all the trouble."

"You've paid for Mum's party with money from Kitchen of Correction? All these good upright citizens are partying thanks to cabbages and clothes pegs and kinky sex?"

Ann's pastor and his wife wave at us and we wave back.

"Oops," I say, and Ollie laughs.

"You are crackers, Katy," he says, putting his arms around me and kissing the tip of my nose. "You don't ever need to make up for things. That isn't how it works. And anyway, the floor and the wiring were accidents. You weren't to blame."

It's kind of Ollie to say this but it's hard to see how my pulling up the floor can be construed as an accident. I mean, it wasn't as though I accidentally grabbed the poker and inadvertently prised up the floorboards, is it? And who plugged in the lava lamp? And went snooping around St Jude's in disguise? I actually think it's just as well he doesn't know quite how much making up I do have to do.

"I'm sorry I kept this party a secret," I say, "especially after what we talked about yesterday. But I kind of had to really, otherwise it wouldn't have been much of a surprise, would it?"

He laughs. "I guess not."

"And you were surprised, weren't you?"

"Not a day passes when you don't surprise me," Ollie replies with feeling.

Hmm, I'm not totally convinced that's a good thing. He might be smiling now but I've seen how stressed he's been lately.

"I know I don't always make life easy for you," I say, "but I always try to do my best."

"I'll make sure I remember that the next time," Ollie tells me.

"O ye of little faith," I tease, going onto tiptoes and kissing him.

Anyway, secret or not, this party's turning out to be a huge success. Ann is beaming from ear to ear while she chats to her guests, the old folk are having a lovely time and even Geoff's having fun without the help of a fine Merlot. There are just two things missing: Nicky and birthday cake. But they'll both be arriving together, of course. Just wait until Ann sees Nicky in his working capacity. She's going to be so surprised! And she'll love the cake. I chose it especially.

Leaving Ollie chatting to a couple of elderly aunts, both of whom are pinching his cheeks and telling him how much he's grown, I make my way to the back of the function room and knock loudly on the door – the cue that Mads and I arranged for the grand entrance of the cake. No sooner have my knuckles rapped on the oak than the strains of Happy Birthday to You strike up.

At least, I think that's Happy Birthday they're playing? It's saxophone music and it sounds a bit odd, kind of slow and exaggerated and... well, a bit more sexy than I was expecting.

My phone vibrates again.

I'M ON MY WAY! STOP THE CAKE!

But Maddy's warning comes too late, because at this point in the proceedings the door flies open and the cake appears in the doorway – the big pink cake with the beautiful white rose icing and trailing ribbons that I know gardener Ann will really love. Right now, she should be staring at it in wonder and gasping with joy.

Yes, that's what she should be doing, but unfortunately Ann isn't gasping with joy: she's gasping with shock.

I know exactly how she feels because I'm in shock too.

What?

WHAT?

I blink in astonishment and rub my eyes just in case I'm having a very weird and rather worrying delusion, but no such luck. I'm wide awake and I really am watching the scene unravel like a slow-motion car crash.

Carrying the cake aloft in his muscular, baby-oiled arms is a young man, groomed, waxed, fake-tanned and plucked to perfection – and wearing little more than a grin and a teeny-weeny apron the size of one of Barbie's tissues. It's not protecting a great deal of his modesty, and his bronzed buttocks are very much on show.

No wonder Maddy was frantic.

But my horrific blunder is a million, gazillion times worse than merely hiring a nearly naked young man to deliver a cake to my churchgoing would-be mother-in-law…

The "waiter" strutting across the room and shaking his naked butt in time to the music is none other than the horrified birthday girl's adored youngest son.

Chapter 23

SOUTHWEST TIMES

Topham's Top Totty!

Tansy delivers the male!

BARELY BUTLERS is the South West's newest and hottest catering company, specialising in hen parties, birthdays, divorce parties and girls' nights. Delicious as the selection of food is, the semi-naked butlers serving it are even more tasty. The boys serve food, mix cocktails, play party games and, most of all, look gorgeous. And they'll even clean up.

"Fit, nearly naked guys who do the washing up! What more could a girl want?" giggles BBs' new owner Tansy Topham, wife of England star striker Tommy.

"I went to a hen do a while back and I liked what I saw so much I bought the company. Just a few little tweaks and a few less clothes and Barely was born!" she adds with a cheeky wink. "It's every woman's dream to have a gorgeous guy as her slave – just like in my books – and this way it can come true. For a few hours anyway!"

Tansy is clearly far more than just a WAG, fashion designer and bestselling writer. Her new catering company has taken the South West by storm and is due to expand nationwide by the autumn.

I actually don't think I can read any more of the article Mads thrust at me when, two minutes after the cake arrived, she came charging into the function room, red in the face and panting like something out of a Throb novel.

"I was just sitting in the kitchen flicking through the local rag and I saw this! You've got to stop everything now!" she'd gasped, brandishing the paper under my nose. "You can't let Ann see – oh!"

She'd suddenly looked around, clocked the stony faces of all the guests and spotted Nicky.

"Bollocks. I'm too late aren't I?"

She certainly was too late. By now Ann was having hysterics, the pastor looked as though he was about to faint, Nicky's cheeks were scarlet with embarrassment (all four of them) and poor Ollie was hastily yanking a curtain down and swaddling his brother in Laura Ashley's finest.

"Stop making a fuss!" Nicky had protested. "It's just a bit of fun."

"Not to me!" Ann had wailed. "I don't think seeing my youngest son naked and oiled up like a stripper is fun!"

"Well, of course not," Nicky had said kindly. "That would just be weird. But seriously, Ma, just chill, yeah? It's all perfectly fine. I just serve a few canapés, chat to ladies and get paid. It's easy."

"It's practically prostitution!" his mother had shrieked.

Nicky had rolled his eyes. "Of course it isn't. The ladies never pay me for the sex. Only kidding! That was a joke!"

"Your jokes aren't helping your mother," Geoff had hissed. "What the hell were you thinking?"

"That I could put some money away for uni and fund my gap year," Nicky had explained. "I've saved a fortune, Dad. You should be congratulating me. 'Take responsibility for yourself for once'; that was what you told me when I was kicked out of school. So I did. I did this because of what *you* said to me. This was really your idea and if you don't like it you've only got yourself to blame. 'Why not seek a little enterprise within a free market economy rather than becoming a left-wing scrounger on benefits' was what you said, wasn't it? I'm confused actually, Pa. I'd have thought you'd be all for this?"

Geoff's mouth had opened and closed at this. He'd been completely lost for words, and I'd looked at Nicky with new respect. He was going to be one very scary politician someday.

"What were you thinking booking a naked butler for Mum?" Ollie had asked me in bewilderment.

"I had no idea the waiters were naked. I just booked Tansy's company," I'd said.

Ollie had groaned in response. "Please tell me that Tansy Topham's not about to rock up too? The church folk will have a fit. You do know she was naked in the papers again this week?"

I hadn't been aware of that, but it was nothing unusual. I'd have thought it would make more headlines if Tansy kept her clothes *on*.

"I didn't know *this* was what Tansy was up to! Of course I didn't!" I'd protested. "I just thought she had a catering company and that it would be another surprise for your mum!"

"Well, you've certainly achieved that," Ollie had remarked grimly. "Although I'd say it was more of a shock than a surprise."

"I did try to warn you, Katy," Mads had piped up. "Why didn't you answer the phone?"

Believe me, not answering her calls is now one of the greatest regrets of my life, along with not writing books about boy wizards and never growing above five feet three.

"Anyway," she'd continued, "I'm here now and I've told you!"

"It's a bit late in the day. I think the damage is done," Ollie had said.

"Shall I go and say sorry to Ann again?" I'd wondered, but my boyfriend had shaken his head.

"Give my mother a bit of space. I think she and Nicky need to have a chat."

"I think we *all* need a chat with Nicky," I'd said darkly. And once it's my turn, that chat will be swiftly followed by me throttling the little git.

Bloody Tansy and her bright ideas. Did it never occur to her to explain just what kind of catering her new company did? It might have been nice to have known that I'd booked a semi-naked butler to serve my boyfriend's mother her birthday cake. And even worse than that, one that just so happened to be her own son.

Anyhow, as I sit in the foyer now, staring miserably at the newspaper article while the fallout continues next door, my stomach twists with mortification. If I live to be a hundred I don't think I'll get over the shock of seeing Nicky strut in with the cake held aloft and wearing a loincloth so small that it was practically microscopic. And I don't think Ann is going to get over the shock any time soon either. When I last saw her she was knocking back brandy like it was going out of fashion, while Geoff yelled at Nicky and Ollie tried to smooth things over. I don't suppose any of them will ever talk to me again, and I don't blame them either.

I don't even want to talk to me ever again.

I put my head in my hands and groan. Why oh why oh why oh *why* didn't I think to ask Tansy what kind of catering her new company actually did? I've known her long enough to realise what a loose cannon she is and that she's the least likely person to be interested in cooking. Tansy never ingests anything apart from salad leaves and champagne, so of course this was never going to be about food – just like her novels were never really about the finest points of the English language, and her fashion designs aren't really about fabric, and her advice column isn't really about… Anyway, you probably get the picture. The point is that if I'd actually *thought* about it of course I would have started to wonder. But my head was so full of secret books and lobsters and Ollie's possible affair that Tansy's credibility as Plymouth's answer to Mary Berry barely figured.

Barely figured. Oh God.

Barely.

Bare. Butlers. Buttocks on view, and not just any old buttocks either. No. Nicky's buttocks. The same Nicky who is living under my roof, attending my school and who is supposedly in my care. Should I expect social services to rock up soon?

"Someone just shoot me now," I groan.

"It's not your fault," says Maddy, for what has to be the thousandth time in the past twenty minutes. "How were you to know? We'd have to have had very strange minds indeed to have even suspected this was what Nicky was up to. You must admit though, he has been very enterprising."

"By taking his clothes off?"

"Oh stop being so melodramatic! He was still dressed."

"I hardly think a pinny covering his crotch and a bow tie count as *dressed*, Maddy!"

She shrugs. "I can't see it as a problem. It's all totally above board. BBs have a strictly no-touching policy and everything. I read it on the website and Tansy promises me it's all very innocent. We could book them for Holly's hen night."

"Tell me you're joking?" I say. Then, as a thought occurs to me, I add, "Hang on. You've talked to Tansy?"

She nods. "I called the company on the way over and told them it was an utter emergency that I spoke to the director. Tansy's on her way at this very moment to put matters right."

Can things get any worse? All I need right now is Tansy rocking up in a pelmet skirt and with her latest boob job on full display. If Uncle Clifford sees her he'll pop for sure. And he's not the only one.

"You do know that Ann's pastor is in there? What on earth will he make of a glamour model appearing on the scene?"

"He'll probably be thrilled. Vicars *are* human you know," Maddy huffs.

You wouldn't think so if you met Richard. Still, I keep quiet. Today is not the day to fall out over my best friend's choice of husband.

"Anyway," she continues, "Tansy's really upset and she wants to sort things out. You know how helpful she can be."

I certainly do. I've had the makeover to prove it, so I think I can be forgiven for not jumping for joy.

I'm frantically trying to figure out how I can stop Tansy from making a bad situation even worse – something that a few moments previously I would have said was totally impossible – when in she skips in sky-high Louboutins and swinging the latest LV handbag from her acrylic-tipped fingers. The rest of today's outfit consists of leather trousers so tight I wince just to look at them and a tiny pink crop top with *BOY TOY!* emblazoned across her chest. At least I think it's her chest under there, although it could be the Mitchell brothers held in captivity and spray-tanned orange. A new set of blonde extensions tumbles down to her minuscule waist, and when she turns to smile at me I'm almost dazzled by the glare from her teeth.

"New veneers," Tansy explains, seeing my face. "Toilet-bowl white, yeah? Tommy says all I need is Armitage Shanks written across them, the cheeky git! Anyway, like I told him, it's the latest look. Flipping agony but all the other girls have got them and you know how it is."

Actually I don't, but it's nice she thinks I might.

"Anyway, babes," Tansy continues, "never mind my teeth. Maddy's told me what's happened and I am beyond shocked. Why didn't you tell me you wanted to book a naked butler? I'd have given you a discount."

"I didn't want to book a naked butler!" I wail. "And I didn't want a discount."

"Eh?" Tansy's forehead would crinkle at this point if it could.

"I didn't want you to feel obliged to take money off. Not when you're building the business," I explain, and she shakes her head despairingly.

"Babes, you are such a muppet. I love giving discounts to my friends; it's part of the fun. Anyway, I'm just about to franchise the lot out and Tommy's been offered to Chelsea for the next transfer window," she says. "I think I can afford to give you a freebie. Besides, who doesn't love a bargain? I could have even thrown in Shane. He's my hottest butler and a dead ringer for a young Brad Pitt. There's no way we'd have sent Nicky down if I'd known this was your booking. Obs!"

"Katy thought BBs did normal catering," Maddy explains. "Neither of us had a clue the waiters were starkers."

"So what exactly did you think *BB* stood for?" Tansy asks me.

"To be honest I hadn't even thought about it. I'd just thought it was a random name," I reply. I must admit this does sound a bit pathetic now.

"Didn't you look at the website? Or ask the staff when you called?" Her eyes are wide. The unspoken question hangs in the air like the patterns of fireworks in a night sky. *Are you really that stupid?*

"I booked this while Katy was away in the States," Maddy confesses. "I was in the middle of trying to stop Rafferty from putting the hamster in the loo at the time, so chatting wasn't high on my list of priorities. To tell you the truth, I was hardly listening to anything."

Those twins are seriously psychotic, the Reggie and Ronnie of the local playgroup, but Tansy's nodding as though this is all entirely normal.

"Shanissa was just the same when she was three. She was obsessed with the khazi. Tommy lost two Rolexes. What happened?"

"It was a close call: Bluebell was about to flush. Honestly, since we went to Center Parcs the twins have been obsessed with flumes. They thought this would be fun for Fluffy."

"Shanissa and Chicago tried to do exactly the same with the gerbil," Tansy nods sympathetically. "Or maybe it was the cat? I'd have to ask the nanny. Tom and I were in Marbs at the time. And don't get me started on the bloody micropig!"

It's looking as though the tales of pet woe might go on and on and on, but luckily Tansy's Swarovski crystal-smothered mobile rings before I have a chance to call the RSPCA. Much smacking of kisses and cries of "Thanks, babes! Love you!" and "You're the best!" later, she ends the call, shoves the phone in her huge bag and beams at me.

"So, Katy had no idea about any of this, it's all a big mistake and we need to make it up to her ma-in-law. Fear not, girls! *Tell it like it is Tansy* is on the case!"

And before I can stop her, she's marching into the function room like an orange-hued, designer-bag-clutching whirlwind. Maddy and I are hard on her heels, but we haven't got a hope. All those hours in the gym haven't been wasted on Tansy; she's across the room in seconds to where Ann is being comforted by her pastor, Geoff is lecturing a mutinous Nicky and poor despairing Ollie is doing his best to mediate. The other guests are plundering the buffet, hacking slices out of the cake and trying to pretend they're not enjoying every dramatic second. This is the most exciting thing that's happened to them since VE Day.

"Mrs Burrows?" Tansy says, holding her hand out to Ann. "May I wish you a very happy birthday?"

She grabs Ann's hand, pumping it up and down with great enthusiasm and chatting away. There's no need for Tansy to introduce herself because anyone who hasn't been living on the moon for the past few years knows exactly who she is. Stunned, Ann and Geoff and their pastor allow their hands to be shaken. Even Great Uncle Clifford reappears, happy to abandon Playboy TV in order to meet the real thing.

"Now, I know today has been a shock," Tansy continues, tossing back her long tresses and batting her false eyelashes at them, "but I really feel I need to explain a few things."

Ollie catches my eye. *Make her stop!* he mouths silently.

I can't, I mouth back. And I'm not exaggerating: Tansy's a force of nature when she gets going, and nothing I could do or say would stop her. I'd have more luck holding back the Severn Bore.

"First of all, Katy had no idea that BBs actually stood for Barely Butlers," Tansy explains, setting herself down on a seat next to Ann. "She really thought I was just serving up canapés and sandwiches. Can you imagine? It's as though all the hours I put into choosing the hottest guys were for nothing! As if! Those interviews were hell, especially the bits when I had to feel their biceps and check out the six-packs."

Oh God. Kill me now.

"So don't be angry with poor Katy, Mrs Burrows! She really wanted to give you a lovely birthday surprise." Tansy flashes the speechless Ann with that dazzling white smile. "She wouldn't even let me give her a discount. She insisted on paying full price. That's how much she thinks of you."

"Blimey," says Nicky, laid out on a sofa and still swaddled in the curtain like a paisley-covered baby Jesus. "You must have spent a fortune, Katy."

"We're very reasonable at BBs actually," Tansy says quickly. "Cheaper than many other companies, and we're available at short notice too. Here, why don't some of you take my card. You never know when you might need us."

She delves into her bag and hands out business cards, which everyone takes dutifully. I can't quite imagine when an octogenarian churchgoer or a pastor might need a naked butler, but I guess you never know. Let's face it, I never thought I'd be booking one either.

"And as for Nicky here," Tansy continues, waving her French-manicured acrylics in his direction, "you really should be proud of him. He has an excellent work ethic."

Ann looks taken aback, which isn't surprising given that the words *work ethic* and *Nicky Burrows* aren't usually found in close proximity. *Idle* and *waster* maybe, but *work ethic*? Never.

"I fail to see how mincing around starkers in a pinny constitutes hard work," huffs Geoff.

"Ah, and that's the final piece of the puzzle," Tansy tells him, leaning forward and revealing a Cheddar Gorge cleavage, seemingly by accident. The poor men in the room don't stand a chance and even the women are mesmerised. Isaac Newton, were he present, might need to rethink the laws of gravity.

"Serving the food and wearing our uniform are the least of the job. Working for BBs is about so much more than that," she explains earnestly. "Nicky has to be on time, talk to clients, sell our brand, make sure he looks after himself, and represent the company to the best of his ability. It's a huge responsibility."

"So it's not just strutting about in the nuddy and being accosted by ladies?" asks Great Uncle Clifford, sounding disappointed. Good Lord, was he about to sign up too?

Tansy looks shocked. "Absolutely not! This is about brand identity and light-hearted fun. It's a way that women can escape from the daily grind of their lives and the reality of being wives and mums, a way for them to forget their age and relive the dreams they once had of being adored and waited on by a handsome prince. It's escapism, pure and simple – no different in essence to reading a Mills and Boon or watching *Gone with the Wind*. What woman doesn't dream of being the sole object of a gorgeous young man's attention, even just for one night? Barely Butlers can deliver that dream for anyone!"

Wow. She's good, and so is whoever wrote that spiel for her. All the women in the room are nodding now, even Ann and the pastor's wife, and the ancient old aunts have gone all misty-eyed too. I'm not convinced myself that the handsome prince needs to have his bum cheeks on display, but maybe I'm just old-fashioned like that?

"Nicky's hard work and dedication have helped many women to enjoy that little escape. It's practically a social service," Tansy concludes, smiling warmly at her curtain-shrouded employee. "He's by far our most booked butler; in fact he's earned himself over ten grand already."

"Bloody hell!" splutters Geoff. "Ten grand?"

"Where do I sign up?" Ollie murmurs to me.

"All to help towards my uni course and to further my education, of course. It's far too much of a financial burden to place my parents under, thanks to successive Tory governments, and I wanted to help you," Nicky says sanctimoniously.

I'm not sure this argument would stand up on *Question Time*, but Geoff looks convinced – and is that a proud tear I see Ann wiping away?

"And nothing at all went on his flash scooter or new clothes or the gap-year fund," Ollie says sotto voce, but his parents pay no attention to this. Neither do they seem to think it odd that their left-wing son has suddenly embraced capitalism (well, except for the jibe at the Tories, which apparently went unnoticed). Instead they appear to be having a change of heart, especially when Nicky mentions that he wants to set up an ISA. Suddenly it's like the second coming and I can practically see his halo. Who cares what he was up to anymore? He was making money! Nicky Burrows is a capitalist and no longer a commie! Their prayers have been answered and all is well for the Surrey contingent!

Ann smiles fondly at him. "Darling, I do understand what you were trying to do and I'm proud you've worked so hard towards your future, even if it was in a rather misguided way."

Ollie snorts. "Chatting up girls and waxing his chest is hardly work!"

But Ann and Geoff aren't listening to Ollie. Geoff's still hanging off Tansy's every word – the conversation having turned to football – and Ann is busy ruffling Nicky's hair and telling him again how proud she is.

"I'm sorry if I embarrassed you, Mum," Nicky says sweetly.

"I still don't think it's appropriate, sweetie, and I'd like it to stop so that you can concentrate on your exams," she replies.

"Of course, Mum," Nicky agrees, all big-eyed and innocent. "My exams must come first. I've been doing well at school though; just ask Katy and Ol."

It's true. Nobody's nagged me about Nicky for weeks. Even Steph hasn't mentioned him. At least something is going right. Then again, maybe they think he's left because he's never there? I make a mental note to ring the attendance secretary first thing on Monday.

"Really well," I say to Ann, crossing my fingers and praying hard. "And I'm so sorry about all this. I really had no idea."

Ann gets up and gives me a hug. "I know you didn't, love. It'll be a story to tell the girls in the WI, I suppose."

"And the moral of the story is that your sins will always find you out," adds her pastor, shooting a suspicious look at Nicky.

"Anyway, I hope that's everything about BBs cleared up now?" Tansy asks, smiling beatifically at her gathered audience. "And before I go, I have a little something for you all with my compliments."

"Is it a free butler?" asks one of the great aunts hopefully.

Tansy laughs. "Far better than that! My Tommy's sending every one of you free tickets to the next England game. You'll all be in the corporate suite with champagne on tap, and afterwards we'll have dinner. You can even meet the team if you like?"

Geoff's eyes light up and I admire Tansy's master stroke. Even the pastor looks thrilled and the old aunts are fondly remembering 1966, while Great Uncle Clifford is getting excited about meeting Posh Spice. I won't mention that Stanley Matthews isn't around anymore or that Victoria Beckham is now a fashion designer; they've had enough shocks for one afternoon.

And just like that, all is immediately forgiven. Ann is even laughing about the horror of seeing her son in a thong, as though it was all just a bit of fun and she wasn't ready to have me tarred and feathered fifteen minutes previously.

"Happy with that?" Tansy asks me, once she's kissed everyone goodbye, signed autographs and posed for pictures. She's also paid for a crate of champagne, so the party's in full swing now – minus a butler, of course. Nicky isn't daft enough to push his luck that far. He's changed back into jeans and handed Tansy his uniform. His bare-butlering days are well and truly over.

"I think 'relieved' comes closer to how I feel than 'happy'," I reply as we air-kiss goodbye.

Ollie puts his hand on my shoulder and together we watch Tansy drive away, top down on the Lotus and blonde hair flying in the wind.

"I have no idea what just went on in there," he says, kissing the top of my head, "but I think we can safely say you've given my mother a party she'll remember for the rest of her life. Now, do you think that from now on in we can have a quiet life?"

I kiss him back and cross my fingers.

"Of course," I say.

And we can, I know it. A quiet life is just around the corner. There's just the small matter of two racy books to deal with first…

Chapter 24

Unfortunately, the corner my quiet life's hiding behind doesn't appear to be close by, and as the weeks pass I begin to worry I may not be approaching it any time soon, if ever. My parents have trundled back to Totnes, the Burrows have returned to Surrey, Ollie's flat out at school as always and even Nicky's allegedly burying himself in revision rather than taking his clothes off – but that's as far as it goes for supposed normality.

I guess nothing in life's normal when suddenly you're the author of a book the media's chosen to hype as the latest big thing. Everyone wants a slice of Isara Lovett and everywhere I go, from the supermarket to the village shop, *Kitchen of Correction* is stacked in tottering piles. My hand aches from squiggling my name across countless copies and if I never do another book signing again it will be too soon. Life has really taken on a bit of a surreal tint since the trip to New York. All the publicity generated there, plus the public's bizarre obsession with Guy as the latest reality-TV star, means that rather than fading into total obscurity as it utterly deserves, my debut novel with Throb is riding high in the charts and selling ridiculously well.

It's a dream come true that's turned out to be something of a nightmare.

There's no way I can get out of writing the next two books now; it seems that people can't get enough of Alexi and Lucinda's culinary capers. I even read somewhere that there's been a rush on clothes pegs and that the price of cabbages has rocketed – which might be good news for farmers but is probably very bad news for the NHS if the tabloids are to be believed.

"You should be thrilled," Holly says when I complain to her during some sisterly bonding in the pub. "This is what you've always wanted. Guy, on the other hand, just wants to go to sea. He's really fed up with all the attention. He's turned down more television work today but everyone wants him. Strange but true, eh?"

Guy, who's wearing dark glasses and a baseball cap, cowers behind his pint and nods miserably.

"They won't bloody leave me alone. All I want to do is go fishing. I've done my bit for publicising the industry. Why can't they all sod off?"

"Because it doesn't work like that," says Holly. "Chin up, baby. You've done wonders for the fishing industry and I bet there's lots of very grateful lobsters too."

She's right. For the past few weeks Guy's been everywhere talking about the plight of British fishermen and sustainable fisheries. The last I heard,

UKIP were trying to persuade him to stand as an MP and *Loose Women* were desperate to have him on the show.

"All because of a bloody lobster," he mutters, giving me an accusing look. "This is all your fault, Katy."

"What isn't?" I wonder sadly. Ann's nearly ruined party, Ollie's stress at school, Nicky's stint as a naked butler – all these things seem to be bouncing back at me like emails from a faulty address.

"Those TV harrises keep calling the house and trying to get me to sign stuff too," Guy adds despairingly. "The words are far too long and I can't be arsed to read any of it. I wish they'd just go away. Maybe they would if I signed?"

"No! Don't sign anything!" Holly and I chorus.

"Of course I won't!" Guy rolls his eyes. "That was a joke. *I'm* not that stupid."

They both look at me pointedly and I sigh.

"OK. I get it. I'm an idiot and I should never have signed the contract without looking at it properly. Nobody knows that better than me."

"Bit late now though," says Holly. "Seriously, Katy, what are you going to do?"

I stare dejectedly into my cider because I cannot for the life of me think how I can get out of writing two more books. Holly's right: this was what I always dreamed of but, like some fairy tale where the heroine gets granted her dearest wish only to learn that it isn't really what she wanted after all, life as a bestselling novelist isn't turning out quite as I'd imagined. I always thought I'd want to sing my success from the rooftops, but apart from the fact that *Kitchen* isn't in the genre I want to write, I also have Ollie to think about. The more publicity *Kitchen* receives, the harder a time he has at work. It's a nightmare for him.

Oh God. I'm going to have to tell him I'm writing two more, aren't I? There's no way I can keep that a secret. No way at all. But it's going to make his life impossible at St Jude's. What if he decides he wants to break up with me because of this? He's been so quiet and distracted lately that I've no idea what he's thinking. He's keeping something from me too, I'm certain of it, but I've no idea what.

And, a nasty little voice reminds me, I never did see him give Ann that necklace…

I gulp a big mouthful of my drink. I am so *not* going down that road right now. I have quite enough to deal with as it is. Besides, if Ol's being quiet then it's because he's having such a tough time at work; of course it's that and nothing more sinister. There have been lots of hushed calls, late meetings and discussions with senior management as St Jude's do their best to field any awkward questions from parents. I know it sounds bonkers and medieval, and quite frankly what his girlfriend does in the twenty-first century is nothing whatsoever to do with Ollie, but unfortunately the school doesn't see it that way. I'm half expecting the Inquisition to knock on my front door at any moment and drag me away for a spot of torture followed by a nice big bonfire.

In any case, the fact of the matter is that there's no hiding my identity now and definitely no way I can get out of the contract. In desperation I even faxed a copy to Frankie and Gabriel's scary agent Seb, just in case he could find a loophole, but no joy.

"Next time do yourself a favour and get an agent before you sign anything," was his (too late) advice. "There's no way I can get you out of this. You'll just have to grit your teeth, do the promo, write the next two books and hire me in the future."

The irony is that if the royalties keep rolling in like they are at the moment then I can probably afford to hire Seb. Like Holly said, I really should be thrilled; even though my percentage of the total profit is tiny, our bank balance is looking the healthiest it's ever been, and my need to dig up floors in search of treasure is a thing of the past. I don't even need to moonlight as a supply teacher at Tregowan Comp anymore, but do you know what?

I wish I did.

I'm missing the way things used to be. I miss having to come up with creative ways to find money and being delighted by a jumble-sale find. I miss chatting to Steph in the staffroom and always having to think on my feet to be one step ahead of my students, and I definitely miss school macaroni cheese. But most of all I miss the way Ollie and I used to be, because we were a team pulling together and we told each other everything. We never had any secrets – apart from my odd splurge with Visa and Barclaycard, although those never really counted – and we were the best of friends even if we had to eat beans on toast and lie awake listening to the *drip drip drip* of water plopping into buckets while we figured out a way we could afford to fix the roof. If only I'd known then just how happy I was. I wish so much I'd appreciated it more and hadn't taken things for granted.

My eyes fill because there's no way a full bank account makes up for the strained atmosphere in the house or the silences that stretch between me and Ollie recently. If Seb can't rescue me, nobody can. I'm going to have to write those bloody books – and keep even more secrets, or else Ollie's career is finished.

There has to be a way out of it all, surely? Or a solution? I just haven't figured it out yet, that's all.

"Shall I tell you what I think?" Guy asks, pushing his shades onto his forehead and giving me a very serious look.

"About what?" I ask nervously. Guy's opinions (although very entertaining on the telly) aren't for the faint-hearted, and I could really do without a lecture on why Cornwall should be independent.

"About what you should do," Guy says. He picks up Holly's hand in his big paw and squeezes it. "I think it's time you just told Ollie everything. Just like I tell my missus everything. Like how much fish I catch, how many pints I've had, when that blonde in Newlyn gave me her phone number—"

"Actually you didn't tell me that." Holly pulls her hand away and glares at him.

"Bollocks," says Guy. "Well, I meant to, baby. Must have slipped my mind. The point is I was going to tell you all about it. She was a right minger anyway."

"So that's all right then?" My sister gives him a look that could freeze lava, and poor Guy slides his glasses down again. "I'm the mother of your unborn child and there you are chatting up other women?"

"I never chatted her up! She wouldn't leave me alone! I don't even know what I did with her twatting number anyway!"

"So you took it then? How typical!" Holly huffs and off they go as usual, bickering and hurling insults at one another while the rest of the pub try to pretend World War Three isn't breaking out over here by the window.

"Err, I hate to interrupt your row," I interject, "but you were saying, Guy? About what I should tell Ollie?"

Guy pauses, mid flow. "What? Oh yeah! I was saying you should tell him the truth."

I stare at him. Just how much has Guy had to drink? Or has all the fame turned his brains to mush?

"The truth?"

"Yeah, you know. It means that you tell somebody what's really happening and don't hold anything back," says Holly. "Unlike Guy here, who conveniently forgets to tell me that random women give him their phone numbers."

"That's fame for you," Guy shrugs. "Bet Frankie gets it all the time."

"Not from women," says my sister sharply. To me she adds, "But actually, Guy's right for once. Just tell Ollie everything about the Throb contract. Tell him that you made a mistake, how worried you are and how hard you've tried to get out of it."

My stomach's knotting like one of Guy's fishing nets just at the thought.

"But things are bad enough as they are. If Ollie thinks there are two more books he'll be horrified!"

"He'll be even more horrified if he finds out once it's too late to make any plans to deal with the fallout," Holly points out. "And it's not good to keep secrets from people you love, is it Guy?"

"Ouch! My ankle!" he yelps as her pointy boot makes contact with his shin. "No! Course not, baby!"

I drain my drink and jump up to my feet, because my sister's right, isn't she? I've been keeping secrets for far too long and so has Ollie, and all it's done is make us both unhappy. Well, from this point on, I am resolved! I will tell the truth, the whole truth and nothing but the truth. At least that way we'll both know what we're dealing with.

But maybe I should have another cider first? Just while I prepare myself? It doesn't do to rush these things.

"Don't put it off," Holly says sternly, some sisterly sixth sense telling her exactly what's going through my mind. "Tell him now before you can chicken out. You'll feel better for it, I promise."

I glance at Guy, who's rubbing his ankle and wincing. Right now he's hardly an advertisement for the benefits of telling your partner the truth. On the other hand, I'm kicking myself daily at the moment. Holly's right. There can't be any more secrets between Ollie and me. No matter what happens, no matter what the consequences, he needs to know everything.

And I am going to tell him.

Chapter 25

"Book Nook in Bristol called. They're expecting you for a signing on Saturday,"
Ollie calls as I let myself into our cottage. "I said you'd phone them back tomorrow to confirm."

He's standing at the Aga stirring something while Sasha sits at his feet, staring up at the pan and drooling. I don't blame her either because it smells delicious. If I wasn't feeling sick with nerves, I'd be drooling too.

"I'm making lasagne," Ollie says, with his back still to me, and my heart sinks a little because Ol always cooks lasagne when he's stressed. He says that the chopping and dicing and making cheese sauce takes so much attention that it's the perfect distraction after a tough day. Judging by the huge pile of chopped veggies and bubbling vat of cheese sauce, he's had a very stressful day indeed.

And I'm about to make it worse.

I can't back out now. Ollie needs to know what I've done and all I have to do is find the courage to tell him. I do wish he wasn't facing away from me though. As I look at him I have a horrible twisting feeling inside because nothing feels quite right anymore. We're not the way we usually are. We're not us.

I can't bear it.

"Do you want a glass of wine?" Ollie's asking, still stirring the cheese sauce vigorously and not turning round to give me a kiss. "I've opened the last of that white Maddy hid here. Lucky she did. I needed a drink so much I'd probably even have raided that stuff you dug up, if Dad hadn't taken it."

"Geoff took Cecily Greville's booze?" This is news to me.

"Yep. He caught Nicky with it, apparently; the bugger was sneaking it out to a sixth-form party, and before I could say anything Pa had confiscated the lot."

Drinking. Naked waiting. Partying when he should be revising. Nicky's life is way more exciting than mine was at his age. Or even now, come to think about it.

"Why did your dad take it away though?"

Ollie takes the saucepan from the hotplate, sets it onto a mat and turns to face me. He looks tired and there are faint lines around his eyes that I'm sure never used to be there.

"You know what a wine buff Dad is. He probably thought it looked interesting. Anyway, there's white open if you want it." He raises his own glass to me. "Thank the Lord for Reverend Richard and his Lenten booze ban. I needed this."

My heart sinks even more. "Bad day?"

He shrugs. "The same as always. I can't see anything changing soon to be honest. I guess I just have to ride it out. It'll calm down in time, I'm sure. The parents will be bored of it all soon and find something else to moan about. Like Carolyn says, it'll all die down and things will go back to normal."

I feel a needle-prick of alarm because he's wrong, isn't he? None of this is going to go away any time soon. In fact, it's all about to get ten times worse.

And hang on. What's it got to do with Carolyn? Why is he talking to her and not me? See, this is where it's all going wrong. What if he prefers her to me? What if she's actually better for him than I am? Let's be honest; I'm hardly enhancing his life lately.

What if once I tell him about the other two Throb books he decides that being with me is more trouble than it's worth?

Wine. I need wine.

Heading to the fridge and retrieving the bottle, I pour myself a very generous glass and then sit down at the table. My hands are shaking.

"I need to tell you something," I say quietly.

Ollie's ladling layers of pasta, meat and sauce into a casserole dish. His brow furrows with concentration and I know his attention is on the dinner not me.

"What's Maddy done now?" he asks.

"This isn't about Maddy. It's about me. Or maybe I should say it's about us. And you're not going to like it."

Splat. A big gloop of meat sauce misses the dish and lands on the floor, and Ollie stares at me.

"What do you mean, about us?" he whispers. His face is very pale all of a sudden.

"Well, not *us* as such but it's about us," I say. "Or more accurately it's about the book."

Ollie exhales heavily and sits down opposite me. His cheese sauce begins to congeal in the pan and neither of us tell Sasha off when she wolfs the spilled sauce up from the quarry tiles. We can both sense that A Big Talk is coming.

"Katy," Ollie says gently, "we've talked ourselves round and around about the bloody book. What's done is done. We're dealing with it at work and you have to stop beating yourself up about everything. I know you didn't do any of it on purpose."

"I didn't! I really didn't," I say. "But Ollie, there's something I haven't told you."

"Oh God," he says. "Why do I have a sudden sense of foreboding? What is it now? Have you smuggled Pinchy back from New York? Should we be expecting the FBI any time soon?"

I try to laugh but sound more like a strangled chicken.

"Hey!" Ollie reaches out and takes my hands. "Don't look so worried. Whatever it is we can sort it, I promise."

"I don't think we can," I say sadly.

"Well, let's try. There's nothing we can't do if we put our minds to it," he promises. "Just tell me, Katy. What is it? What's wrong?"

I take a deep breath. No more secrets; that was what I'd decided and that's how it has to be. And then I tell him everything. All about the contract I can't get out of, the next two books I have to write, how I've pleaded with the publisher, begged Seb to help and basically tried everything I can to get out of writing them.

"I'm so sorry," I finish, hanging my head. "I'd do anything I could to be able to walk away from the contract. I'll never write another book again after this, Ollie. I promise. I know what it's done to you at school and how it's ruining your career. No more books for me again ever. I'm through with writing. Your career has to come first."

Ollie's looking at me with a strange expression on his face.

"Do you really mean that?" he says. "You'd give up writing books for my teaching career?"

How can he even ask?

"Not for your career, for you!"

"But give up writing?" He shakes his head. "I'd never ask that of you, Katy. It's what you've always wanted to do. Remember how you used to write stories in exercise books? Or during staff meetings?"

I still do this actually, but I keep quiet about it. Ollie is, after all, an Assistant Head Teacher and would probably disapprove of such behaviour now.

"You love to write and it's a huge part of who you are," he continues. "This thing with Throb might not be exactly what you've dreamed of, but you've made a success of it and I'm proud of you. Yes, I am," he says, catching sight of me goggling at him. "I'm so sorry if I haven't shown it or if I've let St Jude's get in the way but, yes, I'm proud of how hard you've worked. How many people can actually say they've made their dreams come true? *You've* never given up on yours when lots of other people would have thrown in the towel. You made it work for you."

Golly. I've never thought of it like that before. Go me!

"And I know why you wanted to write that book too," Ollie continues, squeezing my hands. "The digging up of the floor. Going on supply when you didn't want to. I know you did all of that for us and our future."

I guess technically speaking, spying on Carolyn was looking out for our future too, wasn't it?

"I would never ask you to stop writing," Ollie says vehemently. "Never. OK? You write those next two books and make them a big success too, because who knows where they might lead you. They could be the key to your big break with a publisher and then you could be writing the books you really want to write. That could be what makes you happy."

"You make me happy," I reply quietly.

But Ollie shakes his head. "I'm not so sure I do anymore. You've had to hide things from me and that's not right. You should never feel you have to keep secrets."

"That's because I love you!" I cry. "I didn't want to worry you. But the more I tried to put things right the more confused it all became. Besides, you've been keeping secrets too! It's not just me! What about the necklace you never gave Ann? What about all the phone calls to Carolyn? What about the time you met her at school and hadn't told me? What about—"

"What about trust?" Ol cuts me off, so sharply that I'm stunned. His skin is taut across his cheekbones and his eyes glitter behind his glasses. "Whatever happened to that?"

I can't speak. I don't think I've ever seen him so upset.

"What about believing in me and how I feel about you?" he asks fiercely. "And I do love you, Katy, I do, but if you can't trust me, what then?"

He stares at me across the table. In his eyes I see the times we've shared together – laughing at jokes in our tough inner-London school when we were new teachers, Ollie about to boil Pinchy up as a starter course, our first real kiss on the quay, us travelling through Europe in the camper van – and it's as though he's willing me to see these things too rather than all the muddle of the last few months. We were so happy. Surely that hasn't changed?

My stomach clenches. How on earth has everything got so confused? A few months ago I was convinced he was about to propose but now I've never felt further away from him.

"I love you," he says again, softly. "I don't know what's been going on in your head, Katy, but I need you to trust me and believe in me. Even just for a few more weeks."

"I do trust you," I answer.

"Good," says Ollie drily. "I'll try and remember that."

And I do trust him. I do! Except for all the calls to Carolyn, and the late nights at work and the disappearing necklace, of course. I wait for Ollie to give reasons for all these and to set my mind at rest, but he doesn't. Instead he just returns to the Aga and an awkward quiet pools between us. I feel close to tears – which is crazy, isn't it? I've just confessed about the books, and Ollie's told me that I must write them and says he loves me. All should be well.

But if it is, why is the atmosphere between us still so strained and weird? What's going on? There are more undercurrents here than beyond the harbour wall. Why do I still feel as though he's keeping something from me?

And what does he mean, *for a few more weeks*?

"By the way, I need to tell you something," he says, busy stirring the now lumpy sauce. "I've got to go on the Year Nine Paris trip. I know it's short notice but Mick Taylor's dropped out and we need another male teacher to make up the numbers. It's during half-term but I know you'll be really busy with the book, won't you? It'll give you some peace to work."

I don't say anything because I'm too disappointed to even speak. Half-term's next week. Nicky's going to Surrey to revise under the eagle eyes of Ann and Geoff (who understandably don't trust me anymore), and I've been hoping that Ollie and I might have some time alone at long last so that we can start to get life back to normal. I was so looking forward to it.

"How about I come too?" I suggest. "An extra teacher would really help with the pupil-to-adult ratio, wouldn't it? And we could have some time in Paris together. That would be brilliant!"

When Ollie and I were travelling we visited Paris and we had the most amazing and romantic time ever, strolling hand in hand along the banks of the Seine, eating crêpes and kissing the sugar from each other's lips, and later watching the city come alive from the Sacré-Coeur while the sun slipped behind the rooftops. It was magical and beautiful and I can't think of anywhere nicer to be with him. It would bring back so many happy memories and I think it's just what we need.

But Ollie's shaking his head. "That's a nice idea but we've already got Carolyn and Gemma and a couple of teaching assistants. Besides, I don't think it would go down too well if Isara Lovett showed up on a school trip, do you?"

In the past I might have made a quip about Isara Lovett going down very well indeed, but my heart isn't in it and, besides, this just reminds me of how complicated everything has become. In the past too, Ollie wouldn't have dreamed of going away for a week without me; he'd have told school where to stick their trip. But as they say, the past is a foreign country and they certainly do things differently there.

I just wish I could find a way of taking us back.

Chapter 26

I find Maddy arranging flowers in the church. Or maybe I should more accurately say I find Maddy shoving gerberas and carnations into vases and stuffing dead blooms into a bin bag with a mutinous expression on her face. She hates flower arranging with a passion but, along with sorting jumble and organising bake sales, it comes with the territory of being married to Richard. I can't for the life of me think what the trade-off is but Mads obviously reckons there's one, which is the main thing.

"Do you like it?" she asks when she spots me in the doorway. "I thought the usual lilies and roses were a bit dull so I've decided to mix things up a bit. Cool, huh?"

I glance around. The church certainly looks vibrant with its new lurid colour scheme of clashing lilac and orange, but the congregation will probably need their sunglasses on. Still, I don't mention this. It's more than my life's worth. It's probably best not to mention either that Rafferty and Bluebell are busy pulling the pages out of hymn books and poking them through the heating grills in the floor. Hopefully it won't cause a fire before I've managed to bend my best friend's ear.

"Bloody flowers," grumbles Mads, cramming a few more blooms into a vase before pushing it onto a dusty windowsill. "Bane of my life. Honestly, I don't know why the old dears won't let me just order a load of plastic ones from Trago instead. Nobody would notice and it would save hours of time."

"You'd have to dust them," I remark, and she grimaces.

"Fair point. It's bad enough cleaning the sodding brass. I've told Rich we should swap duties for a week. I'll write the sermons and he can do the flowers, deal with the old biddies at the coffee mornings and look after the twins."

"He'd be sobbing behind the lectern by Tuesday," I say and Mads nods, mollified.

"Of course he would. There are some jobs only women can do properly." She brushes pollen off her hands and glances around the church with satisfaction. "Anyway, what are you doing here? Things so bad you've popped in to pray?"

Actually, I haven't ruled it out, although thanks to Throb I'm waiting to be struck down by a bolt of lightning. The way I'm feeling today, that would be a happy relief.

"You *know* they are," I say, following her down the aisle as she tweaks stems and adjusts vases. "Ollie's going to Paris with Carolyn and he doesn't want me to come. Remember?"

To be honest, I'm quite put out that Maddy isn't more offended on my behalf by this. When I called her last night while Ollie was walking Sasha, she didn't seem that interested or outraged, which isn't very best-friendly of her. I mean, if Richard said he was off to Vegas with one of the old biddies from the WI I'd be straight round to the vicarage to sort him out. Not that I can imagine Richard in Vegas or running off with anyone when he has gorgeous Maddy, but you get my point. I'd be furious and ready to do battle for my friend. I wouldn't be arranging flowers!

Maddy sighs. "He isn't strictly going to Paris with Carolyn, is he? There's the small matter of fifty thirteen-year-olds and a load of other teachers as well. It's hardly a romantic tryst."

"But he doesn't want me to come! What does that mean?" I cry.

"That the Throb business makes it awkward? That there isn't room?" Maddy suggests, walking serenely through the nave and repositioning blooms while I scuttle behind her in a stew of fear and resentment. "Honestly, babes, I don't think it means anything. It's just a school trip."

"A school trip with Carolyn," I say bleakly. Good-looking Carolyn with her blonde hair, long legs and lack of embarrassing novel-writing career. That Carolyn.

"She's the Head of Modern Foreign Languages as well as the Deputy Head," Maddy reminds me. "Of course she's going. Honestly, Katy, I think you should relax. I'm sure there's nothing to worry about."

I stare at her. Has being in the church all morning done something to her brain? Maybe she's absorbed all the peace and love and forgiveness by osmosis or something, because this response isn't Maddy's style at all. Usually she'd believe me straight away and do whatever she could to help.

"Whatever happened to her being a floozy?" I ask, taken aback. "Or me kicking her ass?"

"Ssh," says Maddy, glancing upwards and folding her hands. "We're in the church. Anyway, you said yourself that there was no evidence of anything going on."

"That was before he said he was going to Paris with her!"

"He isn't going to Paris *with her*. It's a school trip. Katy, get a grip. Ollie isn't having an affair with Carolyn. It's all in your head!"

I feel as though I've been slapped. In all the years we've been friends Maddy has never, ever told me that I'm imagining things or doubted me.

"Don't hold back," I say, feeling horribly hurt. "Feel free to tell me I'm mad if that's what you think. Would you like it if Richard was off for a week with another woman?"

"I'd *love* it," Mads says with feeling. "No washing, and I could eat toast in bed, buy plastic flowers and binge-watch *Game of Thrones*. If he took the kids as well then it would be perfect. I'm joking!" she says when she sees my face. "No. I'd hate it. But, Katy, I really don't think Ollie's going to Paris because of Carolyn. Why don't you just trust him?"

"And why don't you believe me?" I shoot back. "You usually do."

I don't want to sound resentful but I can't help it. Maddy's my best friend and she ought to be on my side, not sticking up for Ollie. I would have thought she'd have been the first in the queue to march round to the cottage and tell him he's out of order.

"Katy, we've been through this a thousand times." Maddy reaches for her bag and pulls out the church keys. "I've told you what I think. What's the point of asking my opinion if you don't listen to it? Babes, I'd love to chat more but I've got to open the hall up for the Mums and Toddlers group. Rafferty! Bluebell! Put those hymn books down!" She marches up to the twins and grabs them before they can do a runner, leaving me staring after her in shock. What on earth is going on?

I leave the church feeling as though *I'm* the one being unreasonable and unfair. Maddy couldn't have been less interested in my worries – which is weird considering she was the one encouraging me to go into St Jude's and backing me up one hundred percent at the time. What's changed?

Mads hurries down the path, dragging the twins behind her.

"Try not to stress about it," she calls over her shoulder. "It'll be all right! Just have faith, yeah? You gotta have faith."

Who am I, George Michael? I watch Maddy stride away and feel completely lost. What's going on here? My life feels as though it's spinning out of control. Ollie and Maddy are my best friends in the world, the two people I really feel I can count on, and suddenly they're both behaving oddly. In fact, if I didn't know better, I'd say that they're both hiding something from me.

Oh great. Now I'm getting paranoid.

Feeling very hard done by, I set off down the narrow lane that drops down from the church behind the fish market and onto the quay. The village tumbles away and the sea is sparkling in the sunshine but I'm in no mood to appreciate beauty. No, I'm far too cheesed off.

"Cheer up, it might never happen," calls Guy, who's mending a net on the quayside and doing his best to ignore the crowd of day trippers pointing at him and taking sly pictures on their phones.

"It already has," I say grimly.

He tucks his mending needle into the trawl. "I take it Ollie's told you he's off to Paris?"

I goggle at him. "How on earth do you know that?"

Guy's suddenly absolutely fascinated by a boat steaming through the harbour gates.

"Oh look! The netters are in. I'd better given them a hand," he says, looking as though he's about to bolt.

I grab the arm of his smock. "Guy? Who told you about Ollie going to Paris?"

I know gossip travels fast in Tregowan but this has to be a record surely? I've only just told Maddy.

Guy looks a bit shifty. "I think it was Holly."

"Holly? How on earth did she know?"

"I think Ollie might have mentioned it?" He's hopping from rigger-booted foot to rigger-booted foot in agitation now.

"Ollie? When did Ollie tell my sister?" I ask, totally thrown. "He only told *me* last night. Why didn't Holly think to mention it?"

But Guy isn't saying anything else and all of a sudden he's far too busy catching ropes and helping to moor a fishing boat to talk to me. By the time bright yellow fish boxes are swinging out of the ice room and onto the quay I know there's no point trying to press any further. There's no way I'll get any sense out of him now.

My head's spinning and I'm utterly confused. Has Ollie been talking about me to my sister? But why would he do that? I'd go and speak to Holly right now except she's at work. I guess I'll have to wait until Ollie comes home from school and ask him what's going on – not that he'll tell me. So much for trust. And how come nobody other than me thinks it's a major deal that Ollie's off to Paris with a gorgeous blonde colleague?

Oh Lord. I think I'm going mad. If I don't get some answers soon I'm going to go completely doolally.

I know, I'll distract myself with a giant pasty. If ever a girl needed comfort food, it's me. Everything always feels better on a full stomach and then I can worry about being fat rather than stressing about Ollie, which is a result of sorts I suppose.

I'm just sitting on a bench and tucking in to a giant steak pasty when my phone rings. Swallowing pastry and brushing crumbs from my mouth, I answer.

"Frankie! Hello!"

"Darling! What on earth are you eating?" Frankie's kohl-rimmed eye is pressed so close to the screen that I can count his lashes. "Tell me it isn't a pasty? Oh God! It is, isn't it? Are you deliberately trying to torture me? I'd kill for a pasty! And anyway, aren't you supposed to be on a diet?"

Don't you just love Skype? There's no hiding in the twenty-first century. There's Frankie, beautifully made up with blue eyeliner and looking achingly trendy in his spotless white apartment, and here I am on a weathered bench, windswept and scruffy and with a guilty gob full of pastry.

"I thought carbs were the devil?" I say, taking a big bite just to taunt him. Having had this mantra drummed into me while in New York, I'm certain pastry shouldn't be allowed anywhere near Frankie's well-glossed lips.

"Will you stop teasing me?" he wails. "Have you any idea what wheatgrass tastes like? Have you?"

"Not really," I admit. "We don't have a lot of wheatgrass in Cornwall, Frankie, remember?"

But Frankie isn't listening. He's far too busy drooling over my lunch. "Or macrobiotic mung beans?" he continues. "Or tofu flakes with soya shavings? Disgusting. I'm practically fading away here! I can't remember when I last ate something solid. And as for all the colonics—"

"Stop right there. Too much information."

"Am I over-sharing?" he asks. "Sorry, angel. You keep on eating. Don't worry about the fact that meat stays rotting in your colon for years. If you never have an enema you won't have to see it. Or smell it. Oh my God, darling! The stench!"

Do you know, I'm not so excited about my lunch anymore.

"Anyway, never mind my diet," he continues, while I stuff my pasty back into the bag and try very hard not to think about what may or may not be clogging up my colon. "There's far more exciting things to talk about! Congrats on your big book success for a start! Everyone's talking about *Kitchen* over here."

"Is that a good thing?"

"Like duh! Of course it is! Sweetie! You are made!"

"Great," I say, doing my best to sound thrilled. "Brilliant."

"I'm never wrong either. And is Ollie all right with it all now?"

I pause, because is he? I know he said he's proud of me but really? And if he's so proud of me then why's he off to Paris without me? I've done enough school trips in my time to know it's possible to wangle an extra place for a partner.

If you want to, that is.

"He's fine," I say eventually. "Actually he's off to France next week on a school trip."

"*Ooh la la!*" giggles Frankie.

"He's going without me. I don't think he wants me to come."

"You are silly! Of course he does, but if you go too then Ollie would have—" He stops mid-sentence. "Ooo look! A seagull!"

There are millions of seagulls in Tregowan. You can't move without one trying to nick ice cream or mug you for a pasty crust, and my senses are instantly on red alert. Any teacher worth her salt knows when distraction tactics are being employed.

"Don't change the subject when it's just getting interesting," I say. "What would Ollie have done?"

"Lots of paperwork," Frankie replies quickly. "Anyway, never mind all that. I'm inviting you both to a party next week."

"Here? You're coming back to Cornwall?"

"Afraid not, angel. No, the party's in New York. It's our anniversary and Gabe's going to throw a huge bash. We wanted you both to come but since Ollie's off eating snails it'll have to be just you."

"You're asking me to fly to New York for a party?" I laugh at the very idea. "What next? Shall I ask for your M&M's to be sorted into colours?"

"I never eat chocolate," Frankie shudders. "And anyway, it was Gabe who asked for colour-sorted sweets and they were jelly beans, not M&M's. But yes! We want you there. Of course we do. You were with us practically from the beginning. You're family, Katy. How could we celebrate without you? I insist you come."

In spite of feeling low I can't help but experience a little tingle of excitement. Another trip to New York. Really?

"We'll pay for your flights of course," Frankie continues, sensing me weakening. "And your hotel too. It's the least we can do for throwing a party on another continent."

"Seriously?"

"Seriously," he nods. "Come on, Katy. Ollie's in Paris and you're home alone. Why not come out? It'll be fun."

Hang on. Did I mention Paris specifically? I'm pretty sure I didn't. I said France.

"How do you know Ollie's in Paris?"

"Lucky guess," Frankie says quickly. "Anyway, where else in France would you go for a school trip? Oh look! Here's Mufty! Say hello to Katy, Mufty!"

Another distraction, this time in the guise of a fluffy poodle held aloft and having its paw waved at me. Our eyes meet in mutual resignation as I wave back. *Just give in*, Mufty's gaze says, *it's easier*.

"So what do you say? Are you up for a little visit? You know you want to," Frankie urges.

"I'll need to run it by Ollie," I begin, but he flaps his hand dismissively.

"He'll be cool with it. Yay! Amazeballs! I'll get my people to book your ticket and sort a hotel right now. It's going to be wonderful! You'll thank me for this!"

As he rings off, my head's reeling. Conversations with Frankie tend to leave me feeling like I've been inside a washing machine on spin cycle. Have I just agreed to fly to New York for a party? And am I getting super paranoid here, or is Frankie acting just as strangely as Maddy and Guy?

I close my eyes. Of course he isn't. My friends can't all be having an off day. It must be me. Everything's feeling weird and wrong, a bit like a familiar tune played in the wrong key or one of those episodes of *Doctor Who* when the Doctor and his companion rock up in a parallel universe. Of course it's me, not them. It has to be. Maybe the stress of the past few months has got to me and I need a break?

I stay on my bench, watching the waves roll towards the beach and the white clouds scud by. My thoughts are racing too and for a while I just let them whirl. Carolyn. Ollie. Mads. Books. Holly. Naked butlers. Tansy. So much has been going on. No wonder I'm feeling a bit dazed. I think I need everything to just stop so that I can let life settle again. Ollie and I were so happy before when things were simple. I just need to figure out a way to get that back.

Perhaps a break's exactly what I need. Ollie certainly seems pleased to be having one.

I throw the remains of my pasty to the wheeling seagulls, my mind made up. No more sitting around letting things happen to me, and no more agonising over Carolyn and Ollie and what may or may not be going on. It's time to stop and take stock, make a few decisions and get my life back under control.

A tear slips down my cheek because this isn't the way I want it to be, but right now it feels as though there isn't any choice. Ollie might only be going to Paris but he couldn't feel further away from me if it were Mars.

I'm going to go back to New York. Alone.

And I'm missing Ollie before I've even left.

Chapter 27

Frankie's waiting for me in JFK's Arrivals, holding a placard bearing my name on it and waving frantically, just in case I should miss him – which I think would be impossible seeing as he's wearing a bright orange jumpsuit and a Stetson and is flanked by two minders who make The Rock look vertically challenged. Never mind sticking out like a sore thumb; he's as conspicuous as an entire gangrenous hand.

"Darling! Over here!" he cries, hopping from one foot to another (although this could just be the way he has to move in his very pointy cowboy boots). "Howdy!"

I wave back, pleased to see him, if a little taken aback. I'd thought he'd be far too busy arranging his anniversary party to take time out to collect me. I'm honoured.

"Frankie!" I trundle my luggage behind me as fast as I can, so that I can throw my arms around him – but then I recoil instantly. "Ouch! That jumpsuit's really scratchy!"

"Rhinestones," declares Frankie proudly. "All the country and western singers wear them, FYI. This is made by Dolly Parton's own designer actually."

Last time I saw Frankie I seem to remember that he was reinventing himself as A Serious Artist and was wearing smart suits and Italian shoes. I know it was a lifetime ago in rock 'n' roll terms, but I can't say I ever foresaw Frankie's new passion for country and western. It seems rather sudden.

Anyway, hold on! He's English! What on earth does Frankie know about country music? We don't even *have* country music in England, unless you count Morris dancing, which I don't really think the Americans will get.

Let's be fair, I'm English and *I* don't get it.

"I've got a house in Bucks," Frankie says indignantly when I point out that his knowledge of country music might be a little on the sketchy side. "I go there all the time. I'm always in the country."

Frankie so does *not* go to the country all the time. I know for a fact he gets twitchy if there isn't a Starbucks within fifty paces. And anyway, the last time he tried to drive me to his rock-star rural pad he couldn't find it so we gave up and went to the pub instead.

"So what do you know about country music?" I ask, while the minders divvy my luggage up between them, using a novel system of grunts and hand gestures to communicate.

"I know that Ivan and Igor like it," Frankie says, gesturing to his minders, both of whom nod. "They listen to it all the time in the limo and I've got into it too. Hell yeah and yehaw! I love cows and tractors *and* I bought ten copies of the Young Farmers' naked calendar."

"I don't think country music has much to do with cows and tractors," I say doubtfully. "Isn't it about the American way of life?"

"Well, even better because I know all about that," says Frankie airily. "I've even bought a ranch."

I goggle at him. "A ranch?"

"Yep. With horses and everything," he says happily. "It's got thousands of acres."

Frankie can't even keep the basil plant in his kitchen alive for a week. What he'll do with thousands of acres is anyone's guess.

"Anyway," he carries on, "I've got the outfits and the ranch and I've listened to oodles of that country music stuff now. Seb reckons I can pull it off if I write about blue jeans, beer and being working class."

The fact that Frankie normally wears leather trousers, drinks champagne and went to public school doesn't seem to be an issue, which I guess is just as well.

"Seb reckons there's a massive gap in the market, so I've got the gear and I'm off to Nashville tonight to record an album," he adds. "Just you wait; I'll be a country sensation. You'll see."

As we walk across the concourse, the minders lifting my cases as though they're filled with feathers rather than all the clothes I could cram in, Frankie's already causing a sensation. At six feet tall, reed slim and wearing high-heeled cowboy boots he couldn't look more different from all the other smart-suited travellers. I follow him with my head spinning. I know I'm probably totally jet-lagged but surely he can't be going to Nashville tonight. What about the anniversary party?

I must be hearing things wrong. I'm so tired and I've been so stressed about Ollie that I can't even think straight. Ten hours of flying and crossing several time zones will do that to a girl.

Ollie! I must call him and let him know I've landed. I haven't been able to talk to him since he left for France two days ago. He's been on a coach and in the depths of the Channel Tunnel, which is bound to be why he hasn't answered his phone, but we never go this long without talking. I hope he's OK. What if he's choked on a croque-monsieur or drowned in the Seine and I don't know?

"Can I borrow your mobile?" I ask. "I need to call Ollie."

"Right now, angel? Can't it wait?"

"Not really. I haven't spoken to him for almost two days and I want him to know I'm here safely."

Frankie thinks for a moment. "Won't it be night-time in France? He'll be in bed surely? Why don't you just wait until tomorrow rather than disturbing everyone?"

I stare at him. Is it my imagination or is he trying to put me off? But why on earth would he do that? I'm being daft and must be more jet-lagged than I thought.

"It's only a six-hour time difference, Frankie. It'll be the evening in France and the kids will be up until the small hours anyway, so I hardly think I'm disturbing Ollie."

"Sorry, sweetie, I haven't got my phone on me," he says.

"There's one in the limo, boss," grunts Igor (or is it Ivan?).

"That isn't working," Frankie reminds him sharply.

"Fine," I say tightly. "I'll use my phone. It's got roaming."

I dread to think how much this will cost, since I'm calling from New York. I'll probably have to write at least five more Throb novels to pay for this call – but I need to talk to Ollie. I miss him so much and if Frankie won't help then I'll do it myself.

Frankie looks as though he's about to say something, but we're outside the terminal now and the minders are loading my luggage into the boot (or should I say the *trunk*) of a big black limo and the moment is lost.

"Do you want to watch telly?" he asks once we're inside and lolling about on butter-soft white leather seats. "I've got all the channels. Ooo! Look! The Kardashians are on. Kim and Kanye said they'd do their best to come tonight. Exciting!"

This *is* exciting but I can't summon up a drop of enthusiasm. What is wrong with me?

"And I've got a cocktail bar! How about a cosmo?" He leans forward and presses a button, and a mini bar pops out like magic. "Ta-da! What do you think?"

What do I think? I think that I'm being chauffeured in the most luxurious car imaginable, through endless lanes of zooming traffic and towards the most amazing city in the world… and I've never felt unhappier. What am I doing here without Ollie? I don't want to be partying without him or driving through New York or even hanging out with celebrities. I don't want to do anything without Ollie. Ever. While Frankie chatters away and mixes drinks and the car glides soundlessly towards the beating heart of Manhattan, I stare miserably down at my lap and try as hard as I can to bite back the panic rising steadily in my chest.

I want to go home.

Whatever was I thinking, going this far away? I know Ollie's in France and I was annoyed at first, but he had to be there because of his job. He didn't have any choice, did he? I've been totally unreasonable getting upset. Of course he had to go. That extra responsibility is part of being an Assistant Head.

Sod the roaming charges. I'll write ten more novels for Throb and dream up all kinds of dreadful things to do with vegetables and clothes pegs if it means I can tell Ollie I love him and I'm sorry.

"What are you doing?" Frankie asks as I pull my phone out of the bag Tansy gave me.

"Calling Ollie." As if it has a mind of its own, my forefinger scrolls through the contact list and hits *Ollie Mob*. The phone rings and rings before switching to his answerphone. I cancel the call. I've spoken to that answerphone so many times lately that it's starting to feel like an old friend.

"Time difference," Frankie says firmly. "Try tomorrow, angel."

But I'm made of sterner stuff than that. No answerphone or time difference will come between me and the man I love. Nor will anything else, for that matter.

Desperate times call for desperate measures.

I'm going to call the St Jude's emergency mobile number – which, as luck would have it, Carolyn herself gave me on my supply day. The teachers on the Paris trip will definitely have it with them. I know that missing Ollie isn't strictly an emergency but, believe me, it feels like it.

"Can't it wait?" pleads Frankie, starting to look agitated. The way he's carrying on you'd think he didn't want me to call Ollie. Which is just ridiculous.

I shake my head, locate the number and dial while Frankie takes a big swig of his cocktail and regards me dolefully.

"Just remember, none of this was my idea," he says.

I'm just about to ask what this is supposed to mean, seeing as throwing an anniversary party and inviting me to stay was *totally* his idea, when there's a scuffling sound at the end of the line as though somebody's been scrabbling about in their bag to answer, followed by accordion music and chatter. I can practically smell the garlic and see men in stripy sweaters and wearing onion garlands cycling by brandishing baguettes.

Or something like that anyway.

"Hello?" says a female voice. "Can I help you?"

It's Carolyn Miles. My heart plummets because I'd so been hoping that Ollie would answer.

"Hi," I say, turning my back on Frankie. "Is it possible to speak to Ollie?"

"Ollie?" Carolyn sounds surprised. "Ollie Burrows?"

"Yes," I say, before adding quickly, "please."

"He's not here, I'm afraid. Can I help?"

"Not there?" I'm a bit thrown. "Not with you, you mean? So where is he? Watching dancers at the Moulin Rouge?" I mean this as a joke, but it comes out a little harsher than I intend and I hear an intake of breath. "Look, I don't want to be a pain but it's Katy here. His girlfriend? I really need to talk to him. Is he with the kids?"

The following pause is just a beat too long.

"Katy! Oh hi! Yes, I think so! In fact, I'm sure that's where he is. I'll get him to call you when he can."

Now intuition is a powerful thing and mine couldn't be trying to alert me more if it came tap-dancing along the freeway or doing the lambada.

She's fibbing, I know it. But why? I'd just about convinced myself that there was nothing going on between them after all, necklace riddle or not. Was I wrong? Or rather, was I right in the first place? Was it all an elaborate double bluff? Is this why everyone's being so odd lately? I'm sure Mads and Holly have been avoiding me, Guy's conveniently vanished on a week-long fishing trip, Frankie can't look me in the face, Ollie's incommunicado and now even the saintly Carolyn's at it. It feels like my life's turning into one of those trendy grit-lit novels. (You know the ones I mean, with black covers, stark orange typography and heroines on trains/faking going missing/wondering why everyone they know is being weird. I think my title would be *Girl Totally Confused* – and if I ever, ever escape from Throb I might even write it.)

"OK, Carolyn," I say. "This is the thing: I know that there's something going on here, so you may as well admit it and tell me what it is."

There's silence.

Fine. Let's bluff with an old teacher trick that's never known to fail. "To be honest," I add, "there's no point trying to pretend. I actually know everything, so you may as well just be straight. It'll make life easier."

There's another sharp intake of breath at the end of the line. "You know everything?"

"Yes," I say firmly.

"No you don't," mutters Frankie, but I ignore him.

Carolyn groans. "Oh shit. Ollie's going to be devastated. He's tried so hard to keep all this from you for so long. He'll be horrified you've found out! I'm truly sorry."

Can you believe she actually says this with regret? I'm so incensed I could explode and it's exceedingly lucky for Carolyn Miles that she's the other side of the Atlantic.

He's been keeping all this from me, has he? For *so long*? They must have been planning their dirty week away for ages. And where is he now? Having a shower in their hotel room?

"I see," I say grimly. "Just how long has all this been going on?"

She thinks about it for a moment. "I couldn't really say. Certainly since before you went to New York."

A wave of horror breaks over me.

"You've been having an affair with Ollie since I went to New York?"

"What?" screeches Frankie.

"What?" chorus Ivan and Igor before Frankie presses a button that shoots a screen up between us and them. Even the Kardashians seem to pause.

"I'm sorry? What did you say?" stutters Carolyn, sounding stunned. God she's good; she should teach drama, not French.

"You and Ollie. You've been having an affair," I say quietly. My hands are shaking and I think I'm going to be sick. Miles High Club was what Steph called her, wasn't it? I really should have listened.

There's a gasp. "What on earth makes you say that?"

"You! You just told me!"

But rather than agreeing or apologising or even gloating, Carolyn starts to laugh.

"I have absolutely no idea where you got that notion from, but I can assure you that Ollie and I most certainly are *not* having affair! We never have been and I can promise you that we never, ever will either!"

Of course she *would* say that now she's busted, wouldn't she?

"So let me speak to him," I say. "Let me hear his side of the story."

She sighs. "I can't. He isn't here right at this moment. But, Katy, please, you have to trust me on this one. Ollie's the last person who would have an affair. He's totally and utterly devoted to you and even if he wasn't – which he is – I'm the last person he'd be interested in."

Now it's my turn to laugh. I've seen Carolyn and she's gorgeous. Any guy with a pulse would look twice.

"You two spend a lot of time together," I point out. "And then there's all the phone calls and the urgent meetings."

"We work together," she says wearily. "We're colleagues, Katy. Come on, you're a teacher. You know how intense school can get. And there's been a lot to deal with lately too, with the book business as well as helping him with… with other things."

I wait for her to explain what these "other things" are, but instead she just sighs again. "Just take it from me. You're barking up the wrong tree here. And besides, I have a partner. One I'm very happy with, actually."

This is news to me. From what Steph said I thought Carolyn was a real man-eater.

"And doesn't your partner mind you working late with Ollie?" I ask her.

"Sam gets a bit fed up with the workload but he understands that's teaching," Carolyn says thoughtfully. "It's not easy but you make it work, don't you? When you love someone that's what you do. You make sacrifices for them."

"Sam?" I echo.

"My boyfriend," Carolyn explains patiently. "Sam Evans? He owns the Candy Shack in town? You've heard of Candy Shack, of course?"

I live in Tregowan, not on the moon, of course I've heard of Candy

Shack. It's a huge nightclub in Plymouth where all the footballers go and well known for wild parties and excess. Tansy's a regular and she even took me there once. I needed a second mortgage to pay for the drinks so I generally stick to the the village pub but it was great fun – in a short skirted and boozy way.

"Obviously with St Jude's being the *progressive* school it is," she laughs sarcastically here, "I keep my private life pretty close to my chest. Only a few people there know I'm living with the owner of a nightclub. It's the main reason I've just handed in my notice. I want to shout about Sam from the rooftops, not hide away. I'm bloody proud of him – just like Ollie's proud of you and your writing. And he is proud, Katy. Really proud. He's always talking about you."

That lump in my throat's back because I've got it all wrong haven't I? Again. Everything was right there in front of me, as plain as day to see, but I was so busy interpreting things my own way that I simply couldn't see it.

Ollie loves me.

Ollie's proud of me.

Ollie has never let me down.

But I've let him down horribly. I've doubted him and let my own insecurities and paranoia get in the way.

I start to apologise to Carolyn but she won't have any of it.

"Hey, it's all right. I can see how things must have looked," she says kindly. "I'd be jealous if Sam was spending all his time with you! I mean, you're Isara Lovett! How could anyone compete with that?"

Oh Lord. This is worse than I thought. Carolyn is nice. Really nice.

I'd got that wrong too, of course. Like I've got everything wrong.

Once she rings off, promising to ask Ollie to call the next time she sees him, I stare down at my phone and bite my lip. Not even Frankie's reassurances, three cocktails or the soaring glory of Manhattan can make me feel any better. Party plans and reality TV wash over me just like the Hudson washes over the shoreline, and all I can think about is how soon I can get home to the man I love.

Ollie's in France and I'm in the USA, but the distance between us feels even further than that.

What can I do to make things right again?

Chapter 28

"I'm staying *here*? Seriously?"

Frankie's limo turns into Park Avenue and, weaving its way through swarming yellow taxis, draws up alongside a majestic hotel that stretches along the pavement right to the end of the block. A constant stream of stylish women and smart-suited men flows past, and now and again some of them turn left and spin through the building's revolving glass doors.

"Welcome to the Waldorf Astoria," smiles Frankie.

While Ivan/Igor deals with my luggage, I crane my neck and gaze up at the hotel soaring above. It makes me feel quite dizzy. The street we're standing in is a deep canyon walled with the tallest buildings, and from the bottom of this shadowy gorge I can just make out a slither of bright blue sky and sharp sunshine high above us. Flags rustle in the gentle breeze and countless windows stretch heavenwards, up and up and up until the iconic hotel seems as though it's touching the clouds.

"It's amazing," I breathe. "A bit different to the budget hotel I stayed in the last time! Frankie, are you sure? It must have cost you a fortune to put me up here!"

Frankie flaps his hand dismissively and won't look me in the eye.

"Let's not talk about money, sweetie-pie. It makes me feel awkward. Just enjoy!"

Golly, it's not like him to feel embarrassed about splashing the cash. Usually he loves to discuss the bling.

"The Presidential Suite is right at the top," Frankie tells me, following my gaze. "I haven't tried it myself yet but I hear it's stunning."

"The whole hotel's stunning," I say. And it is, it really is, but do you know what? Even one of the most magnificent hotels in the world doesn't glitter as brightly or feel as exciting without Ollie beside me. I'd rather be in a tatty seaside B&B with him than here all alone in luxury.

As I follow Frankie through the doors and up a wide staircase, not even the opulent gold and marble decor or the thick carpet my feet sink into raise my spirits. And neither do the sparkling chandeliers or the elegant mahogany furniture, or even the gentle harp music floating across the lobby.

I feel as though I've been anaesthetised.

While Frankie deals with the reservation and collects my keys, I check my phone for the millionth time – and my heart shrivels a little more when I see that there are no missed calls or texts. Why isn't Ollie calling me back?

Has Carolyn told him what I suspected and he's upset? Maybe he's had enough of all my dramas?

I start to gnaw my thumbnail and Frankie gently pulls my hand away from my mouth.

"I'm going to buy you a set of acrylics," he says sternly. "New Yorkers don't nibble their nails!"

"Ollie still hasn't called," I explain sadly as we ride upwards in the elevator. "Oh, Frankie, I've made such a mess of everything. What on earth am I going to do?"

"Party hard," he says firmly. "You haven't come this far to be miserable, angel – and besides, he's probably just busy."

"Too busy to make a call?"

Frankie shrugs. "You said it yourself: school trips are hectic. Come on, sweetie! Lighten up. You're here to have fun! Stop moping about Ollie. He'll be in touch. He's probably flat out with the kids."

He's right. Of course he is. It's just that I've got the strangest feeling that something isn't quite adding up. Anyway, Frankie might be a bit more supportive than this. After all, he'd have me roaming the streets with search and rescue dogs and sticking pictures onto milk cartons if so much as twenty minutes went by without Gabe ringing him.

I'd have expected a little more sympathy from my friends, but evidently none of them are that interested in my problems. Take Frankie right now, for instance, checking his Rolex and itching to get away. No, my friends have made it very clear that they've all got far more important things to do than listen to me bleating on. As I follow Frankie's jumpsuited back along a sumptuous corridor, I feel very let down.

"Here we are! Your suite!" Frankie unlocks my room and throws the door wide open. "Isn't it incredible! O— err, I chose this one especially because of the view of Park Avenue."

The room is gorgeous. It's beautifully decorated and full of heavy wooden furniture, plus a massive bed piled high with plump cushions. The large windows are framed with curtains that fall from ceiling to floor, and beyond the glass the Big Apple is a constantly shifting sea of cars and humanity and bright blue sky. Walking around the suite, I discover a gleaming bathroom and even a champagne bucket with a full bottle waiting to be opened.

Frankie's right. It *is* incredible and everything that a luxury hotel room ought to be. I should be brimming with excitement and bounding around shrieking. But I'm not, am I? In fact, I feel dangerously tearful because what's the point of this fabulous room if I'm not sharing it with Ollie? The big bed, the lovely surroundings and the cooling champagne aren't any fun on their own.

I wander across to the window and press my forehead against the cold glass. I don't want to be here without Ollie. I don't want to be *anywhere* without Ollie.

"I have to shoot and do party stuff," Frankie is saying. "The concierge will send your luggage up – and do not forget to tip whoever brings it! This is America, remember?" He peels some dollars from his wallet and lays them carefully on the dressing table. "Now, a car's booked to pick you up at seven, so make sure you're in the lobby and dressed to kill. Have a bath, put your glad rags on and prepare to party!"

I don't think I've ever felt less like partying in my life but I nod dutifully. After all, Frankie's flown me here and paid for me to stay in this amazing hotel, so the least I can do is put on a brave face and go to his anniversary party.

Once he's gone (very fast actually, and I'm sure he was on his phone the minute he left my room, telling somebody in a very loud whisper, "The eagle has landed!", but that's probably just jet lag again), I hurl myself onto the bed. I stare up at the ceiling, which reminds me somehow of a perfectly iced wedding cake, and take a few deep breaths.

Breathe calmness in and stress out, Katy, just like in that yoga DVD you watched once. In and out, in and out. See. This stuff really works! Ollie was wrong. You didn't actually need to do the routine at all; the introduction was more than enough to get the gist. You didn't waste your money.

And anyway, that DVD was really useful as a coaster…

I can do this. It's one party and one night. That's all. Then I can go home to Cornwall, tell Throb to do their worst, and finally make things right with Ollie.

At least I hope I can…

By the time my bath has run I'm feeling a little less stressed – which probably has more to do with a glass of the champagne than the breathing techniques – and I'm ready to start my unpacking. I've tipped the bellboy who delivered my case and then I've busied myself organising my belongings and pulling out my trusty little black dress. I'm just deciding whether or not to wedge it in the trouser press to get rid of all the creases when there's a rap of knuckles on the door. Who now?

"Delivery for you, ma'am," announces an enormous box when I open up and peek into the corridor.

A talking box. What on earth? How much champagne did I just drink?

"For me?" I'm confused. Who'd be sending me presents here?

The box wiggles and a liveried bellboy peeps around one side of it. "Miss Carter? This is for you."

I can't deny it. That's me.

Perplexed, I step aside and allow him to deposit the huge box onto the bed. Then he hovers a bit before I twig that I ought to give him a tip. Unfortunately, I've given Frankie's dollars to the last bellboy and all I have is a tatty promo copy of *Kitchen*, but once I've autographed it he assures me this will be worth way more on eBay than a few dollars anyway. In fact he seems thrilled.

My books are a whole new currency. Whoever would have thought?

But anyway, never mind the books. What's this? The box is white and elegantly wrapped with sleek black ribbons, beneath which someone has tucked a crisp white card.

For a very special writer. Wear me!

Wear me?

Intrigued, I tug the end of the ribbon and lift off the lid. White tissue paper rustles as my fingertips delve beneath and reveal a dress. As I shake it my eyes are wide because it's possibly the most beautiful dress I've ever seen. There's a white bodice covered in thousands of tiny glittering beads, with sparkling spaghetti straps to match, and the most amazing full ballerina skirt made of layers and layers of shimmering net.

Oh my goodness! It's a Carrie Bradshaw style tutu dress, the kind I *always* imagined wearing in New York and definitely the sort of dress I would never in a million years buy. The fabric slips through my hands like liquid and the stitches are so fine that I can't even see them. The bodice is boned and the straps are surprisingly strong too. Wow. A dress like this must have cost a fortune.

I hold it up against me and twirl in front of the mirror, feeling like Cinderella. Frankie must have sent it over for me to wear this evening. What a kind thing to do!

Sorry, little black dress, old friend, but I think you may be staying in tonight.

There are shoes in the box as well, glittery strappy shoes with tiny heels and so delicate that I'm almost afraid to pick them up. Goodness, isn't Frankie clever? He even knows my dress and shoe sizes. And there's a floaty silver wrap too, which drifts across my shoulders like gossamer. This outfit is exactly what I'd have chosen for myself and I had no idea Frankie knew me so well. I feel a bit guilty now for thinking he's self-absorbed and shallow. I guess he must have very hidden depths.

There's something about a new dress that lifts a girl's spirits, and even though I haven't got Tansy-style control pants on, I feel a million dollars as I walk through the lobby channelling my inner Sarah Jessica Parker. I've left my hair loose tonight and I'm wearing hardly any make-up because the dress does it all! It's a perfect fit and as the car Frankie's sent sweeps away from the hotel, round a couple of corners and along Madison Avenue I really do feel as though I'm Cinderella on her way to the ball.

I only wish my handsome prince was going to be there.

Chapter 29

Thinking about how much I'm missing Ollie brings a sharp stab of pain that no dress, shoes or New York adventure can ease. As the car glides through the evening city I watch couples walking hand in hand along the sidewalk and my throat feels all tight and strange. I check my phone again just in case he's been in touch but there are still no missed calls or texts. I try his number too but there's no answer, just endless ringing. I suppose Ollie must be asleep by now and I'll have to try again tomorrow.

I gaze out of the car window. This is a bit odd. We're heading through Manhattan and out across the Brooklyn Bridge. Are we going the right way? The journey seems to be taking an awfully long time, and don't Frankie and Gabriel rent an apartment off Central Park? Where is this party being held exactly? I assumed it would be at their place but maybe I'm wrong. Perhaps Frankie and Gabe have far too many guests to fit into a flat? I bet that's it. Movie stars and musicians must know everyone. You'd never fit them all in. Frankie must have mentioned the venue but I've been so worried about Ollie I probably wasn't paying attention – and after everything I've said to my students about listening skills, too!

The sun's lower in the sky now and shadows are starting to slip across the freeway. Soon the clouds are blushed pink and the river's melting into a pool of gold. It's an urban landscape for sure but breathtakingly beautiful in its own right.

The sort of place you should be with somebody special…

"Here we are, Miss," says the driver over his shoulder as the car eventually comes to a halt.

"Here?" I look around, puzzled. Is this where Gabriel and Frankie are holding their party? We're right down near the water. Look! There's the aquarium!

"Are you sure?" I ask. Have Frankie and Gabriel really hired the aquarium for a party?

"If you'd just make your way inside, ma'am," the driver says politely.

I slide out of the car and into the cool evening air, pulling my wrap around me and feeling confused. What an odd choice of venue. It seems ever so quiet and I'd have expected that all the A-list guests would be sweeping up in big shiny cars and posing for photos before waltzing up a red carpet, or something of the sort. Instead, the place looks absolutely deserted.

Moving very slowly in my gorgeous but hopelessly impractical sandals, I wobble my way towards the entrance. Everything looks closed, but when I push the door it swings open easily and I spot a big sign reading *PARTY*. Closer investigation reveals an arrow pointing down the corridor, and attached to this is a piece of string that peels away into the dark depths of the building. OK. I'm in the right place so all I need to do is follow the directions. But where is everyone? Where are all the guests? Never mind spotting a stray Kardashian; I can't even see the aquarium staff.

"Hello?" I call. "Is anyone about?"

But there's no answer. There's not even a cleaner wandering past, or anyone else I can ask. So I dither for moment, wondering what to do. This is so weird. Has my jet lag got to me? Have I got the right day or am I early? No, I can't be. Frankie definitely said to leave at seven and the car was on time too, so I can't have got that wrong. Strange as this is I am in the right place. I guess I just need to follow that string and see where it leads me. Maybe the party's in a room underneath the tank. Yes! I bet that's it! Gabe and Frankie would love to have a party with sharks and stingrays swimming overhead. That's so them.

Feeling certain that this is what's going on, I follow a series of signs and what seems like miles of string through a maze of empty corridors, zigzagging ever deeper into the building. It's dark and quiet, like I'd imagine a zombie apocalypse to be (but set in an aquarium). The air's humid and thick with that odd fishy wet scent and I can't go any further surely? Firstly, my feet are killing me and, secondly, if I go much deeper I'll end up under the foundations.

There's a door ahead of me and the string passes beneath it. There's nowhere left to go except through it. Maybe the party's on the other side?

Hold on. Isn't this where I came before? Back when Guy was filming? It is! This is where Pinchy lives!

Frankie's holding his big anniversary party next to the lobster tanks? That's a bit strange even for him. It's hardly a blinging location and I'm not sure the A-listers will be impressed.

Intrigued, I place my palms on the door and push, stumbling into a dimly lit room. Tanks bubble and my heels tap on the floor, but apart from that all is silent.

The place is deserted.

I'm the only guest in the room. Or maybe I should more accurately say, I'm the only *human* guest in the room.

This is so odd and getting odder by the second. Another note is taped to the floor. *Follow me*, it reads, and below this note is yet more string leading across the tiled floor to a large tank – the very same tank where Pinchy now lives in five-star lobster luxury.

I'm at a party where the only other guest is a lobster?

Oh. I get it. I must be dreaming. I've conked out from jet lag and champagne. My brain makes up some crazy stuff, that's for sure. Still, best go with it. The old subconscious is probably working something through, although I dread to think what. Freud would have a field day wading through this lot.

"What's going on, Pinchy?" I ask the lobster, who stares back at me with his usual black-eyed disdain. "Where's everybody else? Where are all the other guests?"

"All the guests are right here," replies a voice. "And the one who isn't in the tank looks absolutely beautiful."

My heart leaps. I *must* be dreaming, still lying on the bed in the hotel and most likely dribbling too. That's the only explanation because how else could Ollie possibly be stepping from the shadows and walking towards me? He's in France!

I blink. Then I rub my eyes but no! He's still heading towards me, his eyes holding mine and his expression deadly serious. He's in a tuxedo too and he looks so gorgeous. My knees are more watery than Pinchy's tank.

"What are you doing here?" I whisper. "I thought you were in Paris?"

Ollie steps forward and takes my trembling hands in his. "I hoped you'd think that. I have a bit of a confession to make, Katy, because the thing is I never actually went to Paris. I flew straight to New York."

My head is whirling and I hold his hands as tightly as I can, as though only Ollie is keeping me from spinning away. Except that it's not *as though* at all: it's always been Ollie and only Ollie who keeps me steady. Without him I'm as lost as a balloon without its string, drifting away high above the rooftops and blown about with every breeze and current.

"You were in New York all along? Are you here for Frankie and Gabriel?"

Ollie laughs and laces his fingers with mine. "Great as they are – no! The only person I'm here for is standing right in front of me. I've another confession. There isn't a party but I *may* have asked Frankie to help me out a little by telling you there was." He pauses and a worried crease appears between his brows. "I hope you're not too disappointed? You were expecting your Kardashians and you've ended up with me instead."

"You could never disappointment me!" I cry. I haven't a clue what's going on and it's probably all just a dream knowing my luck, but I'm so beyond thrilled to see him that I couldn't care less about parties or celebrities. "Oh, Ollie, it's me who's disappointed you by writing that stupid, stupid book and by not telling you about it in the first place. I know it's made life really hard for you at St Jude's and I'm so sorry I've let you down. I promise it will never happen again."

Ollie pulls me into his arms and holds me tight against his chest. I think I'm smearing the lovely white shirt of his dress suit with mascara, but it's so wonderful to be held by him that there's no chance I'm stepping away. The shirt will just have to be a casualty.

"You could never, ever let me down!" he says fiercely. "I'm so proud of you, and everything you've ever done has been for us, Katy Carter. Don't you think I know that?"

"But it doesn't always end so well," I half sob, half laugh.

"Maybe not," Ollie agrees, tenderly wiping my tears away with his thumb before kissing my nose, "but what a lot of fun we have along the way! Lava-lamp fireworks! Naked butlers! Looking for treasure under the floor! I'd be bored rigid with anyone else, Katy. You've ruined me for life. I'll never love anyone else the way I love you."

I stare up at him. "Really?"

"Really," he says. "Heaven help me!"

I take a deep breath. No more secrets. "Would you still love me if I told you I'd thought you had a thing for Carolyn Miles?"

He raises his eyebrows. "I'd still love you, but I'd wonder a bit about your sanity. *Carolyn Miles*? I hardly think so!"

Well, yes, obviously now and with my hindsight goggles on I feel exactly the same way.

"I might have confronted her about it too," I add. "When I thought you'd run away to Paris with her?"

Ollie whistles. "Whatever's been going on in your head?"

So, because this is all a dream, I tell him and I don't hold back either. I explain how I was worried about him and Carolyn working together, the missed calls from her, the Saturday meeting, his locked phone, the vanishing money, and finally how I called her in Paris and demanded to know the truth.

I know what you're wondering. Did I tell him about spying on them both on my supply-teaching day?

Don't be daft. There are some things a girl has to keep quiet for the sake of her own dignity – even in a dream!

Anyway, even without that particular detail, by the time I've finished recounting everything Ollie's looking a bit shell-shocked.

"Sweetheart, you've been worrying about that all this time?"

I nod and he hugs me hard.

"I'm so, so sorry if anything I've said or done has made you feel insecure. Believe me, that's the total opposite of what I was intending." He shakes his head. "What a bloody irony! I was working all those hours for us, Katy! I wanted to be able to offer you a future."

"And I wanted to do the same with my writing!" I cry.

We stare at each other and burst out laughing.

"What a pair we make," says Ollie. "No more secrets now though, OK?"

"No more secrets," I agree. "So, flights to New York aside, what else have you not been telling me? And don't even try to change the subject. No more secrets, you just said!"

"Sometimes," Ollie says with feeling, "I really need to keep my big mouth shut!"

"I've told you everything," I say, snuggling against him. Wow, this is a vivid dream. He even smells delicious and Ollie-like. "So now it's your turn to tell me what's been going on. After all, you've been keeping secrets too."

"I don't deny it," he nods. "But actually, I think I can go one better. Why don't Pinchy and I show you exactly what I've been keeping secret?"

I stare at him. "What?"

He points to the string. "Why don't you give that a tug and see? Pinchy's been looking after something for me. That's why I needed to get you here. After all, it's really down to Pinchy that we're together in the first place, so it only seems fair he helps out now. I couldn't believe my luck when he showed up again. It was like fate! It was perfect!"

It's official: the stress of teaching has got to Ollie. Still, I'm curious now and sure enough the string is in Pinchy's tank. Right, I'll give it a yank and – oh!

Water splashes onto my bare shoulder as the string whips out of the water so fast that both Pinchy and I leap back. There's a clatter on the floor. What? Something's attached to the string I've just pulled out of the water.

I wonder what it is? I'll just bend down and pick it up…

Hold on. It looks like… looks like…

A ring. A beautiful square-cut ring, exactly like the ones I was looking at in the magazines! It is! It's a ring!

"Is that what I think it is?" I breathe, turning it around in my hands and not able to believe my eyes.

"I don't know," grins Ollie. "What do you think it is?"

My mouth is dry. "A ring?"

"Well done, Miss Marple," he says. "What kind of ring do you deduce this might be?"

"An engagement ring?" I whisper and he nods slowly.

"Of course it is. Phew. What a relief to tell you at last. I really thought the game was up when you saw that bank statement."

Suddenly lots of things are becoming very clear. No wonder Ann never got her necklace.

"I can't think how I got the idea for what kind of ring you wanted," he adds wryly. "It's almost like somebody left some very big hints lying around the house."

"Rubbish – they were incredibly subtle," I protest. "They must have been, since it's taken you five years to get them."

"Ah yes. Time for me to explain all that," Ol says.

Hand in hand, we sit down next to Pinchy's tank and slowly he tells me how all the extra work he was doing at school was to try to pay for the ring and a romantic proposal – but each time he thought the bank balance was looking healthy something happened to wipe it out and take him back to square one. There's quite a list, now he comes to mention it: cars (I never knew that if you drove a diesel through water it could write the engine off, and I swear that puddle looked very shallow); replanting his mother's entire garden (how was I to know what those seeds really were that Dad gave Ann one Christmas?); shorting the wiring (we all know about the lava lamp); and then the floor, of course, as well as all our usual bills and the leaky roof.

"I'd saved for the ring finally and I had enough to take you to New York at half-term," Ollie says, kissing me so tenderly that I melt like ice cream. "I've paid for it all by doing extra marking and tutoring. I didn't want to spend a penny of the money in our usual joint account, because that was both of ours. I wanted all of this to be from me to you, because that's how it should be for a romantic proposal. After all, I can't imagine Darcy would expect Lizzy Bennet to pay for her own ring!"

"The dress, the hotel suite, the flights." I'm blown away. "You paid for all of it, didn't you? Not Frankie?"

Ollie smiles. "Much as I love my cousin I'm not letting him take the credit for this! Look, Katy, I know I've been hard to live with and I've been working long hours but this is why. I hope you can forgive me for keeping all these secrets? That was the bit I really didn't like."

"There's nothing to forgive," I say. "If anything it's me who should be apologising for ever doubting you in the first place."

"Secrets suck," says Ollie. "I should know, since I've been keeping enough of them. I took on exam marking and crammer classes, and I tutored pupils at school in the evening too. I had to put a lock on my phone in case you saw the messages from my tutees' parents. That would have given the game away. Luckily Carolyn knew I was planning this and she made all the arrangements with them and backed me up. She's been brilliant. She and Sam even let me use their house."

Lord. I don't think I could feel much worse. I got it all wrong, didn't I? Just as well I'm not a member of the *Scooby-Doo* team. I'd pull the mask off the villain and it would be totally the wrong person underneath.

"Mads knew too, didn't she? And Holly!" I cry. Now it's all making sense. No wonder they've been so odd recently. "I knew they were up to something!"

Ollie laughs. "Of course they did. I needed them on side to keep you off the scent. And Frankie knew, of course, and Guy – he's been brilliant getting me into here tonight. He's pulled all kinds of strings and I probably owe him gallons of beer, but it's worth it because having Pinchy here completes the journey. Do you know, I'm actually glad I never cooked him!"

We glance at Pinchy. Is it my imagination or does he seem relieved too? At any rate, I'm pretty sure he looks away when we start kissing…

"Ol," I say eventually, when we break apart, "I never want you to have to work that hard again. I have much better things in mind for you than marking extra exam papers! I'll go back to teaching and give up being Isara Lovett, even if the publisher makes a fuss. Your career is more important than writing for Throb."

He traces my cheek tenderly. "I do love my job, Katy, but I love you far, far more. And anyway, I've already handed in my notice at St Jude's. I don't want anything or anyone in my life who isn't proud of my fiancée. Besides, I'm rather looking forward to meeting Isara Lovett! I thought I might even ask the Waldorf's room service if they have any clothes pegs and cabbages!"

I shudder. "I think I'd rather live on cabbages than write another book for Throb. Hope you don't mind starving, Ollie. They'll probably sue me for breaking the contract – and I can't imagine many schools will be keen to hire Isara Lovett to teach English."

Ollie's eyes crinkle at me. "From what I've heard, Isara Lovett has a fine command of Anglo-Saxon. Anyway, I think you might find that Nicky has a solution. I'll say one thing for my little brother: he's enterprising. Why work your naked arse off when you can tell the commissioning editor of Throb that you're really Isara Lovett and earn even more money sitting on your arse typing?"

My jaw drops. "He didn't?"

"He did," says Ollie. "And it looks like they've gone for it and you're off the hook – with Throb anyway. They were so happy with the last book they don't care who really wrote it, just as long as there's more to come. But off the hook with my parents? Now that's another matter. Explaining all this to their friends should be interesting!"

I gulp. "At least it will fund Nicky's gap year."

"And beyond, from what I've heard," Ol smiles. "He'll do very well. This is Nicky we're talking about after all. He'll probably be Prime Minister by the time he's twenty-five. Or inside!"

I feel like an enormous Throb-sized weight's just fallen from my shoulders. OK, so Ollie and I will be jobless and penniless pretty soon, but at least we're free from the burdens we've both been carrying. And that's priceless.

"Talking of money," Ollie continues, "I had a phone call from my father just before I left. Remember I told you Dad confiscated those bottles you'd found under the floor?"

"Cecily Greville's treasure?" I grimace. I think I still have the splinters from pulling up the floorboards that afternoon. The floor looks as though it has a few extra bumps and dents, and my pride certainly does. "I'm still embarrassed about that."

"Don't be," says Ollie. "That's why Dad was calling. You know what a wine buff he is, and when he saw those bottles he was intrigued. He took them away for analysis and guess what? They're full of Sazerac de Forge cognac."

"Great!" I say. Actually I have no idea if this is great or not, but if it puts me in the good books with Geoff then I'm happy. Hooray for Sazerac de Forge, I say!

"It's better than great!" Taking my hands, Ollie pulls me to my feet and starts to waltz me around the room. "Katy! That stuff's worth over ten grand a bottle! You did find the treasure after all! You dug up an absolute fortune!"

I'm stunned. Those dusty old bottles are worth ten grand each?

"Well," I say, giving him my *I told you so* look, "didn't I say there was treasure under that floor?"

"You certainly did – so never, ever doubt yourself," says Ollie, kissing me and twirling me around some more. "Yes, you're crazy and impulsive and impossible to live with but I wouldn't have you any other way. You're Katy Carter and I love you exactly as you are."

Then he lets go of me and drops to one knee. He reaches for my hand. The room feels so very quiet suddenly, and all I can hear is the racing of my heart.

"Katy Carter," Ollie says softly, "five years ago on Tregowan quay I asked you to marry me and I meant it, every word, but I had nothing to offer you except a red setter, a heap of debts and a rusting camper van. You're worth so much more and I wanted to be able to give you everything, to be able to do this properly and in style just like one of your romantic heroes. Darcy perhaps? Or maybe Rochester?" He grins up at me. "Not Alexi though. He's certainly enthusiastic but not very romantic!"

"Lucinda thinks he is," I say defensively. Poor Alexi gets a lot of stick. (Literally, in the scene with the runner beans – but maybe it's best not to think about that at the minute?)

"Can we forget about Alexi and Lucinda for a moment?" asks Ollie. "It's us I'm interested in right now. Katy, do you remember that day on the quay?"

"Of course I remember," I whisper. "I thought *you'd* forgotten."

"Never," Ollie says vehemently. "Travelling and houses and bills all got in the way and time's zoomed by because I have so much fun with you. But I've never forgotten. Never! I love you just as much now as I did then. Actually no! That's wrong. I love you even more and I've never forgotten what I said; I've just been waiting for the time to be right. A time when I can offer you everything. My heart, my life and the few worldly goods I do have."

"You never had to offer me anything, Ollie," I say quietly. "It was enough just to be with you."

He nods ruefully. "I let too much get in the way, didn't I?"

"I think we both have," I reply.

Ollie takes a deep breath. "Well, not anymore. Katy Carter, gifted writer of *interesting* fiction, friend to lobsters and the greatest love of my life, will you marry me?"

If this is a dream, then I am going to be *so* cheesed off. I guess I could stick my hand in the lobster tank and ask Pinchy to give me a nip, but do you know what? I have a feeling that I'm totally and utterly wide awake. More awake than I've ever been in my entire life, because there are no more secrets and no more worries – just the future lying wide open before us.

"Yes!" I tell him. "Of course I will!"

"Phew!" says Ollie and he leaps up, pulls me into his arms and kisses me so deeply I can hardly breathe. "And this time I promise I'm not dragging my heels for five years. What do you say to nipping down to the Caribbean and having a beach wedding? And maybe a big party when we get back to Tregowan? I don't want to waste another second!"

I rise onto my tiptoes and kiss him. White sand, sunshine, blue water and marrying the man I love under dancing palms are all very well, but actually all that matters to me is that it's Ollie I'll make my vows to. In fact, I could make them right now by a lobster tank and with Pinchy as our only witness and it would be more than enough for me.

"When do we go?" I say and Ollie smiles.

"As soon as possible," he promises.

And it's a wonderful thing but all the misunderstandings and fears of the past months slip away just as easily as Ollie is slipping the diamond onto my engagement finger. And when he kisses me, in this room full of bubbling tanks and under the watchful eye of a wise old friend, I know beyond all doubt that Ollie's ring will stay on my hand for the rest of my life.

Isara Lovett herself couldn't have written a better ending.

THE END

Epilogue

Eighteen months later

Golly, but it's hot in the Caribbean! I mean, really, really hot. Not Cornwall hot (which means we all get burned red raw for about an hour a year when the sun finally decides to put his hat on), but more like somebody's turned the oven on, shoved you in, shut the door and left you to cook. Granted sunburn isn't the greatest look when you're ginger, but I'm not going to make a habit of falling asleep by the pool. Or the sea. Or in the garden. Those incidents were just because we've not been here long and I'm still getting used to it all.

I'm not complaining though! No, far from it! When Ollie said he was applying for a teaching job in the Virgin Islands I was packing the factor fifty and humming *Yellow Bird, Up High in Banana Tree* before he'd even downloaded the application form. Getting married here last summer was amazing and the thought of a couple of years in the sunshine, him teaching and me writing, was even better. We both wanted to travel a bit more and have some new adventures, so why not?

And here we are! How incredible is that? St Jude's is just a bad memory, Ollie's loving his new job and, thanks to Cecily Greville's treasure, I'm finally free to write my definitive romantic novel without any distractions from cabbages and clothes pegs. And talking of such things, Nicky's now Isara Lovett and doing a far better job of it than I ever did – and funding his education too. The last I heard, *Bathroom of Bondage* was racing up the charts while Nicky was embarking on his studies at Oxford, thanks to his great A-level grades, and having a marvellous time whipping up left-wing sentiments. I'm not sure what Ann and Geoff make of it all but I have a feeling the luxury cruise Nicky treated them to went a long way towards soothing any misgivings, as did the bottle of cognac we gave Geoff.

So, everyone's happy. Even Sasha has got used to the heat and loves running on the beach and splashing through the waves while Ollie surfs. My days as an erotic novelist are over and it's back to writing romances. Hooray! And there's no time like the present either. I have my laptop, a shady spot in the garden, a romantic hero all of my very own and a big cocktail. I'm all set for literary success.

Right. *Love in Paradise* here we go!
Chapter One.

Hmm, typing in the heat is surprisingly tiring. My fingers keep slipping on the keys. Still, I'm sure I'll get the hang of it in time – and I probably won't stroke iguanas again, because they bite rather hard. My hand's a bit sore to be honest, which isn't good for typing. As pets go I don't think they're really going to work out quite as well as lobsters.

Talking of strange pets, I hope Pinchy's enjoying life in New York. The scientists there have promised me he's going to be safe and pampered, and that he has a home for life. It's a nice end to a story that began with him almost being dinner, and it's the least he deserves for seeing off my horrible ex and clearing the way for me and Ollie to get together. Maybe they'll even find him a lady lobster friend he won't want to eat. Wouldn't that be nice?

Anyway, **Chapter One**.

Oh look! There's Ollie waving at me from the patio. He looks gorgeous, all tanned and muscled from all his surfing and paddle-boarding. Life out here really suits him and he's his old carefree self again. I'm not sure how he manages all those sports in this heat but maybe I'm just built differently and feel the climate more acutely? Yes, I'm sure that's it. I'm designed to sit by the pool, not tear about.

Chapter One.

Maybe I need to listen to some music to get me in the mood? I've got Frankie's new country album downloaded and, since he's huge in the USA now, I really ought to see what all the fuss is about. I know he sings a lot about jeans and beer and his working-class life, which just goes to show that anyone can write fiction if they try hard enough. Besides, like Ollie says, poodles, Louis Vuitton and Botox are probably a bit tricky to rhyme.

Right. Let's try again.

Cha—

Oh! Ollie's peeling off his rash vest and rivulets of water are running down his pecs. Goodness, I'm feeling even hotter than I was before, even though I'm in the shade. Perhaps it's heatstroke? It's not good to overdo it here. Actually, I think I'll leave starting this book for a bit and concentrate on real life instead. That's bound to inspire me.

I know my new husband certainly does!

Husband! Can you believe it? I have a husband! And it's just like when we were best friends, but even better. There are no secrets at all between us now. Well, only the handbag I *might* have bought last week and the stray cats I *accidentally* let into the house, but those things don't really count do they? Of course not.

As I pick up my laptop and head across the spiky grass to our apartment, Ollie beckons me over.

"I think it's time for a siesta," he says, with that slow sexy smile which makes my heart melt like a pina colada in the heat. Putting the laptop down, I follow him into the cool inside.

Do you know what? Something tells me *Love in Paradise* is going to write itself…

Sign up for Ruth's Newsletter to find out about future books as soon as they're released!

I hope you enjoyed reading KATY CARTER KEEPS A SECRET. If you did, you might also enjoy my other books below.

Runaway Summer: Polwenna Bay 1

A Time for Living: Polwenna Bay 2

Winter Wishes: Polwenna Bay 3

Treasure of the Heart: Polwenna Bay 4

Magic in the Mist: Polwenna Bay novella

Escape for the Summer

Escape for Christmas

Hobb's Cottage

Weight Till Christmas

The Wedding Countdown

Dead Romantic

Katy Carter Wants a Hero

Ellie Andrews Has Second Thoughts

Amber Scott is Starting Over

Writing as Jessica Fox

The One That Got Away

Eastern Promise

Hard to Get

Unlucky in Love

Always the Bride

Writing as Holly Cavendish

Looking for Fireworks

Writing as Georgie Carter

The Perfect Christmas

Ruth Saberton is the bestselling author of *Katy Carter Wants a Hero* and *Escape for the Summer*. She also writes upmarket commercial fiction under the pen names Jessica Fox, Georgie Carter and Holly Cavendish.

Born in London, Ruth now lives in beautiful Cornwall. She has travelled to many places and recently returned from living in the Caribbean but nothing compares to the rugged beauty of the Cornish coast. Ruth loves to chat with readers so please do add her as a Facebook friend and follow her on Twitter.

www.ruthsaberton.co.uk

Twitter: @ruthsaberton

Facebook: Ruth Saberton

Printed by Amazon Italia Logistica S.r.l.
Torrazza Piemonte (TO), Italy